3

Three
Verdicts

Three

Ve

3

Donald R Findlay QC

NEIL WILSON PUBLISHING • GLASGOW • SCOTLAND

For Gran, Mum, Dad, Mac and Barney. I still care.

Neil Wilson Publishing
303a The Pentagon Centre
36 Washington Street
GLASGOW
G3 8AZ

Tel: 0141-221-1117
Fax: 0141-221-5363
E-mail: nwp@cqm.co.uk
*http://*www.nwp.co.uk/

A catalogue record for this book is
available from the British Library.

ISBN 1-897784-21-X
Typeset in Melior and
Helvetica Compressed

Designed by Mark Blackadder

Printed by WSOY, Finland

Contents

Chapter One

James Muirhead QC was sitting on a carver in counsel's retiring room in the High Court of Justiciary in Glasgow, his feet up on the imposing oak table which occupied the centre of the room. It had been there for more years than anyone could remember and mourners would have sat around it in its former life as a wake table, no doubt partaking of a glass or two while extolling (or otherwise) the virtues of the departed. Generations of Scots advocates had worn grooves into its polished surface with the heels of their shoes while waiting for juries to return. It had seen many a celebration and more than its fair share of post-trial wakes.

Muirhead had just filled his pipe and was in the process of raising his lighter when the buzzer sounded to announce that the jury was ready to return its verdict. He lowered the flame to the rim of the pipe and stared at his junior counsel, Donald Anderson, through a spiral of blue-grey smoke. He took the pipe from his mouth, cupping the rosebriar bowl in the palm of his right hand and characteristically stroked his greying moustache.

'Just so,' was the only comment he made.

'Must have a chance.' Anderson's observation was as much a question as it was a statement.

'Well, we're about to find out.'

Muirhead pulled on his silk gown and turned to the cheval mirror to don his horsehair wig. His face was showing obvious signs of the strain which the case had imposed. It did not get any easier. He tugged at his constricting waistcoat and frowned. He needed a smaller body or a larger suit.

'Donald?'

'Yes, James.'

'Do you think I'm overweight?'

'What?'

'Do you think I'm...'

'I heard you. How heavy are you?'

'Thirteen and a half...well, fourteen stones. But it's six feet of solid muscle.'

'Then you're too fat.'

2

'Thank you for your moral support.'

'James, can we just go and get the verdict? No point in prolonging the evil hour, is there?'

Anderson took his colleague's grunt as an indication of assent.

Muirhead was in his mid-forties and had been at the Scottish Bar for over twenty years. He was generally regarded as being the best defence counsel of his generation. His formidable reputation was based largely on his enthusiasm for battle. A ferocious cross-examiner, he would fight a client's case to the bitter end, often in the face of apparently insurmountable odds – and seemingly overwhelming evidence. His many celebrated bust-ups with judges were the stuff of tabloid legend, his cases covered assiduously by the press. He had once remarked at a dinner party that judges were like children. 'You mean they should be seen and not heard?', a guest had enquired. 'No. They should respect their betters and be regularly smacked to keep them in order,' Muirhead had replied.

In today's trial, he and the judge, Lord Cowden, had crossed swords more than once. When a police officer was proved to be particularly recalcitrant in the face of persistent interrogation, the judge had sought to come to his rescue, remarking, 'The man has answered your question, Mr Muirhead.'

'Then,' came the instant rejoinder, 'your Lordship's hearing is indeed more acute than that of myself or any of the members of the jury, because we do not seem to have heard it – yet.'

The thinly muffled chortling of the jury made Lord Cowden realise that this was one round he was not going to win.

But now the verdict awaited, and Muirhead steeled himself the few tense minutes which would decide his client's fate. He hated this moment. He always had. The trial of Her Majesty's Advocate against Charles Gallagher was about to come to an end.

●   ●   ●

There are few things in life more dramatic than the end of a murder trial. The speed of events can catch the uninitiated completely unaware. A jury returns – a verdict is delivered. Murder brings a mandatory life sentence with the prospect of nothing more than many years in prison to look forward to. An acquittal and moments later the former accused leaves the building to find his family and freedom awaiting him.

Muirhead had witnessed this play within a play many times. Each time he disliked it a little more. It was the part of the trial he had no control over. Given the choice, he would avoid it. Such an option was never available. If the verdict went against him, he would have to go down to the white-tiled cells below the court and explain to the client why it had all gone so badly wrong. Words of comfort. Platitudes. However well intentioned. Think about an appeal. Take one day at a time. Not the end of the world. Life goes on.

◈　　　　◈　　　　◈

Leaving the retiring room he walked slowly and deliberately along the corridor towards the entrance to the court. Each time he made this journey he was acutely aware of his surroundings. He was about to enter the famous (some would say infamous) North Court of the Justiciary buildings opposite Glasgow Green on the south bank of the River Clyde.

The High Court may be an impressive edifice with columns flanking either side of its imposing entrance but it is not for its architectural splendour or picturesque location that it is noted, but rather the reputation of some of the more notorious visitors who have passed through its marble-floored halls. The very room from which the jury would soon emerge had been occupied in the 1950s by the men and women who had brought in the guilty verdicts which sent mass murderer Peter Manuel to meet his maker at the end of a hangman's rope.

Muirhead paused while the last of the public filed in through the rear door.

Law courts are the last places of free entertainment. In the days of capital murder, the queues of the concerned, the curious and the ghoulish would stretch along the street outside the building, eagerly anticipating the day's events. In recent years, murder trials had become so commonplace that they invariably attracted little public scrutiny and minimal media attention. It was not unknown for the public benches to contain a solitary bored hack and the family of the accused (the latter consisting of a pregnant girlfriend, an alcoholic father and a greetin' mammy with a bad perm).

This case was different. The public galleries had been packed and every word had been reported in the press. A legal cause célèbre was about to reach its conclusion.

Muirhead reached the vestibule which gave access for counsel and solicitors to both the North and South courts. Looking into the courtroom, he watched the comings and goings of the pre-match warm up. The Advocate Depute and his assistant were already seated at their places in court. The Clerk of Justiciary was animatedly arranging documents on his table. Police officers were stationed at the various entrances of the court. The jury box was empty. A policeman appeared at the head of the stairs leading from the cells to the dock, followed by the

4

accused. Charles Gallagher was nearly six feet tall with short dirty fair hair and was as thin as the proverbial rake. (His granny used to say that there wasn't room enough between his shoulders for a pain.) He had a prominent scar which ran the length of his left cheek – a souvenir of some previous skirmish with the pond-life of Glasgow's criminal class.

Throughout most of the trial he had shown no emotion whatsoever. After an initial outburst at a witness, he had sat implacably in the dock, his face betraying nothing of his thoughts and feelings. Now he looked drawn and deathly pale. Before he sat down, he turned to the back of the room and smiled thinly to his family in the gallery. Muirhead noticed that his hands were trembling. He was fighting to keep control – and was determined not to show it.

Muirhead nodded to the macer who headed for the jury room and then paused at the door. Donald Anderson walked straight into the court. He knew his senior's superstition well. Muirhead would not come in for the verdict until everyone was in place and the macer had gone to collect the judge. His practice was invariable. In the far corner, opposite the dock, a door opened and, preceded by the macer, the jury began to file into their places.

There is a theory among lawyers that if jurors cannot look at the man in the dock on returning to court, then they intend to convict him. Muirhead eschewed such notions. There was no way of knowing how juries would behave. Occasionally, very occasionally, you might get a clue. Although juries are always told by judges that punishment is a matter for the court and they should not allow themselves to be influenced by the possible sentence that might be imposed, every juror knows that a guilty verdict in the High Court is likely to result in a lengthy prison sentence. Jurors who returned to their box chattering amongst themselves and appearing relaxed, were usually an encouraging sign. They know that they will not have to witness a man being sent to jail. They know that, for practical purposes, the case is already over.

Muirhead saw no such encouraging sign on this occasion. Every jury member bar one walked in, heads slightly bowed, stony-faced. Only one appeared to show any reaction at all, and Muirhead thought he saw the hint of a smile. The small prissy-looking man who took his seat at the end of the middle of the three rows had an almost perceptible air of triumph about him. The foreman, Muirhead thought … undoubtedly the foreman.

The macer passed on his way to the judge's chambers and paused to take Muirhead aside.

'Dour bunch, sir. Glad to see the back of them. Bet the foreman is the one who looks like Rab C. Nesbitt. Right moaning-faced bastard he's been, sir. Speaking of which, I'm away to get his nibs.' The macer moved on.

'Oh no, he isn't', muttered Muirhead as he took a few deep breaths in an attempt to stop the churning in his stomach. Waste of time, and he knew it.

Resigned, Muirhead walked into court, going over in his mind the events which had brought him here. The death of Kevin Boyle, late and largely unlamented son of Hugh Boyle, one of the last of Glasgow's old-style gangsters, had presented him with his most testing professional challenge ever – and had nearly made him crack in the process.

* * *

On a dark, damp night the East End of Glasgow presents a series of depressing vistas. What town planners had intended as gardens are now barren areas long since devoid of any form of vegetation. All that grows and proliferates are the discarded remnants of rusting cars. Occasional wooden posts mark the boundaries of these once green places. The wooden fences have long since been broken up and used as weapons by local youths in the gang fights which feature as part of Friday and Saturday night's entertainment.

In many areas there hangs a tangible air of menace. Strangers are not welcome. (This covers a broad category of people, including the rent man and the police in particular. Any police car visiting the area will be crewed by three officers – two to carry out the inquiry and a third to keep a careful watch on the car itself.)

The Springfield housing scheme was one such place, a microcosm of the whole of the East End; a close-knit community where every resident appeared in some way to be related to everyone else. This was Boyle territory.

Hugh Boyle had embarked upon a career in crime in the 1940s. It was one which was to be visited with considerable success. Born in the notorious Gorbals in Glasgow where poverty, violence and intense family loyalties co-existed side by side, he was one of seven children and had more aunts, uncles and cousins than he could count, let alone remember. Gangs were a way of life in the Gorbals and membership was obligatory.

Each gang had its own territory and boundaries were jealously and zealously guarded. Every weekend, rival gangs would meet in what would sometimes prove to be mortal combat on Glasgow Green in the shadow of the High Court. Most members bore the scars of battle. The favoured weapon was the cut-throat razor which was often wielded with a breathtaking degree of speed and dexterity. An opponent's cheek could be laid bare to the bone before he knew he had been cut.

In the 1950s, the High Court Judge Lord Carmont decided he would try to remove the razor from the streets of Glasgow. He began handing out longer and longer prison sentences to gang members who appeared before him. Slowly the message sank home. Razors were put away in drawers, never to reappear.

Unfortunately, most gang members still felt it necessary to carry a weapon of some description. After all, a man was naked without one. The knife came to replace the razor. Unfortunately, while the razor could maim, the knife would kill, and while Lord Carmont's sentencing contributed greatly to an improvement in the aesthetic appearance of Glasgow's citizens, it was a significant factor in bringing to many an untimely end.

Hugh Boyle joined the 'Young Cumbie', the youth section of one of the Gorbals' most notorious gangs. It was named after Cumberland Street, the location of its headquarters.

He took part in his fair share of battles, picked up the obligatory scar and could wield both razor and knife with the best of them. However, he swiftly realised that all this violence for the sake of it was ultimately pointless. He had no intention of ending up like so many of his predecessors – in prison or hopelessly alcoholic. His fighting prowess brought him admiration, but it was his intelligence that earned him respect. When he was seventeen he graduated to the Cumbie itself and quickly established himself as a natural leader. He stopped carrying a personal weapon, preferring the company and moral support of two heavily armed body guards. He also improved the gang's finances. Raiding parties were sent around town to relieve the middle classes of their property, houses were broken into, and pedestrians parted from their wallets and handbags.

Hugh Boyle then discovered the magic of credit. People's greed was often far greater than their means, and Boyle was nothing if not generous. He would allow them to incur debts which they could then pay up, with a rate of interest he arbitrarily determined. The unwary (and there was an abundance of them) were trapped. They found themselves having to borrow money in order to meet the weekly instalments. Boyle readily supplied this need and thereby entered the profession of banking. This proved even more lucrative as, realistically the debt had very little chance of being repaid. Occasionally some defaulters would need a gentle reminder.

Boyle found himself growing ever more powerful and more wealthy. He came to appreciate that people were dispensable. His henchmen had no great personal aspirations and were quite content with the money he regularly put their way. It enabled them to have a good bevvy and keep the wife quiet (if not exactly sweet). The foot soldiers, however, regularly fell foul of the law. Despite deals by the police, being a grass in the Gorbals was as good as signing your own death warrant. The police knew of Boyle's activities, but they could prove nothing. A combination of loyalty and terror made a powerful opponent.

He had married a local girl, indeed she was the local beauty. In those days, mixed marriages were frowned upon but the fact that Annie was a Protestant and he was a good Catholic (well, a Catholic anyway) bothered Hugh not at all. The hard man discovered he had a soft spot. He doted on Annie. He worshipped her. She was everything he was not, soft, gentle, and cultured. Hugh's reading was confined to the back pages of newspapers. Annie regularly had her nose in a book by James Joyce or Jane Austen (whoever they might be). She dragged him out to concerts – classical music no less – and the Art Gallery. Hugh accepted his lot gracefully; after all, he loved her.

As time passed, Boyle grew weary of the Gorbals. When the Springfield scheme was built in the mid-sixties, he became one of its first residents, thanks to a generous donation to a local housing official. He was followed by his many relatives and they quickly took over the whole area.

His criminal empire relocated to the heart of the East End and Boyle continued to prosper. Nothing happened in the area without his say so. He also discovered the value of banks, or rather bank managers, not all of whom were upstanding members of the community. One or two liked more of the good things in life than their salary could pay for. Boyle happily made up the difference and in return acquired a series of accounts in a range of fictitious names with equally fictitious addresses.

Boyle's success continued to be based on the money-lending business. He also provided a consultancy service for those who wished to be more adventurous and seek a quick return on investment by robbing a bank or security van. He would supply men and material for a decent percentage of the take. If the turn went bad, Boyle could afford to walk away and put it all down to experience. The risks were virtually non-existent.

Only twice did he find himself in court. The only crime of which he was ever convicted was driving a vehicle while under the influence of alcohol. He lost his licence for twelve months and had to pay a modest fine. Paying his lawyer's bill proved more of a burden. He would probably have got away with it altogether but for the fact that the vehicle he collided with when driving home from the pub had a blue flashing light on its roof.

In 1986 real trouble caught up with him for the one and only time. His son, Kevin, staggered home one night with blood pouring from wounds in his head and arm. He had been out making some collections when the unthinkable happened and he was mugged. Normally, members of the Boyle family did not go about unaccompanied, but the size of Kevin's brain did not match the rest of his physical stature and he liked to strut about on his own playing the part of a hard man. In the East End he was untouchable, but when he strode into a pub in the centre of town and began flashing his money around, he was asking for trouble – and it came looking for him.

On leaving the pub the hapless Kevin was set upon by two youths who hit him on the head with a hammer, stabbed him in the arm and dragged him into a nearby lane, where he was robbed and abandoned like a sack of rubbish. In fact his injuries were not as severe as they had first appeared, but when he arrived home he was mindful that he would have to explain to his father the loss of the three grand. His performance was a bit hammy, but he gave a passable portrayal of the wounded hero.

Hugh Boyle was in a fury. He would have quite cheerfully strangled Kevin for being so stupid. On one hand, his son's injuries would quickly heal. On the other hand, a member of his family, his eldest son, no less, had been publicly humiliated. This was unacceptable. His reputation was at stake. No one laid a hand on a Boyle – not unless they had Hugh's express permission.

Unsurprisingly, the matter was never reported to the police but Boyle allowed some discreet inquiries to be carried out. One name was mentioned. Despite a plethora of offers from his lieutenants, Hugh decided this was a personal matter and as such should receive his personal attention.

Bobby Houliston, small-time crook and short-time local legend, was sitting in the corner of the crowded Tavern Bar in Glasgow's Duke Street, surrounded by many new friends whose admiration and adoration he had secured thanks to the large quantities of drink he had purchased (paid for with Hugh Boyle's money). Had he been facing the door of the bar he might have realised that the silence which descended on the pub ought to have caused him some concern.

'Whit's up? Has some fucker just died?'

Prophetic words.

Bobby glanced over his shoulder and began to speak. Hugh Boyle prevented him from doing so by filling Bobby's open mouth with four bullets fired from a revolver. No one would ever know what Bobby's last meditation on earth might have been. It should have been 'Fuck me!' After swallowing the four bullets, Bobby was well and truly fucked.

Boyle looked round the pub as if to impress on the company that he was unconcerned about being recognised while the stunned witnesses had everything to fear. Slipping the gun into his jacket pocket, he strolled casually from the premises.

The police had their own intelligence sources, and aware of the mugging of Kevin, knew who had murdered the late and largely unlamented Bobby Houliston. He was no great loss to society and in truth he had been an irritation the local constabulary were privately glad to see the back of. However, shootings were not on and the chance to put a major criminal figure like Hugh Boyle away for a long time was too good to miss. Unfortunately, they could not find one witness. Such statements as they had suggested that the pub had been virtually empty at the time. The few people who admitted being there were suddenly stricken with a palsied blindness and an alcoholic amnesia.

On the other hand, Boyle had enough alibi witnesses to make up a decent crowd at a Second Division football match. He was interviewed and cautioned that he was not obliged to say anything, but anything he did say would be noted and would be given in evidence. The interviewing officers did not need the sheets of paper in front of them as Boyle did not open his mouth.

The inquiry was going nowhere till one of the barmaids from the Tavern walked into Stewart Street Police Station and, to the astonishment of the interviewing officers, told the whole story. Hugh Boyle duly found himself arrested, charged with murder and locked up in the notorious Barlinnie prison.

With Boyle out of the way, the police pressurised everyone they believed had been in the pub in an attempt to obtain further evidence. No one would crack. Unfortunately, by chasing a second goal, the police took their eye off the ball. Despite the terrible dangers inherent in the course she had adopted, Betty Brown had received no police protection and was not even under surveillance. She left her home one Friday night to meet a friend and go to the pictures. She failed to arrive and was never seen or heard of again. She shuffled off this mortal coil leaving not a trace behind and the prosecution case, such as it was, collapsed completely.

Hugh Boyle was released from Barlinnie and returned home to Springfield. Publicly, he oozed confidence and righteous indignation, protesting his innocence and demanding a full public inquiry. Privately, the whole episode had greatly alarmed him. He had lost his temper completely and killed a man. This did not trouble his conscience but he appreciated that it made him vulnerable. He had grown accustomed to the good things in life and he certainly did not find prison to his liking. He decided it was time to take more of a back seat and allow his three sons to play a greater part in running the various family businesses.

Kevin, Paul, and Hugh Junior may not have been born with silver spoons in their mouths, but unlike most youngsters from their background, they wanted for nothing. Their mother had tried to bring them up in a disciplined way and to appreciate the real value of things. Their father let them do more or less as they liked and made sure the boys always had plenty of money in their pockets. That the young Boyles had very different natures became very clear during their school days.

The eldest, Kevin, was known to his schoolmates as Podge, at least behind his back. Often a fat kid would be a figure of ridicule among his contemporaries but such treatment was never inflicted on young Master Boyle. He had a vicious temper and liked everyone, except his mother, to know that he carried a knife. His favourite phrase, 'I'll fucking plunge you' was often dismissed as piss and wind – but not always, and not by everyone. After all, big Hugh Boyle was his father.

Kevin hated school, and to be fair, the school returned the compliment. Although he enjoyed being the bully, he heartily disliked his teachers for their efforts in trying to impose discipline on him. He hated his classmates because they would not be his friends. He hated the lessons because he was thick. By the time he was fourteen he seldom bothered to turn up, much to the relief of all concerned. By the age of fifteen he had left to join the family firm. No one mourned his leaving.

Paul was quite different. Academically he was very bright and had a natural aptitude for figures. He was popular with his teachers and fellow pupils, although people still tended to tread warily because of his family's reputation and the fact that Kevin was his big brother.

From an early age, Paul demonstrated a flair for the world of commerce. He always had pencils, rubbers, comics and crisps available for sale at bargain prices. No one much cared how he was able to undercut the local shops – mainly because everyone knew. Following the family tradition, Paul was quite prepared to provide credit for his customers. Few people availed themselves of this facility. Kevin tended to act as debt collector.

In his fourth year at school Paul sat and passed nine 'O' Levels with top marks in arithmetic, mathematics and physics. His teachers expected him to return to school after the summer holidays to sit his Highers and in due course go on to university. Paul left school to join the family firm.

Hugh Junior was very much the baby of the family. He was vaguely aware that he and his brothers were treated differently by the other kids in the neighbourhood. He cared not to know the reasons why. He quickly gave up asking his mother why people pointed at her when they walked down the street.

'Just mind your own interferences, wee one,' was all she ever said. He didn't understand why people pointed, and he didn't understand the reply either. He was a typically easy-going little boy. He did not have much choice. No one ever told him anything anyway. He had asked his father what a 'gangster' was. The reaction told young Hughie that he had said something wrong.

'Who telt ye about gangsters?'

'This kid Davie in my class said you wiz a gangster. So, whit's a gangster?'

'Never you mind, Hughie son. Just you ignore them.'

'But dad!'

'Look Hughie, James Cagney was a gangster, OK?'

'Sure dad, thanks.'

Hughie took it that the matter had been clarified. Certainly, the discussion was clearly at an end but he left wondering who on earth was James Cagney.

Two days after this conversation Hughie noticed that his schoolmate Davie was sporting a splendid black eye. Davie never spoke of gangsters again.

Hughie's passion in life was football. He was small, quick and could juggle a ball as if it were on a piece of elastic. He was a typical example of that breed of Scottish footballer, the tanner ball player. His idol was Celtic winger 'Jinky' Jimmy Johnstone. At twelve he was picked for the local under-sixteen team. Like his idol, he played on the wing and delighted in taking the piss out of all would-be tacklers. Despite being a target for various hatchet men, Hughie could take hefty challenges and bounce straight back. He was tough as well. When he left school, to his father's delight and his mother's chagrin, he signed for Celtic.

●   ●   ●

In the early days of semi-retirement, Hugh was pleased with the way he saw the business being restructured. Kevin dealt with the day-to-day activities while Paul looked after the finances. By now the Boyles had an interest in various public houses and nightclubs while the money-lending side continued to flourish. Paul proved adept at the science of laundering money. To the outsider the brothers ran a small firm which bought and sold cars.

Hugh Senior sat back and enjoyed his role as overlord. Life was good. He would chortle as he read in the *Daily Record* of a mug getting twelve years for failing in an attempt to rob a security van. Drugs – filthy shit. Hugh had watched the rise of the drug trade and readily appreciated that it was a market with an enormous potential for profit. The sprawling housing-schemes of Glasgow were filled with willing and enthusiastic customers. He had a network which could easily have been used to distribute heroin, cocaine, cannabis or whatever the market required. Hugh Boyle would not do drugs.

He did not care if the punters shot themselves full of poison, if their veins rotted and they died in a state of abject misery. He was indifferent to the horror of drug abuse. Equally, he was indifferent to the profits being made by others.

Boyle knew that to become involved in drugs would make him vulnerable again, so did not intend to allow this to happen. Junkies had big mouths, and no loyalty. Most were dealers on the side and were easy prey for the Strathclyde Police Drug Squad. To keep out of jail and to maintain access to a source of supply for their habit they would give the information the police wanted. They were usually so wasted that even the prospect of violent retribution for being a grass was less terrifying than the prospect of being without a hit. They were scum– but they were dangerous.

Boyle let it be known that anyone in his employ who became involved with drugs was out – and he did not mean sacked. None of his people touched the stuff – of that he was confident. His confidence was about to be shattered.

At five o'clock one morning, officers of the Strathclyde Police Drug Squad knocked lightly on the front door of the Boyle house. Unless the occupants had had their ears pressed to the door, they would have heard nothing. The inspector in charge then whispered, 'It's the police. Please open the door'. The necessary formalities having been observed, a Detective Constable knocked on the door again. This time he wielded a nine-pound sledgehammer. The police gained entry. Eight officers moved quickly through the house. Kevin and Paul were not at home, each preferring the company of one of their many girlfriends.

Hughie was the first to react. He reached his bedroom door just as it burst open and found himself confronted by two strangers, one holding a sledgehammer.

'Sit on your fucking arse, Boyle, we're the DS.'

Hughie was pushed back onto his bed.

What the fuck's the DS?, he wondered. His hands being handcuffed behind his back gave him a fair clue.

Hugh Boyle was reaching for the bedside lamp when the main light was switched on. Even though they were casually dressed he knew police officers when he saw them.

'Police. We have a warrant under the Misuse of Drugs Act to search this property. Get up and come downstairs please. Where's your son, Kevin?'

'Are you bastards daft, breaking in here in the middle of the night? I hae nothin tae dae wi' drugs and yous fucking know it. I'm calling my lawyer.'

'No sir,' replied the inspector in charge, moving swiftly to place his hand on the bedside telephone. 'You're not calling anyone for the time being. Please come downstairs both of you. Feel free to put on dressing-gowns if you wish.'

The Boyles followed the police officers downstairs to the lounge where they found Hughie in handcuffs.

'Dad!'

Hugh exploded and lunged at the two officers standing beside his son.

'You fucking scum bastards, get them off him. He's never done fuck all. He's a fitba player for fuck's sake. Try and pit cuffs on me, ye fuckers'.

They did – successfully – but it took four of them to do so.

As the initial shock of the invasion wore off, Boyle's mind kicked into gear. A number of possibilities were occurring to him: the police might be using drugs as a cover to search for something else. But why bother? They must know that he was too streetwise to keep anything incriminating in a kitchen drawer or under the floorboards. The Gallaghers. It had to be!! The Gallagher family from Glasgow's Bridgeton had been rivals for years and had a substantial drugs empire throughout the West of Scotland. But the interests of the rival factions did not clash, and they had for some time tolerated each other in a state of perpetual stand-off. The Gallaghers knew Boyle did not do drugs. Why did they ask about Kevin? His son Kevin…drugs? He thought on.

'Where the fuck is he?'

'What was that?', inquired the officer sitting opposite Hugh.

Boyle stared back malevolently. The man shifted uneasily in the armchair. The search, which would prove fruitless, continued.

◦　　　　◦　　　　◦

The week before, a council of war was held chez Gallagher in Barassie Street, Bridgeton, another part of the East End. Frank Gallagher had invited selected business associates to attend. His invitations bore no RSVP. At his side was his son Charlie.

Just as the Boyles and their extended family dominated the Springfield area, the Gallaghers and their people controlled Bridgeton.

Gallagher Snr was a former bank robber. In former years he had made a lot of money from his trade. He had also served two lengthy terms of imprisonment and regarded this as an occupational hazard, adhering to the philosophy, 'If you can't do the time, don't commit the crime'.

When the drug scene had got going in Glasgow, Frank had come to the conclusion that this was a much easier and less hazardous way to make money than running around banks with a sawn-off shotgun. He had good contacts in London from his blagging days. Most of his robberies had taken place south of the Border. ('Never shit on your own nest', was another of his favourite maxims.) With the assistance of gentlemen in the South, he established an effective network for the importation and distribution of every conceivable type of illegal drug.

The system for transporting the gear, as it was colloquially known, to Glasgow was simple and efficient. Couriers would drive to London and pick up innocent looking packages. They were paid £200 cash and were not told (they did not want to be told) what the package contained. They would do a maximum of three runs before they were replaced. There was no shortage of unemployed men desperate to make a bit of cash, no questions asked.

When the cargo arrived in Glasgow it would be lodged at a neutral venue such as an empty factory or warehouse and observed from a safe distance for a period of time before being uplifted. Thereafter it was taken to a safe house for preparation for onward distribution.

Tablets containing amphetamine sulphate or methylene-dioxyethyleamphetamine, known on the street as 'speed' and 'ecstasy', would be packaged into set quantities before being despatched to the lower level dealers who would sell them to the customers. Blocks of cannabis would be broken up into smaller units. Some of the sub-dealers were in it for the money and never touched the stuff themselves. Others were users who would sell drugs in order to feed their own habit. Powdered drugs such as heroin or cocaine would receive special treatment. A kilo of powder will contain a mixture of the drug itself and various adulterants. Anything could be added to the drug to give it more bulk and thereby increase profit.

When the Gallaghers received a kilo of heroine they would cut it with the equivalent amount of glucose and instantly double the profit. At least glucose did the user no harm. Other dealers were less scrupulous. Some added anything they could get their hands on, such as drain-cleaner or even brick dust. Often the cutting agent did as much damage to the user as the drug itself, sometimes more.

When the adulteration process was complete, the drugs were distributed. As they moved down the chain towards the user, the sub-dealer would add further adulterants and by the time it reached the street about fifteen per cent only of the powder was made up of the drug. The scope for profit was enormous, and everyone made money (apart from the mugs who shot the stuff into their veins).

It was because of concern for this source of income that Frank Gallagher had called the board meeting. He set out the agenda.

'Right, so we're toiling to punt the stuff just now. I'm getting serious grief from the boys down by. They're nudging me to take more and you bastards can't get rid of what we've got.'

Gallagher was not much given to wasting words when he had a point to make.

'Aye, you bastards can't get rid of what we've got'.

Charlie chipped in his tuppence worth, but since he was quite incapable of summoning up an original thought he mimicked his father, parrot fashion. It was manifestly obvious to everyone who knew him that Charlie had failed to find the queue the day the brains were being dished out.

Gallagher shot a filthy look in the direction of his boy. It carried a very clear message, 'Zip it!'

Stupid as he was, Charlie was smart enough to know when he should keep quiet. He contented himself with nodding sagely as if he had just made a telling contribution to the debate.

Charlie was used to living in his father's shadow. Frank Gallagher ran his own show and Charlie had to accept that he was merely the gopher – go for this, go for that. While he may have accepted it, Charlie was not exactly happy with his lot. He wanted to be a big man but did not quite know how to get a start. Everyone in the organisation knew he was just the message boy but one day he intended to show them.

Frank glowered round the table waiting for some response. The recipients of his stare looked at each other, hoping somebody else would respond. Someone had to speak and eventually Mick 'Mad Dog' Clark took up the challenge. Clark was not involved in the actual business of supplying drugs. His particular trade was enforcement.

The Gallagher business was based on a practice known as 'laying on'. Drugs would be supplied to a dealer who would then be responsible for selling them. From the proceeds he would make the necessary payment to Gallagher headquarters. In the event that he was tardy in coming forward with the cash he could expect a visit from Mick Clark.

Mad Dog's reputation for effective ruthlessness preceded his every step; the prospect of his calling was usually sufficient to insure that the funds were forthcoming. If a pointed reminder was required, Clark's favoured weapon was a sharpened screwdriver which he would drive into the thigh or backside of his victims. This usually had the desired effect.

16

'It's the Boyles, gaffer,' someone ventured.

'I know it's the fucking Boyles, or at least it's that shit, Kevin. What I want to know is, what the fuck are you going to do about the Boyles?'

'Why don't we tell the old man about his precious son? He has always claimed he would never do the stuff. He might put the brakes on him.'

'Very good, Mick. What is rattlin' about inside that skull of yours? It's no yer fucking brains. I can just see me phoning Hugh Boyle and saying, "Excuse me, Hughie, but did you know your wee boy is making a mint out of punting drugs and causing me a serious cashflow problem? Any fucking chance you might ask him to give it a rest for a wee while? Frank, I'm sorry to hear about your wee problem. Of course I'll tell him to be a good boy. Would you like me to smack him in the fucking mouth while I'm at it? No bother at a'." Gie's a fucking break, will you! If you've fuck all sensible to say, then say fuck all.'

'Waste the cunt!'

'Eh?' Gallagher stared at his son, not knowing whether to laugh or explode.

'Waste the cunt. Why not?'

'Why not? Why fucking not?'

Gallagher turned to the assembled company spreading his arms wide.

'He asks me why not.'

'Why not?', chipped in Clark. 'At least it would show we meant...' and was abruptly silenced by a look of such ferocity and malice that it would have knocked a lesser man off his seat.

For what seemed an age, Gallagher glared unblinkingly at the man opposite him. Mad Dog was not accustomed to a sense of fear but he had learned over the years that his boss was at his most dangerous when in a cold fury. Shouting and bawling was fine, but when Frank lapsed into silence, anything was possible and often probable. He could feel the sweat begin to trickle down his back.

For Christ's sake, speak, Clark thought to himself while Gallagher sat as if caught on the freeze-frame of a video-recorder.

The others in the room strove not to move a muscle, bat an eyelid or even be seen to be breathing lest the slightest gesture be misconstrued. The silence enveloped them.

'I'll tell you why not, Mr Marlon fucking Brando. This is Glasgow, no fucking Chicago.'

The film buffs among the listeners were puzzled. What had Marlon Brando got to do with Chicago? Surely that was Al Capone? But no one was inclined to correct Gallagher's inexactitude.

Gallagher warmed to his theme.

'You're tubes, no fucking Mafia hit men. You lot seem to think we're a bunch of fucking gangsters.'

This latter assertion came as no surprise to anyone present. A bunch of gangsters was precisely what they thought they were. They awaited the next salvo – it did not arrive.

Gallagher burst into laughter and everyone instantly followed suit, although they were not entirely sure what they were laughing at. The air of tension was replaced by one of near hysteria.

'Aw right. Aw right. Calm down, will ye. This is no gettin' us anywhere. I can just see me as the Godfather – Don Bridgeton – talking a' that Italian shite. I'd sound like that fucker Vince from the chippie round the corner: "Gonna stoppada selling drugs, Kevin, or a ma boy's a gonna make-a ya swim widda fishes, by-a the way." !'

The company collapsed into paroxysms of laughter – all except Charlie. He was only too well aware that he was the brunt of all this merriment. He did not appreciate having the piss taken out of him quite so publicly. Frank Gallagher stopped laughing and the company followed suit.

'Right, we don't want to start World War Three.'

He glanced towards Charlie.

'We don't want the polis climbing all over us but I do want you to start leaning heavily on Boyle's people. Pay them visits. Let them know our intentions are serious and if they won't do business for us, hurt them. Any way you like, but no comebacks.'

Again he glanced at Charlie who by this time had worked himself into his own version of his father's silent fury.

'We'll meet again a week tonight and I want to hear that things have been happening. I'm off to London next week and I intend to tell the boys there that normal service is about to be resumed. So, do not fuck me about. Right, who's for a pint in the Dolphin? My shout.'

Gallagher rose and made his way towards the door followed by his entourage.

All except Charlie. He hung back while the others left. When his father had looked in his direction he indicated he would follow in a minute.

With everyone gone, he sat back down and lit a cigarette. He smoked Balkan Sobranie Black Russian because he thought they were flash, but he actually hated the things and the strong taste of the tobacco did nothing to improve his humour.

'Why not, eh? Fucking gangsters! Don fucking Bridgeton! Swima widda fishes!'

The level of Charlie's voice increased with each phrase, 'Fuck yous! Fuck the fucking lot of yous!'

18

He ground out the partly smoked cigarette on top of a beer can.

'I'll fucking show you,' he whispered. Charlie picked up the telephone and began dialling.

*   *   *

Kevin Boyle was alive. He could hear the ticking of a bedside alarm clock. Each tick exploded inside his head. He risked opening his eyes slowly and very carefully. The room was in semi-darkness, for which he was truly grateful. He waited until the room came into focus. It was in no way familiar to him. He looked at the sleeping form beside him. It was in no way familiar to him.

He lifted the duvet and studied his companion. The girl was lying on her back with her face turned towards him. She was naked. Her blond hair was cut short and as his eyes wandered downwards, Kevin noted she was a real blond.

Nice tits, he thought to himself.

Kevin reached across and squeezed the girl's breast. When he obtained no response he shoved his hand roughly between her legs. The girl moaned and turned away from him.

'Useless bitch,' he muttered, and lay back on the bed. The events of the previous night began to come back to him – or at least some of them did.

It was customary for Kevin to be seen in one of the clubs he owned, buying drink for a group of hangers-on. He delighted in what he perceived to be hero worship. Whenever he entered a club, he would find himself surrounded by people anxious to be seen to be wishing him well.

In reality, the admiration society was composed of two classes of members – those who were quite happy to be bought drink all night, and those who felt safer to be in the company of Kevin Boyle than be perceived as an outsider.

If Kevin was in the mood, he would grandly announce, 'My tab' to the assembled company, and then pretend to be embarrassed by the adulation he received. His tipple was a large vodka and tonic (or a large VAT, as he described it). He did not much care for the taste of the stuff but because that was what Minder's Arthur Daley drank, he reckoned it must be the drink for a villain.

The crowd invariably contained its fair share of females and Kevin seldom encountered any difficulty in obtaining a companion for the night. He had little real regard for the female of the species and had only ever had one regular girlfriend, some years before. Marie had put up with him for six months despite the appalling treatment he dished out.

She only saw Kevin when it suited him. He would phone up and expect her to be ready to go out at a moment's notice. He was as generous with money as he was parsimonious with affection. Marie was tall, raven haired, long legged and stunningly attractive, and Kevin liked to be seen in the company of a beautiful woman. It suited the image he wanted to project. He would bring her presents, usually jewellery or expensive underwear, and take her out to the best restaurants. At the end of the evening Kevin expected Marie to perform sexually for him.

Kevin liked sex. He had no time for the gentler feelings or physical intricacies of lovemaking. He would take Marie back to her flat and tell her to undress as she walked up the stairs in the close. Sometimes he demanded that she strip in the car and walk along the street and into the building wearing only the latest underwear he had bought for her. Kevin liked underwear, especially Basques, stockings and suspenders, all of which he cheerfully bought in large quantities.

Marie was never allowed to wear trousers. Only once did she have the temerity to wear tights. Kevin had phoned to say that he would pick her up in ten minutes to go out for a meal. Marie was just back from her office job and had not had time to do other than have a quick wash and change into a dress. Boyle had parked his BMW outside her door and blasted the horn. When Marie got into the car, he greeted her by putting his hand up her skirt, as usual. When he felt no bare flesh he flew into a rage, told her to get out, sped off and over two weeks elapsed before he made any contact. A phone call announced they were going out for dinner, as if nothing had happened. When Marie got into the car, Kevin was delighted to discover she was wearing stockings. He handed her a box containing some Janet Reger silk underwear. He offered her no apology. She did not expect one.

Initially, all this made her feel quite daring. She was being treated like a tart and she loved it. As time passed, however, she came to realise that she was merely pandering to Kevin's baser instincts and getting very little worthwhile in return. She began to feel used, and she did not care for it.

Eventually she had enough. When Kevin called one night demanding she get ready instantly, Marie's response was succinct. Kevin exploded down the phone, calling her every foul name that she had ever heard of, and quite a few that were new to her. He would have nothing more to do with her. She would regret it.

Kevin was as good as his word.

But Marie didn't regret it.

When he discovered she had gone to Strathclyde University to read business studies it was all the proof he thought he required. She would be mixing with a load of toffee-nosed gits. She wouldn't have two pennies to rub together. She would have to shag the teachers to get through the exams. Better off without her.

Kevin had to content himself with a series of cheap, meaningless relationships but in reality, he missed Marie. He had enough trouble admitting this to himself. He could not admit it to anyone else and certainly would never let Marie find out.

The girl lying next to him was just one more in a long line.

Kevin recollected being in the club knocking back large VATs. He remembered chatting up various females, or at least indulging in what for him passed for chatting up. One of them had been blonde. He had a vague picture in his mind of changing the order to champagne cocktails, a lethal blend of cheap sparkling wine, brandy, Cointreau and Angostura bitters. He knew he would have driven his car – he always did. He recollected rolling around on the floor with a girl, trying to pull her clothes off. He did not remember if he succeeded. As far as sex was concerned neither his memory nor his groin could assist him. If he had done the business, he could only hope that he had enjoyed it at the time. By the look of things he was getting bugger all now.

Kevin climbed out of bed and headed for where he thought the bathroom might be. He was halfway to the door when his hangover caught up with him, swiftly followed by a wave of nausea. He lurched into the hall and luckily found himself facing his intended destination. He made it to the toilet with moments to spare.

Having parted company with the contents of his stomach, he sat on the cool, tiled floor, no longer convinced that he was alive. Indeed, at that precise moment, death would have come as a merciful release. The room was spinning about him. Due to the heavy pounding inside his skull, he thought his head was about to explode. His skin was cold and clammy, his pores oozing a liquid which could have been distilled, bottled and sold. His mouth felt as if a small feathered creature had crawled inside and died.

Kevin bent over the toilet again and retched violently. There was nothing left in his stomach and this exercise only made him feel worse – scarcely possible as this was.

'What the fuck did I drink last night?' he murmured.

Somehow he had to get himself together and get out of there – wherever there was. If he was going to die, he would rather die at home.

Standing under the shower, the hot water created the illusion for Kevin that he was feeling better. He had risked looking in the mirror, but the image which stared back at him had only made him feel sick again.

He dried himself and returned to the bedroom. As he walked

through the doorway, daylight pierced his eyes like sharp needles.

'Hi, Mike! Want some coffee?'

When the pain eased slightly, Kevin was able to observe his hostess, still naked, but now silhouetted against the bedroom window.

'Eh…what? Yeah…coffee would be good.'

'No problem. Shan't be long.'

The girl bounced towards him, her pert little breasts jiggling provocatively, showing no sign that her lack of clothes in front of a comparative stranger was causing her any embarrassment or alarm.

Who the hell are you? he wondered. And who the fuck is Mike?

As she passed him, the girl lightly flicked the end of his penis.

Kevin looked down. He was feeling better. 'Get back into bed. I'll bring it up, so to speak.'

As he sat on the edge of the bed Kevin heard a toilet flush and then footsteps going downstairs.

The girl spoke. 'Your car is parked outside in case you had forgotten. Not in a rush – I hope. You've got promises to keep.'

For reasons he could not explain, even if he had to, Kevin began to feel decidedly uneasy. This bitch must know who I am, he thought, and it's not fucking Mike…the whoor is at it.

It was not exactly unknown for Kevin to spend the night with a strange female. It was unusual for him not to know who she was or where he was. It was unheard of for him to use a false name – he was Kevin Boyle, after all. Maybe it wasn't what he drank but what was in what he drank. Maybe this was a set-up. Maybe he had been poisoned. Maybe his paranoia was out of control.

He came to a decision. 'Time to go, my son!'

It was not in his nature to sneak anywhere, but while the girl made the coffee he dressed and tiptoed down the stairs, then opened and closed the door behind him with all the practised skill of the housebreaker he had been in his younger days. To his relief, the dark metallic blue 3-series M3 BMW was parked directly outside the house. He pointed the key fob at it and three rapid beeps emanated from the car. Only when he was cosseted in the leather driver's seat and had started the 320-bhp engine did he feel he could begin to relax. Looking around, he recognised the street in which he was parked and realised that he was only about half a mile from home.

Kevin caught a glimpse of himself in the rear-view mirror and began to laugh.

'Get a grip of yourself, you tosser. This tart's got you in some fucking state. Fuck it, I'm getting this sorted out.' His sense of anxiety was replaced by more familiar anger. He would find out who this Mike was, and what the girl was up to, even if he had to knock the truth out of her. At least that would make him feel better.

He switched off the ignition and put his hand on the door lever. Had he not been in such a state, he might have taken note of a light-coloured car parked down the street. He might have seen a figure leaving the car and converting a woollen hat into a Balaclava. He might have reacted to the gun which the man carried in his right hand. These oversights were the last ones he would ever make.

The only indication he had of approaching danger was the sound of breaking glass. An instant before two nine-millimetre bullets penetrated his brain, Kevin Boyle issued his last meditation on earth.

'What the fuck…?'

Chapter Two

'Morning Betty, cup of tea and two rolls and bacon please.'

'Sorry son, the bacon's all finished.'

'Give me a couple of rolls and sausage, then.'

'The sausage is all still froze, son, you'll have to wait a wee while.'

'Have you got any eggs, ones that are not still frozen?'

'Oh aye, we've got plenty of eggs.'

'Right, give me a cup of tea and two fried egg rolls, please.'

'Sorry son, the rolls has no arrived yet.'

Grant McAllister was an outstandingly good detective, both in his own opinion and that of his police colleagues. Despite his failure to procure a breakfast, very little avoided his finely-tuned senses. He knew the instant he tasted it that the tepid liquid in the cup was tea. After all, that was what he had asked for. Mind you, if he had just been handed the stuff, far from drinking it, he would almost certainly have sent it to the forensic science laboratory for analysis.

His eyes drifted round the police canteen. He found it a cheerless place. The formica-topped tables, wood and metal chairs combined with the pale and peeling lemon paint on the walls to create an ambience that would depress a saint. It was a place he truly loathed and normally avoided at all costs. He had finished his real work, but was now facing the prospect of tackling a mountain of paper. He enjoyed being a detective. Even as a child it was what he always wanted to be. What he hated was being a clerk. These days police work involved so much bureaucracy and paper that he sometimes felt personally responsible for the felling of half the pulp forests of Finland.

At the end of the night shift, he just wanted to go home for breakfast, a shower and a change. Nineteen years' police service, during which he had steadily but rapidly risen to the rank of Detective Superintendent, had failed to harden him to the scenes of crime he witnessed on a daily basis. He could view a dead body dispassionately, but would touch one only if absolutely necessary. He had never been able to understand why so many people were prepared to live their lives surrounded by filth and squalor. Many of the homes he visited would offend the proprietor of a below-average hovel.

He had all but given up on the tea and was steeling himself for the three hours of pen-pushing which lay ahead. At least when that was done he had the prospect of three days off to savour – three very special days.

Today he was in a police canteen but tomorrow he was off to Milan. For the first time ever he was going abroad – to a football match. McAllister, like many of his colleagues, was a supporter of Glasgow Rangers. He had been a regular at Ibrox since his father bought him his first season ticket when he was sixteen years old. If detection was his passion, football was his obsession.

Work permitting, he would never miss a domestic game, but he had never been able to travel abroad. Now the prospect of Inter Milan against Rangers in the San Siro stadium was more than enough to make him forget the lack of breakfast, the horrendous state of the tea and the prospect of the paperwork. By this time tomorrow he would be on his way to Glasgow Airport and a flight to Italy and not just any old flight but the club's own charter. Thanks to a good friend who was the club doctor, McAllister would be travelling with the official party, players and all. Even a hard-nosed Glasgow detective could become quite excited at the prospect of being in the same company as Richard Gough and Ally McCoist.

The tea had by now lost any appeal it ever had. He decided he would finish what he had to do, get out of the police office and go into hiding. Nothing, but nothing, was going to stop him being on that plane. When he had first been invited to go to Milan, he had been foolish enough to tell the members of his squad. Not normally given to boasting and invariably reticent about anything other than work, McAllister could not resist it. He was not really bragging, but he was like a kid who had been given a new toy and was desperate to show it off to his pals.

The 'boss' was normally a dour individual who was a stickler for discipline and attention to detail. He seldom socialised with his colleagues and the nickname used behind his back, 'Aye on', reflected the fact that whatever he did, he behaved like an on-duty policeman. However, the sight of the Super exhibiting such obvious glee was too much for his men to ignore.

For two weeks now, they had wound him up, mercilessly.

They went around animatedly discussing the fact that the long-range forecast for Europe predicted the worst weather for fifty years with blizzards and sub-zero temperatures. No way a game could be played in these conditions. McAllister made it plain that he was unmoved by this blatant piece of nonsense – but he kept checking with the Meteorological Office, just in case. They had someone pretend to represent Rangers phone him to confirm that he had all the necessary inoculations.

Everyone knew he was terrified of hypodermic needles. They had haunted McAllister since he was a young beat cop.

One Saturday night he had taken the victim of an assault to the casualty department of Glasgow Royal Infirmary, a fairly mundane occurrence. While waiting in the cubicle to take a statement, a nurse came in and began to administer an anti-tetanus injection. McAllister promptly fainted and ended up on the bed next to the assault victim who was exuding alcohol and concern in equal measure.

With all the loyalty for which police officers are noted, his neighbour ensured that the story reached the police office before the two of them returned to book off at the end of their shift. McAllister would blush every time he was reminded of the incident. Since that day, and whenever possible, he had taken steps to avoid being in that position. He had already checked. You did not need any inoculations to visit Italy. Nice try, chaps.

Only one event made him wobble – ever so slightly. A memo from the Assistant Chief Constable landed on his desk informing him of a strategy meeting for senior officers, on the very day he would be in Milan. Although he was scrupulously honest and had never bent, let alone broken a rule, McAllister realised he needed a reason to avoid this gathering. He seriously needed an excuse; he desperately needed a convincing lie. Illness? A family funeral? What if he was seen at the airport? Would he get away with the funeral being abroad? Worse still, what if he was spotted in the crowd by someone watching the game on television? Now he was being ridiculous. There would be eighty thousand people there and the cameras would be concentrating on the play, not the crowd, and almost certainly not on him. But if he was seen, would he be disciplined? His reputation for integrity would be destroyed. He might even be demoted. His income would be reduced. His pension affected. How would he explain it to his wife? This was verging on the ridiculous. He was actually in a mild panic.

'Fucking bastards!' McAllister did not normally swear. Not that he was a prude. He just found the use of foul language in general and the 'F' word in particular, to be unnecessary except in extremis. This time he was prepared to make an exception. The memo he was staring malevolently at had been signed by Assistant Chief Constable Alex Scott, who had retired a year previously. He had allowed himself to be taken in by a fake. But it was a bloody good fake.

'Fucking bastards!', he shouted into the squad room. This profanity from the boss caused a moment of stunned silence, followed swiftly by an outburst of hysterical laughter.

McAllister did not discover the author of the forgery, but strongly suspected Detective Inspector Bob Taylor, his second in command. Taylor had twenty eight years service, was looking forward to his retirement, cared not one whit that his boss was nine years his junior, and was a renowned practical joker. He was the only one who would risk such a thing. If he was found out, he was the only one who would get away with it, and wouldn't care a damn if he didn't.

A chair was drawn back and McAllister was aware of a figure sitting down opposite him.

'Good morning, Bob.'

'Well, that remains to be seen, boss. Do you want the good news or the bad news?'

McAllister was by now focused on his DI. If this was another prank he would be ready for it. He steepled his fingers under his chin in his typical, 'I am now concentrating' pose.

'The good news is there's been a murder.'

McAllister slammed his hands flat down on the table.

'Really, Bob, your sense of humour can be just a bit much at times. I'm going to Italy and that's that. And trying to get me going by putting on this phoney serious face and pretending there's been a killing is just not funny. Now, if you have nothing sensible to say to me, I suggest we both get on with our work.'

'Sorry boss, the word's just come in.'

'Enough! If you've got nothing better to do, I have.'

McAllister stood up abruptly and headed towards the canteen door.

'Boss, the bad news for you, and him I suppose, is that it looks as if Kevin Boyle's been shot. Dead.'

McAllister rounded on the DI. The look on Bob Taylor's face told him everything he didn't want to know.

'Very dead, boss. Sorry.'

Italy.

The San Siro.

Milan.

'I don't bloody believe it. Shit!'

●　　　●　　　●

The small crowd of watchers was stirred by the arrival on the scene of McAllister, Taylor, and two detective sergeants. The general consensus was that the high heid yins had arrived.

The area surrounding Kevin Boyle's BMW had been cordoned off by blue and white plastic tape and resolutely guarded by a number of uniformed police officers. A sergeant detached himself from the group and approached the detectives.

McAllister was relieved when he saw Ben Alexander walking towards him. The two men had joined the police at the same time and had been trained together. Thereafter their careers had taken very different paths. While McAllister had steadily climbed the ranks of the CID, Ben Alexander had been quite content to be an old-fashioned beat cop who eventually, but deservedly, made the rank of sergeant. He had tried the inspector's examinations but, by his own admission, was no scholar and the theoretical side of police work held little appeal for him.

What he was was an outstandingly good thief-catcher. He made a point of knowing everyone in his area, and everything about them. If there was a spate of house-breakings, Alexander would go instantly to the men who were the likely candidates. They were presented with a very simple choice. He could, and would, make their life miserable by being at their back every time they breathed, watching their every move – or a name could be forthcoming. Invariably, a name came forth.

There had been a time when parents who were having problems with unruly sons would speak to Alexander, who would then have 'a quiet word.' The recipient of the quiet word was frequently so shaken by it that he would trip and fall, thereby sustaining a black eye. However, the force of the policeman's personality or the pain of the accidental injury was often more than enough to get a youngster back on the straight and narrow path. This was community policing in operation, long before the powers that be invented the term.

Throughout his career Ben Alexander believed in treating all members of the public with the same degree of respect that he expected them to show to him. He demanded no less from the officers under his command; otherwise they might find themselves invited for a 'quiet word.'

'Painstaking', 'pedantic', 'cautious', were all words which had been applied to him in his annual reports and Alexander would not have regarded these terms as being in any sense critical. His experience had taught him that more crimes were solved by wearing out shoe leather than by Holmesean deduction. He also believed that every man should stick to his trade.

In police forces everywhere, there exists a long standing rivalry between the suits and the uniforms. One lot are flash bastards, the others are woodentops. Alexander had no time for the age-old clichés. In any inquiry, he would play his part, however small, to the best of his ability, and he expected everyone else to do the same. The philosophy was simple, but effective.

He had been out on a routine mobile patrol when he received a radio message about the shooting. He was only two minutes away from the scene and on his arrival a cursory glance into the car told him he had come upon a murder scene. He recognised the car and what remained of the head of Kevin Boyle. The paramedics arrived shortly after him, but they too quickly realised that their part in matters would be a purely formal one.

Alexander secured the scene then sent for a photographer, scenes of crime officers, a police casualty surgeon, forensic scientists and the CID.

'Morning, sir. It is Kevin Boyle. The doc's been sent for to confirm death. I think you'll find that he's been shot. The photographer has arrived and is taking some general views, but no one has been near the car since I got here. Socos are on their way. There are empty cartridge cases on the road. One of my men is standing beside them. It's all yours, sir.'

Grant McAllister smiled thinly. 'Typical Ben Alexander,' he thought. 'Canny soul, does everything by the book and commits himself to absolutely nothing.'

'Thanks, Ben. We'll take a look. See if you can get the spectators back a bit. They're an audience, I can live without.'

As Alexander turned away to do as requested, McAllister could see that the sergeant was pained that the scene had been other than perfect for the arrival of the investigating team.

'Oh, and Ben, I'd like a private word before I leave. This is your patch after all. I'd appreciate your help.'

McAllister knew the sergeant would have access to the local gossip, and many a case had been solved because a rumour was taken seriously. But, more to the point, McAllister was a man-manager par excellence. He was only too well aware that Alexander would enjoy his young officers hearing that their Sergeant had an important part to play in a murder inquiry. He would put himself about to see what he could find out. Noblesse oblige.

McAllister and Taylor walked towards the car. The scene which greeted them was stark in its simplicity. They noted three empty cartridge cases on the road surface, lying about ten feet from the car.

'Looks like nine millimetre. Must have been fired very close to the window. Self-loader.'

Taylor was an authorised firearms officer and indulged in pistol shooting as a hobby. This experience had often come in handy in the professional context. The ballistics experts would analyse the cases and might be able to come up with a good deal of information about the gun which fired them. However, Taylor knew a nine-millimetre when he saw one, and the presence of spent cartridge cases at the scene meant the weapon used was a self-loading pistol which ejected the fired cases. Having been ejected from the gun, the cases would travel on average about eight to ten feet. At least their finding gave the police a starting point. Had a revolver been used, the fired cases would have remained in the chamber of the gun and been removed from the scene by the assailant.

The two officers looked into the car. The driver's window was shattered, the glass lying all over the road and spread around the inside of the vehicle.

The body of the driver was lying slumped towards the passenger seat. The right side of the head was a pulped mass of blood, bone and brain matter. Human tissue was spattered over the cabin. Emanating from the car was a sweet and sickly smell tinged with an odour which those who have experienced it can tell instantly is the aroma of death.

McAllister noted that the front passenger window was shattered. A nod brought this to Taylor's attention.

'Exits?'

'Possibly. No guarantee we will find any of the bullets still inside him. Let's get a search organised and see what we can discover. All the men you need. I don't want anything missed.'

'Do you want the door-to-door started straight away?'

'Absolutely. It looks as if Kevin was parked outside that block of flats over there. Maybe he was visiting. Maybe he was leaving. Who and why? At any rate someone must have heard something or, with a bit of luck, seen something.'

Taylor walked away towards the two waiting detective sergeants.

McAllister stood and stared at the now very late Kevin Boyle. Compassion came naturally to him and he found himself moved by the sight of the shattered remains of a human being. Who he was or what he may have been were now of no importance. Although he had no personal involvement with Kevin Boyle, he knew all about his family's violent history and current criminal activities. From one viewpoint, society would be better off for Kevin's passing. On the other hand, no one deserved a death such as this. This was no exchange of violence. Boyle had not been given a chance. Whoever carried out the shooting had been determined, cold-blooded and cowardly. Was he (or she) driven by revenge, jealousy or some equally powerful motive? Or were they doing a professional job? Already a psychological profile was forming in McAllister's mind. Already he appreciated that 'why?' might be the key to answering the vital question 'who?'.

He became aware of activity behind him, and turned round to see a small bald man wearing a distinctly crumpled suit and carrying a battered leather holdall: obviously the police casualty surgeon to carry out the onerous task of pronouncing life extinct. The good doctor was not about to be overly taxed in earning his callout fee.

'How can I be of assistance? Gunshots, I believe.'

McAllister bristled.

'Not much doubt about this one, doctor. Please don't touch anything unless it is absolutely necessary.'

'I have done this before, you know, inspector,' responded the doctor, somewhat huffily.

'It's Superintendent, actually, and I don't care how often you have done this before. This is a murder scene. Just give me the bit of paper saying he's dead and then the real experts can get on with their work. Thank you, doctor. You'll want to get on, I dare say.'

'Well, really. I thought we were all professionals.'

'Some of us are.'

McAllister watched the crumpled suit sulk off towards the car. If there was a case to be made out for ethnic cleansing, it would be of police casualty surgeons. Normally they were general practitioners who were called out by the police to perform routine tasks such as certifying death, taking blood or hair samples and the like. They were definitely not forensic experts, despite what they might care to think. Too many of them considered themselves to be the re-incarnation of John Glaister, the legendary forensic pathologist, and would proffer all sorts of theories as to how a crime may have been committed. If an inexperienced policeman were not careful, he could easily be misled by such theorising.

'Dead loss,' muttered McAllister, smiling wryly as he realised he had all but made a joke. He checked himself. Murder scenes were not suitable places for any form of levity.

The level of activity in the street was increasing, despite the fact that the uniforms had moved back the small crowd of onlookers. Forensic scientists had arrived and were donning fresh white overalls prior to commencing their painstaking examination. The police photographer was packing away his camera equipment having taken pictures of the scene from every conceivable angle. Taylor was still engaged in conversation. McAllister recognised his companions as being two officers from the firearms section. He walked over to join them.

'The spent cases are definitely nine millimetre. We'll have a quick check of the car here then take it back to headquarters and give it the full treatment. You'll get our preliminary report later today, or tomorrow morning at the latest, depending on what the search and the post-mortem comes up with.' The two men headed off to their work.

'Sorry about this, boss. I guess tomorrow's a no no,' sympathised Taylor.

McAllister shrugged his shoulders.

'Thanks. What progress are we making?'

'There's a low-loader on its way to pick up the car when the scientists have done their bit. They're going to erect screens so that we can get the body removed first. There's some press photographers hanging about. I don't see why we should make it easy for them. The fingerprint boys will do their stuff once we get the car back. Probably won't find anything, but it looks like rain and I don't want to take any chances. The pathologists are on their way to the mortuary. I take it you want to attend the post-mortem?'

'Better, I suppose.'

'At least it won't take long.'

McAllister nodded.

'Professor Walters is going to do it himself. He's coming here for a quick look see first. Should be here any moment. I've arranged to get as many of the troops here as possible to get the door-to-doors done. The HOLMES is being set up.'

The Home Office Larger Major Enquiry System or HOLMES, a computerised system was established by the Home Office in London for use in major criminal investigations. It enabled a mass of data to be collated and cross-referenced thereby avoiding, or at least minimising, the risk of important evidence being overlooked or its significance not appreciated.

'Alex Adams is going to be the office manager and Tom Donaldson will be in charge of the productions.'

Again McAllister nodded. As ever, Bob Taylor was right on the ball. Efficient to a fault.

'Right. I don't think there is much more for us to do here. Let's go break the news to Hugh Boyle that his number one son is no more, then we'll head back to the office. I want everybody on their toes on this one so we can get it wrapped up as soon as possible. I don't want this to develop into a war. I've a sneaky feeling that old Hughie may just jump to conclusions about who was responsible.'

'The Gallaghers?'

'Got it in one.'

'I know there's no love lost between them, but this is way over the top.'

'Maybe so, but I'm thinking of the Gallaghers, and if I am, you can be damn sure that Hugh Boyle will.'

Ben Alexander approached.

'We're just off, Ben. You take charge of the scene until everything is cleared away. Any ideas?'

'Right, sir. Kevin lived at home but had a fair string of, well, girlfriends, I suppose you would call them. Could have been visiting one of them. Lot of people didn't like him but most were too scared to do anything about it. I'll have a quiet word in a few ears. Mind you, one thing is curious. I wonder what happened to that sidekick of Kevin's, Tam whatever his name is. McHarry? No…Tam McGarry. Not like Kevin to go anywhere without him being in close attendance.'

'Interesting. Thanks, Ben. That's just one of the questions I might ask Mr Hugh Boyle, and probably one of the questions he won't answer if he runs true to form. We're off. We'll be in touch.'

●   ●   ●

There are many particularly disagreeable aspects of police work. One of the least pleasant is the bearing of bad news: children killed by drunken drivers, missing relatives turning up dead and dashing all lingering hopes, fathers who have left for work never to return, the victims of a brutal murder. No amount of experience makes the task easier or less painful. The training has not been invented which enables the right words to be found. Even genuine compassion appears false and insincere. Attempts to lend support seem contrived, artificial and are usually rejected. At the moments of our deepest pain we need the company of people we love, who love us, not the company of strangers.

McAllister had performed this duty many times. If asked, he would have claimed confidently that he had seen every conceivable form of reaction – hysteria, rage, total disbelief, outright denial. On one occasion when he broke the news to an elderly man that his wife had been killed by a lorry, the old fellow suffered a massive heart attack and died on the spot.

However, nothing could have prepared him for the scene which now confronted his eyes.

Hugh Boyle, Glasgow hardman of legendary proportions, was curled up in the corner of a settee. His arms were clasped tightly round his knees and he was rocking himself gently backwards and forwards.

When the two officers had arrived at Boyle's door the reception had been as hostile as had been expected. Boyle's hatred of the police was taken as read but he was ranting and raving about a search and his son being handcuffed for fuck all and in the middle of the fucking night – McAllister was totally mystified. When he explained that the visit concerned Kevin, this produced another torrent of abuse. Kevin was a business man…police harassment and victimisation…they were only after him because of who he was, not what he did…filthy police scum…and so on. All par for the course.

Eventually Mrs Boyle appeared at the door. McAllister had never met her before – her slim build, elegant appearance and sparkling blue eyes left him in no doubt that when she was younger, she must have been stunningly attractive. She was still a very striking woman.

Her influence on Hugh Boyle was considerable and instantaneous. Her husband calmed down and made no protest when she invited the two unwelcome guests into the house. Hugh Boyle contented himself with glowering at the officers as one would at something singularly nasty which had been inadvertently trodden on.

When everyone was seated in the comfortably furnished living-room surrounded by paintings which had all the appearance of being originals, McAllister broke the news. Before he could express his condolences, Hugh Boyle let out a primeval scream which came not from the throat, but somewhere deep within his very being. He then pulled himself into the almost textbook foetal position in which he thereafter remained. Since then he had not uttered a comprehensible word, but whimpered to himself like a frightened puppy.

Some hard man, thought McAllister to himself. Typical bully. Quite happy to dish it out but when it comes to their own doorstep they just can't handle it.

The reaction of Annie Boyle had been even more unexpected. No tears. No obvious signs of distress. Pain had appeared in her eyes for a moment but then she caught herself and sat motionless next to her husband.

To him she offered no words or gestures of comfort or sought any from him. Indeed, the only way she acknowledged his existence was to fire him a look which bore all the hallmarks of utter contempt.

The four sat in a silence interrupted only by the moaning of Hugh Boyle. It probably lasted for no more than a few seconds, but seemed to endure for much longer.

McAllister started to speak.

'There are some formalities Mrs...'

Annie Boyle put up her hand.

'As you can see, Superintendent, my husband is very upset.' A statement of fact, said calmly and without a bit of emotion or apparent concern.

'You will require that my son's body is identified. Just let me know where and when. I dare say you have our telephone number even though it's ex-directory.' Again, business-like, almost matter of fact.

'Whatever you think of my family, I expect you to find whoever did this.'

'We will do everything we can, Mrs. Boyle.'

'I expect you to do better than that. After all, it IS what you get paid for. And I suggest you bear very clearly in mind that not everyone may accept that the police will do their duty for people like us.'

The meaning was clear and without any ambiguity. McAllister chose to ignore it.

'We will need statements from…'

'That can wait until I have seen my son and spoken with his brothers. I think that's in everyone's best interests, don't you? Now allow me to show you out.'

* * *

'Hard as fucking nails, that one.'

The two officers were heading back to their office, having received a message that the post-mortem had been scheduled for half past one.

'More than just hard, Bob. She certainly wasn't going to let us see what she was really feeling. But did you see the way she looked at Hughie? It's… I don't know, it's almost as if she was blaming him. There was no concern or compassion in her eyes. I would say that she looked at the miserable sod as if she hated him.'

'Boyle just fell apart. I expected him to go ballistic – mainly at us.'

'Makes you wonder, doesn't it? There's no doubt she was letting us know that if we do not get this sorted out, fast, someone else will. I would have expected a threat like that from Boyle himself.'

'Power behind the throne?'

'Maybe, but it was almost as if she was ready for something like this and had rehearsed the role she intended to play. It wasn't just willpower. It was more deliberate even than that. It was contrived, unnatural. It's bothering me and I don't know why. That bothers me even more.'

'You don't think she knows something about it, do you?'

'I have no doubt that Mrs Boyle knows a great deal more than she will ever tell us. I'm sure she will have her own list of likely suspects. Half of Glasgow will. But it's more than that. OK, she's a Boyle first and foremost. She knows what the family business is and how it's run. So she knows all about the risks. Even so, that lady's self-control was quite extraordinary. The only way I can describe it is that it was almost as if she was expecting us.'

'Maybe she was. Maybe somebody phoned before we got there. Maybe Kevin had a warning. Maybe…'

'Too many maybes, Bob.'

'Maybe.'

* * *

There are good days and bad days in everyone's life, except for Sammy McPhee, who now merely existed rather than lived and had only bad days. Glasgow, in common with most major cities, has its fair share of the homeless. But the Glasgow dosser is a particularly hardy breed. Winter or summer they brave the elements, finding shelter where they can, moving their meagre belongings around with them in plastic carrier bags. Come nightfall, some will seek refuge in one of the city's model lodging houses where at least they will find a reasonably warm bed and something half-decent to eat. During the day, they wander the streets plying their trade as plumbers. Anything that moves they will put a tap on. Any money they come by will be spent on bottles of Buckfast, Lanliq or other brands of fortified wine, known locally as 'electric soup.'

Others, distrustful of anything that smacks of authority, will sleep wherever they can. Shop doorways are preferred because of the warmth emanating from the premises. Unfortunately, such places invariably provide no more than a temporary respite before the occupant is moved on by the police. After all, the citizenry might be offended by the sight of someone setting up home in the entrance to their favourite chic boutique.

Any corner in any alleyway which provides shelter from the worst excesses of the weather becomes a temporary hotel. Room service is non-existent and breakfast is invariably off.

Sammy McPhee had been one of Glasgow's free spirits for over ten years, but it had not always been so.

Sammy and his wife had owned a small newsagent and tobacconist business in Clydebank to the west of the city of Glasgow. They were a devoted couple who were hardly ever out of each other's company, and hated it when they were. Life was good. The shipyards were operating at full capacity and Sammy and his wife Betty worked all hours supplying the workmen with cigarettes, newspapers, filled rolls and, in the morning especially, bottles of Irn Bru, the best known means of dealing with the hangovers left by the previous night's excesses.

Sammy's proudest boast was that he fed the men who built the great Cunard liner Queen Elizabeth II, cleared their heads, polluted their lungs and made 'a right few bob in the process'. Even when the yards went into decline, Sammy and Betty were able to live comfortably. They had always been careful with their money and had enough put by to help them cope with the drop in income forced upon them by the changing economic climate.

The shop became a meeting place for the old men who would hang around reminiscing about what they perceived to be the 'good old days', blaming the Tories for everything and proclaiming how glad they were not to be young and looking for a trade. After all, no more real ships were going to be built on the Clyde.

The local primary school was about a hundred yards away, and two or three times a day hordes of children would flood into Sammy's for lemonade and crisps. The old men viewed them as pests, but Sammy and Betty adored children. They would regularly undercharge their young clientele or give them free sweets. Partly this was altruism, but it was also good business practice. Sammy was developing customer loyalty, and there was never a problem with shoplifters.

They had no children of their own – just one of those things. But hundreds of nieces and nephews meant that Uncle Sammy and Aunty Betty had all the family they could ever want. Sammy's shop was open seven days a week, 364 days a year. He took New Year's Day off. It was traditional, after all.

One day, by nine in the morning, there was no sign of activity at the shop. People knew instantly that something must be wrong and headed round to Sammy's house. No answer led to the arrival of the police to force entry. In the upstairs bedroom they found Sammy sitting on the floor staring blankly into space. He held Betty's lifeless body in his arms. A massive cerebral haemorrhage had taken his beloved wife from him.

Betty was buried on a cold, wet Friday morning. The cemetery was crowded and it seemed as if the whole of the town, young and old, had turned up to say their goodbyes. As Betty, in her oak coffin, was lowered into her grave, she took with her the very essence of her husband's being and his own will to live. That afternoon Sammy re-opened the shop. Everyone advised him to have a rest, go on holiday, take time, heal himself. The advice went unheeded. Although the shop was open, Sammy had no real interest in it. He could see Betty and hear her voice, but she was no longer there. At night he returned to their house, but it was no longer his home, their home.

Sammy had never been a drinker. He enjoyed an occasional dram, but had never been drunk in his entire life. A week after the funeral he woke up in the morning to find himself lying on the hall floor at the foot of the stairs. He had failed to make it to his bed, their bed. When he struggled into the kitchen to make himself some tea, he discovered a scene worthy of a painting by Salvador Dali. There was a pot on the stove filled with washing powder. The door of the washing-machine was open and the clothes inside were covered by the contents of a tin of tomato soup. Everything was covered by foul-smelling vomit. That morning, for the very first time, Sammy experienced the horrors of a hangover. It was to be the first of many. Sammy had heard of the hair of the dog. It bit him with a vengeance. That day the shop stayed closed.

As the weeks passed, Sammy spent more time inside a bottle than he did at his work. The shop ran out of stock. Sammy could not summon up the enthusiasm to replace it. People tried to help, encourage, cajole, but to no avail. Eventually they were forced to take their custom elsewhere. There was nothing in Sammy's shop to buy. The children could not understand what was wrong with their once favourite uncle. Sometimes he would not speak to them at all. On other occasions he would simply snatch their money and tell them to take whatever they wanted – not that there was much of a selection to choose from. Worst of all, he was now dirty and smelled.

One day at noon there was no sign of activity in the shop. Someone phoned the police who eventually made their way to Sammy's home, once again. No answer led them to force entry. There was no sign of Sammy. He was gone and clearly did not intend to return. A scribbled note on the mantelpiece invited the finder to sell everything off and give the money to charity. Wandering round the sad house, the police officer quickly realised that there would not be much worth selling, although the wallpaper and carpets, beneath the dirt and stains, told him it had been a nice house – once.

Sammy McPhee left Clydebank, intending never to return. He took with him only the clothes he stood up in and the good Crombie coat Betty had bought for him. Material possessions had too many memories attached to them, and he had enough of these already. Remembering was easy. It was time to forget.

He travelled into Glasgow, heading he knew not where. Ten years later he had still not made up his mind.

The streets were now the only home he had. He had tried the hostels, but in the confinement of the darkness Betty would come to him. Dreams turned into nightmares and he would be wakened by his own screams. Not surprisingly this tended to upset some of his fellow residents who on occasions sent him back to sleep without the aid of narcotics.

He learned to eke out a meagre living by scavenging abandoned buildings for bits of scrap metal which he could sell on for a few pounds. When times were especially hard, he would visit the rubbish bins of city hotels. You could find food there and sometimes, if your luck was in, there might be a bottle with some wine left in it. A 1976 Chateau Montrose made an agreeable change from the usual gut rot which formed his staple diet.

In more recent years, the streets had become a dangerous place in which to live. Many youngsters were now homeless but were not prepared to try to make the best of their lot. They regarded old winos like Sammy as being easy pickings. Several times he was attacked and robbed of the few coins he had worked so hard to collect. He had no friends. You trust your friends, and trusting people can be dangerous, especially when you are living rough. A man who is desperate for a drink has no respect for or loyalty to someone who may have the means to pay for it.

Among the dosser fraternity, Sammy was known as 'the coat'. The Crombie was now frayed, tattered and filthy, but Sammy was never to be seen without it. There was only one man with whom he had regular contact called Scar. Scar could easily have been around seventy years old. On the other hand, he could have been forty. His face was savagely disfigured by burns. But Scar was a thinker who was undoubtedly well educated and kept abreast of what was happening in the wider world. He always had newspapers or magazines in his pockets and Sammy was fascinated by his ability to expound upon the economy, the state of the Middle East, the latest EU directive and many other topics which were way above Sammy's head.

Although Sammy only spoke with Scar occasionally, their paths frequently crossed in the City centre. Scar canvassed the same rubbish bins as Sammy.

Then Scar disappeared.

Sammy had long since given up reading newspapers. The wider world was of little or no interest to him. By chance he saw a copy of the Evening Times which carried a report of an unidentified vagrant being found dead in the River Clyde. He had been stabbed repeatedly before being dumped in the water. The brief description made reference to the deceased man having a face which was badly scarred. The police were appealing for witnesses. Sammy knew it had to be his friend. Murdered.

Already fearful, Sammy now lived in a state of constant alarm. However irrational it may have been, he was bitter at Scar for abandoning him. People always let you down. He would never let himself get close to anyone ever again. Never, ever, ever.

Sammy turned off Ingram Street down the lane between the High Court Annexe and the Ingram Hotel. He would search the bins before checking out which of his regular haunts were vacant and had bed space available.

The man who knocked him onto his back neither stopped nor apologised. A second man hurrying up the lane tripped over one of Sammy's carrier bags and landed heavily on the now prostrate Sammy. He got to his feet and made to kick this piece of garbage. Before he could do so, his companion instructed him, in no uncertain terms, to get a move on.

'Mick bastard,' thought Sammy as he struggled up off the ground. His bags had spilled out some of their precious contents which he hurriedly scraped back inside. As he walked, he could sense no serious damage. A few more bumps and bruises were neither here nor there. For a moment Sammy thought of heading straight to his bed. However, knowing his luck, there would be good stuff in the hotel's bin, and he would miss out. This was an error of judgement he would swiftly grow to regret.

The first of the bins bore Sammy no fruit. Lifting the second lid, his spirits soared. Some might have said 'Eureka'. Sammy settled for 'fucking magic.' On cursory examination, the leather jacket he had pulled out seemed to be a beauty. It was undoubtedly nearly new and had some form of quilted lining. That this would be a warm garment never entered his head. He would sell the jacket to one of the boys at Paddy's Market. This jacket was money. It never occurred to him to ask himself why such a quality article had been dumped in a bin. Life's rare blessings were to be accepted without hesitation or reservation. In any event, finders keepers, losers greeters.

Actually, it was a pity he could not keep it. It fitted him rather well. But such a garment would only get him mugged and Sammy could do without that, thank you very much.

Having carefully folded the jacket and placed it into a carrier bag, Sammy again dug in to the bin and rummaged around to see what else he could find. The Gods were smiling on him. There was certainly something there.

'Shit.' Sammy swiftly pulled his hand out of the bin. It was wet and sticky. He walked over to a street lamp, but the yellow light only confirmed the presence of a damp and tacky substance.

All his street senses told him to get the hell out of it, but curiosity got the better of him. It required a considerable effort, but Sammy was able to haul the bin under the light. He climbed up on to it and as he peered down into it he started to scream.

Such was his panic that he did not pause to pick up his belongings. He even abandoned the new leather jacket. Sammy's only desire was to run away as fast as his legs would carry him, precisely what he should have done in the first place.

Unfortunately for Sammy, the police officers who had observed this manic dosser tearing towards them had other plans. They grabbed him and Sammy knew that another personal nightmare was only just beginning.

* * *

40

McAllister and Taylor arrived back at the police office and went straight to the room in which they knew HOLMES had been set up and from which the inquiry would be run. Matters were already gathering their own momentum. Several officers were busying themselves with the many mundane duties necessary to get a major investigation under way. Computer screens were switched on, files were being opened, telephones were in constant use.

Having satisfied himself that the operation was well and truly under way, McAllister headed towards his own office.

'Let's have a chat, Bob. See what we've got so far.'

'Cup of cats?' The coffee, tea, soup and hot chocolate produced by the vending machine in the building was disaffectionately known as 'cat's piss.' Each beverage had a similar appearance and, although no one could swear to it from personal experience, the suspicion was that it all tasted the same.

'Why not? Everyone should live dangerously now and again.'

Seated in the Superintendent's room, the two men concluded, having tasted the lukewarm liquid, that life was dangerous enough without taking unnecessary risks.

'Right, Bob, we've got Kevin Boyle shot dead. Whoever did it meant him not to survive. Maybe he was a man with a grudge against the bold boy, who just happened to be passing, just happened to have a nine-millimetre pistol with him, just happened to see yer man and just shot him.'

'Not likely.'

'No, there's nothing due to chance about this. The killer had to be told where Kevin was. Either that or he has been following him. Then he had to get away after the shooting.'

'Hopefully, someone saw the thing actually happen. Even if they can't identify the gunman, they might be able to help us with the car. It's highly unlikely he just casually strolled away.'

'Agreed. We need to know why Kevin was in that particular street in the first place. Who was he visiting? Was he arriving or was he leaving?'

'He was leaving.'

McAllister looked quizzically at his colleague, not because of the comment itself, but the degree of confidence with which it was made.

'I spoke to the cop who first arrived on the scene. Bright lad. Should go far. Might be worth giving him a bit of CID experience in this one. He felt the bonnet of the car. It was stone-cold.'

Again McAllister looked at the DI. This time not quizzically, but with amusement.

'And the name of this bright lad who should go far and who deserves such sudden recognition? I don't suppose his first name would be David by any chance?'

Taylor grinned. His son had joined the police two years earlier, something of which as a father he was inordinately proud.

'OK, OK, good work. We'll see what we can do for the boy. Happy now, you crafty old devil?'

McAllister was inwardly chiding himself. Cold bonnet. He should have thought of that. It seemed that Taylor Junior, like Taylor Senior, had great instincts for the job. It was also the reason why McAllister and the DI had made such a formidable team over the years. The former had an inferential mind. He was adept at understanding the big picture and being able to recognise patterns. He could take a series of apparently unconnected facts and identify the common thread. Although a great believer in diligence and adhering to procedures, many of his successes were down to pure intuition. Taylor on the other hand was meticulous, steady. He would grind away eliminating all possibilities until he was left with what had to be the answer. He might complain about the job, the pay, the hours, the weather, his haemorrhoids, but he let nothing go past him. Put them together and you had the ideal policeman.

'So, who was he visiting and why? Answer these two questions and we could be well on the way.'

'Probably too much to hope for that ballistics will be able to identify the gun. I just get the feeling that this guy is too professional to have a gun that's been used before.'

'Maybe. We'll have to wait and see on that one. We'll start to get some statements in later today. Hopefully that'll give us something.'

'I fancy the Gallaghers being behind this. We know that Kevin Boyle has been eating into their drug business. Want me to check with the Drug Squad to see if they can come up with anything?'

'Yeah. I know it's easy to look at the Gallaghers. Too easy, maybe. But we must check out everything.'

'What about Mummy and Daddy Boyle?'

'I want you to take statements from them after the post-mortem.'

'Thanks, Grant.'

'You stopped me getting to Italy. This is your penance, my boy. Right, let's get down to the mortuary.'

Taylor raised his eyebrows. 'Yes, I know. My favourite pastime. Let's just get it done.'

As the two men got out of their chairs, another detective appeared at the doorway. 'Hang on, boss, you might make Italy yet. We've just had a phone call – no name – but the caller said he lives near the scene of the shooting and can identify the killer.' Alan McNab, one of the squad Detective Constables was sporting a grin as he imparted this piece of information. His senior colleagues sat back down in their chairs as if they were readying themselves to receive bad news.

'Who?' The question was asked in stereo.

'No less a man than Mr Charles Gallagher, villain of the parish.'

'Charlie Gallagher?' again as a twosome.

'Are you two joined at the lip?' McNab responded.

'Very funny. The call's been recorded, I take it?' McAllister continued.

'Of course.'

'Right. Priority now is to find our mystery caller, then find out everything you can about…', McAllister hesitated and looked directly at McNab, '…him.'

'Him.' McNab repeated. 'Glasgow accent, nothing distinctive to me, but I'm going to arrange for all the guys to have a listen, just in case they recognise something. I'm checking with BT to see if they can help to trace the call. Long shot. Even tried 1471, but because the call came through the main switchboard, nothing registered.'

'OK', McAllister said, 'but no stone unturned. Find him.'

'What about young Master Gallagher?' McNab added.

'Leave him alone just now. Anything we might have found on him that would have been of evidential value will be long since disposed of.'

'What about searching the Gallaghers' houses, just in case? We could get a warrant under the Misuse of Drugs Act. Even get the Drug Squad boys to do it for us. They will be expecting us after all. They're bound to know we'll come calling, even on the off chance. We might get lucky.'

'Exactly, and that's why we do nothing just now. Whether Gallagher turns out to be our man or not, he'll be expecting a visitation. Let him wonder and sweat a bit. If we're going to do him, I want to have enough to be able to charge him with the murder, first time of asking. I don't want some smart-assed lawyer accusing us of jumping to conclusions without the evidence to back it up.'

'Fair enough, boss. But I would still be inclined to rattle his cage a bit. Your call, though.'

'And I've made it, Alan, and find me this voice, yesterday. Bob, you and I will try again. Post-mortem time.' McAllister stood up ready to leave.

A shout of, 'Call, Skip', from the outer office, caused Taylor to pick up the nearest phone. McAllister watched his colleague as he listened, nodding regularly but saying nothing apart from, 'I'll tell my boss. He'll love this one.'

'What am I going to love? Don't tell me, someone just shot Charlie Gallagher?'

'Inspirational, but not quite right.' Taylor grinned.

'That was a joke, Bob.'

'Well here's a better one for you. That was Baird Street. They've got a body in the mortuary with its head damn near cut off. Found in the early hours of the morning in a bin behind the Ingram Hotel. Trail of blood up an alley suggests he was taken there by car and then dumped. At least they've managed to find a witness. Some wino bumped into two men in a big hurry running away from the rear of the hotel. Apparently one of them had an Irish accent. Wino then found the body. Poor bastard didn't smell too good before. Smells worse now. He shat himself. When Baird Street heard about Kevin Boyle they thought you might have more than a passing interest in their stiff.'

'So, who is it?'

'No less a man than one Michael Mad Dog Clark. Enforcer extraordinaire to the Gallaghers.'

Once again, McAllister sat back down into his chair.

'Christ, they didn't waste much time did … hang on. You said that Clark was found in the early hours of the morning.'

'Correct.'

'So, he was killed before Boyle.'

'Absolutely.'

'What's going on then?'

'Boyle killed in revenge for Clark?'

'I repeat, they didn't waste much time, did they?'

'Could just be coincidence?'

'Don't believe in it, Bob, and neither do you.'

'I don't suppose that Frank Gallagher would kill one of his best neds just to divert attention from Charlie? Mind you, he is a cold-hearted bastard and would do anything to protect the family.'

'I'm not convinced that if the Gallaghers wanted rid of Kevin Boyle they would do it themselves. I would be more inclined to the view that they would get someone like Clark to do the dirty work for them.'

'One thing's for sure. The Mad Dog didn't kill Kevin Boyle.'

'At least we have one fact in all of this.'

'Pity it doesn't take us very far.'

'It's a start. Now, third time lucky, the mortuary. Before someone else beats us to it.'

Chapter Three

'Rape, according to the law of Scotland, involves the carnal knowledge of a woman, forcibly and against her will. There must be penetration of the vagina by the male private member. Any amount of penetration will be sufficient. There need be no emission of seminal fluid.'

'That's the stuff to give them,' mused James Muirhead. 'Nothing a Glasgow jury likes better of a Friday afternoon than a bit of semen sloshing about the place.'

He looked round the North Court of the High Court building in Glasgow. Seated above him, the trial judge Lord Cowden pressed on with his charge to the jury. In his red and white robes with prominent red crosses, Charles Arthur Blair, judicially styled the Honourable Lord Cowden, was a pinched little man sporting half-moon spectacles and with a voice which sounded as if it was being filtered through rough sand. Not a man who was noted for his sense of humour, he had the air of a man born to be a mute at a funeral. (Indeed, it was rumoured that his entry in *Who's Who* listed 'attending interments' as one of his hobbies.)

Cowden was not James Muirhead's favourite judge. He made little attempt to conceal his view that if the Crown brought an accused man to court, that was reason enough to suppose he was very probably guilty. The prosecuting counsel or advocate depute should be given a free run at satisfying the jury of what his Lordship was inclined to believe was true. The defence, on the other hand, did nothing but cause problems, and defence counsel were a particular irritation. They constantly objected to evidence which pointed to the guilt of their clients. They tricked and bullied hapless witnesses and turned the clearest of evidence into a hideous mass of confusion. They harangued police officers and accused them of all forms of heinous misconduct such as planting evidence and fabricating confessions.

Opposite Muirhead at the table in the well of the court sat the advocate depute, Michael Matthews QC. The two knew each other well and had been admitted to the Faculty of Advocates on the same day, but there all similarities ended. Matthews' father was a judge who had recently retired from the bench. His son had spent most of his legal career dealing with lucrative tax cases and was a recognised specialist in the exciting world of corporate taxation. He was very much an Establishment man who, like his father before him, was undoubtedly destined for the bench. Only dishonesty, indulging in child pornography, or drinking his soup with a dessert spoon could prevent him getting there. His only interest in life was the law. If Matthews had a hobby at all, it was reading a weighty periodical, Current Law, from cover to cover, twice, just in case he missed something the first time around. He was, in short, a boring fart.

He had no affection whatever for the criminal law or its practitioners. He found it and them rather vulgar. This view was not entirely without justification. As a well-known court reporter had remarked, 'If you put the lawyers into the dock and the clients in gowns, who would notice the change?' However, he appreciated that he had to serve his three-year stint as a public prosecutor and 'do his bit', as a necessary evil on his way to the bench.

His father who had been an advocate depute had encouraged Michael to get a bit of width into his practice: 'I know it's a bore doing the criminal stuff for three years but it's good for you to be seen doing it. It will also give you a chance to show these chaps how it should be done and impress the bench. When I became a judge I found it quite useful to have done my bit in the criminal field. Got to know what the buggers are up to.'

Michael had nodded on receiving this advice though he was somewhat confused. Who were the buggers to whom he had been referred – the accused or their lawyers? Probably didn't matter. Probably both.

He had all the trappings of legal Edinburgh: a splendid house in the prestigious New Town, a dull wife who hosted 'At Homes' and busied herself in an endless round of good works for sundry charities (when she wasn't at a coffee morning with other equally dull advocate's wives), 2.4 dull children at the Edinburgh Academy, and membership of the Honourable Company of Edinburgh Golfers (though, in fact, he could not hit a golf ball to save himself), and the most dangerous thing he did with his day was to partake of a small glass of chilled sherry before dinner.

But despite all that, he could be a considerable opponent in court. He possibly lacked a feel for criminal cases in that he was unfamiliar with the lifestyle of the average Glasgow criminal (or for that matter, victim) and his 'bool-in-the-mooth' public-school accent made him appear remote and aloof to many jurors. There was a very good reason for this. He was remote and aloof. However, his preparation for a trial was meticulous and if a piece of evidence was there to be led, Matthews could be relied upon to lead it.

Muirhead, on the other hand, was very definitely not part of legal Edinburgh. Fife-born and bred, his family would probably be described by social commentators and Labour Party activists as 'working class', a term his late father despised. James admired his father more than any man he had ever known.

As a boy, his father, Hugh Muirhead, was an outstandingly bright pupil at school in Cowdenbeath. His teachers had encouraged him to go on to university and his parents were more than happy to make the necessary sacrifices which would have been required to pay for motor-cars and left school to become an apprentice mechanic. During the economic depression of the Thirties, the garage to which he was indentured went out of business, as did many others in Fife, and that was the end of his career as a mechanic.

Thereafter, Hugh spent his life trying to better himself, but without great success. He was a lorry-driver, a bus-driver and ended up as a traffic inspector. He left this secure employment for a better paid job with the National Coal Board and was quickly promoted to a position of administrative responsibility. Then pits began to close and once again Hugh Muirhead moved on. Ultimately, he became a Church Officer, an old-fashioned beadle, in a church in Dundee.

He married Sarah Russell, a kind and gentle girl from Cowdenbeath, and from the day they married till the day he died of a massive heart attack, they were never apart. They had only one child, James. Hugh was determined that his son would not repeat his mistakes, but would go on to university and become a doctor. The Muirheads were never well off – indeed, money was always tight. However, Hugh Muirhead was fiercely independent and would never countenance putting himself or his family into debt. If he could not pay cash for something, he could not afford it. He accepted full responsibility for the decisions he had taken in his life and believed firmly that other people should do the same. He regarded himself as being an individual, not belonging to any class. He encouraged this independence of spirit in his son, and often told him: 'Be yourself, not what people want you to be.'

At secondary school, James was invariably top of his class. Consequently, he was steered towards science subjects and a place at St Andrews University to read medicine. Muirhead applied himself with diligence, but no real enthusiasm. Deep down he knew he did not want to be a doctor. He wanted to be a lawyer.

In the early fifties, when he was a boy, James was fascinated by a programme which he watched through the snow of the black-and-white eleven-inch television his father had bought. Called *Boyd QC* the programme starred Michael Denison as a barrister who donned wig and gown to defend those unjustifiably accused of committing crimes. While other youngsters followed *Watch with Mother* for Andy Pandy or *The Woodentops*, James never missed an episode of *Boyd QC*. He knew there and then that this was what he wanted to be: the man who stood up for the little guy when he was opposed by the big guy.

One day, James Muirhead went to see the rector and returned home to inform his father that he had finished with science in all its forms, was not going to read medicine but intended to become a barrister.

'It's an advocate, unless you are planning to go to England. And what do you know about the law?' his father replied dryly.

'As much as I know about medicine.'

'You've always wanted to be a doctor.'

'No, you've always wanted me to be a doctor.'

'No one in the family has ever had anything to do with the law.'

'No one has had anything to do with medicine.'

'I thought you wanted to go to St Andrews University.'

'I can still go to St Andrews.'

'How do you propose to earn a living? Where will you get a job?'

'Have you ever heard of a poor lawyer?'

Not a proposition his father could readily counter.

Hugh Muirhead feared his son was about to make the same kind of mistake he had made. But James was truly his son and every bit as bloody-minded as his father. Once that mind was made up, there was no changing it. Principle, however, demanded that Hugh had the last word.

'On your own head be it. You'll go your own way whatever I say.'

It was. He did. He became an advocate and that stubborn determination was the hallmark of his career.

University had presented no real problems for him and he graduated with a first-class honours degree in Scots Law, then headed for Edinburgh to embark upon his legal career. After spending two years as an apprentice with a leading firm of solicitors who specialised in court work, he began training for the Bar.

In Scotland, a would-be advocate has to spend nine months devilling, involving working, unpaid, for a practising member of the Faculty of Advocates. Hour after hour is spent in the library dealing with the mountains of paper which seem to be generated by every case which comes to court. Devils are not permitted to appear in court, but have to content themselves with following their Master around, rather like a faithful Labrador.

Muirhead's Devil Master was Richard McGregor, a very successful civil practitioner with a razor sharp mind but an extreme distaste for paperwork. As a result, Muirhead virtually ran the practice. He became very skilled in the technical art of drafting written pleadings and he became even more confirmed in his resolve to become a criminal lawyer. The court room was the theatre which would provide him with a stage.

The day he was admitted to the Faculty was the proudest day of his life and for his parents who saw their son don wig and gown for the first time. Hugh Muirhead was not a demonstrative man but had to wipe away a tear as, for the first time, he shook the hand of Mr James Muirhead, Advocate.

The first twelve months of practice followed a familiar pattern. The time was spent in one of three ways. He was either drafting divorce summonses, waiting for someone to give him something to do, or explaining to the bank manager why his overdraft kept steadily rising despite the promises of the impending arrival of untold riches. These assurances had been given on a regular basis during his devilling days. Muirhead presented copies of the fees he had issued in respect of the modest divorce practice he was building up. The manager was suitably impressed. He would have been less so had James not omitted to advise him that it would be at least a year before any of this paper was actually converted into coin of the realm. The overdraft increased still further.

Despite the indifferent state of his finances, Muirhead married Gill Munro, a secretary for one of the leading Edinburgh Law Firms. She had materialised in front of him one morning as he was waiting to go into court to earn four pounds by trying to get a man admitted to bail.

'Mr Muirhead, I'm Gill Munro from Laird's. Your Clerk said you might be able to draft an urgent summons for us.'

His Clerk was right. By ten fifteen his day's work would be over.

'Sure. I'll bring it to the office this afternoon.'

The slim, petite, very attractive redhead handed over the papers and bounced off, skirt swirling.

As good as his word, Muirhead delivered the papers to Laird's impressive offices in Charlotte Square. Normally these would be left with the receptionist but he specifically asked for Miss Munro. 'Thanks for bringing them down. I'll give them to Mr. Laird.'

'Good. Yes. Fine. I'll just be on my way then.'

'Right.'

'Right.'

Muirhead turned to leave, hesitated and turned back.

'I don't suppose you would like to have a drink tonight.'

'Love to.'

'You would?'

'Yes. I would.'

'Fine. Eight o'clock in Gino's?'

'I always thought you lot were supposed to be gentlemen. Why don't you come and pick me up. Here's my address.'

Had James Muirhead not been so staid, he would have skipped along the pavement. Several times he glanced at the piece of paper, just to make sure and all the while thinking, 'I'm going to marry this girl.'

He did. A small registry office wedding was all they could afford.

It is a fallacy to think that two can live as cheaply as one. But when one has a steady income, it certainly helps. At times Muirhead felt like a kept man but Gill constantly reassured him that all this would soon change. Whenever the lack of instructions drove him to depression, Gill's endless bubbly enthusiasm kept him going.

The nearest he got to a criminal court was taking notes for an advocate depute for a week in Glasgow. This earned him the princely sum of fifty pounds and made him even more impatient to get started. Finally his chance came. The counsel instructed for an assault and robbery fell ill and Muirhead's Clerk persuaded the solicitor that the young man would do a good job for the client, despite his undoubted lack of experience.

Muirhead threw himself into his first criminal trial. His client was an old lag who had a record running to several pages including four convictions for assault and robbery. Not the most auspicious of beginnings. However, he adamantly maintained his innocence and insisted that he had been fitted up by the police.

Muirhead tore into every witness. He was particularly savage in his treatment of the police officers to whom the client had allegedly confessed. So savage in fact that he was regularly rebuked by the judge who was quite taken aback by this aggressive young counsel. Muirhead carried on regardless. This was his big chance and he intended to take it. And, he was defending an innocent man.

When it came to addressing the jury, his speech was reminiscent of an old black-and-white film with Charles Laughton addressing an Old Bailey jury in a capital murder trial. He had ended with a rare flourish: 'Ladies and gentlemen of the jury, the choice is yours. By your verdict you can condemn my client to the bowels of the darkest dungeon, or set him free to walk into the Glasgow sunshine.'

Over-acted, over-dramatic, over-theatrical and basically crap – but it worked. The jury returned a not guilty verdict.

After the trial the old fellow greeted his young saviour warmly, pumped his hand and, with tears in his eyes, delivered his opinion on the matter: 'Mr Muirhead, that was marvellous. Let me tell you sir, you have the makings of a great man. You'll be a QC one day. Probably even a Lordship. If you can do that for me when I'm guilty, I can't imagine what you would have done if I'd been innocent!'

And off he went – not into the Glasgow sunshine but into the mist and rain. He left behind a young lawyer rejoicing in his first victory but aware that the first seeds of cynicism and doubt had been sown. But he also left behind a man whose reputation was beginning to grow. In the years to follow, it flourished.

He became known as someone who would fight for his client regardless of the odds against him, someone who would squeeze every last drop of blood out of a stone if it was necessary for the defence. He became respected and despised in equal measure by police officers, many of whom suffered at his hands in cross-examination. Regardless of rank, Muirhead could demolish a policeman, leaving him to exit court nursing a mixture of bruised ego, frustration and rage. Privately most of them admitted that if they were ever in trouble they would want Muirhead to represent them.

When it came to defending an accused, he had a very simple philosophy to which he stubbornly adhered. It was not for him to decide if the client was guilty or innocent – that was why the jury was there. It was for the Crown to prove guilt, according to the law, and for the defence to put every legitimate hurdle in the way of it succeeding. As a result, if a jury brought back an acquittal verdict despite what might seem to the observer to be overwhelming evidence, then the Crown had failed to prove its case and that was that.

Time and again, he was asked, 'How can you defend all these guilty people?' For years he would try to explain about justice, the right to a fair trial, presumption of innocence and the legal principles which he, at least, held dear. Eventually he grew bored with the glazed eyes and the inevitable retort, 'That's all very well, but you must know they did it?'

He settled for a more simplistic riposte.

'Money!'

Although he hated himself for betraying his principles, at least it had the advantage of bringing many a pointless conversation to a suitably abrupt end.

One evening over dinner, he had been asked the usual question and trundled out the now stock answer with the customary result. Afterwards, one of the company, a doctor chided him: 'I don't believe you about that money business. I suspect you're very much like me. You do the job because you care. Probably you care most about the hopeless cases, the people for whom you can do least.'

Muirhead took this very much to heart and the next time the question was forthcoming, he answered simply, but honestly,

'Compassion.'

This still brought the conversation to an abrupt end, but it certainly made him feel better.

James Muirhead did care. He was born with no silver spoon in his mouth, but his family had fought to give him the best possible start in life. His parents lived by a code of decency, honesty and respect for others, which had become part of his make up without him even realising it. Many youngsters did not get such a start in life and became no more than prisoners of their own background. Bullying, drunken, dishonest fathers tend to produce bullying, drunken, dishonest sons. On and on the cycle goes.

He despised the condescending attitude of some citizens towards their fellow men and women. What did someone with a steady career, living in a comfortable house in one of the upmarket suburbs of Edinburgh or Glasgow really know about life in the concrete ghettos which were built to replace the Victorian slums of the inner cities; of areas where unemployment, despair, domestic violence, crime and drug abuse are as much a way of life as are golf clubs, bridge evenings and parent teacher meetings for those who view themselves as being so superior?

Even more than this, he hated unfairness, wherever and whenever he encountered it, but especially in the law. A trial was meant to be fair; it had to be or there was no point in having the trial in the first place. This view not infrequently brought him onto a collision course with judges, the best of whom will preside over trials in impartial silence and allow the lawyers to get on with their job. Others can't resist the temptation to interfere, often to show just what clever bastards they are.

On one occasion, Muirhead's instructions were that the drugs allegedly found in his client's house had in fact been planted there by the police: without doubt, the most serious allegation to be levelled against any policeman. Not something to be done lightly but, if the allegation was true, it was the most evil thing a policeman could do to a citizen. Under cross-examination the officer was finding it increasingly difficult to explain away the fact that two of his colleagues had searched the cupboard and found nothing before he came along, just for a quick final check, and instantly spotted the heroin.

His discomfiture increased question by question until he was almost at breaking point when the trial judge intervened, just to clarify matters.

'I think that what Mr Muirhead is trying to suggest, no doubt in terms of his instructions and on his professional responsibility, is that you would risk twenty-one years of police service, and your reputation, to bring disgrace on yourself, the police force and your family by planting evidence. Now, would you do that?'

Muirhead had intervened: 'Is your Lordship clarifying some matter which has thus far escaped me or should I now be in a state of confusion as to who is actually prosecuting this case?'

'Mr Muirhead, in my court I will ask such questions as I consider necessary to assist the jury.'

Despite this rebuke, Muirhead did not back off. Would not back off.

'With the greatest of respect, my Lord...', this phrasing being recognised in legal circles as the polite way of advising a judge that he is about to be told he is an idiot, '...your intervention may assist the jury in ways that are beyond my comprehension, but it is certainly going to assist the witness by seeking to portray him in a favourable light when the jury may well be inclined to consider that he is manifestly lying. My client is obliged to be prosecuted by the advocate depute. He is entitled not to be prosecuted by you.'

'That remark is unacceptable.'

'So was your Lordship's question and I invite him to withdraw it.'

The judge knew Muirhead well enough to know that he would not release his grip on this particular bone. If he persisted, the matter would deteriorate into a scene and he was in real danger of losing some of his judicial dignity, and that would never do.

'Carry on, Mr Muirhead.'

A silence settled on the court. Muirhead said nothing despite being the recipient of a stern judicial stare. The jurors sat forward in their seats to await developments. This was what they had hoped to see. This was better than the telly. This was for real.

'Carry on Mr Muirhead!'

Silence.

'Will you carry on with your cross-examination.'

Instruction, not a question.

Silence.

'I will not ask you...'

'When your Lordship has withdrawn his question.'

Silence – apart from the squeaking of His Lordship's chair as he tried not to betray his discomfort.

In a whisper which had to fight its way out from between clenched teeth, the policeman was instructed by His Lordship that he did not have to answer the judge's question.

One or two of the jurors wanted to applaud. The advocate depute winked at his opponent and pretended to remove a tin hat and flak jacket. The accused seated in the dock turned to his police escort and muttered, 'Fucking magic, eh!' Muirhead inwardly savoured his triumph while preparing an outward display of graciousness. The judge was struggling to regain his composure, when up spake the witness who had been totally ignored during this exchange.

'Pardon?'

His Lordship lost it, completely.

'Pardon? Pardon? What do you mean, pardon? Are you deaf? I told you not to answer the question I asked. Don't answer the question! There isn't a question!'

'Sorry, what question don't I have to answer?'

'The one I told you not to answer! The one that is not now a question!'

'I don't remember what it was.'

'What what was?'

'The question. Do you mean the question I don't have to answer?'

'There is no question! So there is no question for you to answer! So do not answer the question! I cannot make it any simpler! Do you understand now?'

'Well, not really, no!'

'Baaaaaaaaaaaaaaaaaaaaah!!'

By now the whole court was verging on hysteria, with everyone choking back the laughter as best as they could. The judge jumped out of his seat and stormed off the bench resisting the temptation to tell Muirhead where to stick his sentiments as the words, 'I'm very much obliged to your Lordship', reached his ears.

Despite such incidents, Muirhead was respected by the Bench as someone who was scrupulously honest and whose integrity was never in doubt. He was undoubtedly his own man. He seldom socialised with his contemporaries and this, allied to the occasional bust-ups with judges in court meant that he was never really accepted by the legal establishment. This state of affairs cost Muirhead not a single wink of sleep.

After thirteen years at the bar, he was elevated to the rank and dignity of Queen's Counsel. It was an honour which was bestowed on Muirhead grudgingly.

In order to become a QC, an advocate must be recommended to the Queen by Scotland's senior judge, the Lord President of the Court of Session. The leader of the Bar, the Dean of Faculty, put Muirhead's name forward to the then Lord President, Lord Fraser, who had never regarded him as being a proper advocate because he spent most of his time defending criminals. Fraser was a man of great intellect but even greater pomposity. He was aware of Muirhead's background, working-class, non-public school educated and considered him too common and vulgar to be one of Her Majesty's Counsel. The establishment was about to bite back.

The application was turned down.

Muirhead could do nothing about his background and, in any event, didn't wish to. He refused to change his attitudes, his method of working or his accent. Nor was he prepared to go away, even to please Lord Fraser. He did make a point of taking on some cases in the Criminal Appeal Court. This brought him into direct conflict with Fraser. Try as he might to put Muirhead down, the advocate fought as hard before the Appeal Court as he did before a jury. Fraser began to appreciate that this man would not go away. A year later, and under pressure from other judges who respected James's ability and integrity, Fraser relented and Muirhead became a QC.

When Muirhead returned with the news, Gill opened a bottle of Bollinger champagne she had kept hidden away. She never doubted that this day would arrive. Even Robert and Sarah, the two children they had 'acquired', as James put it, were allowed a sip. It was a very special occasion. The culmination of years of hard work. Since then he had spent most of his working life not just defending criminals, but mainly those accused of murder.

*   *   *

Muirhead drifted out of his reflective state to return to Lord Cowden's charge. It was drawing to a close.

'There are three verdicts open to you, guilty, not guilty and not proven. Not guilty and not proven are both verdicts of acquittal and mean that the accused goes free and can never be retried. Before you can return a verdict of guilty there must be a majority, that is to say at least eight of you, in favour of such a verdict. When you retire, I suggest you choose one of your number to chair your deliberations and speak for you when you return to court. Will you now retire and consider your verdict which I can take from you at any time.'

When the jury retired, Lord Cowden left the bench and Muirhead walked out of court to be greeted by Jack Morton. Morton was one of Glasgow's leading solicitors, specialising in criminal work.

'Hello, Jack. Have you got a case in the other court?'

'No, I came down to see you. I know your jury's out and you will be a bit pre-occupied, but I'd like a quick word if possible. It's important. Somewhere private.

Muirhead collected his pipe from the retiring room and the two went to one of the dismal little interview rooms located in the bowels of the building. Morton waited till the pipe was well and truly lit, then handed over a document.

'Race meeting on today, Jack?'

As ever, Morton was attired in a loud check suit and tastelessly clashing shirt and tie.

'Very droll. It's my fees suit – small checks! Now read. My client has just had this served upon him. I dare say you've heard something about it. I want you to take the case. It's right up your street. You name it, this one has got it, and then some. He's presently in Barlinnie. I'd like you to go and see him as soon as possible. I was thinking of instructing Donald Anderson as your junior. The old firm. I've checked your availability and his and you are both pretty clear, strangely enough. Trial is set down to begin in just under five weeks.'

'I was hoping for a bit of a break.'

'Jim, you never take holidays, and you certainly won't be heading for sunny Spain when you've read that.'

'The Caribbean, actually.'

'Whatever. Just read.'

Muirhead began to scan the document. It was an indictment against Charles Gallagher, setting out three charges.

Charles Anthony Gallagher, presently a prisoner in the prison of Barlinnie, Glasgow, you are indicted at the instance of the Right Honourable the Lord Haldane of Auchengry, Her Majesty's Advocate, and the charges against you are that:

(1) on 16th March 1996 while acting with others whose identities are to the prosecutor meantime unknown, in Glasgow or elsewhere to the prosecutor unknown, you did assault Michael John Clark residing at 19 St John's Road, Bridgeton, Glasgow, strike him repeatedly on the body with hammers or similar instruments, burn him repeatedly on the body with lit cigarettes, strike and stab him repeatedly on the neck and body with knives or similar instruments, to his severe injury, and you did murder him;

(2) on date above libelled, while acting with others whose identities are to the prosecutor meantime unknown, you, having committed the crime libelled in Charge One above, namely murder, did convey the dead body of said Michael John Clark to a lane behind the Ingram Hotel, Ingram Street, Glasgow, place said body in a wheeled waste bin, and this you did with a view to concealing the commission of said crime, with intent to pervert the course of justice, and you did attempt to pervert the course of justice;

(3) on 17th March 1996 in Mitchell Drive, Glasgow, you did

assault Kevin Patrick Boyle residing at 1 Main Road, Bridgeton, Glasgow, repeatedly discharge a loaded firearm at him, repeatedly shoot him in the head, and you did murder him.

Muirhead reflected for a moment while drawing on his pipe.

'I'd heard he was on petition for the murder of Boyle. Didn't hear about the second one.'

'No, the first two charges came as a complete surprise. They only surfaced with the service of the indictment. Curious thing is, the deceased on charge one actually worked for old man Gallagher. Sort of minder-cum-heavy. I could see they might cobble together a motive for the Boyle killing, commercial rivalry and all that, but I cannot see why Charlie would be involved in killing one of his own people. Nor can I understand what the connection might be between the two killings.'

'I see that Clark was killed first.'

'So we can hardly run the line that it was a revenge attack for Kevin's murder.'

'Just so. Maybe they are going to suggest that Clark was sacrificed to take the heat off the Gallaghers. Point the finger towards Clark's family.'

'You're a devious bastard, James, but Clark was very much the lone wolf. If he had a family at all, I suspect it was the Gallaghers. I'll check that out, of course.'

'What's the evidence looking like?'

'Early doors, yet. We've got a few preliminary statements but mostly formal stuff. Bob Blythe from Edinburgh did post-mortems for us. Actually there's some interesting stuff in his reports. I've got initial briefs made up, if you want the case. I can get them to you over the weekend. I phoned the Fiscal to get a summary of the evidence but he wouldn't tell me anything. They're keeping this one very tight.'

'Interesting.'

'I thought you'd like this one.'

'Consultation, Monday evening.'

'Absolutely.'

The high pitched whine of a buzzer announced that the jury was ready to return its verdict.

'Christ, James, that was quick.'

'Not guilty. Lot of nonsense. During the act of rape, the victim was actually on top.'

'Go on, explain.'

'She claimed she was terrified of my client, who just happened to be her boyfriend.'

'But why was she on top?'

'Because he had a bad back.'

'Eh?'

'Because he had a bad back. I do wish you would listen.'

'Sounds like a good night in rather than a rape.'

'Case should never have been prosecuted.'

'Here's hoping you say the same thing at the end of this one. Never can tell.'

'We'll see. I'll have a look at the papers this weekend. See you Monday night at Barlinnie.'

'Just one more thing,' Morton continued, 'I don't think he did it.'

'Jack, you always tell me that.'

'This time I believe it. I don't know why. Just a gut feeling, having spoken to the boy. He's shit scared.'

'He's entitled to be, facing two murder charges.'

'I know, I know, but there's just something about him. Judge for yourself when you meet him.'

'We'll see.'

Muirhead headed towards court, and a verdict. As he proceeded he was struck by the way his colleague seemed to be so uptight about the case. Strange.

Despite being conscientious to the nth degree and meticulous to a fault in his preparation of cases, Morton always appeared to be completely laid back. Someone once suggested that he had been almost excited by an incident which happened in a case, but this was generally dismissed as mere scurrilous rumour. Everyone knew he cared about his clients and worried about their cases. He just did not show it. He preferred to devote his energies to preparation rather than perspiration.

Muirhead remained puzzled as he strode along the corridor. Suddenly and inexplicably he shivered. For no reason he could have explained, he had a bad feeling about the case he was to undertake. What it was – he did not know. Just that he had never experienced this before – and he did not like it one bit. He shivered again.

'Behave yourself, you silly bugger,' he mouthed to himself.

       ●   ●   ●

The driving rain which fell incessantly had already soaked the waiting crowd. There was no shelter to be had from wind or rain. Yet no one made any attempt to seek respite from the biting cold. Spring was late in coming this year. The crowd stood in an eerie silence broken only by the occasional shuffling of feet or a hacking cough, quickly stifled by a gloved hand. The faces were as grey as the weather which enveloped them. The casual observer would have instantly noted a total absence of emotion. The astute observer would have detected a concentrated effort to display no emotion. Men, women and children, yet not a flicker anywhere. Not a tear in any eye.

They had gathered together for a single purpose, but for a variety of reasons. Some to be able to say they were there when local legend was created – some to watch – some to be seen – and some to watch the watchers.

Many were local residents who were in attendance because they feared their absence would be noted, and in some way commented upon at some future date. Their numbers were swollen by a curious mixture of the leading and lesser lights of Glasgow's criminal fraternity and officers of the Serious Crime Squad, several of whom were armed. Indeed there was every likelihood that some of the crowd were also armed.

At least it was a simple matter to distinguish between the good guys and the bad guys: the bad guys were more expensively dressed.

The police were watching the villains watching the police watching the villains. Everyone was waiting and becoming colder and more miserable by the minute.

A child's voice broke the silence. He was instantly grabbed by his mother who held him close lest he make some further comment of a less innocuous nature. Suddenly there was a dramatic increase in the general noise level as the members of the crowd shuffled about trying to get the circulation back into frozen feet and shifting slightly to get the best possible view of the drama which was about to unfold.

Sixty yards away in an unmarked police car, McAllister and Taylor were studying the scene.

'They're coming out. Looks like we're about to get some activity, Bob.'

'About time, my feet are like lumps of lead.'

'At least you're in the dry,' McAllister responded testily.

Taylor was indifferent to the mild rebuke. If Detective Inspectors did not stand around in the pissing rain, Superintendents had forgotten the pissing rain existed.

'I hope they've got plenty of rolls of film.'

Police photographers had been located at various points in order to compile a complete record of those who braved the elements to be part of this sombre scene.

'Quite a collection. There's more previous convictions here than in the Scottish Criminal Records Office. If you locked up the whole bloody lot of them you would cut the crime rate in Glasgow by at least fifty per cent.'

This time McAllister ignored his colleague's flippancy. Despite being something of an exaggeration, there was a good deal of truth to it and in many respects the sentiments were entirely laudable and shared by the Superintendent.

The two men lapsed into silence and continued watching.

The door to the Boyle home opened and two men in full black morning dress and black silk top hats emerged followed by a coffin laden in flowers and carried by six other men similarly attired. Had they been followed by Edward G. Robinson, George Raft, Humphrey Bogart and the Kray Twins, no one would have batted an eyelid. This was to be a gangland funeral in the grand manner worthy of a classic gangster movie.

It was as if some unseen director had shouted, 'Action!'. The crowd of extras edged imperceptibly forward as if attempting to get their faces on screen. The principal players emerged from the house.

Annie Boyle, her face hidden by a black veil, walked upright and elegantly beside an old man who was stooped and shuffled forward with the aid of a silver-handled walking stick. No one who knew him could fail to notice that Hugh Boyle had aged many years in the few days since the death of his first born. He appeared to stumble and two pairs of hands grabbed him to prevent what would otherwise have been an undignified fall. Paul and Hugh Junior took their father's arms and with their aid he struggled to walk. Annie displayed no reaction to her husband's plight. She offered neither helping hand nor word of comfort.

At a suitably respectful distance, the rest of the official mourners made their way from the house to take up position behind the waiting hearse.

The brothers left their father's side and stood opposite each other at the vehicle's rear doors to assist in placing the coffin inside between wreaths of white flowers spelling out the words 'SON' and 'BROTHER'. When they had taken up station behind their parents, the cortège moved off. Slowly and sedately it began its sombre journey towards the cemetery.

As it left the street, known locally as 'Boyle Boulevard', the crowd of watchers began to disperse. Some headed for home or the nearest pub, satisfied that they had done their duty. Others out of curiosity or enforced loyalty and a few, a very few, out of genuine sympathy, joined the end of the procession along with the police. Kevin Boyle was leaving home for the last time.

The journey was short. Whereas his life had been lived amid violence and disorder, his departure from it was a model of peace and tranquillity. The freshly-dug grave awaited no hero, despite the abundance of floral tributes carefully placed around it. An enormous headstone of grey granite already stood at its head, bearing the legend,

'Kevin Boyle, a beloved son, a gentle brother and a loyal friend, at home with the Lord. Missed by all.'

As a wag subsequently remarked, 'At least they got the bastard's name right.'

Kevin Boyle was to receive the Christian burial he had scarcely earned by his earthly deeds. The local priest had heard of him but had never actually met him and had certainly never seen him in church. When invited to perform the funeral service his reluctance had been expressed in the simple word, 'No.' However, the offer of an indecently large donation to his chapel had swiftly convinced him that there may have been some merit to this man's life after all.

He was spared the ordeal of having to fabricate then deliver a eulogy. After the body had been lowered into the ground, the company was addressed by Paul. Glowing tributes were delivered for a young man who put others first and himself last. Devoted. Loving. Honest. Most of those who actually listened began to wonder if they had come to the right funeral.

The pathos of the moment was somewhat marred when a stray dog wandered among the wreathes and crapped in full view of the mourners just as Kevin's many virtues were being extolled. The symbolism of the gesture was not lost on many, including McAllister and Taylor who were now parked just outside the cemetery gate.

'Strange', muttered the DI, 'no sign of the minder. He's buggered off but you would have thought he'd resurface for his master's funeral do.'

'We'll find him. They can keep on pretending all they like that they have no idea where he's gone, but he'll turn up one way or another.'

'It's beginning to look as if it may be the other.'

'Let's get out of here. It's nearly over and, in any event, I've seen enough. We've got a murder charge to think about.'

'Another one?'

Across the city, another funeral was taking place. It was a much less grand affair and somewhat poorly attended.

An elderly lady was assisted to the front row of the Linn Crematorium by her son. He had flown up from London the previous night and intended to return home just as soon as he had done his filial duty.

'It's nice to see that Michael's friends have come along. He will be pleased.'

'Yes, Mum. He will be pleased.'

The kindly tone of his voice masked the inner feelings. Craig Clark could recognise police officers when he saw them. He might have been away from Glasgow for over ten years, but he could still spot the polis at a hundred yards. As a boy, he had seen plenty of them – usually looking for his brother who seemed to have been in trouble since he was old enough to walk and talk, or at least steal and lie.

He had never had much of a relationship with his brother. In fact the two had cheerfully hated the sight of each other. Craig applied himself at school, was popular with his teachers and in his brother's considered opinion was a 'crawling little cunt.' He had always refused to become involved in the various dishonest enterprises which occupied every waking hour of Michael and his gang. As a result he was invariably referred to simply as 'The Wanker.'

When he left school, Craig spent his nights loading vans for City Bakeries in order to pay his way through college. He obtained a diploma in accountancy, got himself a job and devoted his energies to becoming a fully qualified chartered accountant.

He stayed at home only to protect his mother from the drunken violence of his father, and when the latter died he left home and headed for London. This was his first trip back to Glasgow. He had kept in touch with his mother by phone and letter and received the occasional report from friends about his brother's nefarious activities. His mother was convinced that Michael was a good boy about the house who, for some reason, was being picked on by the police. Craig knew differently.

The news of his brother's violent demise came as no real surprise to him. He had long known it was only a question of when, not if. He had come to the funeral for his mother's sake, not out of any sense of brotherly love or loyalty. Sitting in the stark surroundings of the crematorium listening to the resident minister going through the necessary formalities and watching the shrouded coffin sink into the floor to be burned, only one thought kept coming into his mind:

I hope I don't miss that fucking plane.

Chapter Four

Charlie Gallagher did not attend either funeral – for two good and compelling reasons. One, he was not invited. Two, more significantly, he was locked up in prison having been remanded on a charge of murdering Kevin Boyle.

He had not been in the least surprised by the arrival of the police at his front door – even at six in the morning. Police officers delight in dawn raids. If asked in court, they will trundle out the stock excuse that at this hour there are less people about and consequently less risk of interference. In addition, it is also to spare the blushes of the target and save him the embarrassment of being arrested in the full public gaze that they choose the hour. Both explanations are fatuous. Quite simply, police officers delight in the drama of dawn raids.

The Gallaghers, as a family had been expecting such a visit. Most of their people had been invited to attend one police station or another to assist with inquiries. They had taken the precaution of visiting their lawyers and putting on record where each of them had been at the time of Boyle's death. This is what they would tell the police, and in the event of any funny business or inaccurate recording of their statements, the lawyer would be able to produce their sworn affidavits. A practical illustration of the old footballing maxim – get your retaliation in first.

No one thought to even comment on the death of the Mad Dog. After all, even Strathclyde CID could not be stupid enough to think that was down to one of them.

That is not to imply they were completely indifferent to his demise. True, his death had not been mourned. Easy come, easy go! But the fact that he had apparently been murdered before Kevin, according to reliable rumour, was the cause of much debate if 'What the fuck's going on?' can amount to debate. No sufficient answer was forthcoming.

Suggestions abounded and included the notion of someone with a private grievance. There were many who might have attended the audition for this part, someone in their own organisation looking for a fast track to promotion and a quick way of building a reputation. As yet, no claimants to the Mad Dog's throne had come forward. Among the more bizarre suggestions were: the police, (to get Mad Dog out of the way), and Kevin Boyle himself who was then shot as an act of revenge by someone no one could put a name to. The simple fact of the matter was, the Gallaghers did not have a clue.

Charlie had been detained under the powers afforded to the police by the Criminal Procedure (Scotland) Act 1995 which allowed for the holding of a suspect for up to six hours for questioning before being released or charged with a crime. The police are under no obligation to allow a solicitor to be present during such questioning.

None of this had presented Charlie with any difficulties. He answered all their questions. Repeatedly, he told his interrogators where he had been and who had been with him. As expected, they were interested in the death of Kevin Boyle. As expected, Mick Clark was never mentioned.

He had been questioned for about three hours by two detective sergeants. No problem. They were getting nowhere and eventually walked out of the interview room for a time leaving him in the company of a uniformed constable. Charlie attempted to engage his watcher in conversation, but the uniform was filled by someone who was deaf, dumb, stupid or a combination of all three. Charlie was banging his head against a wall of silence. The opposition returned and went over the whole routine again. Everything was tape-recorded. No problem. The atmosphere had been professional but pleasant – almost cordial. Not exactly what he had expected – but no problem.

Again he was left alone with the dummy. This time Charlie chose to ignore him. That was certainly no problem and in any event his diamond-studded Rolex told him that the six hours were nearly up and he would soon be on his way home, or at least on to the nearest pub. Thirsty work answering all these daft questions. Job done, out of here couple of pints, no problem. Good night, good luck and cheerio to you all!

The two question masters returned to the interview room accompanied by a new suit who sat down while the others stood behind him. The tape-recorder was switched on.

'My name is Detective Superintendent Grant McAllister and I am presently in interview room number two at London Road Police Office. I will now ask the others present to identify themselves.'

'Detective Sergeant Ian Scott, Strathclyde Police CID.'

'Detective Sergeant Leslie Walker, CID.'

The new suit nodded at Charlie.

'We've done this bit. If you don't know who I am by now, what are you doing here wasting my time and yours, Mr Detective Superintendent Grant McAllister Sir?'

'For the record please, just a formality but a necessary one, I'm afraid, please state your name. Otherwise somebody might think that I was talking to an empty chair.'

Charlie ostentatiously looked at his watch.

'In six minutes you will be.'

'Your name, if you don't mind.'

The tone was relaxed, again almost cordial. Charlie's initial anxiety at being confronted by a new policeman, and a senior one at that, began to ease. He would play along. This guy obviously had some official spiel to deliver. Maybe he was even going to apologise for keeping him here so long. This was no problem. After all, he would be out of here very soon – in five minutes to be precise.

'Charles Gallagher.'

'Mr Gallagher, up till now you have been detained here in terms of the Criminal Procedure (Scotland) Act. I propose now to release you from that detention.'

'About time too. Not that I mind helping you lot out, always happy to oblige, but basically I've got better things to do with my time, know what I mean? If you need me you know where to find me. Now if you'll excuse me, I am out of here. Thank you!'

Charlie went to stand up. He was the only one who moved. He looked at each of the officers in turn. Expressionless. Blank. Suddenly the penny began to drop. Something was wrong. Something was very wrong.

'Please sit down, Mr Gallagher. I'm afraid that for the time being, you are not going anywhere.'

The tone was now cold. This man meant what he was saying. This might just be about to turn a bit nasty.

'Mr Gallagher, you are now under arrest and I am about to prefer a charge against you. Before I do so I must caution you that you are not obliged...'

'What do you mean, a charge? What fucking charge? I've done fuck all and you cunts know it. You're fucking trying to fit me up, you fucking bastards!'

He was standing leaning over the table and spitting his words into McAllister's face. The latter remained resolutely calm.

'I am going to prefer a charge against you...'

'Charge! Charge!! You, ya piece of shite, you couldnae charge a fucking battery!'

Charlie had lost it, and might have blown it completely had the corner or his eye not registered the presence of the tape-recorder. His brain snapped back into gear and he slumped down onto his chair. Breathing heavily, he gripped the table in front of him with both hands and stared venomously at the policeman. He would say nothing more but he would let this bastard know just how much he hated him.

'I am going to prefer a charge against you. I must caution you that you are not obliged to say anything in answer to the charge, but anything you do say will be tape-recorded, noted and may be given in evidence. Do you understand the words of the caution?'

Gallagher had said all he was going to say.

'Mr Gallagher, do you understand the words of the caution?'

Nothing.

'No response. Very well. The charge against you is that you did, on 17th March 1996 in Mitchell Drive, Glasgow, discharge a loaded firearm at Kevin Boyle, now deceased, shoot him repeatedly in the head whereby he was so severely injured that he died there and then and you did murder him. Do you understand the charge?'

Nothing.

'Do you have anything to say in answer to the charge?'

Nothing.

'Very well. You will now be detained in custody till you appear in court tomorrow. You will be photographed and finger printed, and I am going to arrange for a police casualty surgeon to take samples of blood and hair from you. I can obtain an order from the court to allow these samples to be taken if you do not provide them voluntarily. Will you allow such samples to be taken?'

Nothing.

'I must advise you that I will make application to the Sheriff Court for the necessary warrant. This is Detective Superintendent Grant McAllister concluding the interview with the now accused Charles Gallagher.'

When the tape-recorder was switched off, Gallagher was desperate to tell the police just what he thought of them. He decided to bide his time. They were bluffing. They didn't have anything on him. They had to be bluffing. His father would get the lawyer and he would sort it out – at least he would get him bail. If Charlie had applied any rational thought to his predicament, he would have remembered that in Scotland, people charged with murder are kept in custody until their trial. He would not get bail – as he would very soon find out.

Later that afternoon he was taken from his cell for an interview with his solicitor. Despite his high hopes, matters did not improve. He expected to see Jack Morton, but instead he was greeted by one of his minions. Morton was out of town. This was a piece of news Charlie did not want to hear.

'Then get the bastard back here, fucking now!'

'I have spoken to him on the phone and he knows the situation. He will see you tomorrow before you appear in court.'

'Look, wanker, I want to see him now. He gets paid plenty. I want the organ grinder not his bloody monkey.'

'There is nothing he could do just now. But tomorrow he will explain what is likely to happen. You will be put through a judicial examination before a Sheriff and Mr Morton will advise you...'

'Likely to happen! I'll tell you what IS going to happen. What is going to happen is that you are going to get back on that fucking phone and tell him to get me out of here.'

Jack Morton's assistant wanted to tell this arsehole what to do with himself, but his job paid well. He also thought of trying to explain that getting out was not really an option since the following day the court would follow normal practice and remand him in custody for a week to allow the Crown to carry out further inquiries. Thereafter he would be taken back to court and fully committed: in other words, locked up in Barlinnie until the trial. He wisely decided that he had spread enough gloom for one day. The boss could deal with it. As the client had succinctly put it, Morton got paid plenty.

Had he chosen the gloomy path, he would have had the satisfaction of knowing that everything he had prophesied came to pass. Despite his many vociferous and violent denunciations of the police, the courts, the law, lawyers and anyone else he could think of, Charlie Gallagher was fully committed for trial on a charge of murdering Kevin Boyle.

Hence on the day of the funerals he was in the visiting room of Barlinnie sitting in a sullen silence while his sister and young brother George endeavoured, without success, to cheer him up. Their chances of success could be measured on a scale running from zero to less than zero. Even the news that Kevin Boyle would soon be pushing up the daisies raised his spirits not one whit.

'What's your QC saying?', his brother asked cautiously.

'He never says anything.'

'He must say something.'

'OK, OK, he asks a whole load of stupid fucking questions. Sucks his stinking fucking pipe. Asks more stupid fucking questions. When I tell him I know fuck all about fuck all, he goes on about the jury needing "rather more than that". Rather more than fucking what? Whose side is the bastard on anyway?'

'Come on, Charlie, take it easy. He's just doing his job. He's supposed to be the best there is.'

'If he's so fucking smart, why doesn't he get me out of this shithole?'

'You know why, Charlie. Jack has explained it to you umpteen times.'

'Words. All I get are fucking words. When is some fucker going to do something. This place is doing my head in and you tell me to take it easy. Well fuck you! Fuck the lot of you!'

Charlie motioned to his sister and stormed out of the room. The visit was over.

●   ●   ●

The mobile phone was answered on the first ring. The conversation was abrupt but conveyed everything the parties had to say to each other.

'That you?'

'Of course.'

'You got the message?'

'Yes.'

'Enough?'

'Very generous.'

'Don't make any plans to return to Glasgow, ever.'

'No need, for now.'

'Ever.'

'Fair enough. Charlie?'

'Charged.'

'Kevin's?'

'Yes.'

'What about the other one?'

'Not your concern.'

'If you say so. You're the boss.'

'Believe it.'

The line went dead.

●   ●   ●

'James, it's Jack Morton, sorry to call you so late.'

'Yes, Jack. What can I do for you?'

'We need to have a chat fairly urgently. I've just discovered two new pieces of evidence.'

'Why do I get the distinct impression that I'm not going to like what you are about to tell me?'

'Your client has appar...'.

'Oh I get it! Suddenly he's *my* client. There was me thinking he was *our* client.'

'James, this is serious. There's a confession. Actually there's two confessions.'

'I thought we had all the police statements – there's no hint of any admission.'

'It's not quite as simple as that. Only one is a cop, the other is a civilian. And it gets better than that. The cop is someone we might not even have bothered interviewing. On the face of it he was just a boy who watched Gallagher during a gap in the taped interview. Seems the client decided to confess all to him.'

'Highly unlikely, I would have thought. If he did, he deserves the jail for being stupid.'

'Quite. I've only got the bare bones of it so far. Nearly shat myself when I read the precognition. I've sent my investigator to see this guy again to get as much detail as he can. Mind you, the next one's even better.'

'Do you mean worse?'

'Probably. It's certainly a beauty. It seems we may have a supergrass.'

'A super... go on.'

'Thought you'd like it. There's a guy who is now in Perth awaiting trial. He claims that when he was on remand in Barlinnie he was in the segregation unit at the same time as Gallagher. Says the two of them became friendly and he was given the whole story about the murder – chapter and bloody verse.'

'Christ! Have you spoken to the client about this?'

'Claims he has never heard of this guy. I've asked the Crown for a photograph to see if Gallagher recognises him.'

'Obviously you've checked that the two were in the same unit for a time – how long?'

'Ten days.'

'Ten days, and we become so bloody pally with him that we appoint him our father confessor. That'll no do.'

'It gets even better. This guy is apparently called Alan Warwick.'

'Apparently?'

'I'm having it checked out, but apparently that is not his real name, or at least it may not be his real name. It seems that he has given evidence before, in England, would you believe? On that occasion his name was Beswick. Nice one, huh?'

'Nice one indeed. I think you're right. We'd better meet and discuss this. I don't want to talk any more on the phone. In cases like this I'm never convinced that someone isn't listening in.'

'James, you're getting paranoid.'

'Just past experience,' Muirhead intoned as he recalled a major trial some years before, when he had become convinced that his phone was tapped. For no good reason, it contracted the habit of making a series of odd clicks and, during one conversation, he was sure he could hear talking in the background. He decided to set a trap. His client had completed his evidence in chief and was about to be cross-examined by the advocate depute. Muirhead arranged for his instructing solicitor to phone him at home. They discussed a variety of mundane matters and then, as arranged, the solicitor asked how Muirhead felt the client had done thus far and how he thought he might fare in cross.

'As long as he doesn't try to be too smart he'll be fine. As long as he is not asked about his dealings with Owen McGuire. I'm not too sure we have an answer for that.'

The following day the cross-examination proceeded. The accused had little difficulty in dealing with the early matters put to him Suddenly he was asked, 'How long have you known Owen McGuire?'

'Who?'

'Owen McGuire. How long have you known him?'

'I don't know anybody called Owen McGuire. I've never heard of Owen McGuire.'

'Please be very careful. Have you had any dealings of any kind with someone called Owen McGuire or who uses the name Owen McGuire?'

'I am being careful. Very careful. Now watch my lips. I have never met, dealt with or heard of someone called Owen McGuire, Owen anything or anything McGuire. Is that clear enough for you? Is that being careful ?'

Looking decidedly puzzled, the advocate depute realised it was time to move on to potentially more fruitful ground.

He would have been even more puzzled if he had glanced at his opponent. Muirhead's expression was a bizarre mixture of amusement and rage. Owen McGuire was a figment of his imagination.

From that day forth, he had a deep and abiding dislike of the telephone. He did not trust it, or rather did not trust the people who might be listening in to it. Hence he wanted to meet Jack Morton face to face.

'As you please. Tomorrow night. Six o'clock. My office.'

'Suits me. I'll arrange for Donald Anderson to be there.'

'Things are getting interesting, n'est ce pas?'

'Ain't they just.'

'See you tomorrow night.'

Muirhead sank back into his battered old armchair and began the ritual of emptying, filling and lighting his favourite pipe.

The preparation of the case was well under way and in his study he was surrounded by bundles of papers, maps and photographs. He had already identified the various areas of potential difficulty as well as the parts of the evidence which could assist the defence. In his mind he was developing the possible strategies which might be available to tackle the prosecution case.

Grasping the defence case had not proved overly taxing. The client knew nothing about either crime and was claiming to have been at home when each murder was committed. He had been surrounded by members of his family and a variety of friends and acquaintances, each of whom was more than willing to testify to this effect. That was the easy bit.

Muirhead did not go into trials with a detailed battle plan. His preparation was faultless and he would be familiar with all the minutiae of the case. He would know the strengths and weaknesses and would have worked out how to highlight the former and paper over the latter.

Once the trial started he did not rely on preconceived notions. He had to be able to react to events as they happened, deal with evidence as it appeared, expect surprises at every turn. If a plan went awry, it was all too easy to find himself with nothing to fall back on.

Preparing for a criminal trial is a laborious process, yet it has to be carried out in a comparatively short period of time. When a person is committed to prison to await trial, the prosecution in Scotland has 110 days to start the trial. By the eightieth day of his incarceration an indictment must be served specifying the charges, listing the witnesses and productions and stating where and when the trial will take place. Only then do the accused and his legal advisers begin to find out the exact nature of the case they have to meet. Prior to this the independent prosecutor, the Procurator Fiscal, collates the Crown evidence and prepares the case.

The indictment is served on the accused in prison. This is a ceremony attended by no solemnity whatsoever. A prison officer will visit the cell and hand over the document accompanied by the utterance of formal words such as 'There's yer indictment. Be lucky'.

The defence have a month to interview the prosecution witnesses, obtain copies of and study the various documentary productions and decide what evidence must be led by the defence to meet the charges.

Each of these stages had been passed through and Jack Morton, as ever, was ahead of schedule. Ten days before the trial, as required by law, the prosecutor and court would be formally advised of the two special defences of alibi. Alibi is a special category of defence which is special only in the sense that the Crown is entitled to receive advance notice of it.

In reality, there are only three defences to any criminal charge – 'It wisnae me' – 'I wisnae there' – 'A big boy done it and run away'. There is a hybrid many accused persons seek to use, but in reality it is not a defence in the true sense. It runs, 'Well, aye, I done it, but I dinnae want tae go to jail for it.'

In relation to each of the charges of murder, Charlie Gallagher was maintaining that he was elsewhere when each of the murders was committed. If the Crown was to establish his guilt, it would not only have to prove it, it would also have to disprove the alibis.

From what he knew so far, Muirhead was not convinced that the prosecution case was particularly strong. Now it appeared that matters were about to take a turn for the worse. The problem with confessions is that jurors tend to take a rather strict view of them. For some reason (a reason which irritates the hell out of defence lawyers) they seem to think that only guilty people confess to crimes.

What on earth was Charlie supposed to have said to some boy policeman? Could he really have been that stupid? Possibly; although he seemed to have dealt reasonably with all the formal interviews. Would a young cop have the balls to make something up? And what about this supergrass? Gallagher had been warned time and time again not to discuss the case with anyone apart from his lawyer. People awaiting trial are under constant scrutiny, their telephone calls may be listened into, letters are read. Certainly their fellow inmates will show little loyalty and will cheerfully trade information to the authorities in the hope of gaining some benefit for themselves. Absolute caution is always necessary. Maybe the idiot had dropped his guard. If he had, it could prove to be a very costly lapse in concentration.

Muirhead drew on his pipe and grimaced. The tobacco was spent. Time for bed, although he doubted if he would sleep much. Too many thoughts in his head. Things were getting interesting, to say the least. He had just turned out the lights in the study when the phone rang. Muirhead lifted the handset and said, 'James Muirhead.'

'Mr Muirhead, I've got a piece of advice for you. Get out of the Gallagher case or you could find your health deteriorating – rapidly.'

'Very funny – who is this?'

'Never mind who this is, just take the advice. This is not a joke, Mr Muirhead.'

'If you think I'm going to pay attention to some idiot who won't tell me who he is, you're off your head. Now, tell me who you are and what you want or frankly I suggest you fuck off, to put not too fine a point on it.'

'You're being very stupid, Muirhead. I was giving you some advice, friendly like. Now I'm telling you. Drop the Gallagher case.'

The line went dead.

Muirhead dialled 1471 but was not overly surprised to find that the caller had withheld the number.

Nutcase...has to be, he told himself. Nonetheless, he felt a distinct sense of unease. He had received letters from cranks before calling him every name under the sun and casting serious doubts on his parentage. But to actually hear the voice conveying the threat, that was different.

And yet, it was, to say the least, an odd demand. Even if he did withdraw from the case, could withdraw from the case, another counsel would be instructed to take over. Muirhead knew that life was anything but predictable when you are dealing with juries. Maybe he would win, but equally maybe he could lose. Maybe somebody else would win. Maybe not. What could possibly be the reason for someone wanting him to pull out? Yes, he was good, very good, but there were no guarantees.

How did the caller know he was defending Gallagher? Who would know he was defending Gallagher? The client, the family, his solicitor and his staff, some of his colleagues, the prosecution, the police, even some journalists. He began to realise that the list was endless. So, who would have a motive to want him out of the case?

What to do? Call the police? And what could they do about it? Get an intercept put on the phone? Sledgehammer to crack a nut. Anyway, there was no guarantee he would call back. No reason to suppose he would call back.

Muirhead was getting nowhere. He stared at the phone, half expecting it to ring. Nothing.

'Nutter, James, probably a nutter. Forget it, my son. More than enough to worry about.'

As he switched off the study lights for the second time, Muirhead shivered again. This was becoming a habit, and he didn't like it. More to the point, he didn't know why.

Had he taken the trouble to look out of the window he might have discovered part of the reason for his agitation. The figure hurrying down the driveway had left behind a message, scratched into the paintwork on the boot of Muirhead's Jaguar. It was as clear as it was unequivocal.

R I P

Chapter Five

Barlinnie prison sits in the East End of Glasgow in a district known as Riddrie. The area is dull, drab and totally without charm. It provides an ideal backdrop for its most infamous architectural structure.

Barlinnie, the Bar-L, the Big House, is a Victorian jail whose halls leave even the casual observer in no doubt whatsoever as to their purpose. It is surrounded by a high wall topped with razor wire. Video cameras observe its every nook and cranny. It is an easy place to get into. Getting out again is the tricky bit.

C Hall in Barlinnie is the most depressing of all. It contains those who have been convicted of nothing, but have been remanded in custody to await trial. Charlie Gallagher was one such inmate.

He sat across the table from Muirhead who sat quietly, exuding calm tinged with concern. Gallagher was slowly running out of steam. He had delivered himself of a peroration, railing against the Boyles, the police, judges, jurors, prosecutors, justice, injustice, and anyone or anything else he could think of or take a swipe at.

The three lawyers had spent two hours with their client going over the evidence at the heart of the Crown case. Every time they tried to explain the difficulties and sought answers to some pertinent questions, they were greeted with a stream of invective. Gallagher was not prepared to face the realities of the situation. His final outburst had been prompted by Muirhead's attempt to encourage him to face up to some potentially awkward issues.

'Mr Gallagher, there really is no point in shouting at me. I'm only trying to help you. You really must make some effort to help yourself.'

'You're the fucking QC! I've told you. These bastards are all fucking lying, so why don't you just fucking prove it, if you're so fucking smart.'

'Something a little more constructive would help, you know. I appreciate this man Warwick or Beswick may be a liar, but why do you think he is lying about you?'

'Because the polis have fucking paid him, that's why. How many times do I have to fucking tell you that, for fuck's sake?'

'Well, I have to tell you that in my view there is sufficient evidence to get you to a jury. If you have to give evidence, telling a jury that the police have 'fucking paid him' is not exactly a complete answer.'

'Enough to get to a fucking jury! How can this get to a fucking jury? Have you bastards just been pissing about wasting your fucking time and my old man's fucking money?'

'Mr Gallagher, we can deal with the evidence. I cannot simply make it disappear. I'm not a magician. As you might say, I'm not Tommy fucking Cooper!'

'You're not a fucking QC either and who the fuck's Tommy Cooper and what the fuck's he got to do with it...!?'

There was nothing the lawyers could do but weather the storm. When it had all but blown out, Muirhead gathered his papers together, and the two others followed suit.

'Look, Mr Gallagher, I appreciate how you feel about this. I understand the frustration of being locked up in this place, and before you say I don't, please remember I've been visiting clients here for over twenty years and most of them have felt just as you do. So, please calm down and take it easy.

'The case has been well prepared, we know what we have to do and more importantly we know what we're doing. In short, we're ready to go. We will do our best. I don't go into cases intending to come second. You will receive the best possible defence. Of that, you may rest assured.'

He held up his hand to indicate that a further contribution from Gallagher was going to serve little useful purpose.

'We'll leave it there just now, I think, but we'll come and see you on Monday morning before the trial starts. Please remember, when you are in court, just sit there and listen to the evidence. Do not react to it in any way. No outbursts. Do not even nod or shake your head. If there is anything you remember you have not told us, just attract Mr Anderson's attention. He will be sitting very close to you. You can assume we know everything we have discussed, so do not, please, call him over unless there is something new. I do not want the jury to think that we are making the script up as we are going along. Take it easy over the weekend and we will see you on Monday morning. OK?'

Gallagher stared at the table in front of him.

'OK?'

'OK. Just get me out of here.'

'I'll do my best.'

The lawyers left the interview room. They walked in silence across the prison yard to the main gate. Once outside, Morton summed up the situation.

'You're on your own with that one, Mr Muirhead!'

Anyone watching might have thought it curious that three eminent legal figures would leave a prison and almost immediately burst into laughter. The comment had reminded each of them of a case they had been involved in some years earlier.

A man had entered a bank in the centre of Glasgow intending to rob it. He was wearing a Balaclava. Unfortunately it was an open-face Balaclava and did virtually nothing to conceal his identity. On approaching the young female teller he pretended to have a gun in his pocket and demanded money. As he did not have an account, his request was denied. He then endeavoured to climb over the bandit screen, but when he had one leg on either side of the glass the young lady grabbed his leg, pulled hard and refused to let go. Only with considerable difficulty did he make good his escape in the getaway vehicle which bore more than a passing resemblance to a Glasgow Corporation bus heading to Easterhouse. Needless to say he was arrested. Jack Morton, Donald Anderson, and Muirhead had all gone to see the client in Barlinnie. Muirhead reviewed the not inconsiderable body of evidence.

'Eight witnesses identify you as the robber.'

'They're mugs, Mr Muirhead. You'll destroy them.'

Muirhead noted this helpful contribution.

'In your house, the police found a Balaclava mask identical to that worn by the robber.'

'It belongs to my wee boy, he wears it in the winter.'

Reasonable. It was noted.

'When you were arrested you were examined by a police casualty surgeon who found that the insides of your thighs were covered in bruises and abrasions and your genitalia were swollen to twice their normal dimensions.'

Sweat was beginning to appear on the client's furrowed brow. This was proving a bit tricky.

'I was playing football with my wee boy and he kicked me between the legs.'

Plausible...barely, but still plausible.

'Your fingerprints were found at the top of the bandit screen on the inside of the glass.'

The client thought long and hard before declaring: 'You're on your own with that one, Mr Muirhead.'

The laughter subsided.

'Ah well, nothing new in that Jack, nothing new at all. Donald and I will get together on Sunday and go over everything again.'

'If you need me, give me a call.'

'Fine. As we say in the trade, we'll see you in court.'

'I see you've got the Jag back. Any more funny phone calls?'

'No. Just some crank I suspect. Strangely enough, I thought it was going to bother me, but since nothing else has happened I've just ignored it.'

'Didn't tell the police then?'

'No, they've enough to do rounding up more business for us without wasting time on rubbish like this.'

'Quite sure?'

'Absolutely. No problem.'

'Monday then?'

'Monday.'

●　　　●　　　●

'The person you recommended had proved unsatisfactory. Not up to the job.'

'So?'

'So, what are you going to do about it?'

'What am I going to do about it? I wasn't aware it was my problem. You asked for a name, so I gave you a name. If I'd been there it would have been well sorted by now. You're the one who told me to keep away.'

'Don't get fucking smart.'

'Look, I told you it was a daft idea and it wouldn't work. I also told you if you wanted it done right, I would come and do it. But no, no, you were the big man. You would see to it. Now you're blaming me for a fuck-up. Well, old son, there are two words and the second one is, off.'

'It's in both our interests that Gallagher goes down.'

'From where I'm sitting, I couldn't give a rat's arse one way or another.'

'It won't be that if he gets off and the filth start digging again. You never know, someone might just blow in their ear.'

'Don't threaten me, you little bastard.'

'Take it easy, take it easy. I wasn't getting at you.'

'No, you were fucking threatening me. No one does that, especially not the likes of you. If anything happens to me, I won't go down alone, and you better fucking believe it.'

'OK. OK. I'm sorry. I'm grateful. You did me a big favour.'

'Don't be smart.'

'Can we talk, sensibly?'

'I can – can you?'

'I need your help. Will you help me...please?'

'That's better. Fifty K.'

'Fifty grand!'

'Plus expenses.'

'Are you off your fucking head?'

'This line seems to be breaking up. I didn't hear you say yes.'

'OK. OK.'

'Pardon!'

'YES.'

'Consider it done. Leave the money at the usual place. English fifties. No cheques. No credit cards. Cash, that'll do nicely, thank you.'

'Very bloody funny.'

'Line's breaking up again.'

'Yes.'

'Pardon.'

'Yes...thank you.'

The line went dead.

        ●   ●   ●

'Court!'

The macer preceded Lord Cowden to the bench to begin the trial of Her Majesty's Advocate against Charles Gallagher.

Having bowed to the judge, the various counsel and solicitors settled into their places. Charlie sat in the dock flanked by two uniformed officers of Strathclyde Police. They held batons between their white gloved hands. Gallagher was wearing a plain blue single-breasted suit, white shirt and sensible tie. In a different context he would have been taken for a man of business. Unfortunately, his business was allegedly murder.

In the well of the court the lawyers sat round a table littered with papers.

In front of the dock were arranged the various productions in the case: photographs, maps, reports and a quantity of bloodstained clothing.

In the benches behind the dock, the unempanelled jurors shifted nervously in their seats, waiting, wondering, trying to catch a glimpse of the accused. The three front rows were occupied by the members of the fourth estate armed with their shorthand notebooks and copies of the indictment. A motley collection of cheap suits and short skirts were all eager for some juicy titbit early in the evidence which would provide them with a decent headline for the early editions or the lunchtime news.

One young reporter who, judging by his accent, had been sent north by an English newspaper, displayed a total lack of familiarity with quaint Scottish customs.

'Will he be pleading guilty?'

78

The response from a veteran hack, 'With James Muirhead in the case, there's more chance of Ally McCoist becoming Pope', left him a mite nonplussed and certainly no better informed.

The judge looked down towards defence counsel.

'Mr Muirhead,' he intoned.

'My Lord, I appear with my learned friend Mr Anderson on behalf of the Pannel Charles Gallagher who pleads not guilty to the various charges libelled against him. There are special defences of alibi and reference may be made to these in the course of the evidence.'

The trial had begun.

The Clerk proceeded to ballot the jury by picking pieces of paper out of a plastic bowl and reading out the names each contained. The unfortunate nominees made their way nervously to the jury box and settled uncomfortably in their places.

When fifteen had been chosen, the Clerk invited them to stand while the charges were formally read over to them. Then they were put on oath.

'Do you swear by Almighty God that you will well and truly try the accused and deliver a true verdict according to the evidence? Please say I do.'

They did.

Lord Cowden then proceeded to growl at the jury in his customarily charmless manner as if he was lecturing his servants on their lack of breeding and manners.

There would be no opening speeches. Straight to the evidence. The Advocate Depute and his assistant appeared for the Crown, Mr Muirhead with his junior for the defence. Junior counsel were not mentioned by name, and solicitors, being in his Lordship's opinion a lower form of life, were ignored totally.

Witnesses would be called, examination, cross-examination, re-examination. End of Crown case. Defence case. No obligation on the accused to give evidence or prove anything. Onus of proof on the Crown throughout. Speeches. Charge to set out the legal framework.

Muirhead picked up the occasional word. No need to pay close attention. He had heard it before – many times.

He was concentrating on his opponent. Matthews as ever was sitting exuding an air of supreme confidence.

You arrogant bugger, thought Muirhead. But you're nervous, you devious sod. He had noticed that the Advocate Depute was fiddling with a piece of tape which had been used to bind some of his papers. He was tying it into a series of knots while plainly lost in thought.

Muirhead gave his attention to the jury. There was not much you could tell at this stage. Mostly, the jurors looked bemused. Two did catch his eye. One man was leaning forward listening intently to every word said to him. He nodded occasionally as if he understood and then actually began to take notes. A foreman in the making if there ever was one.

Another man was lounging back in his seat staring round the court, clearly paying no attention to anything said to him. A know-all. A troublemaker. There's always one.

Muirhead glanced up to the public gallery. He noticed only that it was packed. A rare event these days. Had he paid more attention, he might have observed a bearded figure with eyes focused intently on one of the leading actors rather than the play which was about to unfold before him. As he turned his gaze back to the jury, Muirhead shivered.

'It's cold in here.'

Anderson was busy organising his papers.

'Is it? Hadn't noticed.'

'Well, I think it's cold.'

'Eh? OK it's cold – if you say so.'

'It is cold.'

'Look, if you're trying to tell me you're coming down with something, you're not on. Too late to get out of this one now. We're in this together – up to our necks.'

Muirhead smiled thinly.

'Take more than feeling the cold to get me out of this case, I fear.'

'Death wouldn't get you out of this case, James.'

Both men smiled. Anderson meant it. Muirhead didn't – the notion was not even vaguely amusing. He turned his mind to the matters in hand.

He had met with his client that morning in the cell area below the High Court building. It is a singularly cheerless place. The concrete floors and white tiled walls combined to give it the impression of a Victorian public lavatory. Sometimes it smelt like one.

Gallagher had been surprisingly laid back, at least in outward appearance. He had no questions to ask and Muirhead contented himself with reminding the client of the need to keep calm in court and reassuring him that everything and everyone was ready to go. Gallagher asked only one question: 'What do you think?'

'I'm not here to get second prize.'

Charlie nodded.

His Lordship completed his opening salvo and invited the Depute to open his case, who then proceeded to do so. The morning was occupied with the evidence of scenes-of-crime officers who would take the court through a series of photographs graphically illustrating the horror which is a murder scene.

The jurors watched in varying degrees of shock as they were shown Kevin Boyle slumped in his car with most of his skull and brain matter splattered over the inside. The scene had been copiously photographed.

The pictures from the mortuary proved too much for one of the female jurors who turned very pale and would probably have fainted had she not been swiftly ushered out of court. It took some time for her to recover sufficiently to be able to view Boyle lying naked on the stainless-steel mortuary table. From the neck down there was not a mark upon him. However, as one of the jurors later cynically remarked, 'He must have been in the dick queue when the good looks were being handed out.' Above the neck there was little to indicate that this had once been a human being – a mess of blood, tissue and splintered bone which looked as though it had been put through a mincer.

The jury were also shown photographs of the inside of a flat, respectable enough, comfortably furnished with a bed which had clearly just been slept in. No sign of violence here.

The scenes from the Clark murder scene were equally gruesome. The Mad Dog was to be seen crammed into the bin, arms and legs contorted into bizarre shapes. His head was slumped forward on his chest. His hair, face and upper body was covered in congealed blood. There was no obvious source of the bleeding but clearly he had sustained some major injury.

On this occasion, the mortuary photographs revealed that his throat had been cut with such ferocity that his spine could be seen through the gaping wound which had once been his neck. There were more photographs of a lane showing a trail of blood which ended at the kerbside.

A set of four photographs displayed a burned-out motor car framed by the background of some rural scene.

When allowed Muirhead asked a few questions on largely inconsequential matters. He had no particular points he wished to make but liked to give the jury a chance to become accustomed to the sound of his voice. It also enabled him to begin to attempt to strike up a rapport with the jurors, to let them know he would be trying to assist them, to help them through the complexities which lay ahead.

The Advocate Depute had fired off a series of questions, obtained the answers and sat down, without giving any indication that he realised the jury actually existed.

Muirhead, on the other hand, tried to involve the jurors. He wanted to appear interested in them, without pretension, basically just an ordinary chap with no airs and graces who just happened to be wearing a wig and gown. He knew this approach would be in stark contrast to his opponent who would appear stiff and aloof with his superior air and New Town accent.

The photographer was replaced by the Police Casualty Surgeon who described being called to the scene, examining the body of Kevin Boyle and pronouncing life extinct. When he came into court he had been ready to expound upon his theories as to how this may have come to pass. He had gone to the lengths of buying a book on firearms and had convinced himself he knew all about trajectory, angles of entry and exit, bullet calibre and the like. He left the court more than a little peeved that he was not called upon to demonstrate his new-found expertise.

The luncheon adjournment was reached with the defence position unscathed. It would have taken some kind of cataclysmic disaster for a photographer and a doctor to do much damage. It might not be so easy as the afternoon wore on.

After lunch, the girl Boyle had spent his last night with was called in to court. Barbara Potter was blonde, pretty, smartly dressed and very nervous. As she answered questions she constantly twisted a ring round and round the middle finger of her left hand.

She lived in a flat in Mitchell Place in Glasgow and had stayed there for just over two years. She was employed as a pub manageress and did some part-time modelling.

'Fashion?', Matthews enquired.

'Nude.'

She knew Kevin Boyle by sight. She had been to pubs and clubs he apparently owned and he had been pointed out to her. She could not remember by whom. No particular reason. At the time it had not been important.

She had only met Boyle once, and this had been on the night before he was shot. This was at Arbuckle's club and she was there on her own. Boyle had come up to her and started chatting. He was drunk. He bought her champagne. (Actually it was fizzy wine but he had fobbed it off on her as champagne.) She got drunk and began to fancy him. His chat-up lines were so awful they were quite funny. She took him back to her flat. In his fancy car. He frightened her, he was driving so badly. They ended up in bed. Nothing much happened. Boyle was too pissed. He passed out almost immediately. Next morning he simply got up and left saying he would call her – sometime. Then she heard the commotion in the street.

Matthews continued with his staccato questioning. Why had she gone to that particular club? Her nervousness turned to agitation.

'I was asked to go.'

'What do you mean, you were asked to go?'

'I was given money.'

'You were paid?'

'Yes.'

'How did that come about?'

'There was a man who used to come into the pub where I worked. I went for a drink with him now and again.'

'What was his name?'

'I don't know. I just knew him as Bob.'

'How could you go out with a man and not know his name?'

For a moment it looked as if the girl would faint. She turned white and her legs were shaking so violently it appeared as if they would buckle underneath her at any moment.

'Money.'

'Speak up please. Say that again.'

'Money. He paid me to go with him.'

'Did he pay you just to go out with him or did he pay for more than that?'

'Not just to go out.'

'He paid you for sex?'

'Yes.'

'You were acting as a prostitute?'

'I needed the money. I was into money lenders and they were threatening me. I wasn't doing anybody any harm.'

'So you say.'

Muirhead cringed at the Advocate Depute's pompous dismissal of the girl's explanation for her plight. With a bit of luck, that would not endear him to the jury.

'Is there anything more you can tell me about this man Bob?'

'He was tall, about forty, dressed well. He seemed to have lots of money. He had an accent. Irish, I would say.'

'How often did he pay you for sexual favours?'

'Three or four times.'

'You can't remember?' Matthews appeared to have smelt something nasty under his nose.

'Three.'

'And he paid you to go to this club?'

'Yes.'

'What did he tell you to do?'

'He told me he had been involved in a business deal with Kevin Boyle who had cheated him. He had heard that Boyle was a poof, a homosexual, and was going to put this in the papers. I was to get him back to my flat and offer him sex. When he wasn't interested, that would show he was bent. He said he had a mate who was a reporter and who would do the story because Boyle was supposed to be a hard man and a villain. He said he would phone me afterwards and then introduce me to the reporter. I just wanted the money. That's all.'

'How much were you to be paid for this?'

'Five hundred pounds.'

Muirhead was prepared for this story. When he read it in the girl's statement he found it highly improbable. Now that he heard it he found it almost nonsensical. However, he was not prepared for what happened next.

'When this man offered you the five hundred pounds, was he alone or was there someone with him?'

'There was another man with him. He sat at a table while Bob spoke to me. Then the two of them left.'

'Do you see that man in court?'

'Yes.'

'Will you point him out?'

The girl raised a tremulous hand and pointed to Charles Gallagher.

Gallagher leapt to his feet. 'You lying bitch. I've never seen you before in my fucking life. Who's paying you, you fucking whore! Slag, fucking lying slag. Who's paying you now, you cow.' The dock escorts moved quickly to restrain him.

'Sit down, Gallagher. I will not tolerate outbursts in my court. If you cannot behave yourself, I will have you removed.'

The officers struggled to get Charlie back into his seat. The jurors had been shocked by this explosion and were taking time to settle themselves. While Muirhead was annoyed at the very behaviour he had warned against, it had afforded him the opportunity to confer with his solicitor.

'This is not in my precognition, Jack.'

'I saw her personally and she said she did not know Gallagher. She was taken to an identification parade and didn't pick out anyone, never mind him.'

'Great! This is all I need,' and turning to face the witness, Muirhead rose to his feet.

Cross-examination is an art-form with its own canons and principles. Asking questions is a simple matter. You can take a man off the street, put a gown on his back, send him into court and he could ask questions all day. The trick is to ask the right question in accordance with the golden rule, 'If you don't know the answer, don't ask the question.' When a witness is being co-operative and supplying all the right answers, the temptation is to push too far and ask one question too many thereby destroying all the previous good work at one fell swoop. The art lies in knowing when to stop or when to ask no questions at all.

Accused persons sitting in the dock expect their lawyers to be constantly on their feet, tearing into witnesses. In reality, the able lawyer aims to spend as much time as possible sitting on his backside. As a lawyer, when you are on your feet your client is in trouble. When you are seated, it means there is nothing to worry about.

Muirhead would normally begin by stroking a witness gently, teasing out such information as he could. Gradually he would turn the screw. Only if necessary would he resort to the mailed fist.

He began by asking Potter a number of general questions about her background. His tone was pleasant, affable, as if he was apologising for troubling her. He could see the girl begin to relax.

'You have identified the accused, my client, as being someone who was at your place of work when you were offered this bribe?'

'Yes.'

'It will be clear to the members of the jury that you were doing your best to tell the truth. Would that be fair?'

'I hope so.'

'Of course. Of course. And no doubt you told us the truth about the reasons for and the nature of your encounter with Kevin Boyle?'

'Yes. Certainly.'

'And presumably the jury should have no difficulty in accepting that they heard from you the whole truth?'

'They should.'

This was easy, Potter thought. This man was clearly on her side. It did not dawn on her to ask why. She dropped her guard.

'Then why are you lying?'

'What?'

'It's a very simple question – why are you lying ?'

'I'm not. What about?'

'Who is Sharon McColl?'

'I don't know.'

Now it was not only her legs which were shaking – her whole body was shaking.

'You know no one called Sharon McColl?'

'I don't think so.'

'What do you mean, you don't think so? Do you – yes or no?'

'No...I can't remember.'

The fifteen jurors sat forward expectantly. They knew something was about to happen. They were anxious to see what. The Crown team thought they knew what was coming as they had a statement from Sharon McColl. They too were in for a surprise.

'You made a phone call to Sharon McColl on the morning Kevin Boyle died.'

'Is that a question, Mr Muirhead?' Lord Cowden also knew that something was about to happen and he was not keen to see Muirhead demolish a potentially crucial Crown witness.

'Of course it's a question – and I am entitled to an answer.'

'Maybe. I…I can't remember.'

'You can't remember phoning someone, you can't remember if you do know or do not know. Have I got that right?'

'I phoned her.'

'You suddenly remember this, do you?'

'Yes…sorry.'

'What did you talk about?'

'Nothing.'

'I see. You phoned this person and then the two of you sat silently at the opposite end of a phone line. Yes?'

'Nothing much.'

'What much?'

'I told you, I can't remember.'

'Who is Mike?' A swift change of tack.

'Mike who?'

'Yes, that was my question, now can I have an answer?'

Muirhead was in full cry and Barbara Potter would have done anything to be somewhere else – anywhere else.

'I know a lot of people called Mike.'

'Doubtless, but which one did you speak to Sharon McColl about?'

Barbara's face carried the clear message, 'How the fuck do you know about this'. She wanted to say something and although her mouth was open, nothing came out.

'You phoned Miss McColl to tell her that you had just made an easy few quid. You had been paid to screw some guy called Mike and he had been too pissed to get it up.'

She still did not know how he knew, but clearly he knew – too much.

'Yes.'

'Louder please, so we can ALL hear you.' Muirhead stared directly at the judge.

'YES.'

'So why did you lie?'

'I don't know.' Her answer was whispered, but this time she was not asked to speak up.

'You attended an identification parade at London Road Police Office, did you not?' Another sudden change of topic made her think that perhaps the worst was past. She was sadly mistaken.

'Did you pick anyone out at the parade?'

'No.'

'Why not?'

'I was nervous. I didn't know what to do.'

Muirhead feigned incredulity.

'What do you mean you didn't know what to do? A policeman would tell you that if you saw the person you had referred to in your statement to the police you should pick him out by number. Correct?'

'Yes.'

'So what were you too nervous to do?'

'Say anything, I suppose.'

'That's just another lie, Miss Potter, isn't it?'

'I can't remember.'

'A policeman took a note of what you did say at the parade and it is, "He's not here, I'm certain".'

'Yes.'

'So the man you claim you saw in the disco was not at the ID Parade?'

'No.'

The jury were now totally enthralled. None of its members had known quite what to expect when they came to court. Some thought it would be like the telly. In reality this was better than the telly because they were part of it.

Muirhead was about to embark upon uncharted territory. He knew about the conversation with Sharon McColl and the witness's response at the parade. He knew that she had lied in her evidence. He did not know why. He was about to try to find out. This could be a hazardous exercise.

He looked down at the papers in front of him as if he was looking for some important piece of information. He knew the question he wanted to ask. Unfortunately, he didn't know what the answer would be. This was too early in the trial to be breaking the golden rule. Sometimes though, needs must.

From the corner of his eye he could see the Advocate Depute. Since he was sitting facing the jury, he was trying to remain calm. The piece of tape he was fiddling with was now twisted into a large knot. It was perfectly obvious that the Crown did not know what might be about to come its way.

Although only a few seconds had elapsed, Muirhead was well aware that to the people in court this could seem like an age. The witness might take this opportunity to pull herself together. It was important to keep the momentum going.

'Then why did you point to the accused as being the man in the pub?'

'I don't know.'

'Why did you point to the accused as being the man in the pub?'

Muirhead's voice now had a distinctly harsh edge to it. Barbara Potter would have given up her very soul if she could just run, faint, die, anything to get away from this man who was tormenting her. Her head was spinning. She felt she had to do something. She fell back onto the wooden benchseat in the witness box and burst into tears, sobbing into her hands.

Through her fingers she could see someone standing beside her. A saviour. She raised her head to be confronted by the macer holding a plastic cup of water – the courtroom panacea for all ills. It was becoming obvious that no one was coming to save her. She waved away the water and, with an air of resignation, stood up.

'You must answer counsel's question, Miss Potter. Are you ready to continue? We really must get on.' As ever his Lordship was all heart.

'What did he ask me?'

'I want to know why you identified Mr Gallagher, the accused, in court?'

'I was told to.'

The answer was barely audible to most people in the court. Muirhead heard it and exploded with his response.

'What! What did you just say?' Muirhead had not been sure what to expect, but he certainly had not expected this.

'I was threatened.'

'By whom?'

'I told you, I don't know. The man with the Irish accent, Bob, came to my flat. I didn't know I'd been with Kevin Boyle till the police spoke to me. I realised I'd been set up. This man told me that when I came to court, I was to pick out the accused and say that I saw him in the pub on the night I was paid to sleep with this guy Mike. The bit about him being a poof is true. I didn't know it was Kevin Boyle. He gave me a photograph and told me where I could meet Mike. If I didn't point out Mr Gallagher, he would come back and cut me. He had a knife with him and he drew it down my face. He wasn't joking. I was scared. I'm still scared. I didn't know what to do.'

'When did this happen?'

'Last night. He told me not to tell anyone.'

'The man in court – have you ever seen him before in your life?'

'No. I'm sorry. I'm so sorry.'

Muirhead returned slowly and deliberately to his seat and sat down.

'Great stuff. One to the bad guys, methinks!'

Muirhead nodded his appreciation to his junior.

The Advocate Depute prolonged her torment and re-examined for the better part of an hour, but the girl would not budge. Yes, she had lied but now she was telling the truth.

The first day of the case came to an end with the defence unscathed. Indeed, the fact that a crucial prosecution witness had been discredited meant that, with luck, the defence was a goal up in the minds of the jury. However, there was still a long way to go.

As the court prepared to adjourn, a lone figure slipped out of the public gallery and hurried down the stairs.

● ● ●

Muirhead was driving home, reflecting on the day's events. When he came out of court it took his mind some time to slow down. He would go over and over the day's evidence trying to assess its impact, where it fitted into the scheme of things, checking in case anything had been overlooked.

So far, so good. The dock identification had been a considerable shock, especially so early in the trial. He knew he had taken a gamble, but it had paid handsome dividends. However, he could do without more surprises like that. There was still some very difficult evidence waiting in the wings.

'A man with an Irish accent,' he mused. Interesting coincidence. The wino who had found the body of Mick Clark had mentioned in his statement a man with an Irish accent. Coincidence? Maybe. Maybe not. Irishmen weren't exactly thin on the ground in Glasgow.

In many criminal investigations there are suggestions of witnesses being intimidated, usually in an attempt to prevent them speaking to the police. It was quite novel to hear a witness claim that she had been forced to give evidence against an accused. Someone, somewhere clearly had an interest in getting Gallagher done. But who and why? If the two men with the Irish accents were one and the same person, he would like to find him – maybe. Maybe not. One day down and still he had no notion of the connection between the two murders – up to now. But now there was the germ of a connection – the mystery man with the Irish accent. Somewhere in the papers he had seen another reference to an Irishman. For the moment he could not recollect where. He would find it later.

As he turned into Allison Street there was a loud bang as the car pitched down at the front and lurched to the nearside. Muirhead fought for control but there was no response. He hit the brakes and the car came to an abrupt halt. Fortunately, no one was coming towards him and, other than banging against the kerb, he thought he and the car had survived relatively unscathed.

As he checked round about him he looked in his rear-view mirror to see a car behind him swerving to avoid an object lying in its path.

'What in the name of God is that?' he muttered. As he got out of the car to check for the damage, he found out.

The Jaguar was minus a front wheel.

Chapter Six

The second morning of the trial was taken up by the pathologists.

Pathology is the strangest of medical specialities. Its practitioners spend their time surrounded by dead, mutilated bodies. Confront them with a living specimen and they run the proverbial mile. A pathologist encountering a child with a grazed knee could tell the angle of the wound, its age and the nature of the surface which caused the damage, but would not have a plaster to stick on it.

Julian Walker was the Regius Professor of Forensic Medicine at Glasgow University. He was a small, dapper man who habitually wore a spotted bow tie. As he gave his evidence he peered over the top of his gold-rimmed half-spectacles. His enthusiastic performance conveyed the impression of a man who loved his work – strange as that work might be.

He had read out the technical description of his external examination of the body of Kevin Boyle from his report. He was now explaining, in layman's terms, exactly what this meant. Making reference to the post-mortem photographs, he described the two gunshot entry wounds on the right side of the head in the part of the skull known as the temporal bone. On the left side and to the rear, there were two corresponding injuries which were clearly exit wounds. Brain matter was extruding from each of the exit wounds. There were no other significant injuries on the body surface.

The two bullets had passed through the brain causing extensive damage en route. By the time they had exited, the damage they left behind was non-survivable. Death would have been virtually instantaneous.

He was asked if he could give an opinion as to the sequence of events. From his examination of the scene and the body, it was clear that Boyle had been seated in the driver's seat of the car. He felt it probable that the gunman had approached from the rear of the vehicle. He probably got to a point opposite the centre pillar. Kevin Boyle had then turned slightly to his right, no doubt to look at the person standing beside him. He was shot twice in the head. The Professor could not say how many shots had actually been fired, but two had been sufficient to despatch Boyle.

He then turned to deal with Clark. However appalling the scene of Boyle's death may have been, it was nothing compared to the horrors surrounding the Mad Dog's final hours. Photographs showed his twisted body stuffed head down in the bin. Mortuary photographs revealed his body on the mortuary table, arms, legs and spine contorted into a bizarre shape.

His body was covered by a total of sixty-three bruises and abrasions. His wrists and ankles bore marks consistent with his having been tied with rope or some similar material. Walker described how each of his arms and legs were broken, as was his back. On his neck were a number of small round burns which had all the appearance of being caused by a lit cigarette being placed against the skin. His throat had been cut.

A sharp-bladed weapon had been used to sever completely the windpipe, the jugular vein, the carotid artery and various other vital structures. Death was caused by a combination of massive haemorrhage and oxygen deprivation due to the damage to the windpipe. Death would have followed within a minute or so of the throat being cut.

Mitchell continued. 'How would you describe the nature of the injuries inflicted on this man?'

'I would say that he was tortured then executed.'

'Why do you say tortured?'

'The burns to the neck are quite clearly non-accidental. Their infliction would have been excruciatingly painful. There were five different sites and this would have required five different applications. When the body was found, it had been violently deposited in the bin and I initially thought that the limbs and back might have been fractured during this exercise.'

'What changed your mind?'

'The deceased had exsanguinated.'

'Meaning?'

'There was virtually no blood left in his body. It was clear from the locus that, although there were a few blood spots leading from the pavement to where the body was found, putting it simply, there was not enough blood. I have no doubt that he was assaulted and killed elsewhere. Since death would have been very rapid, I am quite satisfied that he was dead when he was put in the bin. When we dissected his back there was no reaction, no blood in the tissues surrounding the fracture. This was caused after death. However, there was extensive bleeding into the tissues surrounding the broken arms and legs and bleeding around the edges of the broken bones. He was very much alive when he sustained these injuries.'

'How do you think they may have been caused?'

'I find that a more difficult question to answer. The fractures are remarkably clean and above each site there is surface bruising as well as bruising into the tissues themselves. I think that his arms and legs were securely held or braced in some way and he was struck with a heavy object such as a hammer.'

'What degree of force would have been involved?'

'On a scale of mild, moderate and severe, I would say very severe force. These were acts of considerable brutality. Taking everything into account, I have seldom seen anyone so badly beaten before they were killed.'

'Finally, can you tell me whether one person, acting alone, was capable of inflicting the injuries on Mr Clark?'

'I suppose it could be said that most things are possible, but I find it very difficult to conceive that one person could have caused all this damage. Bear in mind that his hands and feet had been bound at some point and presumably he would have offered some resistance. More importantly, I believe that his arms and legs were supported while they were broken. I am quite satisfied it would require at least two people to carry this out.'

'Two people at least?'

'At least...in my opinion.'

This was enough to make some jurors wince. Muirhead knew that this could produce hostility in their minds. Some people can appreciate that in a rage or if severely provoked, one person is capable of inflicting the most awful violence on another. Some might not be unduly bothered by the notion that one bad man could shoot another in cold blood. Live by the sword and all that. None of this would necessarily prejudice their consideration of the evidence. But the Mad Dog's killer or killers had been sadists, and sick ones at that. Even if they had some doubts at the end of the day, a jury might not be prepared to risk releasing such a monster back into their midst.

As he left court for the luncheon adjournment, Muirhead was approached by a man who introduced himself as Detective Superintendent McAllister.

'I know who you are, Superintendent. We have met a number of times before, even if we have not been formally introduced.'

'Could I have a private word?'

'If it's about the case you must speak to my solicitor. You ought to know that.'

'It's not about the Gallagher case. At least not directly. I have received a report that you were involved in an accident last night.'

'And how does a Detective Superintendent come to know about a minor road traffic matter? I did not even call the police. A traffic car just happened to turn up. Or did it?'

'I don't know anything about that, but the officers put in a report. Because your name featured in it, you're defending Gallagher and I'm the officer in charge, it was passed to me.'

'Detective Superintendents do not normally receive reports about traffic accidents.'

'Mr Muirhead, there is no need to be so defensive. I'll speak plainly.'

'I wish you would.'

'Please. I am concerned that a wheel should come off your car on the first day of this trial. I do not believe in coincidences or in bizarre accidents. I think there is a possibility that the wheel nuts were loosened deliberately in order to cause the accident.'

'That's ridiculous. It was an accident, pure and simple. Even if it wasn't, it doesn't mean it has anything to do with this trial. Probably kids playing at silly buggers.'

'Mr Muirhead, I don't think that you believe that for a moment. Has anyone approached you about the Gallagher case? Tried to put pressure on you?'

'I really don't need to waste my time listening to this nonsense. I suggest you keep your insinuations to yourself and get on with your real work and let me get on with mine. You and I have nothing more to say to each other.'

McAllister was left staring at Muirhead's back as he strode off.

'Thank you, Mr Muirhead. Very helpful,' he mused. 'So something is going on and you believe it's connected to this little matter. Stomp off if you like. We'll talk again – soon I suspect.'

Muirhead walked straight into the retiring room, changed out of his court dress in silence and left the building.

Morton and Anderson watched him go. They were used to his moods and knew there were times in a case when he could be totally uncommunicative. Normally, however, they could hazard some guess at the reason. They exchanged quizzical glances. Nothing in the morning's evidence should have produced this reaction.

'What's that all about?'

'Don't know, Jack. Something or someone has clearly rattled our leader's cage. He'll be fine by two o'clock. Probably just being his usual grumpy self. Maybe didn't get his leg over last night.'

'Maybe.'

'He'll be fine. You know how he is. Gets worked up about something. Stomps off. Calms down. Back to normal.'

Muirhead would not have agreed. He strode across Glasgow Green.

He was trying to light his pipe as he walked and meeting with no success. This only served to increase his anger. When he reached one of the bridges over the river he aimed a kick at the parapet. The pain which shot up his leg snapped him out of his fury. He paused and looked down to the Clyde. 'What the hell is going on?', he murmured to himself. The question was addressed at the flowing water – it sullenly failed to respond.

Although he could become completely wrapped up in his day's work and could be oblivious to whatever else was going on round about him, he was not normally discourteous – at least not intentionally. He was angry that McAllister knew about the incident with the car. He was angry that McAllister rightly suspected that something was going on. He was angry at himself for lending credence by over-reacting. He was angry at himself for being angry. And yet he was troubled. The phone call, the vandalising of the car and now the wheel. Normally he did not believe in coincidence either, so who was he kidding and more to the point, why? Maybe he should get the police involved. But the last thing he wanted was Strathclyde's finest tramping in and out of his life when he was involved in a complicated case like this. There was really nothing concrete to tell them. No one could influence the way he conducted a trial. But he was becoming agitated by it all. Maybe that was someone's idea. But why? And who?

He glanced at his watch. It was a quarter to two. Time to get back. Get a grip of yourself, you silly arse. Work to be done.

He turned round and bumped into a passer-by.

'Sorry!', Muirhead exclaimed.

'No problem, pal.'

As he walked back to court he snorted, 'Another guy with an Irish accent!'

●　　　　　●　　　　　●

Muirhead rose and commenced his cross-examination of the pathologist. 'Professor Walker, can we deal with your examination of Mr Boyle? His death was caused by two gunshot wounds?'

'Yes.'

'I think you suggested that the gunman approached the car from the rear and fired through the driver's window?'

'Yes, that is my view.'

'Presumably the fact that the window was shot out would assist you in that regard?'

'Clearly.'

'Can you tell the jury anything about the range involved here?'

'When a firearm is discharged, flame comes out of the end of the barrel along with a certain amount of unburnt propellant as well as the projectile. There was no sign of burning on the skin surface, nor was there any trace of unburnt propellant. This means that the person who discharged the firearm was two feet or more away from the victim.'

'Inside the car there is blood and brain matter splattered on various surfaces?'

'Yes.'

'I take it that the spread and pattern are consistent with the gun being fired into the car?'

'From my examination, yes. The forensic scientists and ballistics people would carry out a more detailed examination.'

'Did you see any sign that blood had sprayed out of the car?'

'I'm not sure what you mean.'

'Was there any blood spotting on the outside of the driver's door or wing mirror, for example?'

'Not that I saw.'

'Or on the outside edges of the driver's door pillar?'

'Not that I saw.'

'Was there any blood on the road surface beside the car?'

'Not that I saw.'

'May the jury take it that there is no basis for concluding that any of the deceased's blood would have landed on the gunman?'

'Anything is possible.'

'No doubt it is, but can you answer my question?'

'I could not rule it out totally.'

'Did you observe anything to show that blood or tissue had sprayed out of the car?'

'As I said, I can't rule it out.'

Muirhead allowed his irritation to show and snapped back. 'I did not ask you what you could rule in or out. Now will you answer the question I did ask you?'

The professor bristled. He did not care to be treated in this abrupt manner. He was not any old witness. He was the Regius Professor of Forensic Medicine at Glasgow University, after all. His reply was clipped.

'No, there was no such sign.'

'Thank you. I'm very much obliged. As far as Clark is concerned, you are satisfied that he was dead when he was dumped in the bin?'

The now slightly sarcastic tone did not improve Walker's humour. Being roughly treated by counsel was inconsistent with the good professor's perception of his status and dignity and he allowed his irritation to show.

'I thought I had made that abundantly clear.'

'Indeed you did. But is it possible to determine how long he had been dead at that point?'

'That is a very difficult matter.'

'I appreciate that, but I am sure that, drawing on your vast experience, you can assist me and the jury.'

'A little ego massaging,' Anderson muttered to Morton. 'I told you he would be fine.'

'The ladies and gentleman of the jury may have watched television programmes and seen a pathologist come along, look at a body and state that the time of death was two minutes past eight. Why can't you do that?'

'I'm afraid that bears little resemblance to reality. At best one can only give an approximate estimate of the time of death depending on the body temperature, the ambient temperature, the state of rigor mortis and a number of other factors. All of these in turn can be affected by the conditions in which the body has been kept.'

'Please, will you help us with your best estimate?'

'After death the muscles of the body stiffen and enter a state called rigor mortis. This usually develops within three to six hours and is fully established within twelve. Normally it will last for two to three days. When I saw the body being removed from the bin, rigor was present in the facial muscles and developing in the limbs. This was at about five in the morning. I would put the time of death at round about midnight. The jury must understand that this is only an approximation.'

'So if the body was found just after one in the morning, he was probably dead for about an hour by that time?'

'That would be reasonable.'

'You tell us that death was due primarily to exsanguination?'

'It was a major cause, yes.'

'But there are spots of blood leading towards the bin where the body was found.'

'On death, blood is no longer pumped by the heart but it will leak from any damaged vessels. Even where there is significant blood loss, there may yet be sufficient to leak out in drops when, for example, a body is moved.'

'But it does mean that somewhere there was deposited a massive quantity of this man's blood?'

'The scene of the killing would be heavily contaminated with his blood. Yes.'

'And so would anyone who was involved in the killing or, for that matter, the disposal of the body?'

'Possibly.'

'Oh, not possibly – undoubtedly?'

'Probably.'

'Almost certainly, to the extent that it would take a minor miracle to avoid being bloodstained. Isn't that right?'

'I would expect anyone involved in the actual killing to be bloodstained.'

'Heavily?'

'Probably.'

'Thank you, Professor Walker.' Muirhead sat down.

In his re-examination, the Advocate Depute led the Professor on a Cook's tour of the world of bloodstains. Blood travelling through the air would land on a surface as a spot. Such spots might appear to have tails giving an indication of the direction of travel. Bloodstains resulting from direct contact would appear as a smear. On the other hand a spot could be smudged or might soak into material and appear as a smear.

Muirhead listened as the discourse developed. He also watched the jurors and was pleased to note that their eyes were gradually glazing over. Nothing in this was going to cause him any concern. He had made the points he wished to make. Charlie Gallagher must have killed Clark round about midnight at a place awash with blood and he himself would have been heavily bloodstained. So far everything was going according to plan. If only he could be convinced that he knew exactly what the plan was.

●   ●   ●

'I don't see much sign of progress.'

'Patience, my boy. The world wasn't built in a day.'

'Rome.'

'What?'

'Rome...Rome wasn't built in a day.'

'Whatever.'

'You fucked up badly with the girl.'

'I've told you before, if you're not satisfied, then do the job yourself.'

'I'm paying you money, good money to do it for me.'

'That's why I have employed plan B.'

'I trust it is a fucking sight better than plan A.'

'Look, you want Gallagher to go down. Stand on it, he will. Unlike you, I know what I am about and if you would stop wasting my time with stupid fucking phone calls I can get on with it.'

'What are you doing next?'

'Are you daft? This is a mobile phone. What do you want me to do – take out an advert in the Evening Times?'

'I just want to know what I'm getting for my money.'

'You're going to get results.'

'I've seen precious little sign of that so far.'

'Look, arsehole, I won't tell you again. The job will be done. Now piss off and give me peace!'

'Don't speak to me like that. Just who the fuck do you think you are...'

The line went dead.

●　　　●　　　●

Criminal trials bear an uncanny resemblance to honeymoons – bursts of frantic activity producing varying degrees of satisfaction followed by periods of boredom where action is hoped for rather than realistically anticipated. For two days the trial had gone into the doldrums. The Crown led a series of witnesses dealing with a variety of background and peripheral matters. The trial was becalmed in its boring phase as facts were established.

Kevin arrived in the club, was his usual self, life and soul and all that, was seen chatting away to some female, no one had seen her before, left in her company. Nothing unusual in that. Just Kevin being Kevin.

A local worthy and his dog (the dog did not give evidence) had seen the BMW M3 parked in the street in the early hours of the morning and again at breakfast time. Whether the man or his dog was the insomniac was never clearly established and probably didn't matter.

With an impish twinkle in his eye, Muirhead rose to his feet to inquire what kind of dog it was and obtained the answer, 'The wife's'. His feigned embarrassment amused the jury. When the Advocate Depute pushed further: 'I think my learned friend was inquiring as to the breed of dog,' and received the response, 'It wiz a black dug,' then allowed his irritation to show by slamming his papers shut, Muirhead was confirmed in his view that the jury would think his opponent a pompous prat.

A number of local residents spoke of hearing a series of loud bangs, looking out of windows, but seeing absolutely nothing. Three witnesses did enable the Crown to put a little more colour into the picture.

Mrs Jessie Brown was a typical Glasgow busybody. She lived alone with her four cats and spent most of her waking hours sitting at the window of her flat observing the various comings and goings in the street below. She would have been asleep when the drunken Kevin arrived the previous night, but noted the flashy car sitting parked in the street the following morning. She had no idea of what kind of car it was. She knew nothing about cars. It was black or blue and she thought it would be expensive.

She was feeding her cats when she heard a series of loud bangs and hurried to her observation point. A man was getting into the rear seat of a car which then drove off at speed. She could give no detailed description of either man or vehicle.

He was tall(ish), average build and his hair was dark. He was wearing dark clothing. The car was blue or green, but it could have been grey. It could have been a saloon or a hatchback because she did not know the difference between the two. It had headed off in the general direction of the city centre.

Robert Scott, the next witness was getting ready to go to work when the gunshots brought him to his window. He knew that he heard gunfire as he had served as a regular soldier for six years. He had seen the car speeding off and had actually observed a man running along the street and diving into the front passenger seat of the vehicle.

His description bore not even a passing resemblance to that of his predecessor. The man had been in his forties, about five feet eight inches tall, thickset and with ginger hair. He distinctly remembered the ginger hair. He was wearing jeans and a light coloured jacket. The car was a Ford Sierra, silver in colour and had a 'B' somewhere in the registration number. It headed out of town. No, he could not identify the man who had jumped into the car.

Yet a further version was provided by a delivery driver who had been parked about one hundred yards down the road. The car was a silver-coloured Volkswagen Golf. His brother used to own one. He only caught a brief glimpse of the man getting into the car, he knew not by which door, but it had registered with him that the man had some kind of hat on. He could not remember in which direction the car had gone.

No one had seen a gun or anything remotely resembling a gun.

None of them would have been in a position to identify the man getting into the car. Each of them had been to the identification parade but had not even picked out a stand-in. None of the descriptions were of sufficient accuracy to be of any real assistance.

Eye-witness evidence has the capacity to be the best and worst of testimony. When a witness points to a man in court and says, 'Him', it invariably has a telling impact on the jury. On the other hand, people regularly make mistakes. Many of the great miscarriages of justice have been brought about by mistaken identity. It is one thing to recognise someone we know, but to pick out anyone based on a fleeting glimpse in circumstances of agitation or alarm, is an exercise fraught with difficulty and danger – not the least of it for the person picked out. Show ten people the same scene and they will each remember different details and disagree about significant aspects of these details.

The Crown was left with a man, probably the gunman, of indeterminate height, age, build and general appearance, getting into a car of uncertain make and even less certain colour, heading at speed into the centre of town or maybe away from the centre of Glasgow.

None of this had in any way assisted the Crown in proving the case against the man in the dock. Suffice it to say, no one had given a description which bore any manner of resemblance to Charlie Gallagher.

At the end of day four, Muirhead made eye contact with his client just before the latter was taken downstairs to the waiting cells. Gallagher nodded, imperceptibly, but he nodded nonetheless. Clearly, he felt that things had been going a little better but was still seeking some confirmation and reassurance.

Muirhead returned the nod and the two parted company.

●   ●   ●

It was to be Sammy's big day. Since he had fallen into the hands of the constabulary his lifestyle had not been to his pleasing. He had been required to stay in one of the City's lodging houses. Although the authorities were picking up the bill, Sammy did not care for this restriction on his freedom of movement. To make matters worse, he had to report to a police station every other day.

The police had pretended to be concerned for his welfare. Sammy was unimpressed. He was only too well aware that they were keeping an eye on him. He began to get paranoid. He was sure he was being followed. Everywhere he went there seemed to be uniforms – watching him.

On one of his visits to the police station, Sammy had been handed a citation ordering him to attend court as a witness in the case of Her Majesty's Advocate against Charles Gallagher (whoever the fuck he was). Ah yes, the identity parade thing. All this bother just because he found a leather jacket. That was all he wanted. He hadn't touched the guy in the bin, didn't want anything to do with him then – or now. Yet he was having to go to court.

On the Thursday afternoon he had reported as usual and was told he had to be at the High Court the next day. Police officers would pick him up from the lodging house and conduct him there personally. He was getting the chauffeur treatment and was to be ready at nine o'clock. Sammy had got himself caught up in something that he wanted to be no part of. He had kept hoping that it would just go away and leave him alone.

Alone! Yes, he was alone, but he had got used to it. He preferred it that way. Be your own man. Have as little as possible to do with people and certainly nothing to do with the authorities.

He was afraid. Not of giving evidence in a court. That was easy enough. People would ask him questions. He would answer them. God knows he had answered plenty of late. A few more were not going to hurt. No one could do him any harm, no matter what he said. He remembered one of the old men who used to come into his shop. He was due to start work at eight o'clock, but after a particularly heavy night he would wander in mid-morning for an Irn Bru and a bacon roll before drifting gently and warily towards the shipyard.

'You'll get yourself into bother one of these days.'

'Maybe so, but they canny shoot ye, can they?'

Sammy wandered towards his model.

'They canny shoot ye, can they?'

No, but he was afraid of something else – memories. Memories meant pain, and pain was an ever-present companion in Sammy's life. Loneliness produced the greatest pain of all. A strength-sapping mixture of a constant dull ache fractured by deep shafts of fiery agony. He had learned, forced himself to learn, to live with the loneliness – but not tonight. Tonight he could not face the pain. He needed to talk. He needed some comfort. He desperately craved the company of the only person he had ever cared for and who truly cared for him. He needed his Betty.

In the course of his dealings with the police, Sammy had discovered that he could usually tap a few coins from them. Buggers probably put it down as expenses. He had spent some of this money on a few luxuries like an occasional roll and sausage and some real cigarettes. But he had managed to save some, not much, but some, just in case. He had never been sure what the 'just in case was'. Now he knew.

Sammy changed direction and headed towards Central Station. It was a place he had visited on many a scavenging trip, but it was a long time since he had purchased a train ticket. He had not the slightest inkling as to what one might actually cost. What if he did not have enough money? Damn it, he would get there somehow.

Sammy joined a queue at the ticket office. Very quickly he was the queue. Clearly some of his potential fellow travellers were being put off by his underarm deodorant – or the lack of it.

'Single to Clydebank, please.'

'A single to Clydebank?'

'Is there an echo in here?'

The counter clerkess produced the ticket but seemed reluctant to part with it. She eyed Sammy up and down.

'£1.75.'

'How much?'

'I just told you. Do you have the money to pay for the ticket?'

'I want to travel on the train, not buy the bloody thing.'

The girl behind the counter clearly had reservations about Sammy's financial status. She also seemed to think he was deaf, daft, foreign or a combination of all three. She lapsed into the mode adopted by the British when addressing anyone perceived to be from another jurisdiction. She shouted.

'Have — you — the — money — for — the — ticket? If — not...if not — go — away — please.'

Sammy dumped a selection of grubby coins on the counter.

'Help yourself, darling.'

Making no attempt to conceal her disgust, the girl began to select the necessary fare using the end of a pencil.

Sammy could not resist the temptation. Maybe it was because he was excited at the prospect of going home. Suddenly he felt mischievous.

'What you doing later, darling?'

'Mind your own business – and I'm certainly not your darling.'

She pushed the change towards him, having extracted the necessary funds and looked up at Sammy ready to tell this tramp what she thought of him before presenting him with his ticket and getting rid of him.

'Take your money. I suggest you go and wash before you get on a train with decent people you disgusting little man!'

Clutching his ticket and the remnants of his savings, he headed for the platform. He glanced up at the clock. Twenty-five to. Ten minutes till the train left. Sammy contemplated blowing more of his savings on a cup of tea, but he recalled that station tea was generally foul – and expensive.

By the time the train pulled into Clydebank after its twenty-minute journey, Sammy was in an even worse state of confusion. The sign had said Clydebank but he scarcely had any idea where he was. This was certainly not the town he had left. He hardly recognised the place. As he wandered out of the station his sense of being in a foreign land increased with every step.

Many of the old buildings he had known were quite simply gone. They had been replaced by ghastly modern structures. Flats which looked as if they had been designed for rabbits rather than people. Shops (he supposed they were shops) all glass and neon lights. He could have been anywhere – or nowhere. The place had lost its character – it had no soul. This was certainly not his Clydebank. It was not where he and Betty had had their home.

As he stared at his shop, the tears welled in his eyes and trickled down his cheeks.

Finnegans Wake Irish Pub.

Live Irish Music.

Grub served all day.

Happy hour 5-7.

Sammy stared, memories flooding back. He could picture the crowds of men walking to and from the shipyards. He could hear the voices of the children in his shop as they chattered excitedly, arguing about which sweets or comics they would buy. And there was Betty, standing in the shop window, looking up and down the street, smiling. Betty always smiled.

He thought of the years they had spent building up the business. Sammy was the one who wanted to take all the latest offers from the sales reps. Betty was always the prudent one.

'But if we buy two cases of these shampoos we get them for less than half price.'

'Sammy, we sell two bottles a week, if we're lucky. We'll be sixty before we break even, never mind make a profit.'

Betty would never put her husband down, even if she did have to restrain him occasionally.

'Let's take six bottles just now and see how they go.'

Honour was satisfied all round.

Sammy smiled. Betty bullied him – just a bit – but he did not really mind. Together they were a great team.

'Together.'

That was what he missed. That was what he wanted. For him and Betty to be together again. Sammy was so lost in his own thoughts that he was unaware of everything going on around him. People on the street, customers entering and leaving the pub – none of them existed as far as he was concerned. None of them gave the old tramp more than a cursory and slightly disdainful glance. Sammy did not even register their presence.

Had he been slightly more aware, he might have spotted that the dark blue Ford Sierra which had followed him from the station was now parked across the street, its two occupants watching him intently. He might even have noticed as it U-turned and began to approach him.

Suddenly his mind snapped from his reflective melancholy into a state of sheer panic. Hands were grabbing his arms. He was roughly turned around, bent over and pushed into the back seat of the car which then sped off. Sammy was half on the seat, half on the floor. When he tried to get up, he was hauled upright. To his right and left were grinning faces.

'It's OK, Sammy, my son. We're just giving you a lift. As they say, just sit back, relax and enjoy the flight.'

Once again, Sammy was leaving Clydebank. In his confused state, he could think but one coherent thought.

'Fucking waste of £1.75!'

❋   ❋   ❋

'He's changed his running order. We're getting the wino to tell us about Clark,' Anderson informed Muirhead.

'McPhee?', Muirhead responded.

'Yes. Seems odd that he's going on to Clark when he's still got to lead some of his best stuff on the Boyle charge.'

'Maybe.'

During a trial, the Crown, as a matter of courtesy, will normally tell the defence the order in which it is proposed to call the witnesses. The prosecutor can, of course, change his mind and call who he likes, when he likes.

Anderson was excited by this apparent tactical shift. Muirhead was unimpressed. Maybe there was something to this. Maybe not. One thing was certain, if he asked the Advocate Depute why, he would not be told.

The door to the retiring room opened and Jack Morton rushed in.

'McPhee's here.'

'We know.'

Morton looked slightly peeved that his news had preceded him.

'Sorry, Jack, but the Crown junior told Donald this morning that he was calling McPhee.'

'Why the change of direction?'

'Could be for any one of a variety of reasons, Jack. It's a bit early to be getting paranoid about things like the order of witnesses.'

'James, this is not any old witness, this guy could put us in deep shit. We were not expecting him till next week but he's here – now! If there is something going on, I suggest we try to find out what. Why don't you get an adjournment to give me the chance to carry out some inquiries.'

'Jack, do what you think your job requires, but don't tell me how to do mine. I'm not some bloody amateur who needs spoon-fed.'

'Hang on, you don't have to talk to me...'

'Come on Jim, Jack's only trying to...'

'Leave it, Donald. If McPhee is giving evidence I want to read his statement and get ready to cross-examine him. I do not need to be told how to do my job. If I want advice I will ask for it. Now if you will excuse me, I'm going to the library.'

When the door closed over Morton and Anderson stared at each other.

'I wasn't trying to tell him how to do his job, for Christ's sake. He knows me better than that.'

'I know that, Jack, so does he. He's helluva uptight for some reason. Crabbit, yes. But this is not like him. Not like him at all. Even I'm getting slightly concerned. I've never seen him quite like this.'

'I'm uptight, too, but that's no reason for us to fall out with each other, and no reason for him to speak to me as if I was the bloody amateur.'

'Steady on, Jack. He didn't mean anything personal, any more than you did.'

Morton sighed deeply.

'Oh, I know. Gets to you though.'

'Sure.'

'I'll go and sniff around Mr McPhee, if you'll pardon the expression.'

'Take your hankie, Jack.'

Left alone, Anderson stared out of the window over Glasgow Green. It was a day to match his mood – grey.

'Something is wrong with you, James, old friend. But you'll tell no one, will you? So why should I get my head bitten off for asking?'

The buzzer saved him from having to answer his own question.

❀   ❀   ❀

When Sammy had gone to the lavatory before being called into court, he had hardly recognised the image in the mirror. Clean-shaven, hair combed, a suit which almost fitted him and a collar and tie – and bloody uncomfortable they were too.

His appearance in court might have caused no stir amongst the jurors, but it had certainly taken James Muirhead aback. He had been expecting to see a tramp. Instead the witness reminded him of a shopkeeper.

Sammy had had to ask the judge to repeat the words of the oath twice. Not because his lordship's diction was other than a model of crystal clarity, but because his ears were ringing with the words, 'Do yourself a favour, just get it right'.

Sammy described his lifestyle over the past few years. He got by, scavenging for items he could sell. He often visited hotels and the like.

Yes, he supposed he could be described as a tramp. He preferred the term, homeless person. All of this took the jury by surprise. The image did not fit the reality.

He recounted his visit to the bins, his finding of the jacket and then his more grisly discovery.

They had been right. It was easy. Just answer the questions.

He explained how two men had knocked him over as he had entered the lane beside the hotel. They had spoken, abuse, he could not remember the details. It was dark but he got a look at them. Tall man, young, early twenties probably, thin. He had some kind of a hat on. The other man was older, a bit taller, dark-haired and had an Irish accent.

He was shown the leather jacket and identified it as the one he had removed.

As the macer returned the jacket to the production table, Sammy stared after it. All this trouble for a leather jacket.

'Now, Mr McPhee, do you see in court either of the two men who were in the lane that night?', Matthews asked.

Sammy hesitated.

'Take your time, just look around the court and point out in court anyone who was in the lane that night.'

Turning to the dock, Sammy raised his right arm and pointed.

'Him there.'

'How sure are you, Mr McPhee?'

'Quite sure.'

This evidence impressed the jury. None of them thought it possible that Sammy could have been set up like Barbara Potter. A few jurors looked directly at Gallagher. Was he capable of such butchery? They tried to imagine the scene as Mad Dog was tortured. Could they picture Gallagher's hand on a razor-sharp knife as it cut through a man's throat spewing out his life's blood? One or two cringed. Undoubtedly, the Crown had scored a goal.

His questioner returned to his seat. Sammy knew there was more to come, but at least he was halfway there. He was breathing a relieving sigh as he waited for the next onslaught. Prepared as he thought he was, Sammy was rocked back on his heels by a question which was asked even before its asker had risen to his feet. Whatever opening gambit Sammy had been expecting, it was certainly not this. It also made the jury sit up and take notice. Which was the general idea.

'Where did you get the suit?'

'Eh? I don't quite follow.'

'It seems a simple enough question. Where did you get the suit?'

'I found it.'

'Where?'

'I don't remember.'

If Sammy did not know what this was about, neither did the jury. They knew it was about something and by now they could tell when a witness was uncomfortable. Mike Matthews asked a question of his junior. She clearly didn't know either.

'When did you get it?'

'Some time ago.'

'Where do you live, Mr McPhee?'

'Where I can. You know that, I suspect.'

'For some years now, you have slept rough, living on the streets. Homeless. Carrying your belongings about with you. Is that right?'

'Yes.'

'Your suit looks very clean and well-pressed.'

Sammy was just a few minutes into the second half and already his defence was falling apart.

Matthews rose to his feet, clearly feeling the need to protect one of his star witnesses, or at least afford him some respite.

'My Lord, I fail to see the relevance of this whimsical exchange.'

'Precisely what I was thinking myself, Advocate Depute. Mr Muirhead, where is this taking us, if anywhere?' His Lordship affected an exasperated sigh.

'It's taken me to the knowledge that this witness is a liar, and very soon it will take the jury to the same conclusion.'

Matthews tried to struggle back to his feet. His Lordship choked on the intended admonition. The jury chortled..

'It was like this when they gave it to me.'

'Who? When who gave it to you?'

In court, moments of silence seem to last for ever, even if they are but a few seconds long. By his answer, Sammy had taken himself to the end of the pier. Now all eyes were focused upon him waiting for him to fall off. He duly obliged.

'The polis.'

'Who?' His Lordship's voice was virtually at screaming pitch.

'In effect, my Lord, as I indicated, the witness has just admitted that he has been lying and now accepts he got the suit from the police.'

'I don't follow this.'

'If your Lordship will bear with me, all will be revealed.'

Rounding on Sammy, he barked: 'When?'

'Last night.'

'Where?'

'In a police station.'

'Which one?'

'I don't know. Honestly.'

'Which policeman?'

'Three of them.'

'Names?'

'I don't know. They didn't tell me their names.'

'Why were you there?'

'I went to Clydebank to visit Betty, my wife. They shoved me in the back of a car and took me to a polis station in Glasgow.'

'Why?'

'They said they wanted a word. I got a shower and a meal and they gave me this suit to wear to court.'

'Anything else?'

'Aye. I could keep it if I got it right.'

'Got what right?'

'What they wanted me to say.'

'What was that?'

Again Sammy paused, but clearly he was heading for the water in an uncontrollable dive. Even his Lordship was now intrigued. He added, 'Neither can I' to Muirhead's 'I can't hear an answer.'

'They sat me at a table and went over my statement, time after time. My head was getting sore, but they wouldn't give it a rest. They wouldn't let me have a sleep. They told me I had to get it right. If I did, I could keep the suit.'

'You could keep the suit. Hardly much of a reward, was it?'

'What do you mean, reward?'

'I mean a reward for doing your duty and coming to court to give evidence.'

'I don't have much.'

'So, as a result of this generous offer, have you told us the whole truth?'

'I took an oath.'

'I know that, but have you told us the truth, the whole truth?' Muirhead's voice carried an edge like a honed blade.

'Yes.'

'Really?'

'I told you, yes.'

'Apart from the lies you have admitted telling us?'

'I think so.'

'You think so. When you identified the man in court, you said you were sure. Are you sure?'

'Yes.'

'May the jury take it that you would not allow your evidence on such a crucial matter to be influenced by the offer of a second-hand suit?'

'Of course not.'

'I thought so.'

The slightly kinder tone of voice made Sammy think that the worst might be past. He was about to be proved very wrong.

◆   ◆   ◆

Grant McAllister was sitting in the corner of the waiting room used by police witnesses. His junior colleagues sat together chatting about the topics which most occupied their minds – football, drink and sex, but not necessarily in that order. McAllister sat alone, wrapped up in his thoughts.

The investigation had been speedy and efficient. A man had been charged and was standing trial. On the face of it, the case looked solid. Not overwhelming, but solid enough. And yet! And yet he had a bad feeling about it, a sense of unease which was steadily deepening.

He was only too well aware that there were machinations going on behind the scenes and he could not get any kind of a grip on what or who or, more to the point, why.

Someone was trying to put pressure on Muirhead and the arrogant bastard knew it, but he would not co-operate with the police. He had often known of witnesses being threatened, but a lawyer, that was different, and how. In one way this did not evoke much sympathy within him. Perhaps the likes of James Muirhead, Queen's Counsel, might come to appreciate what the real world was really like.

Equally, he knew that this could only be intended to have some effect on the trial. What the hell could it be? What? What? What?

Then there was the girl, Barbara Potter – she too had been got at. Something of which the police had had no inkling. It was quite unacceptable that any Crown witness should be pressurised and not only had the police done nothing about it, they knew nothing about it.

McAllister recognised that the crucial evidence was yet to come. Arguably the case had gone in favour of the defence thus far. He did not regard this as a particularly serious problem, and was often to be expected. He had had a meeting with the Procurator Fiscal and the Advocate Depute and was aware that the plan was to lead the background and general evidence before turning to the matters which best linked Gallagher to the murders.

He had watched Muirhead in action for many years and had often faced him across a courtroom. One of his tactics would be to seek to muddy the waters by talking up every piece of evidence, however insignificant, which tended to exculpate the accused. Any minor or trivial detail which did not point conclusively to guilt would be portrayed as if it was a fatal blow to the very heart of the Crown case.

Good evidence, from the prosecution standpoint, would have sarcasm and scorn poured upon it as if it was unworthy of even passing consideration. He recollected a particular case when he and other officers had been tipped off about a pending bank robbery. They were lying in wait when the robbers arrived and arrested two of them when they entered the premises. The getaway driver hastily abandoned his vehicle and ran off. He was a well-known Glasgow face and was identified by seven police officers at his subsequent trial when he returned from a holiday in Spain which he had arranged with an indecent degree of haste.

When addressing the jury, Muirhead had been almost contemptuous in his dismissive treatment of the police witnesses, 'In this, the clearest case imaginable of mistaken identity based on no more than a passing glimpse of the back of an indistinct figure vanishing into the far distance...a blatant attempt by the police to turn a shadow into a figure of substance...to convert the unknown into the certain...turning an unfounded belief into a matter of certainty...such is what passes for a case against my client.'

The theory ran thus. If one policeman thought he knew who the driver was, they would all get to know who the driver was. One policeman, seven policemen, a hundred policemen, so what?

'Ladies and gentlemen, seven officers claim to have recognised my client. That does not for a moment make it so. Imagine Ibrox Stadium on a Saturday afternoon. Rangers are on the attack. Brown sends Durie free with a perfectly weighted pass. He sprints into the opposition penalty box and is brought crashing down by the onrushing goalkeeper. The referee waves 'play on'. The following day, you could produce forty thousand witnesses to swear blind that it was a penalty kick. It would not make it so.'

For the second time the driver got away from the police.

McAllister appreciated that, given half a chance, Muirhead was capable of doing considerable damage to an otherwise perfectly good case. The most reliable of witnesses could be made to appear as if they did not know what day of the week it was. The most honest of witnesses could be portrayed as someone you would not trust to tell you what day of the week it was.

What would he do to McPhee? McAllister had interviewed Sammy personally. He may have smelt pretty bad, but he was nobody's fool. He knew what he had seen and had no reason to elaborate, let alone lie. He would make a good impression on the jury. He ought to appear as a sympathetic character. He could provide the beginnings of a link between Gallagher and the death of Clark. Muirhead ought not to be able to damage him – too much.

McAllister was beginning to feel a bit more confident when a movement at the door caught his eye. He looked up to see one of his Detective Constables beckoning him out of the room. Something was wrong. McAllister just knew it.

He ushered the DC to the far end of the corridor.

'What is it?'

'I thought you'd want to hear this, Boss. There's a problem with the witness – the wino.'

'McPhee,' McAllister corrected.

'Yes. Sorry, Boss.'

'What's going on in there?'

'He's claiming that he spent last night with some cops going over his statement. They told him to make sure he got it right.'

'What the fuck! Who?'

'And they gave him a suit to wear, would you believe?'

After the momentary loss of control, McAllister's voice ran cold.

'Who did the asking?'

'Muirhead.'

'Has McPhee named them?'

'Not yet.'

'You mean he's not finished?'

'No. I suspect he's got something more up his sleeve.'

'Get back in there.'

In theory, persons waiting to give evidence are not supposed to know what is actually happening in court. True, they may glean snippets from newspapers, radio and television. But, so far as possible, their evidence should be their evidence, untainted by the testimony of other witnesses. However, in the real world, police officers, especially senior officers, do not care for being caught cold. They prefer to have as much advance notice as possible of lines of attack which may be adopted by the defence. To this end, lines of communication between the court and the witness room are usually set up, and kept open.

McAllister paced up and down the corridor. His normally well-ordered mind was now in a complete turmoil. None of his squad would dare do such a stupid thing. If they did, they would know that if they were found out, they would end up on permanent points duty for the rest of their careers, if they were lucky. So, who? And more to the point, why?

And if Muirhead did indeed have something else up his sleeve, what was it? He almost dreaded to think how much worse things could become. Time to do something. He strode purposefully to the telephone.

He issued some terse instructions and turned away to find himself once again confronted by his DC.

The look on his face ought to have told him the next question was going to prove superfluous.

'Don't tell me, it just got worse?'

'Shit, Boss, and how!'

●   ●   ●

Sammy had been answering questions about the area where he had found the Mad Dog's mortal remains. None of these had caused him any difficulty and he had gained in confidence sufficiently to convince himself he had weathered the storm. After the initial hostility his interrogator had been the model of civility. He had to be nearing the end of the road. He was nearly there.

'Finally, Mr McPhee, you went to an identification parade, did you not?'

'Yes.'

'Just two weeks after the events you have been telling us about?'

'Yes.'

'And on that parade there was a total of six people?'

'Yes, I think so.'

'As opposed to one man sitting in the dock flanked by two police officers?'

'I don't know what you mean.'

'What I mean is that it is very easy to pick out a man sitting in a dock. A man who virtually has a sign pointing at his head saying "accused".'

'I picked him out.'

'I know you picked him out here, but did you pick him out at the parade?'

'Yes.'

'Why?'

'He was there.'

'Where?'

'In the lane that night. The night I've been telling you about.'

'You're sure?'

'Yes.'

'If you were sure, why did you pick out two people at the parade?'

'Did I?'

'Don't you know?'

'I don't remember.'

'That is not an answer. At the parade, you said "Number three or number five. I'm not sure, possibly number five". You said that, didn't you?'

'I don't know.'

'Not an answer. Didn't you?'

'I could have. Maybe. Look, I'm not sure. You're confusing me.'

'Number five was Mr Gallagher. Number three was a stand-in, just a member of the public brought in to make up the numbers. You picked out two men, and the best you could say was possibly number five. Do you accept that you said that?'

'Possibly.'

'Why did you say that?'

'I can't remember.'

'You are avoiding my questions. Why?'

The pause became a delay which seemed to turn into an eternity.

'WHY?'

'I wasn't sure. I did my best. I only saw him for a second. It was dark. I did my best.'

'So you were not sure then, not sure at all, but you claim to be sure now. Why the change?'

'I just am, that's all.'

'How sure do you think you may have been if you hadn't been given the suit?'

'That's got nothing to do with it.'

'Really?'

'Yes. Really.'

The questions had been coming at him with such speed that once again Sammy felt himself beginning to panic. It was as if the floor of the witness box had turned to sand and Sammy was struggling to avoid sinking into it.

Muirhead could see the witness shifting uneasily. If he was going to get him, it was now. He could have settled for leaving matters where they were, but he had the feeling it was time to chance his arm. For the second time in the case he was about to take a flier.

'Have you been coerced into changing your evidence?'

The Advocate Depute snapped to his feet.

'My Lord, in light of the previous questions asked, the thrust of this question must be directed at police officers. I trust my learned friend has some basis for that very serious allegation.'

'So do I, Mr Depute.'

So do I, thought Muirhead to himself, or the shit you've lived in, Mr McPhee, will be nothing compared to the shit I'll end up in.

Counsel are not permitted to fire off allegations unless there is some evidential basis to support them. Muirhead had a suspicion. That would have to do. The rule was not being broken, just bent a bit.

'Answer my question, truthfully please.'

Every pair of eyes in the room was now focused upon Sammy. The sand beneath his feet was shifting again. His mouth was dry. He would have taken a drink of water but he knew his hand would shake so much that the glass would have been empty before it reached his lips. He was trying very hard to look straight ahead of him but almost involuntarily his eyes flickered in the direction of the public gallery. He could not make up his mind if he was relieved to see there were no faces he recognised.

'We're waiting patiently, Mr McPhee.'

Sammy made one more attempt to stem the tide.

'I wasn't so sure at the police station. I was nervous. When I looked at him here I was sure.'

'Are you nervous today?'

'Of course I am. You're making me nervous.'

'So, what's the difference?'

'What difference?'

'You were nervous at the police station and you weren't sure. You're nervous in court and now you are sure. Why? Why Mr McPhee? What has really happened?'

Too late. The ball was well and truly burst.

'I had to.'

'Had to do what, Mr McPhee?'

'Say I was sure. They told me to say I was sure.'

Muirhead asked the question. The judge, the Depute and the jury mouthed the word in unison.

'Who?'

'The police. The police told me to say it. When they went over my statement last night, it said that I wasn't sure about the guy I saw. They told me that was no fucking good, sorry about the language. I must be sure. I had to be sure. They had got the right guy, so why wasn't I sure? They told me that I had better say I was sure or they would make my life hell.'

'Did they say how they would make your life hell?'

'No, but I just knew they would. I'm sorry. I just want to be left alone.'

'And are you sure?'

'No. It could be him, but no, I'm not at all sure.'

'It might not be him?'

'Maybe not.'

As Muirhead sat down, Sammy actually felt as if a great weight had been lifted from his shoulders.

The Depute and the Judge badgered him for a time but he could not tell them to which police station he had been taken, he had been given no names and could only give a vague description of the officers. In truth, he did not try very hard to remember. In truth, he no longer cared. As he walked out of the building wearing his new suit and clutching his carrier bags, he had decided it was time to join Betty. He had had enough.

The Advocate Depute asked the judge to adjourn for the day as he wished to consider this unexpected development. His motion was granted. Apart from any other considerations, Lord Cowden had had enough excitement for the time being.

As the court room was emptying, Morton turned to Muirhead.

'Come on, James. How did you know all that?'

'I told you Jack, I know what I'm about. Sorry about my mood earlier on.'

'No problem, James. But why don't I believe you?'

'I'm sorry.'

'That's not what I mean and you know it.'

'I hope you're not suggesting I just took a flier and got lucky?'

'You, James. Never!'

The first week of the trial of Her Majesty's Advocate against Charles Gallagher had come to an end.

Chapter Seven

Bob Taylor was liked and respected by every officer who had ever worked under him. He was trusted by his superiors and the members of the Procurator Fiscal service. While his approach to his work, and indeed life in general, might seem easygoing, he was a conscientious detective who would work at a case until he was satisfied he had all the right answers.

If a case was going nowhere, he would tell his team to 'guddle around a bit and see what comes up'. The team members knew that they were being told to go right back to the beginning and check everything in intimate detail. The notion that a case might not be solved was something he would never countenance.

'A crime is like a crossword puzzle. Every answer is connected to another. Solve one clue and you get help with the next. Every puzzle can be completed: it just takes time and patience. The harder it is, the greater the satisfaction. Anyway, it's good to lock the bastards up just when they think they've got away with it.'

The main reason for his popularity was that he was intensely loyal to his men. He demanded 100 per cent effort. Success belonged to the team. But if someone made a mistake, the team would accept responsibility. He did not believe in public admonitions, let alone bollickings. A telling-off would be delivered in private and invariably left the recipient feeling humbled and embarrassed rather than chastised.

When a young officer had contrived to lose an important document in a case, he had been asked to see the DI. When he returned, his equally young colleagues had gleefully examined the front of his trousers to see if there were any bloodstains where his balls had been cut off. There was no evidence of trauma.

'He told me I had been very careless and would have to do better if I wanted to get on in the job. I had let everyone down but myself most of all. Then he said he wasn't angry with me, just very disappointed in me.'

The old heads nodded sagely. Typical Taylor. A boot up the arse would have been painful but quickly forgotten. Instead, the young cop had been made to feel six inches tall, clearly didn't like it, and certainly would not forget it. He would learn. He would do better.

Bob Taylor was straight. If he could not crack a case by sheer hard work, he certainly would not do it by cutting corners. His men knew better than to try. It was widely known that he once suspected a Detective Sergeant of bullying an accused into making a confession. Nothing was said at the time, but the Sergeant did not turn up for duty one morning and shortly thereafter was discovered to be back in uniform, somewhere in the outer limits.

Now Taylor was in a quandary, the like of which he had never known. He sat in the corner of the bar staring into a double whisky. He knew that if he drank it, it could prove to be one too many. He picked up the glass and poured the entire contents down his throat. As the liquid burned its way to his stomach, the prospect of a monumental hangover the following morning was nothing compared to the pain and torment which were now threatening to tear him apart. Loyalty was important to him, perhaps of paramount importance. But of critical importance was loyalty to the law it was his duty to maintain. Being a policeman meant you had duties and responsibilities to the law, to the public, to your colleagues, to the force, but most of all to the rule of law. And yet, he had forgotten something. What about family and family loyalty? And if that clashed with other loyalties, what then? What indeed?

He left the pub and checked that his car was locked. He would never dream of driving, not in his state. As he walked, his mind rehearsed the events of the evening, desperately seeking a solution. Every puzzle had a solution somewhere.

When David entered the pub, his relaxed air and cheery greeting told Taylor that his son was unaware of the storm he was about to run into.

Sitting down with a pint for himself and a half and a half for his father, he casually opened the conversation.

'Not that it's other than nice to see you for a drink, but what do you want, and why this dump? Christ, this is the back of bloody beyond. You haven't gone and got some WPC in the club have you, dad?'

'That was stupid, bloody stupid!'

'It was only a joke.'

'Don't fuck with me, David. You know what I'm talking about. You know fucking well what I'm talking about. Now tell me what you thought you were playing at and why. I also want to know who else was involved. Don't make matters worse by lying to me. Right now I'm speaking to you as your father, but don't think for a second that I can forget that we are both police officers and I am your superior. Talk to me. Make me understand what this is all about. Think before you speak. Think very bloody carefully, but speak.'

David Taylor felt as if an icy hand had reached inside him, grasped his bowels and began to twist and squeeze. He wanted to run, anywhere, but his heart was beating at such a rate that he was sure it would burst if even the slightest strain was placed upon it. In any event, he knew his legs would not support his weight.

Lifting his glass he choked down a mouthful of the beer which suddenly tasted stale. He fought to control the shaking as his hand returned the glass to the table. He knew he was caught, and lying was pointless.

'I'm waiting, David.'

'What's the problem here? Gallagher is guilty. Either he did it or he ordered it. I know it and you know it. We had a word with a witness just to make sure he didn't screw it. Don't tell me you have never had a word in the odd ear?'

'The problem is you didn't just have a word. You put the frighteners on a Crown witness. You threatened him. More to the point you made him change his evidence.'

'We just told him to say that he was sure. What's the problem?'

'I repeat, you idiot, the problem is that you perverted the course of justice. The problem is, it all came out in court thanks to that smart bastard Muirhead. The problem is, you have been found out. The problem is, you fucked up. You may have fucked up the whole case. The problem is, McAllister wants answers. The real problem is, I've got the answers he wants. Don't ask me what the problem is. I know what the problem is. The problem is, what am I going to do about it?'

There are moments when the mind seems to go into free fall. Ideas flash before the eyes at a rate which defies comprehension let alone analysis. David Taylor was a skydiver whose parachute would not open. The downward spiral of his altitude was mirrored by a corresponding increase in his level of panic. If he had an emergency chute, he forgot all about it. He hit the ground with a bone-shattering thump. He had survived the fall but was terrified to move lest the extent of the damage was revealed to him. Only his eyes were capable of independent movement and they found themselves locked onto his father's withering stare. This was a look he had not seen before, a chilling mixture of anger, anxiety, sadness and something he struggled to identify as he had not seen it before. The realisation hit him harder than the fall itself. Contempt!

When there is no available means of escape, the cornered animal will attack.

'Problem, dad. You're the one with the problem. We, I, OK, we, we picked up this drunk, cleaned him up a bit, took him through his statement, and that was it. Don't tell me you've never gone over a witness statement before someone gave evidence? As I see it, there is no fucking problem. Why are you giving me all this pious, holier than thou crap? All my life I've heard you talking about villains. How they deserved all they got. How they were scum. How it was your job to make the streets safer. How it was a war between the good guys and the bad guys. All I did was to try to make sure one of the bad guys goes away for a long time. Now, tell me straight. What is so wrong with that? What is so fucking wrong with that?'

'You told him he was to say he was sure when you knew perfectly well he wasn't. You leant on him. You threatened him, damn it. You told him to lie for Christ's sake!'

'If, if he lied, that was his decision. I just wanted to make sure he was clear about his story. I repeat, this bastard Gallagher deserves to be put away, does he not?'

'Of course he does, but by the rules, THE rules. Not by you bending the rules. And because of what you've done, he may well get away with it.'

'Come on!'

'He may well get away with it. Is that what you want me to tell McAllister?'

'Tell him you couldn't find anything. He'll believe you.'

'I got you your chance in this case. You fucked up. Now you want me to lie for you. You want to make me as bad as you are. Is that what you think of me?'

The younger man had for some time realised he could not talk his way out of his predicament. He had to get away from his father's anger and that awful stare, preserving such self-confidence as he could.

'Why don't you do what you've always done? Exactly what you bloody want and to hell with everyone else. McAllister is a superintendent, so what? I'm your son, damn it. Or is the job more important to you than I am? I guess we're going to find out.'

Driving himself to his feet, David Taylor was hit by a wave of nausea. He knew that what he had said was horribly untrue, and worse still, unfair. He was heading for the door when his father's voice stopped him.

'David, when you go into the witness box, you will be telling the truth, won't you?'

'What do you think?'

These were the words which most troubled Bob Taylor as he walked towards his home. He did not know what to think. As he turned up his collar against the rain, he didn't know what to do either.

Bob Taylor was not alone in having a bad night. As the policeman headed home, James Muirhead was in the centre of the city in a largely deserted car park. He had gone for dinner alone as he wished to reflect upon the week's events. Now he wished he hadn't bothered. He had been unable to establish any clear picture of where the case was going other than confirming to himself that things were going on behind the scenes. Since he was driving, he had no wine and consequently had not enjoyed the meal. Now he had a flat tyre. He had called the RAC who had informed him that they would be on the scene as soon as possible. Unfortunately, they were busy and this could take a couple of hours. He had decided to change the wheel by himself. Not a smart move.

A trained chimp would possess a greater degree of knowledge of things mechanical. After twenty minutes of confusion, effort, loss of temper and failed attempts to make sense of the Jaguar's manual which was now turning into a soggy mess, he had managed to remove the spare wheel and jack from the boot, located the latter under the car, and was now heaving and straining to loosen the wheel nuts. He was soaking.

The noise of a vehicle entering the car park momentarily attracted his attention. He quickly lost interest when it was plainly not the RAC. Even the approaching footsteps failed to distract him from the war he was waging with a recalcitrant wheel nut. The cold metal being pressed against neck had a wonderfully focusing effect on his mind.

'Do yourself a favour, Mr Muirhead. Just stay where you are and listen very, very carefully.'

Someone playing a daft joke at this time of night and in the pissing rain was the last thing Muirhead needed. This idiot with the phoney Irish accent was going to get a mouthful, whoever he was. Muirhead started to move.

'Very funny. I'm stuck here in the pissing rain and you're...'

The metal was jammed roughly into the back of his neck causing his forehead to collide with the wheel arch of the car.

'This is no joke, believe me. What you can feel is a gun. It's loaded and if you want me to use it, I will. Personally, I don't care if I blow your fucking head off, or not. In fact, Mr Muirhead, that will be your decision at the end of the day. Just think on this. Your puncture was no accident. I made it happen. I caused you to be here, alone, at my mercy, so to speak. I did this to you. I can just as easily finish with you and then do the same to Gill and the children. Robert and Sarah, I believe.'

Thoughts of his family flashed through his mind. The notion that someone might harm his family caused the bile to rise in Muirhead's throat. Gill, so full of life and fun. How easily she could take the mickey out of him and make him smile when she felt he was being boring or pompous. Robbie, easygoing Robbie. Nothing ever seemed to worry him. School, sport, getting a row, everything taken in his stride. And Sarah, daddy's little girl. She would sit beside him at his desk while he ploughed through bundles of papers. Asking questions. Sensible questions for an adult, never mind a ten year old.

'That's good, Mr M. I can see you're thinking. I take it we understand each other?'

Muirhead tried to nod his head, but was shaking so much he could not make even such an insignificant voluntary gesture.

The gun was pressed in again.

'I understand. What do you want?'

'I've sent you a number of messages and you chose to ignore them. This is your last chance. Some very important people, friends of mine, are very upset by the way you are handling the Gallagher case.'

'I'm doing my best.'

'That's the problem, Mr Muirhead. You are doing rather too well. In short, you are just too good at your job. Gallagher has to get done. My friends will be very upset if he doesn't get done. My friends will be very upset with you if he doesn't get done.'

'That's up to the jury, not me, for Christ's sake.'

The gun was driven harder into his neck. The tone of the voice hardened.

'Don't be fucking stupid, Muirhead. You're the only one who can stop him being convicted. And that's going to change. You're going to take a dive. You're going to sell the jerseys. You're going to fuck it up, Mr M. Or I'm going to fuck up you and your family.'

'What am I supposed to do?'

'I told you not to be fucking stupid. Do whatever you have to do. Just make sure Gallagher goes down. Got it?'

'What?'

'Understand?'

'Yes, I understand, but how can I guarantee...?'

A sharp metallic click stopped him short.

'I can guarantee it, Mr Muirhead, if that's what you want. But I'm sure you're a man of your word. Tell me my friends have nothing to worry about. Tell me that Gallagher's defence is about to take a nose-dive. Tell me that Gallagher is going to get done. Tell me that your family will be safe.'

Again the gun was jammed into the back of Muirhead's neck.

'I'll do what I can.'

'Not good enough. I've tried to be reasonable. Maybe I should just shoot your kneecaps off now and go tell your wife all about it?'

'All right. All right. Whatever you want.'

'You know what I want.'

'Gallagher will go down, if I have anything to do with it.'

Another prod from the gun.

'Gallagher will go down.'

'Get in the back seat face down. I'll be leaving you now, but don't worry, I'll never be very far away. I'm going to count to a hundred. If I see any part of you before I get there, I will shoot it. If I was you, I wouldn't go mentioning this conversation to anyone. Let's just keep it to ourselves. Confidential, like. Our own private bonding. Oh, and here's something to remember me by.'

Muirhead struggled into the back of the car. He felt something land lightly on the back of his hand. The back door was slammed shut, then the front door was opened and he heard a ripping noise. He was not going to be able to use the car phone. Footsteps headed away from him. An engine fired into life and a car drove off.

Muirhead hauled himself up and looked out of the back window. Tail-lights disappearing into the distance. Nothing else. He slumped down into the back seat and forced himself to breathe deeply until he regained some self-control.

He had spent all his working life dealing with violence: people committing acts of violence, victims of violence, photographs of injuries and death, weapons and blood stained clothing. This was the first time he had stared violence in the face, experienced the terror and horror of it, been the victim of it. He fought to clear his mind. Gradually his sense of shock and fear was replaced by one of anger and disbelief.

He opened the car door and vomited, violently. An object fluttered to the ground. He picked it up and in the interior light he saw a Polaroid photograph of his wife and daughter leaving his house.

Who was this guy? Whoever he was, he was serious about what he had said. He had just had a gun pointed at his head. It couldn't be much more serious than that. The phone calls, the car, now this. But why him? Terrorising a witness was one thing, common enough, after all. But to threaten the defence lawyer! This was sheer insanity, but the threat was very real, not just to him but to his family.

He had tried to ignore what had gone on. Put it down to some crank. Brushed aside the police when they offered help. Now someone had threatened to kill him and his family. And yet he was still gripped by the unreality of it all. Trying to get at him for some crazy purpose was one thing, even threatening him with a gun, but to actually use it. No way would that be allowed to happen.

Muirhead was slowly getting a grip of himself. He began to review his options. Plainly he would allow nothing and no one to influence his conduct of the case. He could explain the situation to the Crown and his solicitor and then get the judge to stop the trial which could then be re-run with new counsel. However, things had gone well and it would not be in Gallagher's interests to have the trial aborted. The witnesses who had been through the box had been alerted to the line of defence and the element of surprise would be totally lost second time around. On the face of it, the answer was simple. Detective Superintendent McAllister seemed to think he knew everything about everything, so why not dump the problem in his lap and then get on with the job in hand? McAllister could devote his time to chasing a ghost with a phoney Irish accent.

With his head in order, Muirhead was aware that he was still shaking. His stomach was churning. Staring at the image which still confronted him, a thought nagged at the back of his mind.

Maybe the Irish accent wasn't phoney.

      ❋   ❋   ❋

'I think you'll find that matters have been taken care of.'

'Sure?'

'What do you want? A written guarantee?'

'I want to know that the job has been done, properly.'

'I just told you that. It's hardly my fault if you can't grasp it.'

'I don't want to be told about it. I want to see evidence of it.'

'You'll get that next week. Now, the rest of my money. I'm bored with this climate, and the Guinness in the pub stinks.'

'You've already had money. You're getting fuck all more until I decide that you've done what I'm paying you to do.'

'I must have misheard you. For a moment there I got the impression you were going back on our deal. I can feel myself getting quite upset. I do so hate to feel that someone has let me down.'

'I'm not going back on anything. I agreed to pay you for results, not promises and certainly not ifs, buts and bloody maybes.'

'I told you, the job's done. That's all you need to know. I'm good at what I do. If I say I'll do something, I will. If I say I've done something, I have. Now, I expect to be paid, promptly and in full. I will not take it kindly if I am not paid or if I have to wait. Do I make myself clear?'

'I will pay you in full, but only when I am satisfied with the quality of the workmanship. Do I make myself very clear?'

'I'd think about that very carefully, if I were you.'

'I have and I think I am fucked off with your bullshitting. When our mutual friend is safely out of harm's way on a long-term basis, call me and then I will settle your bill. OK? Did you hear me? Answer me damn it!'

'You just fucked up. The deal's off, but the debt is still due. I'll settle it my way. I'll be in touch. You'll know when.'

'Look, there's no need for that. Just be patient. I've no intention of cheating you. Why should I?...You still there?'

The phone was dead.

●　　　　　●　　　　　●

Grant McAllister was awaiting Bob Taylor's arrival. It was Sunday afternoon and the squad room beyond his office was reasonably quiet with only two or three officers on the phone or reading reports. McAllister stared at the notepad in front of him. The page was blank. Never before had he been so troubled by a case. Too many unexplained and apparently unrelated events. But were they truly unrelated? And why was he uncomfortable every time he thought of Gallagher in the dock?

He had no doubt that someone was trying to get at James Muirhead. The answers to the questions who and why eluded him for the time being. Matters were not helped by the fact that the arrogant sod would not co-operate. Indeed, he was being intentionally obstructive. If he wanted to play silly buggers, maybe he should just let him get on with it. Unfortunately, the bogey wheels of this prosecution were beginning to work their way loose and were threatening to fall off. McAllister needed to know who had the spanner.

Two witnesses had been the subject of interference. To have someone like Barbara Potter being threatened was, unfortunately, not unusual. She was weak, vulnerable and had become caught up in events which were way out of her league. One of the biggest problems facing the police was the pressure put on witnesses by accused persons and their cohorts. But Sammy McPhee, this was quite different. It was certainly not normal for witnesses to be got at by police officers. He was determined to find out who was responsible for this, and when he did he would make it his personal business to retire them from the force, permanently.

It troubled him deeply that the police had been unable to find any trace of Tam McGarry, Kevin Boyle's minder. Why had he not been with his boss when he was shot? Why had he apparently disappeared immediately after the shooting? McAllister did not believe in coincidences, and certainly not of this magnitude.

Most of all he was beginning to develop a nagging doubt about Gallagher. He had never been convinced that there was enough evidence to link him to the death of Clark. In any event, he could not work out any real motive that Gallagher might have for wanting the death of his father's best henchman. The Boyle case ought to be strong enough to secure a conviction. At least there was evidence and motive, and that combination was never a bad start.

Arguably the best evidence was yet to come: one more eyewitness, who on the face of it should be independent and, hopefully, untainted by outside interference. The forensic evidence should stand up. Then, of course, the confessions. The confessions!

He could accept that in an unguarded moment Gallagher might have said something to a police officer which he would later regret. But Warwick? Now, this was very different.

There is a popular myth that a code of silence is operated by the criminal classes. Honour among thieves. Omerta. Not so. Criminals will readily provide the police with information against their best friend in an attempt to secure a favour from the officer concerned or to do the dirty on a professional rival. Informers are usually secretive, nocturnal creatures. This is one business in which it does not pay to advertise. The subjects of their reports do not take kindly to having their activities discussed. Frequently they express their disapproval in clear and painful terms.

Arnold Warwick was about to enter the witness box and grass in the most spectacular manner. He would know that the Gallaghers would never forgive him and make it their business to exact appropriate revenge. Why this man was taking such a risk was an unknown factor. He himself was awaiting trial on a charge of armed robbery. Initially he had offered to give a statement if this charge was dropped. This offer was declined. Then he indicated he was prepared to speak if the judge at his trial was told of his co-operation. This was acceptable. Warwick agreed to testify even although he was aware that there was no guarantee the hoped-for benefit would live up to expectations.

McAllister glanced at his watch. Taylor was late. Not like him at all. He continued staring at the notepad. He looked up when he heard footsteps hurrying towards his office. Tom Donaldson, the Productions Officer, hurried in. The look on his face sent an involuntary shiver down McAllister's spine.

'Boss, there's been an accident at Hillhead underground station. It's Bob Taylor. Boss, he's dead.'

The impact of this news struck him like a punch in the solar plexus. Before he could gather his thoughts or utter any comment, the ringing of the telephone made him reach instinctively for it.

'Superintendent McAllister?'

'Yes.'

'It's James Muirhead. I think we had better meet. I have something to tell you.'

'Yes, of course. Look, I'm sorry, but I'm dealing with something just now. I'll get back to you just as soon as I possibly can.'

So now you want to talk to me, Mr Muirhead, thought McAllister. Well for the time being, you can damn well wait.

Chapter Eight

'Advocate Depute.'

'My Lord, the next witness is number seventy-six, Arnold Warwick.'

Monday morning and the scene was set for one of the most crucial stages of the trial.

As he awaited the arrival of the prosecution's star witness, Muirhead reflected on the events of the previous night.

McAllister had come to his home about 10.30. Business-like and formal, he had refused a drink or even tea or coffee. He had sat silently, taking no notes, and listened as Muirhead recounted the history of recent happenings. He had asked only two or three questions about matters of detail. He showed no surprise at anything he was told. Indeed, his face had displayed little reaction of any kind.

At the end of the meeting, which lasted no more than twenty minutes, he stood up, shook hands, indicated he would be in touch and left.

Then, and now, Muirhead could have convinced himself without difficulty that McAllister was completely uninterested in the information he had received. Yet the more he thought about it, the more he realised that McAllister was a man with many things on his mind. He appeared preoccupied – but with what? He had absorbed the information given to him and had no doubt filed it away to be dealt with in due course.

To his right at the table, Donald Anderson was busy arranging the papers needed for the cross-examination to come. Jack Morton was standing beside the dock conversing with his client. Both were glancing towards the door of the court.

Arnold Warwick entered, accompanied by two prison officers. As he entered the witness box his escorts took up positions on either side of it. If he intended to seek a means of escape or retreat he would find he was going nowhere. A small man with short dark hair, he was dressed in an open-necked shirt and a dark blue suit, not in its first bloom of youth.

Warwick's eyes darted nervously round the court, but Muirhead noted he pointedly avoided looking towards the dock. When he raised his hand to take the oath from Lord Cowden, his hand, like the rest of him, trembled.

'Your full name is Arnold Joseph Warwick, is that correct?'

'Yes.'

'Your age?'

'Thirty-eight.'

'You are presently a prisoner in Perth awaiting trial on a charge of assault and robbery?'

'What's that got to do with it?'

'Just answer my question, please.'

'You know I am – yes.'

'Are you married?'

'No.'

'In August of this year were you a remand prisoner in Barlinnie prison in Glasgow?'

'Yes.'

'Were you held in what is known as the segregation unit?'

'I don't know what they call it. It was a dump. They call it the Wendy House.'

The accent was clearly English, probably London, but not Cockney. The voice displayed distinct traces of nervousness but was gaining in confidence. He stood upright in the witness box but his hands firmly grasped the ledge in front of him. He was fighting to keep control of himself.

'This is going to be interesting,' whispered Muirhead to his junior.

'Looks an aggressive little bastard,' came the reply.

Mike Matthews cleared his throat.

'Which cell were you in?'

'Sixteen.'

'Did you get the opportunity to meet any other prisoners in the unit?'

'Some chance. You only get to meet the screws face-to-face, and only when they're telling you to do something or taking the piss out of you, know what I mean!'

'Did you get the chance to converse with, to speak with any fellow prisoners?'

Warwick paused and looked down at his hands which had released their grip on the witness box. He rubbed his palms together before wiping them on his trousers. He was now sweating profusely.

'Yes.'

It was almost a whisper.

'Pardon?'

'Look, I don't need this. I was promised protection and no one has done a damn thing. They got my statement and you Mr smart arsed Prosecutor and your poxy Scottish police don't give a rat's arse any more.'

'Mr Warwick!'

Both Matthews and the Judge barked at the witness, but for the moment there was no stopping him.

'I've been threatened, called a fucking grass, had shite shoved under my cell door. The bastards even spat in my food. That's what I got for co-operating. Well, I'm not co-operating any more.'

'Mr Warwick, you will calm down, you will behave decorously and you will answer questions, in a civil manner using temperate language.'

Warwick fired a contemptuous glance towards the bench.

Mike Matthews realised this intervention from his Lordship was likely to make matters worse. He decided to adopt a more conciliatory tone.

'I appreciate this must be difficult for you. It cannot be easy for you to give evidence against a fellow prisoner, especially when you have been threatened and treated in this appalling manner.'

Muirhead shot out of his seat like a ballistic missile.

'I object to the learned Advocate Depute giving evidence in this matter. If that is what he wishes to do, he should go into the witness box and take the oath.'

'Mr Muirhead, the Advocate Depute is trying to do his job and it is difficult enough without your unnecessary interruptions.'

'His job, as my Lord puts it, is to ask questions without leading the witness or giving the evidence himself. Your Lordship's job, if I may remind him, is to insure that that is precisely what happens.'

'I do not need you to tell me...'

'Perhaps if I rephrase the matter.'

Matthews was determined to retain some control over the situation.

'I'll keep the questions simple, Mr Warwick. Please just calm down and try to answer them as best as you can. Did you converse with a particular prisoner?'

Warwick hesitated, clearly unsure as to whether there was any merit in a further outburst. He thought better of it.

'Yes, I did.'

'Who was that?'

'Charles Gallagher.'

'Can you point him out if he is in court?'

Warwick thrust his arm towards the dock, but his eyes stared resolutely ahead of him.

'In what circumstances did you have a conversation with the accused?'

'There's a caged-in yard next to the cells. You get to walk about inside it for an hour each day. It's what they call exercise. Bloody farce, more like. Anyway, his cell had a little window thing which looked onto the yard. He used to talk to me through it.'

'Were there any prison officers present?'

'The yard is enclosed. Sometimes one would hang around the door for a bit but normally they left you to it and went for a cup of tea or something.'

'What did you and the accused speak about?'

'The first few times, nothing much. Just where we came from, what family we had, football, that sort of thing.'

'Who instigated the conversations?'

'He did.'

'Did you talk about your respective cases?'

'Yes, we spoke about what we were in for.'

'Did he ever tell you anything about his own case?'

'Once.'

'What did he tell you?'

'Everything.'

'Tell the jury what he said, please.'

Warwick was beginning to look more relaxed. He was warming to his task.

'He told me he was a big noise in Glasgow.'

'Big noise?'

'He was making out that he was this big time villain. He said that this guy Boyle had been causing him serious grief. Muscling in on his business. He said he had decided to get rid of him. He had some of his people follow him. He got a phone call one morning that this guy was shacked up with some tart. He was picked up, driven to some street in a stolen car, waited for the guy to come out of her gaff, got out of his car, walked up to him and shot the cunt in the head. He said it was easy, dead fucking simple. Walked away, cool as you like.'

'Did he say what he did with the gun?'

'He said one of his boys dumped it in the Clyde.'

'Did he say anything else?'

'Sure. I said he had taken some risk doing this himself as he might have been recognised. He told me there was no chance of that. He had pulled on some kind of mask thing. Said he wasn't daft. He'd worn gloves to stop any powder staining on his hands. The gloves got dumped along with the gun. This showed what a smart operator he was.'

'Did he mention anyone else?'

'Yes. He told me there was this guy, didn't name him or anything. Said he worked for his daddy. Said he found out that he was going to kill this guy, Boyle, and tried to stop him. Daddy's instructions. Now, he didn't like that. Didn't like that one little bit. So he and two of his boys battered fuck out of him. Said they made him scream and scream like a stuck pig. He was crying for his mother. They cut his throat and then dumped him in a bin. Said they just threw some rubbish away.'

'When did you report this conversation to the authorities?'

'I thought about it for a while. Few hours probably. I decided this was too heavy for me. I told one of the screws in the unit. Just enough to get him interested. Next day the police came to see me.'

The Advocate Depute sat down and Muirhead rose to cross-examine. The temperature had dropped markedly. A chill wind had just blown through the court. Thus far, he felt that most of the members of the jury were on his side, apart from one individual he had already noted. Now the jury were puzzled. Clearly they had not expected to hear such evidence. One or two were staring at the dock – wondering. Just the first hint of hostility perhaps?

Even before the witness had come into court, Muirhead had decided that attack would be the best form of defence. Having seen and heard the evidence, he saw no reason to change the plan.

'What do you expect to get out of this?'

'Meaning what?'

'Meaning, what do you expect to get out of this?'

'Nothing from you, that's for sure.'

'Then, what do you expect to get from the authorities?'

'The same. Nothing.'

'Then, what do you hope to get?'

'Watch my lips – nothing.'

Warwick spat out the last word. He was once again clenching the front of the witness box. White-knuckled, he was leaning forward thrusting his head towards Muirhead. He was ready for the battle ahead.

'You gave a statement to the police?'

'Yes.'

'Did you ask for anything in return? A favour perhaps?'

'No way.'

'No way. I see. When you gave the statement, you were awaiting trial and indeed you are still awaiting trial?'

'Yes.' Cautious. A hint of suspicion. Muirhead's tone was light, almost conversational.

'You are English, I believe.'

'And proud of it.'

'Indeed. Indeed. Ever been in prison in England?'

'Wait a minute. I'm not on trial here. What I've done or not done in the past has got nothing to do with this. You've no right to pry. Are you going to let him get away with this? I thought you were on my side?'

The Advocate Depute, to whom the question was directed, remained impassive and immovable.

It was Lord Cowden who intervened.

'Mr Muirhead's question is a fair one: just answer it.'

'I thought judges was supposed to be fair. Some system of justice this. Yes, I've been in prison in England.'

'And you've given evidence in court on other occasions, in England?'

'In my own cases, yes. And I always told the truth. So there.'

'Have you previously given evidence in cases involving other accused persons?'

Warwick was beginning to look a little less confident. He knew something was coming; he was just not sure what. Both judge and jury were clearly intrigued. Developments were awaited with undisguised interest.

'Yes.'

'Do you know a man called Paul Tomzack?'

'You are in trouble, pal. You're scraping the barrel now. Yes, I know him – he's a crook.'

'Have you ever spoken with him?'

'Once or twice.'

'Four times, I think?'

'OK. Four times. So what?'

'So you met with this crook – four times?'

'I just told you that.'

'No, I told you that, but never mind. Why did you meet with this crook?'

'He came to see me. I don't know what he wanted.'

'I see. On four occasions this crook came to see you, and at the end of these meetings you were none the wiser?'

'Correct.'

'You did not think to ask him what he wanted? Is this what the jury are to believe?'

'The jury can believe what it likes.'

'Quite. But the ladies and gentlemen should believe that you did not ask for any of these meetings?'

'Correct. Arsehole!'

'Mr Warwick, you will refrain from making derogatory remarks.' Cowden exclaimed.

'You're letting him do what he likes. Old Scots fart.'

The Lord Cowden was not a man accustomed to being spoken to in such a manner. Certainly not in his own court. His normally florid complexion turned a deep shade of purple and it looked as if he might have a seizure. Muirhead did not wish to lose his momentum because of a judicial outburst. He poured oil on the troubled waters.

'Come now, Mr Warwick. I'm sure you did not mean to offend.'

Warwick opened his mouth to fire off another salvo but was immediately confronted by another question. This one took everyone by surprise. Especially the witness.

'What is your name? I know the name you gave us, but that is not your real name, is it now?'

Before the witness could react, he was hit by a follow-up.

'Your real name is Arthur John Beswick. Isn't it?'

The last two words were uttered in a voice which now had a distinct edge to it.

'I don't use that name.'

'Maybe not, but that is your given name, isn't it?'

Warwick stared down at his feet. His grip on the witness box tightened. He was shaking – not with nerves – with rage.

'Yes.'

'And you have previously been in court under the name Arthur John Beswick?'

Warwick took several deep breaths, and fought for control.

'I did silly things when I was a boy.'

'Doubtless, but I was thinking of occasions when you appeared as a witness using the name Arthur John Beswick?'

'What's all that got to do with this case? He told me he done a murder. If you're supposed to be defending him why don't you get on and ask me about that?'

'Oh, rest assured, I will, but for the moment, just tell the ladies and gentlemen on how many occasions you have given evidence for the prosecution?'

'I can't remember.'

'Come now, be fair to yourself, how many times, or do you wish me to assist your recollection?'

Muirhead's voice had now taken on a tone heavy with sarcasm. Warwick was clearly rattled. His eyes darted around the court as if looking for a means of escape. None was available to him. He would have to stand and fight.

'Tell me then if you are so smart.'

'Newcastle Crown Court, December 4th 1987, you gave evidence against a man called Frederick Charles Love, did you not?'

'So what?'

'The "so what" is that you claimed in that case that you had had a conversation with Mr Love in a cell and he told you about his part in a bank robbery.'

'Something like that.'

'Carlisle Crown Court, April 10th, 1989, you reappear as a witness, this time in a case against one Hugh Thomas. This time you claimed that you met Thomas on a number of occasions in a prison exercise yard. He apparently felt able to confess to you the fact that he was responsible for a slashing which took place in a pub.'

'What does all this prove?'

'It proves you are a remarkable man, Mr Warwick. You must have an extremely sympathetic nature. People have an almost uncanny need to unburden their souls to you.'

'I know what I know.'

'Yes, but why did you tell the authorities? Why did you grass?'

'Who are you to call a grass, you wanker?'

'And more to the point, why are you grassing unless you hope to get something out of it ?'

'I never asked for nothing. Bloody listen, will you.'

'London, this time. The Old Bailey, no less.'

The tone now light. Almost casual.

'September 3rd 1992, and once again you appear as a witness. The accused was Philippe St André, a black man. He too confessed to you. This time about a murder. A man you claimed you only spoke to once, confessed that he had killed a rival drug dealer. All sounds a bit familiar, doesn't it?'

'Maybe to your twisted mind, it does.'

'When your own cases come to court, on each occasion after you had given evidence, the judge was told in mitigation of your sentence that you had co-operated with the authorities in a serious criminal inquiry.'

'Prove it.'

Muirhead did.

He spent the next hour taking the witness through transcripts of his previous court appearances. The jury were enthralled. Even his Lordship was impressed at the total control Muirhead was exercising over his victim.

By the end of this particular chapter the jurors could be left in no doubt that the man before them was a strange mixture indeed.

By the lunch adjournment Warwick, or Beswick, looked like an English opening batsman who had survived a whole morning against a West Indian pace attack, but did not know how. If he enjoyed his lunch it soon turned to acid in his stomach, as Muirhead resumed his questions.

'Did you read newspapers while you were in prison?'

'Sometimes.'

'If you read the newspaper reports of the death of Clark and Boyle you will find many of the details you claim to have obtained from Mr Gallagher. Don't you think that is interesting?'

'He told me things.'

Muirhead ostentatiously opened a newspaper.

'I'm looking at an article from the *Daily Record*, a paper I'm sure you are familiar with.'

He did not pause for an answer.

'Published just a few days after the two murders and an article under the byline of Scott Thomas which claims to disclose the story behind the two murders. Interestingly, it reveals that Kevin Boyle was shot in a car, at close range. It names the street where the body was found. It claims to reveal that Boyle was shot in the head. It also describes the finding of the body of Mr Clark in a bin in a lane behind the Ingram Hotel. The author writes that a police source has revealed that Clark was tortured and had his throat cut. Interesting, don't you think?'

'He told me. So go on with your little games Mr Hotshot or is it Hot Shit?'

'Did you read this particular newspaper?'

'No.'

'Did you read this newspaper?'

'Are you deaf as well as stupid? I told you – NO.'

'I propose to lead evidence from the staff at Barlinnie prison to the effect that while you were in the Segregation Unit at Barlinnie, the one newspaper that you did have access to was the Daily Record. Any smart answers, now?'

'He's a killer. I know it. You know it. You just get paid to pretend to believe he didn't do it. I've had a lot of briefs like you. None of them were any good.'

Despite the anger and sense of loathing welling inside him, Muirhead kept his voice very calm and even.

'What you have told the jury is a mixture of what you read, prison gossip and some inspired guesswork, isn't it?'

'Bullshit.'

'Do you read the *News of the World*?'

'What?'

'Ever read about yourself in the *News of the World*?'

'Oh yes, here we go again!'

'Indeed. Look at defence production twenty-one. Is that a copy of the *News of the World* from April 1994 with a headline "Super Cheat" above an article which appears to be an interview with you in the course of which you explain to the reporter how you made a series of false confessions and conned the police and the courts into treating you leniently?'

'Tough luck, sonny. I conned them – for money. More money than even you will earn for this case, pal.'

'Meaning?'

'I told the paper a load of shit, lies, pure lies and would you believe it, they paid me for the story.'

An air of triumph.

'So, by your own admission, you are someone who will lie and cheat if you think you can gain some advantage?'

Instant deflation.

'I've told you the truth.'

'But you are quite prepared to lie when it suits you – aren't you?'

'No.'

'And you've lied here today, a series of deliberate, vicious, lies, in order to advance your own selfish ends and you have no qualms about convicting an innocent man of murder?'

'No chance.'

'Another lie. At the end of your interview with the police you told them to make sure they noted that you had volunteered the information you had just given.'

'Did I fuck.'

'Indeed you did, or at least that is what the police officers noted.'

'They're liars.'

'I see. But you did volunteer the information, important information, and you are now claiming that the police have made up a lie to the effect that you wanted them to stress the voluntary nature of your actions. Doesn't make a lot of sense, does it?'

'They're liars.'

'Someone is certainly lying. So when your case comes to court, you will not wish the judge to be told about your co-operation in this case?'

'That's my business.'

'Why should Mr Gallagher choose you to confess to?'

'Ask him.'

'I'm asking you.'

'Ask him.'

'When you are exercising, where is the officer escort?'

The sudden change of tack caught Warwick by surprise.

'What? Eh, sometimes he stands in the doorway. Sometimes he goes for a cup of tea or whatever. I said that. So what?'

'Comes back to check on you from time to time?'

'Yes. I suppose.'

'Did your cell look into the yard?'

'Yes.'

'A small window looking into the yard. Not much of a view I suppose?'

'Very droll. What's your point?'

'You were in cell sixteen?'

'Yes.'

'Mr Gallagher was in cell eight?'

'Yes.'

'Obviously he could see into the yard or he would not have been able to talk to you?'

'Obviously. You're getting better at this.'

'Thank you. I am trying. From the windows of these cells you can't see the door to the yard, can you?'

'Clever boy. Done your homework.'

Again the witness was gaining in confidence. Alas, a custard pie was just around the next corner.

'So, when Mr Gallagher was making this great confession to you, for all he knew, a prison officer could have been listening to his every word well?'

'I suppose.'

'Now, why should he do such a remarkably stupid thing, take such a remarkably dangerous risk, just to tell his story to a complete stranger who might have informed on him anyway?'

'You're just playing lawyer's games.'

'Answer the question, will you?,' barked Muirhead.

'I don't know,' was the response of a man whose legs were beginning to buckle. Muirhead was about to cut him off at the knees.

'Well, if you don't know that, you certainly know this. Paul Tomzack, far from being a crook, is in fact an English solicitor, isn't he?'

'So he claimed. But I reckon he's bent.'

'Come on now, Warwick, he came to see you because he was preparing a fresh appeal for the man I asked you about earlier, Frederick Love.'

'So he said.'

'And he told you that he had discovered you had given evidence against other accused persons.'

'I think so.'

'He asked if you were prepared to give a statement about these matters?'

'No.'

'No? Didn't you give him a statement? A statement in which you accepted that the evidence you had given about your conversation with Lane was a downright lie, a piece of pure fabrication?'

'NO.'

'Be careful, Mr Warwick. Look at defence production twelve.'

Warwick glanced at the document handed to him and his eyes instantly lit up. Brandishing the paper, he rounded on the jury.

'There you are, members of the jury. You are being tricked. A typewritten sheet of paper. No signatures – nothing. Could have been typed by anyone. He probably typed it himself.'

Anderson tugged Muirhead's gown.

'James, we've got the original!'

'I know, my boy. Patience! Man's entitled to a bit of sport.'

'Is that a statement...?'

'It's nothing.'

'Is that a statement, just look at it, in which you appear to retract the evidence you gave against Frederick Love, Hugh Thomas and Philippe St André? You accept you told lies and that you did this in order to gain an advantage for yourself in cases pending before the courts?'

'This is pure crap and you know it. I feel almost sorry for your client, Muirhead. If you're a lawyer, mate, Crippen was innocent.'

'Is that so, Mr Warwick? Is that so? Well look at defence production thirteen. That IS a handwritten version of the same document, but in YOUR handwriting, signed by you and counter-signed by Paul Tomzack, solicitor. Still think Crippen was innocent?'

Mike Matthews sank into his chair. He looked and felt like a man who had eight draws on the coupon only to find that he had forgotten to post the thing. He knew that one of his star witnesses had just fallen out of the sky. Lord Cowden was forced into a wry smile. Much as he disliked Muirhead, he respected a professional on top of his job.

Everyone in court knew that Warwick was beaten, but like a wounded, dying animal, he summoned up one last strike.

'So, I gave that statement. It's all lies. I got paid to make that statement.'

'Paid. I see, and who paid you?'

'Tomzack. I told you he was a crook.'

'He is a solicitor. And how much did he pay you?'

'Ten grand.'

'Cheque or cash?'

Muirhead's voice was now dripping with sarcasm.

'He never paid me. He said he would pay me. He cheated me. Every bastard cheats me. You're trying to cheat me. He offered money as well.'

'Who offered you money?' Muirhead spat the words at him.

'Him. The lawyer. Morton. He came to see me in prison and said the Gallaghers would pay me whatever I wanted to withdraw my statement.'

'Warwick, you really are a contemptible creature.'

'Mr Muirhead, you must not abuse the witness – however much he may deserve it.' It was clear to all that Lord Cowden had formed his own view of Mr Warwick and, for that matter, Mr Beswick.

'You are, in effect, accusing my instructing solicitor, Mr Jack Morton, a respected lawyer, of being a party to you being offered a bribe in an attempt to pervert the course of justice?'

'That's what happened.'

'Mr Warwick or Beswick or whatever your name is, that is just the last in a series of vicious lies you have told in this witness box.'

Muirhead sat down before the witness could respond.

Mike Matthews had already decided that he was asking no further questions of his witness. Any attempt to repair the damage caused would probably end up making matters worse.

Arnold Warwick left the witness box. As he walked from the court he glanced at Muirhead but his eyes continued to avoid any contact with the dock.

*   *   *

While Warwick was being tormented in the witness box, McAllister was suffering his own private hell. Seated at his desk, he was reading the report on the death of Bob Taylor. The life of his friend and colleague was brought to an end by a simple matter-of-fact sentence in the post-mortem report.

Cause of death: crushing injuries due to being run over by a train.

He could feel the tears welling in his eyes as he read the conclusions of the officers who carried out the investigation.

> At the time of his death Detective Inspector Taylor was significantly affected by alcohol. We have been unable to trace the licensed premises we assume he must have visited.
>
> The witnesses at the station are consistent in their account that they saw him standing alone at the end of the platform which would be reached by the oncoming train. No one was nearer to him than fifteen or twenty yards. As the train approached the

station, DI Taylor walked to the edge of the platform and stepped over the edge, falling in front of the train. There is no basis for thinking that he tripped or fell off the platform accidentally. Undoubtedly, it was a deliberate action.

No one to whom we have spoken from among his colleagues had any reason to be concerned about his mental state in the days prior to his death.

His widow expected him home that evening.

His son, a serving officer, is very distressed by his father's death and has not been interviewed.

We are given to understand that Mr Taylor was engaged on an inquiry for Detective Superintendent McAllister.

In the whole circumstances, we have no doubt that DI Taylor committed suicide for a reason or reasons we have not yet been able to discover.

SUICIDE

The word leapt off the page. McAllister had no doubt that Bob Taylor had killed himself. He also knew that something horrendous must have happened to this man to cause him to step into oblivion in front of a train.

Just a few hours before, he and Taylor had been discussing the problems in the case. He had entrusted his DI with the task of discovering the identity of the officers who had been leaning on Sammy McPhee. In every sense, he had been his usual self.

'When I find them, I'll nail their bollocks to the floor.'

'Just get them in here Bob, sharpish, till we find out what they thought they were up to. Then we can both nail their bollocks to the floor.'

'After you, boss. After you.'

Just Bob.

Now he was dead.

He picked up the other file on his desk. It contained the notes he had prepared after his meeting with James Muirhead. The phone calls, the threats, the incident with the car, and finally the gun man with the Irish accent.

For reasons he could not yet explain, he was confident that the key to all of this was Tam McGarry. He desperately wanted him found, but the extensive inquiries carried out so far had revealed not a single trace of the man. People do not normally disappear. They may go into hiding for a time, but inevitably they surface. McGarry was proving unusually elusive.

The minder of the late Kevin Boyle had not been at his master's side and now his master was dead. A mysterious figure with an Irish accent was moving around in the shadows leaning on James Muirhead. McGarry. He had to find McGarry. McAllister urgently needed the answers to a few critical questions.

He had a fair idea that he knew who was in possession of the information he so urgently required. Problem was, he also had a fair idea that he would encounter a good deal of hostility before the information would be imparted to him, if at all.

    ●   ●   ●

Mike Matthews stared out of the window at the passing countryside. The 17.00 train from Queen Street Station in Glasgow was taking him to Edinburgh. He was not enjoying the journey, but was beginning to relish the large gin and tonic cradled in his right hand. Normally, he would never have countenanced such a thing but when the trolley had arrived beside him he had ordered a large one without much thought.

'Had a bad day then,' the salesgirl cheerfully inquired.

Matthews rounded on the girl and was about to tell this impertinent creature to mind her own business when he found himself confronted by a very pretty blonde nineteen or twenty year-old. A swift glance down told him that a short skirt was revealing a goodly area of shapely leg and a cream blouse was well filled by firm young breasts.

'Not the best of days, actually.'

'You a lawyer, are you?'

'QC.'

'I thought that was a cheap wine.'

'No, it means Queens Counsel. I'm prosecuting a case in Glasgow.'

The girl's cheeky grin told him he had just had the mickey taken out of him.

'Sorry. I didn't mean to sound so dreadfully pompous.'

'That's OK. My dad's a consultant surgeon. He says that most lawyers are pompous pricks.'

'He's probably right.'

'Not all the time. I bet you're not pompous really. Bet you know how to let your hair down.'

'Oh yes. Of course.'

Handing Matthews his change the girl leant over conspiratorially.

'Here, have these – on Scotrail. Cheer up. Tomorrow's another day.'

Matthews looked down at the packet of peanuts. Tomorrow's another day – Christ, what a thought! He was on his way home to another evening of listening to his wife prattling on about the endless trivia she had involved herself in that day. At ten o'clock she would go off to bed. By the time he got there, having worked on his papers for the obligatory three or four hours, she would be sound asleep – or at least pretending to be asleep. Any attempt to arouse her or coax her into some sexual activity would be met with a total rebuff. It mattered not, Matthews had long since given up trying.

He sipped on the gin and chewed the peanuts. Let his hair down. Thinking about it, he doubted he had ever let his hair down. At school, he had been a swot, a prefect, and head boy, and was largely despised by his class mates. At university, he took no part in clubs or societies, never went to the union bar, didn't go to parties, didn't get pissed, didn't chase women and certainly didn't do drugs. He had spent four years attending lectures, writing up his notes or reading in the library. He knew what was expected of him by his father – he was told often enough. His wife was the daughter of his father's closest friend, an eminent Edinburgh surgeon. She was considered to be suitable wife material. He married her – it was expected of him. He didn't love her, certainly didn't lust after her and did not even like her very much. But she was suitable, had produced the necessary offspring, could host a dinner party with the best of them and when her father died a few years previously, had been left sufficient money to be financially independent. At least she did not cost him much.

She bought her own clothes which were invariably sensible as opposed to haute couture. She had no interest in jewellery or perfume. More importantly, she did not expect anything from him. She had her own circle of friends and was happy to accept it as being her duty to prepare an evening meal and make social chat while it was being consumed. Truth to tell, she cared for her husband no more than he cared for her, but he provided her with the social position and lifestyle which she found acceptable.

Actually, she found it very acceptable. For years she had been screwing the family dentist whose obnoxious wife had, to his great relief, walked out on him. He had no wish to become involved in a serious relationship but had no desire to take an oath of celibacy. When he had first told her of his attraction, she was appalled, flattered and excited, all at the same time. She was persuaded to visit him in his flat one morning. They would have coffee. Within half an hour the coffee was going cold while they thrashed around on the leather sofa. Such sessions became fortnightly occurrences. Only occasionally was she concerned that her husband might find out but only because she was not entirely sure what his reaction might be. The effect on his feelings or ego she could cheerfully ignore. If her friends found out that she had a bit on the side, she could tolerate the gossip. In any event it would be born of jealousy rather than genuine horror. But a messy divorce! She need not have bothered.

Matthews had known for some time. He was screwing the dentist's receptionist, Shona, a plump, jolly twenty-three year-old who was perfectly happy to accommodate him occasionally between her ample thighs. She was as generous as she was undemanding. She was genuinely embarrassed when given some expensive perfume or the occasional conscience bauble when Matthews had not visited for a time. With his wife, sex was something to be done occasionally, swiftly, in the dark and in the strict missionary position. Shona would make love on the floor, on the kitchen table, against a radiator. She was without inhibition, would wander around her flat naked and delighted in Matthew's inability to keep his hands off her or his dick out of her.

On one occasion as they cuddled in front of the gas fire, Matthews had nervously posed a question.

'What do you see in me?'

Shona grinned and slid her hands between his legs.

'Your big cock.'

'I'm being serious.'

Shona thought for a moment.

'You're kind to me. You don't expect anything from me, other than a good shag. You're a great lover and you're fun.'

Matthews let the matter rest. 'Fun,' he mused. 'I've been called many things – but never fun!'

Matthews drained his glass of its last drops of gin. Had there been a bar handy, he might have risked another. Just as well – he had work to do. The case thus far was a mess. In fact it was verging upon being a shambles.

He had been rather pleased when he fell heir to this particular brief. A high-profile trial, good media coverage, a case which on paper looked rock solid and a chance to work it right up James Muirhead. He had almost completed his stint as an Advocate Depute and this ought to have been a splendid conclusion to three years of public service.

Now it was in very grave danger of becoming a total disaster. None of his main witnesses had produced the goods and he feared that the jury might begin to think the whole thing was ridiculous. Normally he would have comforted himself with the knowledge that he still had a card or three to play. In this case, he realised he could take nothing for granted.

Before he left the High Court building his instruction to the Procurator Fiscal in charge of the preparation of the case had been simple.

'For tomorrow, just find me a witness who can do Gallagher some real harm and who will not leap about like a demented puppet when Muirhead gets his hands on him.'

● ● ●

Muirhead sat in his study nursing a large Hine Antique brandy. He reflected on the fact that the case was going well. There were still problems to deal with and much might yet go awry. For the time being, at least, the jury must be wondering. Only a pretty perverse bunch could be thinking that the Crown was proving its case. That would do for the time being. He ought to feel satisfied, even confident. He had taken a gamble or two. The first week of the trial had undoubtedly gone in favour of the defence.

Matthews had obviously decided to start the week with Warwick in an attempt to maximise his impact and counteract some of the failures of the preceding week. Well, that plan had gone up in smoke in the most spectacular fashion. Where would he go now? Time alone would reveal the answer to that question. But there were many other 'whys', and the lack of answers was deeply troubling.

Muirhead found it most suspicious that a man with a track record of being an informant and an unreliable witness (all of which must have been known to the Crown) happened to find himself in the segregation unit in close proximity to Charlie Gallagher. Whoever arranged this was bound to suspect that Warwick would run true to form and claim some connection with Gallagher. He concluded that there was every reason to suppose he had been located there for this very specific purpose. Such a decision had to be taken high up the tree of authority. Someone was playing games – dangerous, devious games.

There was the most extraordinary behind-the-scenes activity in this case. Someone, some people, had clearly been leaning on Crown witnesses. Police officers had put pressure on Sammy McPhee and arguably had tried to get him to change or at least modify his evidence.

And then there was the voice. The mysterious Irish voice. The voice which had tried to force him out of the trial. The voice of the hand which had held a gun to his head. The voice which had threatened his family.

He had given up wondering why someone was trying to influence his conduct of the case. Sometimes before you ask 'why' it is better to ask 'who.' Clearly it was vital to some person that Charlie Gallagher was convicted.

Muirhead filled his pipe, lit it and slowly and deliberately inhaled and exhaled the smoke. He stared into the now empty brandy glass. No. This exercise required calm reflection – and a clear head. Fuck it, it also required another brandy.

With the glass suitably charged, Muirhead settled down in his chair. Who?

This was no 'outraged of Kelvinside', anxious to see justice done and seeking to put lead in the pencil of those charged with its administration. Too much effort had gone into this for it to be a nutter. So, not a nutter.

He could rule out the Boyles. If anything, they would probably want Gallagher on the outside so they could get to him more easily. Kevin's death was not something which could be avenged by the imposition of a term of imprisonment – however lengthy that might be. So, not the Boyles.

Some police officers might bend the rules and the evidence as they had tried to do with Sammy McPhee. It was not unheard of for policemen to be convinced of the identity of the perpetrator of a crime but find themselves frustrated by their inability to prove it. In such circumstances, a scrap of highly-incriminating evidence might unexpectedly be found in a pocket, a drawer, a motor car.

Before the advent of tape recorders in police stations, a myth was created that when a suspect was in custody, his dealings with the police were conducted in a monastic silence. Only when the individual was to be charged and cautioned that they did not need to say anything, did the suspect feel obliged to speak – usually in order to admit his guilt in a few carefully chosen words. Inevitably this brought the claim, 'I've been fucking verballed up!'

Nowadays, interviews are recorded. People are encouraged to tell their side of the story and preferably to admit guilt. Yet there remains the temptation to insert an on-line admission when the machine is switched off.

OK, so the police might have massaged some evidence, might have leant on a witness or two, but they did not normally run around putting guns to lawyers' heads. So, not the police.

'So, who the hell is left? The Gallaghers?', Muirhead muttered to himself. 'They'd hardly want one of their own going down the bloody tubes. You're missing something, James, and you're talking to yourself. Bed for you!'

Muirhead went to rise from his chair but felt weighed down by a great weariness. This case was getting to him – badly. The threats had alarmed him. The behind-the-scenes activities gave him the feeling that he was not in control. The case was going well, yet there was every danger that it might blow up in his face.

He was tired – very tired. How much violence could you tolerate before you had had enough? To how much death could you remain insensitive? How many times could you bear the responsibility for a man's liberty before the burden becomes too great? How many judges could you fight with, how many witnesses could you cross-examine, how many juries could you address before the supply of adrenaline finally dried up?

Would he go to court one day and say to himself: 'I can't do this any more.'? What if this happened during the present case? What if it happened tomorrow?

This spiral into a slough of depression was interrupted by the ringing of the telephone.

'Mr Muirhead?'

'Yes.'

'Do you recognise my voice? No names please.'

'Yes.'

'I have some information for you concerning our mutual acquaintance. What you make of it is up to you.'

Muirhead listened intently for the next twenty seconds.

'Why are you telling me this?'

The caller was gone.

Chapter Nine

Annie Boyle sat in a cafeteria in the St Enoch's Shopping Centre, staring into a polystyrene cup of lukewarm coffee, oblivious to the comings and goings of the early-morning shoppers. She was reflecting upon the changes in her life since the death of her son – the turmoil into which her family had been plunged; the decline of her husband; the pointing fingers; the whispers; the endless phone calls from journalists, and the never-ending stream of police officers. Questions! Questions! Questions! Annie had always been aware of the nature of the family business but had never felt the need or desire to become involved with its nuts and bolts.

She had disapproved of the freedom her husband had always afforded to Kevin, even from an early age. She had grown weary of the sound of her own voice telling Hugh that if he did not keep a firmer grip on the business and on Kevin, both were likely to end up in serious bother. She fought to control her irritation when Hugh attempted to placate her with hollow promises that he would 'sort it.'

She knew only too well that nothing would be done. Nothing would change. Kevin would be allowed and indeed encouraged, to go his own sweet way. Hugh did not see past his eldest son and anything Kevin did which might be even vaguely injudicious was justified by an endless series of fatuous excuses. Kevin was able to behave exactly as he chose.

For some time prior to the murder, Annie had become aware of some kind of tension between Kevin and his brother Paul.

Paul was the business man, the money man. He preferred to keep a low profile and firmly believed that if you did not upset the authorities, the authorities were unlikely to upset you. The brothers had never been particularly close and Paul and Kevin frequently argued about some of the latter's activities. These arguments were invariably heated but recently there had been an edge to their disputes that she could not put her finger on. Too often for her liking, she felt as if she was listening to two people conducting a private debate.

'We're the Boyles, we do what we like.'

'No, you do what you like. I'm trying to run a business that is making us, you, a bloody fortune and you fuck about attracting attention to yourself, to us.'

'So what, who's going to touch us?'

'The law won't touch us, Kevin, it will jump all over us.'

'Christ, you can be a total wimp. The polis have tried before. They failed before. Stop shiting yourself, will you, and go back to your books and computer games.'

'This is serious Kevin.'

'I'm being serious. Give it a rest, will you!'

'If we just stick to what we know we'll have more money than even you could ever spend. Why the hell do you want to take risks just to make more? Risks which could ruin everything?'

'Listen Mister Yuppified Middle-Class Wankhead, you can't stand still. You've got to keep on the move. Change with the times. Go with the flow, all that shite. There's business out there and I'm going to make damn sure we get our share of it, and some. It's how the old man worked. It's how I work. Like father, like son – this son.'

'We run things now and in any case you know dad wouldn't touch things that were too risky. That is why we are where we are. That's how I do business. Like father, like son – this son.'

'I do things differently. That's it – and if the polis want to get in the way, they can be dealt with.'

'How?'

'I know how.'

'Kevin, this is crazy. How ?'

'That's my problem.'

'No, it isn't. It will be our problem. You're talking pish and you know it. And it's not just the polis. You're getting right up the noses of other people.'

'I'll deal with them too.'

'Talk sense, Kevin.'

'Enough. Fucking leave it. You're not the boss. You tell me fuck all what to do. No cunt tells me fuck all what to do. Got it? Have you got it Paul?'

'I've got it, but you're heading for deep shit, Kevin. Someone's going to stop you.'

'They can fucking try.'

She sipped at the coffee, ignoring the fact that it was now stone-cold. Despite her concerns over Kevin's activities, Annie had loved her son. He would always be her wee boy – mischievous, petulant, needing constant reassurance from her that he was special. She could picture him, tousle-haired, clothing dirtied and torn, hands and face bloodspattered as the result of yet another scrap. Tears welled in her eyes as she recollected the last time she saw him – in the mortuary. Her little boy had no longer appeared mischievous. His head was an horrific mutilation. He had been brutally violated. His eyes seemed to be crying out to her in pain and terror. His mouth was open and she could hear the voice calling 'Ma! Ma!' as it had done so many years before. An observer would have found the scene horrific, sickening, obscene. Not Annie. She saw her son and felt his pain.

Time to go.

She walked to the escalator, descended to the ground floor and left the Centre. She looked across the large open car park towards the High Court building some six hundred yards away. There, the man who had killed her son was on trial. The man they said had killed her son. Since the trial had started, Annie had deliberately avoided newspapers, televisions and radios. She had certainly not ventured anywhere near the court. Now it was time to find out what was going on – for herself.

   ❋   ❋   ❋

Everyone is afraid of something: open spaces, heights, spiders, living, dying, the VAT man. Nothing chills the blood of the defence lawyer more than the spectre of the apparently genuine independent eye-witness. The public should adhere to the three golden rules for witnesses to a crime: do not get involved by telling the police; if you must tell the police, do not give your name and address; if you must give your name and address, do not give your real name and address.

Barclay Thomson had chosen to ignore each of these rules in turn, in a big way, and now found himself opening the batting on the seventh day of the trial.

Thirty-something, he gave all the outward appearance of being a product of the sixties. Long straggly hair, thin, droopy Zapata moustache, combat jacket, jeans and a T-shirt bearing a picture of Che Guevara – he looked as if he was about to audition for the lead role in a remake of Citizen Smith.

'Power to the people!', muttered Anderson.

'It may be my elbow which needs the power,' came his senior's surly response.

He deponed that he was a musician, a drummer, with a Glasgow rock band which rejoiced in the name of the Culture Vultures.

'The who?,' inquired the Advocate Depute.

The reply, 'No, the Culture Vultures', caused much mirth amongst the jurors, especially as it sailed above the heads of both counsel and judge.

His manner of speech disclosed he was not uneducated as he

confirmed when questioned on the subject. He parents were professional people and he had attended Glasgow Academy before graduating from the London School of Economics with a BA degree in Politics and Economics. The Depute was setting this man up as a sane, sensible witness, despite his singular appearance. Instinctively, the jury knew something was about to happen.

After describing where he lived and confirming that from his lounge window he had had a clear view of the BMW, he was asked about the critical matters.

'I write songs and I was working at my keyboard. I had been at it all night but nothing was happening for me. The room was smoky and I went to the window to get a breath of fresh air, and it all just happened. Like, man, I thought to begin with it must be the telly, making something like Taggart. It looked seriously real.'

'What did you see when you looked from the window?'

'Nothing much at first, just parked cars, not many people about. I saw a man with a dog. Local, I think. Then something caught my eye.'

'What?'

'I saw this guy walking along the street and all of a sudden he pulled at this woolly hat and it just became a balaclava mask. He walked up to a car, the BMW, briskly, then pulled something out of his pocket and there was a series of bangs.'

'How many bangs?'

'I can't be sure, but four, five or six.'

'More than two?'

'For sure. For sure.'

'Did there seem to be anyone in the BMW?'

'Yes. There was someone sitting in the driver's seat.'

'What did the gunman do next?'

'He turned on his heels and ran along the road for about fifty yards. As he got to a parked car, he pulled off the mask and literally jumped into the rear passenger seat. The car shot off along the street and then turned right as if heading to the town centre.

'It was then I realised that there was something very wrong. Nothing happened. There was no camera. No people. Just a kind of a weird stillness. My phone wasn't working. I ran downstairs to a phone box. I had to pass the BMW. There was blood everywhere. I dialled **999** then went back to my flat.'

'Can you tell us about the getaway car?'

'It was grey. Hatchback. I'm not very good at makes. The number did not register at all.'

'Can you describe the gunman?'

'Tall, about six feet. Quite thin. Fair hair. He was wearing dark clothing. Black bomber jacket perhaps.'

'Would you recognise him if you saw him again?'

'Yes. For sure.'

'Do you see him here in court?'

'Yes.'

'Can you point him out?'

Thomson turned immediately to the dock, raised his right arm and pronounced, 'There. Charles Gallagher.'

There was considerable agitation in the public gallery. A number of jurors scribbled notes. Lord Cowden was ostentatiously marking his notebook with a red pencil. Muirhead tried to exude an air of outward calm.

'How sure are you, Mr Thomson?'

'As sure as I can be.'

'Why?'

'I went to school with him. I knew him. I recognised him.'

' "I knew him. I recognised him," ' repeated the Advocate Depute, slowly and deliberately.

'Yes.'

'Thank you very much.'

His Lordship adjourned for lunch and left the bench to a rising level of noise emanating from every corner of the court. There was much to discuss, for players and spectators alike.

Muirhead confined himself to a single pertinent question: 'Why the hell didn't I know that was coming?'

The blank looks on the faces of his solicitor and junior told him the question would prove to be rhetorical.

One person did not join in the chattering as the spectators walked down the stairs from the public gallery and into the street. Annie Boyle's mind was racing.

She had stared at the back of the man who had killed her son. The man they said had killed her son. She tried to hate, tried to be angry, tried to feel – something.

She had studied Barclay Thomson while he gave his evidence. Watched his body language. Listened intently to his voice. Very convincing. None of this had given her any sense of satisfaction. She had come to the court seeking answers. Perhaps in search of some peace of mind. She had found neither. More questions – fewer answers. More agitation – less peace. This was wrong – very wrong.

Nothing could bring her son back. She had spent her life trying to protect her family. She had fought to persuade her husband that he should keep the boys out of the business. She had failed. She had tried to encourage her sons to be careful. To avoid making enemies. She had failed.

She had grown weary of the name 'Boyle' being spat out or whispered as if it was a word to be spoken only in hatred or fear. She had prayed for this to change. Her prayers had gone unanswered. She had failed and failed and failed again. She had always given Hugh his rightful place as head of the family. She knew she could not tie her children to her indefinitely. She had recognised and respected the fact that the boys were now men and must be allowed to take decisions for themselves and make their own mistakes. She had taken a back seat – but had sat on it for far too long. She knew she could not turn the clock back. But no longer was she prepared simply to be an observer. Never again would she allow her family's name to be synonymous with dishonesty, wrongdoing, violence or terror. One Boyle at least would do what was right.

She walked purposefully away from the High Court. She knew what she must do. She did not know how, or what the ultimate consequences might be.

*   *   *

'Jack, have we nothing to throw at this chap?'

'Only what you know already. I did find out that he has two previous convictions. Unfortunately, they date back a few years and were both for simple possession of drugs. Probably when he was a student. Admonished once, then fined twenty pounds. Hardly makes him a major-league criminal.'

'Or a dishonest witness. No suggestion at all that he has any connection with the Boyles, for example?'

'My inquiry agent has dug and dug but come up with nothing. This guy is an ageing hippie, probably smokes a bit of hash. Apart from that he seems to be a genuine eye-witness who...'

'Yes, I've got that bit. I was hoping for just a little assistance. And don't say, "You're on your own with that one Mr Muirhead." Of that fact, I'm well aware.'

'I remember acting for one of those so-called terrorist chaps in trials some years ago. They took all sorts of bits and pieces from his home. Old Charlie Brewster was my senior. Great chap, old Charlie. Give him two large gins and he would go on for hours about his army days. The way he talked, you would think he had been in every regiment in the British Army. Actually, I suspect he was a cook or something. Anyway, Charlie was running this defence that the client was just a collector of militaria.

Sat in court day after day shaking his head and striking poses of horror and disbelief every time it was suggested that our man might be involved in anything even vaguely naughty.

'Well, everything seemed to be going fine until Turnbull, the Strathclyde ballistics chap, came in to give evidence. The Depute handed him Charlie's man's collection of militaria, and Turnbull built a bloody sten gun out of it. You should have seen Charlie. He went apoplectic. We got out of court and I started to laugh. Well, it was quite funny. Not the evidence – that was a bit serious. But Charlie's face – absolutely priceless.

'Christ, he rounded on me and told me it was all my fault. I had let him make a fool of himself. I should have spotted that this junk could be assembled into a gun. Didn't follow this myself. Seemed to me that Charlie should have spotted it, what with his vast military experience and all. Maybe they didn't have sten guns in the catering corps. Unless it was for the squaddies who had to eat old Charlie's gravy. There you go.'

'Donald, what the hell are you on about?'

'Charlie Brewster. You know Charlie...'

'Of course I bloody know Charlie Brewster. I've known him for twenty years. What has all this to do with what might be seen as our present predicament?'

'I forget. There was some point to it, I think.'

'Jesus Christ. If you have any other contributions to make, keep them to yourself.'

'Sorry I bothered.'

'Let's just get on with it – shall we?'

'That's it!'

'That's what?'

'Charlie Brewster. He used to have this saying: "the hotter the war the sooner the peace".'

'What?'

'It sort of means that the darkest part of the night is just before the dawn, I think. It will get worse before it gets better. That sort of thing.'

'And how does this help me to cross-examine Mr Thomson?'

'Not directly, perhaps. But it makes you think. Doesn't it?'

'Donald, have you ever thought of becoming a philosopher?'

'Not really, no.'

'Very wise!'

*   *   *

An hour into his cross-examination, James Muirhead was getting nowhere fast. Barclay Thomson resolutely maintained that he knew what he had seen. He had an uninterrupted view of the incident. He had the gunman in sight for about a minute. He had a good opportunity to see his face. He may have been tired, having been up all night, but he recognised the man he saw. Not quite the minute he saw him but certainly by the time he turned away from the car after the bangs. He had not been alarmed at that stage because he thought he was watching the making of some television programme.

By the time he phoned the police he realised he had witnessed something very serious and that he knew one of the people responsible. He was quite confident about his identification. He had been at the same secondary school as Gallagher. They were in the same year and had attended the same classes. No, they were not friends, but there had never been any problems between them. He did not like him, did not dislike him. His feelings were entirely neutral.

He readily accepted that he had not spoken to Gallagher since their school days, but he had seen him in and around Glasgow and was in no doubt that he knew who he was and that he had been the man with the gun. He was quite confident he was not mistaken.

The atmosphere in the court had taken on rather a different character. Lord Cowden was sitting back in his chair. He had long since put down his fountain pen. For once in this case Muirhead was producing nothing which was worthy of noting.

Gallagher was becoming increasingly agitated. He sat hunched forward in the dock, his hands tightly clasped in front of him. At several aspects of Thomson's evidence, he vigorously shook his head. He avoided any eye contact with the witness. He knew that if he looked at this bastard in the witness box he would explode. If he could just get his hands round his throat he would get the truth out of him – then kill him. He was fighting an internal battle to hold on to his self-control. He also wanted to tell his useless fucking QC what he thought of him. The guy in the witness box was trying to bury him and his lawyer was doing nothing about it. For the first time in the trial, the Advocate Depute looked relaxed and confident. There were no skeletons in Thomson's cupboard. There could surely be no suggestion that he had been got at. On the face of it, he was an independent eye-witness and the fact that he actually knew the accused was a bonus. And what a bonus.

However, behind the calm exterior, Matthews was still worried. This witness had to be accepted by the jury. He was arguably the best the Crown had. He had to survive reasonably intact. So far so good. 'Just keep it going my boy, but watch your back. Don't be fooled. He's not done with you yet.'

Muirhead resumed the cross-examination.

'Why did you make the treble nine call?'

'I thought something was wrong. It is not usual to see people firing guns in the street – even in Glasgow.'

'Did you think that someone had been hurt?'

'I suppose so, yes.'

'When you made the call, did you ask for the ambulance or the police?'

'I can't remember. An ambulance I think.'

'The treble nine call was tape-recorded, as such things are. Look at production 37. Do you see that that is a transcript of the call?'

'Yes.'

'It is clear from that document that you asked for the police.'

'Yes. I see that. I thought I asked for an ambulance.'

'When you made the treble nine call you were simply trying to do the right thing?'

'I saw something serious happen. I decided to call the police. I think that's perfectly reasonable.'

'No doubt, but you told the jury you called the ambulance?'

'I made a mistake. I apologise.'

'A mistake. I see. Presumably you would call the ambulance if you thought someone was injured and needed medical aid?'

'Yes.'

'But according to the transcript you asked for the police. At no time did you mention an ambulance. Did you think that someone had been shot?'

'Possibly.'

'Could be badly hurt? Dying?'

'Possibly.'

'Did you tell that to the police?'

'Yes.'

'Did you?'

'I believe so.'

'Look at the transcript. You were put through to the police and you said, "There's been a shooting in Mitchell Road. This guy just fired a gun." "Is he still there?" "No, he drove off." "Has anyone been injured?" "I don't know." How does that square with what you told the jury to the effect that you asked for an ambulance and that there was "blood everywhere"?'

'When I realised that the gun was real, I got a fright. I did not expect to have to remember all the details, months later.'

'Surely, if you saw blood everywhere, your priority would be an ambulance?'

'I assumed the police would get an ambulance.'

'Even although you gave no indication that someone had been injured, badly injured?'

'Yes.'

'I see. When did you realise you knew the gunman?'

'Certainly by the time he got in the car.'

'By the time he turned away from the BMW?'

'Maybe.'

'Not when you first saw him walking towards the BMW?'

'Not really.'

'Not really, or not at all?'

'He looked familiar.'

'Why didn't you tell the police that you knew who the gunman was?'

'They did not ask me.'

'If we assume you had recognised the gunman, surely you would appreciate this would be information which would be of great interest to the police? Were you asked for your name?'

'Don't remember.'

'Back to the transcript. You were asked, "Can I have your name please?" Read over your answer.'

' "No, that's all right. I don't think I'll bother." '

'Why did you refuse to give your name?'

'I didn't want to get involved, man. What's wrong with that?'

'Why not? What was the problem? What did you have to hide?'

'Nothing. I just did not want to be involved. I had done what I could. What I thought was right. I might not have bothered at all if I had known I was going to have to stand here and be abused by you.'

'Mr Thomson, rest assured that his Lordship will not allow me to abuse you. I am entitled to ask you questions and examine your evidence – in detail.'

Muirhead was keeping the pressure on, probing with the skill of a swordsman wielding a blade with artistry and control. He had drawn some blood but had inflicted no major wounds. His opponent lacked his dexterity but was mounting a stout defence while remaining remarkably calm under the persistent attacks. The jury was fixated.

'On how many occasions did you speak to the police?'

'I made one treble-nine call.'

'I did not ask you that. I asked on how many occasions you spoke to the police. Answer the question, please.'

'I gave the police a statement, then later on I saw the procurator fiscal. I also went to an identification parade. That's it.'

'Will you just answer my question?'

The Advocate Depute was on his feet.

'My Lord, the witness has answered my learned friend's question. There is no need for him to badger the man.'

'It certainly seems to me that he has answered your question Mr Muirhead.'

'My Lord, there is the world of difference between giving an answer to a straight question and giving a straight answer to a straight question. I would prefer the latter.'

'You have had an answer. Move on please.'

'How many times did you phone the police?'

'I made one treble nine call. I told you, man.'

Again the Depute was on his feet.

'My Lord, you have already ruled on this matter.'

'Mr Muirhead, I have told you to move on. Did you understand my ruling?'

'I did, of course, and I will move on if your Lordship is telling me as a matter of law that I am not entitled to have an answer to the perfectly reasonable question I asked in cross-examination on behalf of a client charged with murder.' (Because if you are you old bastard you know I'll be off to the Appeal Court the first chance I get.)

His Lordship got the message, loud and clear.

'Advocate Depute, I think this is a difficult area and I will allow Mr Muirhead to pursue it – for the time being.'

'I am very much obliged to your Lordship.' Muirhead accompanied this with a slight bow. (This was lawyer-speak for 'Up yours, my Lord!)

'The answer to my question Mr Thomson, please...I'm waiting...we are all waiting.'

'I made a second phone call – to the police.'

'When?'

'Later the same day.'

'And during that short call, did you give the police the name of the gunman?'

'I told the police that the man with the gun was Charlie Gallagher.'

'That's not entirely true. You told the police that the man who shot Kevin Boyle was Charles Gallagher.'

'I may have done. I don't remember my exact words. That's too much to expect.'

'Well, is it too much to expect you to tell the jury how you knew it was Kevin Boyle who had been shot?'

'I think I heard it on the radio.'

'When?'

Three Verdicts

'When what?'

'When did you hear it?'

'I'm not sure.'

'How long before you called the police?'

'I can't remember exactly.'

'You called the police at 17.20. The name of Kevin Boyle was not released to the press until 21.00 hours.'

'Then, it was after I went to the local shop for cigarettes. Maybe I heard the name there. People were talking about the shooting.'

'Which do you wish it to be? The radio? Gossip? Something else? Which?'

'I can't remember.'

'Too easy. Which?'

'I can't remember. You can raise your voice all you like. I am telling you – I can't remember – so carry on with your amateur theatricals.'

The first sign that Thomson was becoming rattled. Muirhead took his best shot. A full-blooded lunge.

'You made this call anonymously, didn't you? You refused to give your name, your address or your phone number. Doesn't seem like a citizen just doing his duty? What is this all about? What were you hiding?'

'Nothing.'

'Then why did you hide your identity?'

'I didn't want involved.'

'Then why make the call?'

'I thought it was the right thing to do.'

'You knew Kevin Boyle, didn't you?'

'I knew who he was.'

'You drank with him in his night clubs?'

'I've had a drink with lots of people.'

'Kevin Boyle?'

'Once or twice. Other people were there.'

'You heard the local gossip about it being Gallagher who had done the shooting?'

'No, the gossip was about Kevin Boyle.'

'And you decided to pass this gossip on to the police – anonymously?'

'Nonsense, man.'

'And it was some weeks later that you went to the police to give a statement identifying yourself as the maker of the anonymous call?'

'It was some time later I gave the statement.'

'And that was after Mr Gallagher was arrested and this had been on the television, radio and in the papers?'

'It could have been.'

'It was – wasn't it?'

'Yes.'

'And I suppose you will say, that despite all these matters I have discussed with you, the jury are to accept your evidence when you claim to identify Charles Gallagher as the man with the gun?'

'That is for the jury to decide.'

'Indeed it is. Thank you very much.'

'That was superb, James. Christ, you had virtually nothing to work with but you made him look as if he doesn't know whether it's New Year or New York. Surely to God a jury can't convict on the basis of that evidence?'

'I wish I could be that confident.'

'Come on, James, this is the worst bit of the case on one view and we've got through it with their star man rocking all over the place.'

'He still says we killed Boyle.'

'Yes, but...'

Muirhead held up his hand. The Advocate Depute was ready to re-examine.

'Just a few questions, Mr Thomson. You have known Mr Gallagher since school days?'

'Yes.'

'Let us try to imagine that this shooting had not happened. If you had seen Mr Gallagher in the street, a casual encounter, would you have recognised him?'

'I believe so.'

'Did you get a good view of the man who fired the gun into the BMW?'

'Yes'

'And even although it may have taken you some time, did you eventually go to the police and give a statement?'

'I did.'

'And did you attend an identification parade?'

'Yes.'

'And did you pick someone out?'

'Yes.'

'Why?'

'He was the man with the gun.'

'Is he here in court?'

'Yes he is.'

'Who is he?'

'He's there, man. The accused. Charles Gallagher.'

'Thank you. Thank you, very much indeed.'

For the first time since the trial had started, the Advocate Depute returned confidently to his seat. Today he might even enjoy his lunch. He looked across at Muirhead. He hoped, expected, to see some signs of anxiety. Muirhead's face was fixed into a mask of calm serenity as if he was at peace with the world and had not a care in it.

'Pretend all you like', muttered Matthews. 'I may not have a firm grip of your balls, but at least, now, I can give them a bit of a squeeze.'

His junior nudged him and he looked down at her notebook.

30 – 30?

He made a minor amendment.

40 – 30!

A series of police witnesses occupied the afternoon which drifted by without a hint of the excitement which had been produced by the events of the morning session.

Ben Alexander explained how he had arrived at the scene of the shooting and secured the area. He identified the spent cartridge cases which he had found on the roadway adjacent to the BMW. It had been drawn to his attention that the bonnet of the car was cold, thereby revealing that Kevin Boyle was about to leave the street when he was shot.

Detectives explained how they had detained Gallagher at home in relation to the murder of Kevin Boyle, then taken him to a police station where he had been interviewed under tape-recorded conditions. The transcripts of the interviews were produced in court and certain extracts were read to the jury. The officers confirmed that Gallagher had answered all the questions put to him and had maintained that he was at home at the time of Boyle's murder. He had been in the company of persons whose names and addresses he freely, and indeed willingly, provided. They confirmed that at no time in their presence did Gallagher say anything which suggested he might be involved in the murder. He had repeatedly denied having any direct knowledge of it. Indeed, he had gone further and claimed that there was no bad blood between himself and Kevin Boyle or indeed any member of his family and the Boyles.

The latter assertion prompted a measure of debate in the public gallery. Any potential insurrection was swiftly quelled by a steely glare from the bench.

The officers explained that after the interviews were concluded they reported to their superior, Detective Superintendent Grant McAllister. He had taken the decision that Gallagher was to be charged with the murder. He had not explained his reasons. As a rule,

Superintendents were not in the habit of justifying themselves to junior officers, and it was not prudent to ask them to do so.

It was the boss himself who had prepared the charge. Gallagher had lost his temper when the murder charge was put to him. He had shouted and become abusive and refused to answer any further questions. The officers readily conceded that being interviewed in a police station could prove to be extremely stressful. It was not unusual for someone to snap when actually confronted by a serious charge. In fairness, they would not read anything into this.

After being charged, Gallagher was fingerprinted, allowed an interview with a lawyer and then kept in custody pending his appearance in court.

Inspector Malcolm McDonald explained that he had been in charge of a number of uniformed officers who had gone with the CID to detain Gallagher at his home. When the latter had been removed, he and his men had carried out a thorough search of the house. A variety of items had been seized as potential productions.

He was shown a number of magazines on the subject of guns, but accepted that they were such as could have been purchased in any half-decent newsagents. They were all standard publications and in his view would be purchased by someone who had an interest in guns and shooting, but there was nothing illegal or illicit about them.

He was then shown a black leather jacket. This had been found in the back of a wardrobe in a bedroom which he understood was occupied by Charlie Gallagher. When asked why he had taken this particular jacket he explained that it was one of a number of articles of dark clothing and that he had been instructed to search for and take possession of any such items. He agreed that in the time between the death of Boyle and the search of the Gallagher house there had been ample opportunity for someone to arrange for the cleaning of all the articles of clothing he had seized. Indeed, it would have been a simple matter to dispose of the jacket completely.

He had been specifically told to look for gloves and a woollen balaclava. He had found neither. Needless to say, no gun or ammunition was found.

The Advocate Depute rose to his feet.

'At this juncture, in order to assist the Court and the ladies and gentlemen of the jury, I would advise that while I have further evidence to lead, I would anticipate that the Crown case will close tomorrow.'

'Thank you, Mr Depute, that is most helpful. I am indebted to you. Well, ladies and gentlemen, you have heard what was said. The end of the Crown case is in sight. Tomorrow morning. Ten o'clock.'

'Yes, my Lord. No, my Lord. If my Lord will part his cheeks, I will lick his arse, helpfully. Not at all, Advocate Depute, I will be indebted to you if you will graciously permit me to lick your arse. What a mutual admiration society!'

'Don't be so cynical, Donald. I'm sure the two of them will be very happy together.'

'Oh indeed, they make a lovely couple.'

'I do hope that you are not suggesting that his Lordship might be mildly favouring the nice prosecutor as opposed to the nasty defence lawyer?'

'Dear me, no, old bean, perish the thought, perish the thought. I was simply noting that it seemed to me, on mature reflection, and having regard to all the relevant circumstances, and without giving undue weight to any particular factors, and, on a fair and balanced consideration of such matters as should be weighed in the scales, his Lordship was merely displaying his – customary level – of impartiality.'

'Thank you, Sir Humphrey Appleby. I think we have your position.'

'Well, James, it doesn't matter how often I appear in front of him, he gets on my bloody nerves. Judges are paid to be impartial. He gets his money under false pretences!'

'Enough of this, we have more important matters to think about. Jack, we will have to see the client tomorrow evening.'

'Are you proposing to put him in the witness box?'

'I'm not sure, yet. As you know, I don't normally advise a client to give evidence. Too easy to make mistakes, get caught out. I'm not convinced he will be able to control his temper.'

'That's my fear. Mind you, I haven't seen Matthews prosecute many cases.'

'He's not a shout and bawl merchant, but he is thorough. He'll niggle away at him. Gallagher could probably cope with being shouted at a bit but if Matthews keeps at him he might just blow. What do you think?'

'Difficult one. Normally I would agree that we should keep him out, but I assume we're leading the alibi witnesses?'

'Some of them, certainly.'

'I think it can look bad if you call the monkeys but not the organ-grinder.'

'Always a danger, Jim.'

'We'll have a chat with him tomorrow. By then he will have seen the whole of the Crown case.'

'Do you think there is enough evidence to go to the jury on both murders?'

'It may not be the greatest evidence in the world, but there is just enough and in any event, if there is a doubt about it at all, Cowden will let it go.'

'Well, at least tomorrow we get to half time. Do you reckon we're ahead?'

'Maybe. Maybe not.'

'Pessimist!'

'Realist.'

❋   ❋   ❋

Again there was the disembodied mechanical voice.

'Thank you for calling 0608 614 519, please leave your message after the tone.'

'I'm getting seriously pissed off with this. I've left twenty fucking messages on this poxy machine. Now, call me – urgently. I don't want to have to come looking for you. Do I make myself plain. And remember this: I can play games, too.'

The man listening to the messages switched off the mobile phone. His face remained impassive and he stared ahead. He stood for a few moments reflecting on what he had just heard.

'So you can play games too, can you? Well, we will just have to see about that. Won't we?'

❋   ❋   ❋

'How did you get on, Ma?'

'I saw all I needed to see.'

'Sorry?'

'I'm not putting up with any more of this. I've had enough.'

'I don't understand what you...'

'You know exactly what I mean. I know you too well. If I had had any doubts, your eyes just eliminated them.'

'This is silly. You're upset. It's understandable. I told you not to go. I said to you that it was not the place for you.'

'Don't patronise me. Just don't bloody patronise me.'

'Look, it'll be OK. I'm getting it sorted out.'

'What do you mean, you're getting it sorted out? What are you getting sorted out? What have you been up to? I want to know.'

'I haven't been up to anything. All I'm trying to do is keep the business going and that is not easy. That was all I meant. Please, just trust me. I know what I am doing.'

'Trust you! Trust you! Trust you to do what? Haven't you done enough already? Done enough harm? You're acting as if nothing has happened. As if we are all to pretend that nothing has happened. Well, I've pretended for too long. Pretended to be deaf, dumb and blind. No more. No more. Trust you! After all this, you want me to trust you. No, I will not trust you to do anything. Now I'm going to do things. Things that need to be done. Things that should have been done – a long time ago.'

'There's no need for you to interfere.'

'Interfere! Just remember who you are talking to and don't you ever, ever accuse me of interfering.'

'I'm sorry, I didn't mean...'

'Just remember this. I'm not taking a back seat any longer. I will be watching you, watching your every move. And I intend to get some answers – for myself.'

'Look, I really don't know what you're talking about. You're just upset. You won't do anything silly, will you ?'

'Silly? No I won't do anything – silly.'

*   *   *

His every instinct told McGarry this was foolish and dangerous. If the authorities had been able to prove a fraction of the things he had done in the past, most of his life would be spent as a guest of Her Majesty. His police file ran to several pages. Suspected of involvement in armed robbery, extortion, serious assaults and even a suggestion that in the mid-seventies he had been the getaway driver when a notorious gangland figure had gunned down a rival right in the centre of Glasgow one busy Saturday afternoon. Rumours abounded, but no one actually managed to see anything. A combination of luck, intimidation and the low cunning he had been blessed with had enabled him to avoid the inside of courts, never mind prisons.

Five minor convictions, which had cost him a few quid in fines, were all the police actually had to show for the hundreds of man hours they had devoted to trying to nail his arse to the wall. He did not make mistakes and left no traces or loose tongues. If he found himself the centre of attention, he would slip away to sunnier climes until obscurity was again ready to embrace him. He was well aware that the attention of officers of law was never far away. Occupational hazard. You kept the fox at bay, you didn't invite it into the henhouse. Money was certainly not a problem. He had deposits in various discreet banks and had amassed a wide share portfolio, in an equally wide variety of names. He was a skilled financial manipulator and was quite at home in the equity, currency and commodity markets. Indeed, he read the *Financial Times* more often than he read the sports pages. Had he not been a criminal, he would have been a ruthlessly successful business man.

Every job he had ever done was done for money. Emotion played no part in it. No doubts. No regrets. Certainly, no sense of guilt. Do it, calmly, efficiently, then walk away. Simple principles which had served him well. Now he was ripping them into tiny pieces and scattering them to the wind.

Foolish!

Dangerous!

But that little bastard had tried to shaft him. After all he had done. And all he knew. That was not acceptable and that could not be allowed to pass. He might wish to return one day and he would need his reputation intact. This was not business. This was personal.

Foolish!

Dangerous!

Necessary!

❋   ❋   ❋

The professional informant is precisely that – a professional. He trades off information in return for a reward from the police tout fund. Most officers, especially those of senior rank, will run their own network of touts whose identities are jealously guarded. A single informer may work for several officers without any of them being aware of this fact. McAllister was no exception.

His best tout, whom he only ever referred to as Shugs, was himself a well-known Glasgow criminal figure with a long record. Several officers were working very hard to connect him with a series of armed post-office robberies. When he was a young cop, McAllister had arrested the equally young Shugs for car theft (actually for several car thefts). Shugs had been desperate to get bail and had offered information if McAllister arranged this. He spoke to the Procurator Fiscal who indicated that Shugs would get bail anyway. Claiming the credit, McAllister conveyed the good news to Shugs who, in his gratitude, provided a barrel load of nuggets about his friends and enemies alike. Shugs had been turned. McAllister climbed several rungs up the career ladder.

As the years passed, Shugs proved invaluable. There was little going on he did not know about. There was little he knew about he was not prepared to sell.

McAllister had summoned Shugs to a meeting. As ever, they met late at night in the largely deserted carpark behind the Forth Bridges Hotel.

'New car, Shugs?'

'Jaguar. XK8. Nice, isn't it?'

'Business must be on the up and up. Should I take an interest?'

'From what I hear, you've got your own problems to deal with.'

'Meaning?'

'Please, let's not play games. Gallagher walking out of the High Court is not going to look good for you, now is it?'

'Gallagher will get done. He's guilty.'

'He didn't kill the Mad Dog.'

'How do you know?'

'Take my word for it'

'Did he kill Boyle?'

'You're the detective.'

'I can probably increase the payment, if the info is good.'

Shugs swept his hand towards the car.

'As you said, business must be good. I'm thinking of rationalising some of my activities. Closing down on some options. Modernisation programme, so to speak.'

'Meaning?'

'Meaning, I'm serving you notice that our partnership is hereby dissolved. Not that you can complain: you've done well out of it, Superintendent.'

'I've always made sure you were well rewarded.'

'This will be our last meeting. You want McGarry don't you?'

'You know?'

'I know he's a sicko. He would chop his granny's tits off just to see if his knife needed sharpened.'

'Is he in Glasgow?'

'Christ, for a PO-LICE Superintendent you can be clueless at times. Of course he's in Glasgow. Your lawyer pal knows that.'

'Why has McGarry been at Muirhead?'

'I repeat. You're the detective.'

'Is he working on his own? For someone? I know, I'm the detective.'

Shugs went into his jacket and pulled out an envelope.

'As you can see, I'm wearing gloves. The stuff inside was not written by me and I haven't handled it or the envelope. It will not self-destruct, so I'd be grateful if you would not leave it lying around.'

'How much?'

'Please. I'm offended. Let's say it's a farewell gift from me to you.'

Shugs turned and walked towards his car.

'I may come after you one day.'

Shugs stopped. He turned round slowly.

'As you said, the partnership is dissolved. That means we're business rivals.'

McAllister held out his hand.

'Rivals I can live with. Enemies?'

'Rivals.'

Shugs nodded and walked towards the Jaguar.

Back in his more modest vehicle, McAllister watched as Shugs drove out of the carpark. He switched on his map light, opened the envelope and read the contents with increasing interest.

'Well, well, well. Right, young man. Time for you and I to have a few words, I think. And soon!'

Chapter Ten

'Your full name is David Ian Taylor?', Matthews commenced.

'Yes.'

'An Acting Detective Constable with Strathclyde Police, twenty-four years old, five years police service.'

'Yes sir.'

'On the 16th of March were you one of a number of officers who attended the scene of the shooting of the now deceased Kevin Boyle?'

'Yes.'

'You would perform various duties, I've no doubt, but there is only one matter I want to ask you about. Did you examine the bonnet of the BMW car?'

'Yes.'

'Why?'

'I wanted to see if it was warm or cold to get some idea of how long the car may have been there.'

'And?'

'It was stone cold.'

'Now, some time later, were you on duty in an interview room when Mr Gallagher was being questioned by detective officers?'

'I was.'

'We have heard evidence about the contents of these interviews, but what was your function there?'

'I was to supervise the prisoner. Sometimes the CID like to leave the room to discuss things. I was there to keep an eye on Gallagher.'

'At any time did you engage him in conversation?'

'No. In these situations you are expected to say nothing.'

'How many times were you alone with Mr Gallagher?'

'Three, perhaps four.'

'Did he say anything to you?'

'The first two or three times he made some comments, about nothing in particular.'

'Give the jury some examples.'

'He asked me why I was there, why he could not be trusted on his own, whether they thought he would steal the tape recorder. He said he was bored answering the questions, that he wasn't going to hang around much longer. That sort of thing.'

'And you said nothing?'

'Nothing.'

'Indeed, did you really pay much attention to what was being said?'

'I paid attention just in case he said something important. But there was nothing to make a note of, for example.'

'Were you alone with Gallagher shortly before he was charged with murder?'

'I was.'

'Did he say something then?'

'Yes.'

'Did his demeanour change?'

'He had been quite relaxed. Laid-back, I suppose. When the two CID officers left again he became quite agitated. He started to walk about the room. He began to mutter about the officers. He said they were stupid. They knew fuck all. He asked me if I agreed. The only time I spoke was to ask him to be patient. Then he became angry and shouted at me. He told me I was just a dummy standing there. That he was willing to bet I thought I was just as smart as the rest of them.'

'What else did he say?'

'He said, "Well, I'll show you who the smart bastard really is. I gave Boyle what he deserved and neither you nor they wankers will ever prove it".'

' "I gave Boyle what he deserved and neither you nor they wankers will ever prove it?" ' Matthews enunciated the words slowly and deliberately to allow them to sink in and to maximise their effect.

'Yes.'

'What was your reaction to this?'

'I could not believe it. I was in a bit of a panic, I suppose. I just did not know what to do.'

'What did you do?'

Just after he said this, Superintendent McAllister came in to charge Mr Gallagher.'

'What was Mr Gallagher's demeanour when Mr McAllister came in?'

'The instant the door opened he switched to being laid-back though he did blow up when he was charged.'

'When did you report what had been said to you?'

'When the accused was taken to be finger-printed.'

'Who did you tell?'

'The two officers who had been doing the interviewing. They told me to put it in a statement at once.'

'Is there any doubt that Mr Gallagher said these words to you?'

'No sir, none at all. He said it.'

Matthews sat down.

Muirhead glanced at the jury as he prepared to cross-examine. Once again he could feel a number of icy stares emanating from them.

'It would seem, constable, that Mr Gallagher confessed to you, confessed to murder, indeed.'

'I thought so.'

'Why do you think he wanted to confess to you?'

'You better ask him, sir, with respect.'

'No, I'm asking you.'

'I don't know. I repeat, ask him.'

'The two of you were alone when this was said?'

'When what was said?'

'Don't play games with me, constable. When he confessed.'

'Yes, we were alone.'

'The rest of the time there were at least four of you in the interview room.'

'Yes.'

'And when four of you were present, Gallagher repeatedly and constantly denied involvement in the death of Kevin Boyle?'

'You could say that.'

'I just did.'

The battle was joined.

'There was a tape recorder present. Wasn't there?'

'Yes.'

'Yet that tape recorder does not seem to have heard any confession from Mr Gallagher?'

'It was only switched on when the CID were present.'

'What is the normal procedure when a person says something important, something incriminating?'

'I'm not sure I understand.'

'I'm sure you do. Are police officers still issued with notebooks, despite this technological age in which we live?'

'Yes.'

'Then let me try again. What is the procedure when someone, such as a prime suspect in a murder inquiry, says something important, something incriminating?'

'You make a note of it in your notebook, if you can.'

'Why?'

'So you have a record of it and to act as an aide memoire.'

'Did you make a note?'

'No.'

'Could you have noted it down?'

'Not in the interview room.'

'Why not?'

'If I had tried to take out my notebook and write down what Gallagher had said, he would have seen me and he would just have denied it.'

'So you thought about noting it?'

'Well no, not really.'

'And are you seriously suggesting that by not noting the comment you thought Mr Gallagher was more likely to admit it?'

'No, I suppose not.'

'So you chose to ignore – procedure?'

'I just didn't make a note of it. I didn't think it was necessary.'

'Have you ever ignored any other police procedures?'

'I don't understand.'

'Your father was a policeman, a senior policeman.'

'My father is dead.'

'I know that. I knew him. He was a fine officer. It was a tragedy he killed himself. Why did he kill himself?'

'I've heard you were hard Mr Muirhead. I didn't know you were ruthless. Is there nothing you won't do to win? We haven't been able to bury my father yet and you drag his memory into this just to upset me, soften me up...'

Cowden intervened. 'Calm yourself, Constable Taylor. Mr Muirhead, this line of questioning is disgraceful. What is the relevance, if any, of this and think before you answer. I intend to note it carefully – very carefully indeed.'

'I won't pursue it.'

'What?'

'I won't pursue it – for the time being.'

Lord Cowden was seething with rage. Not because of the questions or their nature. Not because there was a compassionate side to his nature. Not even because he thought that the evidence of a policeman should simply be accepted. He knew Muirhead was up to something and, yet again, he did not know what.

During the lull occasioned by this exchange, Taylor had taken the opportunity to suck in a few calming breaths. This bastard couldn't know – could he?

'Back to police procedures then. When you take a statement from a witness, is it important to find out what that person actually knows? To avoid putting ideas into his head? Not to pressure him into saying what the police believe the evidence to be? What the police want the evidence to be?'

He knows!

'Well?'

'Mr Muirhead, which of these questions do you want answered?'

Oh, Jesus Christ, he knows!

'Your father would know. Wouldn't he?'

'Mr Muirhead!'

His Lordship's voice was raised, but Taylor was almost screaming.

'I just wanted the wino to tell the truth!'

Taylor slumped onto the seat in the witness box. With his head in his hands he continued to talk, but not to the court. This was a very private conversation. It could only be heard because of the silence which had descended around him. Every listener felt as if he was an interloper intruding into private grief.

'I had to keep an eye on him. I knew he wouldn't turn up. If he did – drunk probably. Weak. Say anything. Anything. Dirty. Smelly. Not believe him. Just cleaned him up. He saw him. He must have seen him. Evil. Evil. Do what they like. Dad said they deserved what they got. Dad would have done it too. Arrogant bastards, think they can get away with anything. Walk around the streets as if they owned them. Gallagher did it. Killed him. Even if he was rubbish. No loss, really. But a chance to put Gallagher away. For good. I just wanted him to tell the truth.'

Without prompting, Taylor rose to his feet. His expression disclosed that only part of his mind was still in the court room. Muirhead continued.

'You wanted him to say what you thought was the truth. Isn't that right?'

'He must have seen him.'

'You had been a uniformed constable, had you not?'

'Yes.'

'Then you were given a chance to work with the CID, by your father, and you decided to make a name for yourself?'

'No.'

'You threatened Mr McPhee?'

'He's weak. He's nothing. A nobody. An old drunk. Why would I waste my career on the likes of him?'

'Did your father ask you that?'

'Leave him out of it.'

'Your father found out that you had tried to pervert the course of justice.'

'Lies.'

'Did he confront you with it?'

'No.'

'What was he going to do? An honest cop. Forget what he knew or report that his son, a policeman, a policeman's son, had committed a serious crime?'

'Liar. You think you're clever. What do you know about the streets? What goes on out there? If I was trying to make a name for myself, as you imply, why would I care if anyone found out? You deny that Mr Muirhead.'

Muirhead had been firing questions at the witness. His voice now slowed right down. So calm, it was almost matter of fact.

'You tried to make a name for yourself, all right. You fabricated evidence against my client. You were alone with him for a few moments. Alone. No tape recorder. You made up his confession. Deliberately. Wickedly. Cynically. Then, not satisfied with that, you leant on Sammy McPhee. Your twisted mind wasn't prepared just to do Mr Gallagher for one murder, you wanted to do him for two. You didn't just pervert the course of justice. You came into this court and lied and lied and lied again. You committed perjury. You deny that Mr Taylor?'

The whole court waited for the reply.

The whole court waited – in vain.

'We're waiting – patiently.'

'It's not true.'

'Well, I think we'll leave that to the jury, shall we?'

When Grant McAllister entered the witness box he could tell from the atmosphere in court that something dramatic had happened. He had passed Taylor in the corridor on his way out. His face was ashen. He turned his eyes away from his superior. Just as well. McAllister shot him a look which would have knocked him flat on his back.

McAllister's appearance was essentially a formality. He described what he had seen when he arrived at the scene of the shooting, the various measures he had instructed to set the inquiry in motion and his decision to have Gallagher brought in for interview. The officers conducting the interrogation had kept him advised of Gallagher's answers. In consultation with the Procurator Fiscal he had taken the decision to prefer the charge of murder.

He described Gallagher's reaction to the news that he was to face such a charge but expressed the view that this was neither unusual nor unexpected. As with his colleagues, he would not hold it against a man that he became upset when charged with such a serious matter.

'You did not charge Mr Gallagher with the murder of the man, Clark.'

'That is correct, Mr Muirhead.'

'Indeed, at no time did you put such a charge of murder to Mr Gallagher'

'That is correct.'

'When did you discover that Mr Gallagher was to be charged with the two killings?'

'Before the indictment was served, I was telephoned by Mr Harris, the Procurator Fiscal, and told that this was the decision of Crown Office.'

'So, the decision was taken in Edinburgh, at the Crown Office, the office of the Lord Advocate?'

'Yes.'

'But you, the officer in charge of the investigation, did not deem it appropriate to charge Mr Gallagher with Clark's murder?'

'Correct.'

'Did you know Kevin Boyle, in a professional capacity?'

'I knew of him.'

'Did the police believe him to be involved in criminal activity?'

Muirhead felt a tug at his gown.

'If I may have a moment, my Lord?'

His Lordship nodded, none too graciously.

'What is it, Jack?'

'James, you can shout at me if you like, but is this question altogether wise? If we put Boyle's character in issue, the Depute will do a tit for tat. We're not exactly as white as the driven snow. If they lead evidence that we are a bloody gangster, is that not going to make Warwick more credible? Surely the boy has to give evidence? The Depute will have a field day if he can ask him about some of his past activities.'

'He's not giving evidence.'

'What?'

'He's not...'

'I heard you. Am I not allowed a say in this? I am the man's solicitor.'

'You will get your say, Jack, but he will not be giving evidence. At least, he'll have to climb over me to get to that box.'

'OK, James, you're the boss, I suppose.'

'Yes, Jack, I am the boss. Sorry.'

'When you're ready, Mr Muirhead. We don't have all day.'

'Of course, my Lord. Can you answer my question, Superintendent?'

'Kevin Boyle and other members of his family have been significant criminal figures in Glasgow for many years.'

'Involved in what kind of activities?'

'Illegal money-lending. Extortion. Intimidation. The use of violence in a variety of ways. Take your pick really.'

'May the ladies and gentlemen of the jury take it that a man like Kevin Boyle would have a number of enemies?'

'Occupational hazard, I should have thought.'

'Would these enemies tend to be criminals?'

'A fair percentage of them would be, yes.'

'And would be people who might be prepared to use violence?'

'Yes.'

'Lethal violence?'

'Possibly.'

Mike Matthews was scribbling away furiously. Had the maestro actually played a bum note? Normally the Crown cannot disclose the previous character of an accused until after a verdict has been returned. A man must not be convicted of a particular robbery just because that is what he ordinarily does for a living. However, if an accused brings out the bad character of his alleged victim, then he runs the risk that the prosecution will be entitled to expose his character, warts and all, to the public gaze.

Matthews not only had a list of Gallagher's previous convictions, thefts, breaches of the peace and a number of assaults, but was sitting on a bulky police file listing his other activities which had not resulted in court appearances. He was running an alibi defence. He was claiming to have been elsewhere. He had to go into the witness box. Matthews relished the prospect. It never occurred to him to ask himself why Muirhead was prepared to risk leaving his client so badly exposed. He had done so, and that was good enough. Matthews had been handed a gift horse and, given the chance, he would ride it for all he was worth.

'Was Kevin Boyle involved in drug dealing?'

'There was information to that effect, but there was not enough evidence to justify charges.'

'Have any other members of the Boyle family been involved in illegal drug dealing?'

'Not so far as we know.'

'And would we be right in understanding that there are large sums of money to be made in dealing in illegal drugs?'

'Undoubtedly. Some people make a very large profit.'

'And are some people prepared to use violence to protect their financial interests?'

'Certainly.'

'So, Kevin Boyle was a man who probably had a number of enemies who would be men capable of using significant violence to further their own ends?'

'That's fair.'

'Did Mr Boyle have a man working for him by the name of Thomas McGarry?'

'Yes.'

'Would it be fair to describe him as a minder, a bodyguard?'

'Yes.'

'Someone who was paid to be with Mr Boyle, to look after him, shall we say?'

'I suppose so.'

'Where is Mr McGarry?'

'I do not know.'

'Have the police been looking for him?'

'Don't answer that question, please.'

The Depute was on his feet.

'My Lord, I object to this. I do not know what my learned friend is suggesting, but if he is seeking to implicate this man McGarry in some way, then he has lodged no special defence of incrimination against him.'

'My Lord, I am not suggesting anything. I am simply asking about the whereabouts of someone one might have expected to be near Mr Boyle at the time of the incident.'

'Mr Muirhead, I cannot ever remember you asking a question in which you were not suggesting anything. I will allow you to proceed, but I will be keeping a very careful watch on the direction in which this is going.'

His Lordship could smell a rat when one scampered across his court.

'I am, as ever, very much obliged to your Lordship for his forbearance and indulgence.'

'Just get on with it.'

'Well, Superintendent?'

'We have been looking for Mr McGarry since the death of Kevin Boyle. So far we have found no trace of him.'

'Does he have an accent, so far as you know?'

'Yes. Irish.'

'Thank you.'

Muirhead walked towards his seat, nodding sagely as he went.

'Oh, just one other matter. Your former colleague, DI Taylor, committed suicide, tragically?'

'Tragically, yes.'

'During the course of this trial?'

'Yes.'

'After the witness Samuel McPhee had given evidence?'

'Yes.'

'Did you become aware of the allegations made by Mr McPhee to the effect that he had been threatened or at least pressured by police officers?'

'Yes.'

'Was DI Taylor investigating these allegations?'

'On my instructions, yes.'

The animated conversation in the jury box and public gallery was interrupted by the Advocate Depute rising to re-examine.

'Mr McAllister, you say that Kevin Boyle would have had a number of enemies among the criminal fraternity?'

'That is correct, yes.'

'Would these enemies include Charlie Gallagher, the accused? The man charged with his murder?'

'I believe so, yes.'

'Thank you, Superintendent.'

'Members of the jury. Lunch.'

         ●   ●   ●

The door to the retiring room was slammed with such force it nearly bounced off its hinges.

'Christ, James, why?'

'Why what, Jack?'

'Why the high-risk strategy? You've done a superb job so far. You've had the Crown on the run since we started. The jury must be wondering what is going on. Surely it would take a pretty perverse bunch to convict the boy in the face of that evidence?'

'You can never be sure. You know that as well as I do, Jack.'

'Exactly my point. The Crown have no real motive in this case and you're in danger of giving them one. The Depute might now be able to bring out that the Gallaghers have been into drugs for bloody years. There's your motive. Business rivalry. Criminal business rivalry.'

'Calm down, Jack.'

'Calm down! Calm down! I don't mind you being an arrogant sod, James, but you're not infallible. You're not God. You just occasionally think you are.'

'Will you listen?'

'Why should I listen to you? You paid no bloody attention to me back there in court. I thought this was supposed to be a team effort?'

'Come on, guys, take it easy. The enemy is out there. No point in arguing amongst ourselves.'

'It's OK, Donald. Listen, Jack. I know the case seems to be going better than we might have hoped. I agree with what you say about motive.'

'So...'

'The so is, we've still got a client who has been identified and who has confessed – twice. And there is still the forensic evidence to come. Think about it. What single factor gets a man done more than anything else?'

'Go on.'

'It's a jury thinking, "If it wasn't him, who was it?" Add to that, the fact, and it is a fact, that no Glasgow jury is going to think that a man charged with two gangland murders is an innocent abroad. Of course they'll think he's a villain. They may even think he and Boyle were deadly rivals. In fact, I don't care if they think that Gallagher hated Boyle more than any other man living or dead. The point is, he is not alone. The jury know now that all sorts of people out there had good reason to bear ill-will towards Kevin – to want him out of the way.'

'That's all very well, James, but what if Gallagher gives evidence? He'll be bad enough as a witness if he gets wound up. Now that you've put character in issue, Matthews will crucify him.'

'I'm not putting him in the box.'

'Christ, we've got an alibi! He has to give evidence.'

'No, he does not. I never intended to lead him as a witness – unless things went so badly there was no choice. If he goes in the box, he'll be bloody hopeless. He'll lose the place and come over as the evil little shit he is. If the jury don't like him, and you can put your mortgage on that, there is every danger they will do him regardless of the state of the Crown case.'

'Are you proposing to call any of his witnesses?'

'Yes. Some.'

'Then the Depute and Cowden will jump up and down if you don't call Gallagher.'

'That is a risk I'm prepared to take. Better that than have Gallagher ending up in bits in the witness box.'

'Makes a lot of sense.'

'So you go along with this?'

'Not just because the man thinks he's God, but yes, I do. Absolutely.'

'Two against one.'

Morton stared out of the window across Glasgow Green. The silence was interrupted only by the sound of Muirhead lighting his pipe. Anderson gestured to his senior. The suggestion was plain. Make the peace.

'Jack...'

'It's all right. I wouldn't have instructed you guys, wouldn't ever instruct you guys, if I didn't trust you, and your judgement. I just feel we are so close. And I still don't believe he did it. I want to win this case. I badly want to win this case.'

'So do we, Jack. So do we – just as badly. Let's go and poison ourselves with the canteen pie, beans and chips.'

'I'll pass that.'

'Very droll, Jack.'

'Forensic this afternoon?'

'Yes. And if it's of any interest to you, I don't think he killed them – either of them.'

'See you after lunch...What did you just say?'

      ❀   ❀   ❀

'My Lord, the final witness for the prosecution is Dr Malcolm Bruce.'

The senior forensic scientist from Strathclyde Police took the oath, peering at the judge through bottle-glass spectacles. His shirt-collar looked as if it had never seen an iron, his tie was askew and the suit he wore only fitted where it touched. He looked the part of the eccentric boffin. In reality he was one of the country's leading forensic experts and had a mind like a steel trap. He was one of the few people who enjoyed being cross-examined by James Muirhead. He relished the challenge, even although he regarded the lawyer as his intellectual inferior in all matters scientific.

He was asked to identify two blood samples, one taken from Kevin Boyle and one from Charlie Gallagher. He explained that on analysis it was revealed that the men had blood groups which could be readily distinguished.

'Kevin Boyle had the blood group EAP BA. This can be found in 42.6% of the population. Gallagher had the group EAP A.'

He then confirmed that he had examined the car in which Boyle's body had been found and had taken a series of blood and tissue samples from inside the vehicle. Not surprisingly these were entirely consistent with having come from Kevin Boyle.

'Look please at label seventy-one.'

A black leather jacket was handed to him by the macer.

'That is a black leather jacket which you examined?'

'Yes.'

'A police label is attached to it. Please tell us where it was found.'

'It says that it was found in a wardrobe in a bedroom belonging to Charles Gallagher.'

'Did you find any blood on the jacket?'

Bruce spread out the garment so that it could be clearly seen by judge and jury. He had given evidence many times and knew how to present it to best effect.

'On the left front, just below the breast pocket, I found three blood spots. These were cut out for analysis and the holes are now circled in yellow chalk.'

'What, if anything, is the significance of the blood appearing as spots?'

'If blood is transferred by direct contact, it will appear as an ill-defined smear. When blood is airborne and lands on an object it will appear as a spot.'

'So the blood you found had travelled through the air and landed on the jacket?'

'That is correct.'

'Were you able to group the blood?'

'There was insufficient material for conventional testing but we subjected it to DNA analysis.'

'Now, what is that?'

'Deoxyribonucleic acid or DNA is the term used for the genetic material which makes up the human body. Except in the case of identical twins, each individual's DNA is unique. Putting it very simply, it explains why we are all different, why some of us have blue eyes, some brown, some have fair hair, some black and so on. If you could unravel a person's DNA it would stretch to the moon. We take a piece of DNA and identify certain characteristics, then we can make comparisons. After testing, we can produce a picture of the DNA which looks a bit like a supermarket barcode.'

'Did you do that in the present case?'

'We DNA-tested the blood samples from Gallagher and Boyle. Unfortunately, the spots were so small that we could not carry out a full test on them. We used a procedure known as DNA amplification or Polymerase Chain Reaction.'

'That's a bit complicated for me.'

'We target specific areas of DNA which we know vary between individuals. We then copy this area many times with the result that the initial quantity of targeted DNA is greatly increased.'

'You then have material which you can test?'

'Precisely.'

'What were your findings?'

'Mr Boyle's blood had the types HUMVWA 14,19 HUMTHO1 7,8 HUMF133A1 7,7 HUMFES 11,12.

'Mr Gallagher's blood had the types HUMUWA 14,15 HUMTHO1 9,9 HUMF13A1 5,6 HUMFES 11,12.'

'They appear different?'

'Quite distinguishable.'

'Did you obtain a result for the spots on the jacket?'

'We were partially successful. We identified two types. HUMVWA 14,19 and HUMTHO1 7,8.'

'What does this mean?'

'It means that the blood spots did not come from Charles Gallagher but could have come from Kevin Boyle.'

'Can you put a figure on the chances of these coming from Mr Boyle?'

'We estimate that it is seven hundred times more likely that the blood spots came from Kevin Boyle than an unrelated individual.'

'Does that mean you are saying it is Kevin Boyle's blood?'

'No, it means I am saying that it is seven hundred times more likely to be the blood of Kevin Boyle rather than an unrelated individual. I can say that it is certainly not the blood of the person whose sample bears the name of Charles Gallagher.'

'Thank you.'

'Mr Muirhead?'

'Putting it bluntly, if I may; one in every seven hundred people have blood which could match the results you obtained for the spots.'

'Correct. I said we were only partially successful.'

'I heard you the first time. What is the population of Scotland?'

'I'm not exactly sure. Around five million or so.'

'Assuming it is just over five million, then over seven thousand two hundred people would have blood which would fit your results?'

'That seems right.'

'And in Britain alone, never mind anywhere else, nearly one hundred thousand people would fit?'

'Again, that is correct.'

'How many of them live in Glasgow?'

'I really have no idea.'

'For all you know, they all live in Glasgow?'

'I would have thought, statistically, that is most unlikely.'

'I'm talking facts, not statistics. Do you know how many of them do live in the Glasgow area?'

'As a matter of fact – no.'

'More to the point, how many of them were in Glasgow on the day that Kevin Boyle died?'

'Really, Mr Muirhead, that is a ridiculous question to ask me. How am I supposed to know?'

'As you know I ask the questions and you answer them, but let me turn the tables. You haven't got a clue. Have you?'

'If you say so.'

'These spots, they were tiny?'

'They were very small.'

'How long had they been on the jacket?'

'I could not say.'

'Weeks, months, years?'

'If the jacket was not cleaned, they could certainly have been there for a number of months.'

'You examined them at the end of May?'

'Yes.'

'So they could have been there for some months prior to the 16th of March?'

'They could have been, yes.'

'Did you visit the locus before the car was removed?'

'Yes.'

'And carried out an examination?'

'Yes.'

'Did you find any traces of blood on the outside of the car or on the roadway beside the car?'

'None at all.'

'Let us assume this blood came from Kevin Boyle. These three tiny, nay, minuscule, spots were the only spots to fly from Mr Boyle's head and land on an object outside the vehicle, that object, as luck would have it, being a jacket worn by the alleged gunman?'

'I wouldn't go that far.'

'Why not? There was no trace of blood anywhere else outside the car.'

'None that was found.'

'Does that mean there may have been blood there and you managed to miss it?'

'We conduct our business in a thorough manner.'

'You told me that. So if there was blood on the car or the roadway you would have expected to find it?'

'We would have hoped to find it, but if the spot was very small, it may not have been possible to detect it.'

'Look at the book of photographs taken at the locus. We can see a mass of blood, bone and brain tissue spattered inside the car. Despite that, only three tiny, minuscule spots were detected on a jacket belonging to Mr Gallagher, and nowhere else?'

'With that, I agree.'

'And these spots are of indeterminate age?'

'Yes.'

'And they could have come from thousands of people?'

'Including Mr Boyle.'

'But thousands and thousands of people?'

'Statistically, yes.'

'Factually, yes?'

'I suppose so.'

The Advocate Depute rose to ask his last question in the presentation of the Crown case.

'Could the blood spots on the jacket belonging to Mr Gallagher have come from Kevin Boyle?'

'Yes, they could.'

When the witness left the court, Matthews got to his feet.

'My Lord, as I indicated, I have no other evidence to lead. I have carefully considered the material available to the Crown on charges one and two. I am not satisfied it would be right for the Crown to proceed on either of these charges and consequently I withdraw them. I do intend to proceed on the charge of the murder of Kevin Boyle.'

'Very well, Mr Depute. It is a matter for you. Stand up, Gallagher. The Crown having withdrawn charges one and two, I acquit you in respect of each of these matters. You may sit down.'

The noise level in court increased dramatically accompanied by a flurry of activity.

Gallagher sat in the dock staring anxiously towards Jack Morton who hurried to explain this latest development to his client.

Anderson turned to speak to Muirhead but was halted in his tracks by the slightest movement of the hand of his senior who remained stony-faced and impassive.

The public gallery was debating exactly what had occurred and its significance. No one seemed entirely sure what they had just witnessed. The body language of the jury clearly demonstrated a lack of comprehension.

Lord Cowden turned to face them.

'Ladies and gentlemen, in our procedure the Advocate Depute is the master of the instance. He is perfectly entitled to evaluate the evidence available to him and to decide upon which charges he wishes to proceed. His reasoning is a matter for him. He has withdrawn charges one and two and it was my duty to acquit the panel in respect of these matters. This I have done. As a result, you will only be required to reach a decision in respect of charge three.

'Now, ladies and gentlemen, it has been a long day and I have no doubt Mr Muirhead will wish to consider his position before embarking upon his defence case, if that is what he intends to do. Tomorrow morning, ten o'clock.'

●　　　●　　　●

The interview room in the bowels of Glasgow High Court is a cheerless place bathed in a stygian gloom. The concrete floor, high ceiling, white-tiled walls, sixty-watt bulb lighting all combine to give it the character of a Victorian public toilet – minus the urinals.

'If I don't fucking tell them I had fuck all to do with this, I'm going to get done. You bastards don't seem to give a shit about that.'

'Mr Gallagher...'

'I keep telling you, I never fucking shot him.'

'Mr Gallagher! Sit down. Calm down. Listen – please.'

'Come on, Charlie. There's no point in shouting and bawling at Mr Muirhead. He's done a great job so far – as you know perfectly well. He's already got you off one murder charge, for goodness sake. We must decide what we are going to do now. It's sort of important to get it right. Now just listen to what the man has to say to you.'

Gallagher sat down heavily on a rickety chair at the small wooden table located in the centre of the room.

'Mr Gallagher, we must decide if you are going to go into the witness box. Ultimately, it is your decision. I cannot tell you what to do. I can only advise you and certainly I will not force you one way or another. Is that clear?'

'Look, I'm not fucking stupid. Don't treat me like a fucking...'

'Come on, Mr Gallagher, do us all a favour and stop this nonsense. No one has treated you in any way other than with respect. Christ, we've all done our best for you, but every time there are difficult decisions to take, all you do is shout and bawl at me. No thanks to you, you have been acquitted of one murder and you have a good chance of being acquitted of another one. Now, if you want to go into the witness box and blow it to hell and back, that is up to you. All I want to do is give you the best advice I can.'

'I've been locked up for months – doing my head in.'

'I appreciate that.'

'Fuck it, I'm shiting myself, man. If I don't take the stand they'll think I've got something to hide. I'll get done.'

'That is just not so, Mr Gallagher. Please listen to me.'

Gallagher's outburst was born of terror and frustration – not anger or resentment. He sat clenching and unclenching his hands. He stared wildly ahead. He seemed to be locked into his own private world. His shirt was soaked with sweat. He was not a pretty sight and smelt worse.

Jack Morton handed him a cigarette. Gallagher's hands shook so much he could not navigate it towards his mouth. Morton took it, lit it and placed it between Gallagher's lips. He inhaled deeply. Four long drags later, the cigarette was almost finished. The combination of deep breathing and nicotine had a calming effect upon him.

'Go on.'

'If you give evidence and you are believed – you win – problem solved. But Matthews will have a go at you. He will push and prod and get right under your skin, quite deliberately. If you cannot keep your temper, you know what happens when you blow. If the jury think you're lying or if they don't like you, you are in deep, deep trouble. No matter how bad the Crown case is, they may convict you on the basis that if you're not telling the truth when you say you weren't there, you must be guilty. It's not supposed to work that way – but often it does. It is a very dangerous game we play and you are right in the middle of it.'

'What do you want me to do?'

'I think you should stay in the dock. Play safe.'

'What about my alibi? Are you just going to ditch it?'

'I think you know that some of your witnesses will not be terribly impressive. Their granny wouldn't believe them if they told her the Pope was a Catholic. One or two will stand up, just. I think we call the best of them and leave it at that. It's the old "better safe than sorry" principle. At least that's my advice. But you should ask Mr Anderson and especially Mr Morton. After all, he is your solicitor.'

Gallagher looked towards Jack Morton, plaintively.

'I've had to give this a lot of thought, naturally. Normally I believe that a jury will want to hear the accused's side of the story. But Mr Muirhead is right. You won't be a very good witness. I don't think you'll do yourself justice. If you lose your temper, and you will, that could be enough to kill off our chances. I don't honestly see you convincing a jury, Charlie. I go along with senior counsel – stay out of the box.'

'Mr Gallagher, I'm only junior counsel, but for what it's worth, I agree with the advice you have just been given.'

Gallagher returned his attention to Muirhead.

'Am I going to get off?'

'I can't give you a guarantee.'

'Christ!'

'The case is better than I could have hoped for. I just don't want to do anything to ruin what we have achieved. I suspect most of the jury will have made up their minds already. If we can lead some reasonable alibi evidence together with one or two bits and pieces I have up my sleeve, I think you have a very fair chance.'

'A very fair chance! What the fuck is that?'

'It's a damn sight more than many people get in this place. But you must bear this in mind. You get one shot at it. If you give evidence and it goes bad, you can't change your mind afterwards. The clock does not go backwards. If you don't give evidence and you get done, same thing applies. No third umpire. No stewards' inquiry. Think on this.

'You know if you will be telling the truth in the witness box. I've only got your word for it. If you're not telling the truth, the whole truth, you are the one who runs the risk of being caught out. You must do what you think is best.'

'This is my life we are talking about.'

'I know.'

'I could get done – couldn't I?'

'Yes.'

'At least that's honest. You're the lawyer. Do what you think is best. Just be fucking right!'

⚫   ⚫   ⚫

'Are you ready to charge them?'

McAllister looked from the papers in front of him to the Detective Constable.

' I think so, Boss. It looks pretty solid to me. They've just been interviewed and the story is wonderful.'

'What's the background?'

'Two guys are seen hanging around outside the Bank of Scotland in Anderson Drive. Woman gets suspicious, dials treble nine. Before the cavalry gets there, security firm has arrived and starts carting the money inside. One of the two guys produces an iron bar, whacks a guard on the leg, his mate grabs the money, off they go. Uniforms arrive, see the two running so they chase them up the street. Pair of them jump in a taxi, would you believe, which gets all of fifty yards before it stops at traffic lights. Nicked – money and all.'

'Pretty solid indeed – more like cast iron. Do we know them?'

'No, not really. Few minor thefts each, nothing in this league. Looks like a get-rich quick scheme that didn't quite make it.'

'It'll do for six years a-piece.'

'I would have thought so.'

'OK, charge them and get them locked up. Do they want a lawyer?'

'Yes. I'll call the duty solicitor.'

'Fair enough. Oh, you said the story was wonderful. Give me the punch-line. I need cheering up.'

'They accept they were running up the street – but only to get a taxi. When the cab stopped at the lights, two complete strangers run past. One of them stops, turns back, shoves a bag into the back of the cab and says "Here boys, it's fucking Christmas!" Then, crivvens, jings, help ma Boab, the polis arrive and all this is a terrible misunderstanding.'

McAllister laughed. He actually enjoyed the experience. It was quite some time since he had laughed.

'Not bad, is it, Boss.'

'It's different. You know, it's just daft enough to take a jury's fancy. Cut no corners. ID parade for the witnesses. Do the whole bit. Meantime, charge them.'

'Right, Boss.'

McAllister returned to the file of papers on his desk. He read them because he had to, not because they held any real interest for him.

'Vin ordinaire!'

Castlemilk in Glasgow. Apache country. Two drunks had been wending their way home after a night's refreshing. They came upon the house of a man who had once allegedly offended the relative of a friend of a pal of one or other of them – it was not clear which. Probably didn't matter. They proceeded to demonstrate their disapproval of this perceived slight by throwing bricks through a window.

The householder, not surprisingly, took offence and left his abode to discuss the issue. Unfortunately, to emphasise any point he wished to make, he took with him a machete and a butcher's cleaver, the kind of implements everyone in Castlemilk seems to have readily to hand. During the ensuing debate, one of the two brick chuckers sustained a wound to his neck which severed his carotid artery. He died – of course.

'Windows,' muttered McAllister. 'Single biggest cause of serious crime in the West of Scotland. If they boarded up all the windows you would cut the crime rate by half. Waste! Total bloody waste! One dead, one going down for murder, and all because of a window.'

'Call for you, Boss, line two.'

'Superintendent McAllister.'

'Mr McAllister, I assume that you're still looking for Tom McGarry?'

'Who is this please?'

'I'm sure if you think about it you will remember my voice.'

'Yes… I apologise. I did not really expect you to be telephoning me.'

'Perhaps not.'

'Are you still looking for Tom McGarry? No games please.'

'Yes, I am.'

'I can tell you how to find him.'

'Where?'

'Patience, Superintendent. Certainly not over the telephone.'

'What do you suggest?'

'I have things I want to say to you, to discuss with you. If you meet me, I'll tell you how to find McGarry.'

'Where and when?'

'I'll come alone. I expect you to do likewise. No tape recorders. No cameras in the distance with telescopic lenses. No gasvans with people pretending to be working. Come alone or not at all.'

'How do I know I can trust you?'

'Please, Superintendent. I'm prepared to trust you. Don't hardly imagine that I'm going to attack you in some way. Nor am I likely to pull down my knickers and scream rape. For all I know, you may be recording this conversation. If I wanted to do you harm, I'm sure you don't doubt that I could arrange it without giving you advance notice.'

'That sounds like a threat.'

'Not at all.'

Sharper tone.

'I repeat – no games, please. I need an answer.'

McAllister reflected for a moment. It was seriously bad practice to meet someone in circumstances such as those requested without some form of back-up. On the other hand, this was a potentially significant development. It was something he could not ignore and he had little doubt that the terms of the contract were not open for negotiation.

'Well?'

'Where and when?'

'You will come alone.'

A statement.

'I will come alone. As you would say, no games.'

'Good. Tomorrow night. The car park at the Exhibition Centre. 11.30. I'll be driving a red N-registered Volkswagen Golf. It'll be up to you to find me.'

'I will.'

'I don't doubt it. Goodnight, Superintendent.'

McAllister was relieved that the proposed meeting place was not in the back of beyond. At least he would not be totally isolated. On the other hand, he suspected he was not likely to be in any real danger. Nonetheless, he found himself excited at the prospect of the events which lay ahead. The prospect of getting McGarry was highly pleasing. The prospect of what he might be told was intriguing.

'Well, Mr McGarry, perhaps you and I will get the chance to have a bit of a chat – at long last. Enjoy your night – the good guys are coming to get you, I hope.'

A head appeared round his door.

'You said something, Boss?'

'Just wishing someone a good night.'

'Eh?'

'Forget it. It's this vin ordinaire going to my head.'

'What kind of a van?'

'I said forget it!'

Chapter Eleven

Muirhead was a solitary creature. He seldom socialised with his colleagues. He had many acquaintances but very few friends. Social niceties bored him, polite conversation irritated him, enforced gaiety annoyed him. Normally, he was perfectly at ease with his own company. And yet? And yet he was gripped by a wholly unfamiliar sensation. He felt alone. No, he felt lonely.

This case was getting to him as no other he had ever experienced. He had been threatened. His family had been threatened. He had had a gun pointed at his head. He had fallen out with his solicitor. He was fighting a running battle with the prosecutor, the judge and even his client. If he had given the wrong advice, Charlie Gallagher could go down for murder – a murder he may not have committed.

He thought of Gallagher in his cell. Solitary. Isolated. What thoughts were going through his mind? He would have to sit in the dock, his future entrusted to a man he hardly knew and fifteen strangers who owed him nothing. Fear and uncertainty eating in to him. Powerless. Impotent.

He, the lawyer, had decided Gallagher, the accused, would not give evidence. He had made sure that the man could not give evidence. Charlie would never have a more difficult choice to make, and Muirhead had taken the decision for him. Now he would have to live with it. They would both have to live with it. But for only one of them were the consequences very real.

He thought of Gallagher and shivered.

Two men from opposite backgrounds, with different lifestyles, linked together and sharing one common bond. At this moment in time, they were each very much alone.

●   ●   ●

The metallic voice – again.

'Thank you for calling 0686 174 582. Please leave your message after the tone.'

'Look, I'm getting seriously pissed off leaving messages on this damned thing. Will you make contact with me – like yesterday? I have to talk to you. Things can be sorted out. Just give me a call. Eh, please.'

The caller banged down the handset.

'Where are you, you bastard, and what the fuck are you up to?'

The phone was snatched up and a number angrily dialled.

'Any sign of him?'

'Nothing. All the boys have been out looking. We've left word everywhere we can think of. He's gone to ground and is staying there.'

'I want him underground and the sooner the better.'

'He'll surface soon. When he does, we'll get him. He's not going anywhere.'

'He has gone somewhere. Somewhere you can't find him, apparently.'

'Relax. He's no threat. He can't get to you with the boys around you and he's hardly likely to run to the polis, is he? If he stays hidden – no problem. When he surfaces – problem solved.'

'I don't want the problem solved. I want it and him eliminated – as in permanently.'

'Who do you want eliminated?'

'What?'

'I asked you who you want eliminated?'

'I didn't hear you come in.'

'That's obvious. Now tell me what you were talking about. And don't lie to me.'

'Nothing to worry about. It's just a bit of business. I'm taking care of it.'

'Don't patronise me. I've told you before that I've kept my mouth shut for far too long. No more. I want to know what's going on. If you don't tell me I WILL make it my business to find out. It's taking care of business that has got us into this mess. Now, what the hell's going on?'

'There's nothing for you to worry about.'

'Jesus Christ! Just tell me!'

'I've never heard you swear before.'

'Maybe not, but you've heard it now. There's going to be many new things around here, starting right now. So tell me, what is going on?'

'It's McGarry. I think he could cause us some trouble. Serious trouble.'

'Us?'

'Well, OK. Me then. I'm scared of him and what he might do. Not that he has any reason to want to harm you or me, for that matter.'

'Look, I think you better tell me the truth. And remember, I know a lot more than you think, and I know you – I'll know if you lie.'

*   *   *

Tom McGarry switched off the mobile phone having collected his messages – again.

'So, you're desperate to speak to me now, you little bastard. Well, it's too late, my son. It's payback time.'

He turned his attention to the horseracing on the television and snarled as the winner was announced.

'Just as well I couldn't get to the bookies. Lucky Again – would be better off in a tin of dogfood than on a racecourse.'

He cut off the sound and stared at the screen. It was time to get out of Glasgow. Back to Ireland was the best bet. Out of harm's way there were one or two people who could make good use of his special talents, as they had done in the past.

McGarry was the archetypal mercenary. He had no interest whatever in the politics of the North or the South. He favoured neither Protestant nor Catholic and worked for each against the other, sometimes simultaneously.

He looked around the depressing bedsit. It was not of the standard he preferred but as boltholes went, it was passably comfortable. Compared with the rat-infested barns he had hidden in near the Irish border, it was verging on the luxurious. But it was undoubtedly time to go.

His escape route was in place. He had dyed his hair and his beard. He was well aware that the police were crawling over the City looking for him. Not that this was a cause for concern. He had spent his life outwitting smarter opponents than the Glasgow polis. He had a car garaged less than a hundred yards away, and had stolen it himself – a piece of Japanese crap which was indistinguishable from every other piece of Japanese crap. The tax disc had been skilfully altered to match the new number plate which in turn matched the number of a car which he knew to be owned by a newsagent in Paisley. Only a very thorough examination would disclose the forged disc and nothing in a Police National Computer check would suggest the car was stolen. When he was ready, he would drive to Stranraer. He had false identity documents. He would walk casually onto the ferry and then home. No problem – he had done it many times before.

And yet his normally supreme confidence was lacking its customary authority. Agitation was not a sensation with which he was overly familiar. But he was agitated and he did not care for it, one little bit. Yes, he was leaving Scotland, but he had no intention of running off with his tail between his legs. He intended to leave a message behind. A reminder. A lasting monument to his ruthless efficiency. This meant he had to take to the streets and therein lay danger. The police he could deal with but there were other eyes out there, eyes connected to mouths which were bought and paid for. For all the time he had spent in Glasgow, it was not his city. Friend and foe could be indistinguishable and were frequently one and the same. He had contempt for his failed paymaster but did not underestimate the perils of his situation. A cornered rat is at its most dangerous and is capable of the most irrational attack, and McGarry could sense danger. He could almost smell it. He had survived so far because of his ability to manoeuvre around any potential threat. Now this may not be possible. He would have to take risks. He had been treated with disrespect. Such a wrong could not be allowed to pass. It was a matter of professional pride.

He stroked the handle of the Browning pistol which lay on the seat at his side.

'Time for you and me to have a bit of a chat – a rather one-sided chat.'

*　　　*　　　*

'Staring at it won't make it any better.'

'At least we'd get ten out of ten for neatness.'

'Thank you, Donald.'

'You keep telling me to be positive.'

'Positive, yes. Sarky, no!'

'Oooooooooooh!'

'Come on chaps. We've got a pretty document listing eight witnesses and apart from Tomzack, none of them is any bloody use.'

'It's got to be the mother for starters. Hasn't it?'

'What do you think, Jack?'

'Well, on the plus side, she doesn't have a record.'

'But?'

'She has a tongue on her like a brickie's labourer.'

'Rough?'

'Could strip the varnish off your furniture. Doesn't call a spade a spade – more like a fucking shovel. She's known locally as the screaming skull. She doesn't shut the door on Jehovah's Witnesses, she eats them up and spits out the...'

'Thank you, Jack. Got the picture.'

'So, we start with the skull?'

'We start with the skull. Next?'

'The best of them is probably uncle Eddie. He is a sort of a cousin of Frank Gallagher. Has never been involved in any of the business ventures. Bit dolly dimple really. He has a kind of granny flat at the back of the Gallagher house. He potters around the garden, washes the cars, that sort of thing. He will certainly stick to the story that Charlie was at the party all the time. I think he could come over reasonably well. If Matthews tries to bully him, the jury might just be sympathetic. It's your decision, James, of course.'

'Is this a dagger I see before me, the handle turned toward my hand? Uncle Eddie then. After that, Paul Tomzack. End of story.'

'What about Jack?'

'Jack?'

'Me!'

'Should we try to get Jack in as a late witness to deny the bribe he is supposed to have offered Warwick?'

'Fair point, Donald.'

'Wait a minute – no way – no fucking chance. You're not getting me into a witness box. Let that smart-arsed bastard prosecutor take the piss out of me? Not on your life.'

'Well, Jack, we've got to think of the client's best interests.'

'If you want blood, you can have blood. You can sleep with my wife, my secretary, the dog, if you prefer. But you're not putting me in a witness box.'

'Jack, I do believe you are in a panic.'

'No, I'm not! I'm not in a panic. I'm not! I've been in court all the time. I've heard the evidence. I'm your instructing solicitor. I can't give evidence. Can I?'

'There's nothing to it, Jack. Christ, you've seen more people give evidence than the two of us put together. You just take the oath, stand there and answer a few simple questions. Well, maybe just the odd tricky one.'

'I bloody know how to give evidence. I also know how you bastards delight in making an idiot out of any solicitor who is mad enough to give you the chance.'

Muirhead donned a worried mien.

'I take it that what Warwick said was a lie?'

'Of course it was a bloody lie. Have you gone mad, James?'

'Now, now, Jack. I'm sure it's a lie, but the jury might just wonder, you know. Better safe than sorry.'

'Jesus Christ!'

'What do you think, James?'

'It's a tricky one.'

'I'm fairly clear in my mind.'

'Yes, I've come to a view on the matter. I'd prefer the dog.'

'Me too.'

'Right, let's get the show on the road.'

'Bastards! Fucking bastards!'

'Such coarse language, old chap.'

'Shocked and appalled, Donald. Shocked and appalled.'

❖   ❖   ❖

'Mr Muirhead, is it your intention to lead evidence?'

'It is, my Lord. The first witness will be Hilda Gallagher, number one on the defence list of witnesses.'

'Are you calling your client?'

'The first witness will be Hilda Gallagher.'

'Mr Muirhead, I asked you if it was your intention to call your client to give evidence.'

'Whether I call my client is something of which I will advise the Court at the appropriate time. Or rather, the time I consider to be appropriate.'

'Ladies and gentlemen of the jury, no doubt you are anxious to hear from the accused. Unfortunately, you are not to be told when that will happen – if at all.'

Oh, no you don't!, Muirhead thought to himself.

'As my Lord is, I have no doubt, well aware, there is no obligation upon an accused person to give evidence. In the event that he – elects – to go into the witness box, his counsel, namely me, and no one else is entitled to determine when that should be.'

'Mr...'

'I noted, as no doubt the jury noted, that your Lordship, very properly, made no comment on the order in which the Crown called witnesses...'

'Mr...'

A tidal wave is hard to resist.

'I am sure your Lordship is not seeking to imply that there is anything wrong with the way in which I propose to conduct my case, otherwise he would be ruling against me on a point of law. I have received no such ruling from your Lordship and indeed it is difficult to conceive how there could be such a ruling.'

'Mr Muir...'

'Accordingly, I assume that I may now proceed with my case and as I have indicated, twice, the first witness will be Hilda Gallagher.'

'Mr Muirhead, I was only trying to help by clarifying...'

'I am, as ever, obliged to your Lordship for his assistance, but help like that I can do without, with the greatest of respect.'

The day had begun.

Hilda Gallagher was a striking figure as she strode into the witness box and took the oath. The chemist who had concocted the liquid which had produced her red hair was a man with a very sick sense of humour. She wore a tight-fitting emerald green suit with a skirt length which would have turned many a head if worn by a twenty year old. All it turned were stomachs. Her fingers were dripping with ostentatiously large gold rings – as vulgar as they had been expensive. Only a minor miracle could prevent her falling off her six-inch heels.

Muirhead glowered at Morton who had inexplicably contrived to find something of all consuming interest in the file in front of him.

'...and nothing but the truth.'

'That'll make a change, I suspect,' muttered Anderson.

'Now, now, this is our defence.'

'Should I panic now or wait till she starts?'

'Christ's sake, Donald!'

'Mr Muirhead.'

He began with the usual background details. Name, age, address, relationship to the accused. He began to wonder if Anderson had, perhaps, been right. Mother Gallagher had a voice which could grate cheese and to complete the image was affecting a BBC2 accent.

Matthews was struggling to conceal a grin which conveyed the clearest of meanings.

'Your turn to suffer, old chap.'

'You are aware that your son has been charged with murder arising out of an incident which occurred on the 16th of March?'

'Eh em aware he has had that hanging over him like wan of they sword things.'

'Madam, do you mean Damocles?'

'No, your honour, Charles, my boy.'

Matthews was stuffing his gown into his mouth to choke the laughter, himself or both.

Muirhead looked down at the floor in the fond hope it would swallow him up. No such luck. No option but to return to the fray and carry on regardless.

'Was the 16th a special day for you?'

'My, yes, we had this lovely party in the house. All the family and friends were there – well not all our friends, just one or two close friends, you know. We had a lovely buffet, proper caterers, not cheap I can tell you, but as I always say, a thing worth doing is worth doing right. Don't you agree?'

'Yes, probably, but I was thinking more of the reason for the party.'

'Oh, no reason. Well you don't need a reason to get together with the family, do you? I think families are so important. I think they are the most important thing, don't you?'

'Yes, yes. Was it your wedding anniversary?'

'Yes.'

'Well, was that the reason for the party?'

'Oh, I see. Yes.'

'Look at defence production number eight. Is that a copy of your marriage certificate?'

'Yes.'

'Does it show you were married on the 16th of March, the same day as the party?'

'Yes.'

'And was the party held in your house?'

'It was held in our home. In our home.'

'When did it begin?'

'Well, it didn't really begin. Our front door is always open. Anyone will tell you that. People just come and go, come and go.'

Muirhead was beginning to lose patience.

'Mrs Gallagher, please just listen to my questions. I appreciate that you are nervous but we will get on better if you just try to answer the questions you are asked. Now, did your guests arrive in the evening, the afternoon, the middle of the night, for breakfast the next day?'

'Some people did stay overnight. I'm maybe not the greatest cook in the world but, if I do say so, I can lay on a nice bit of breakfast. Most important meal of the day, I always say.'

'Mrs Gallagher! When did they arrive?'

Hilda Gallagher was not accustomed to being shouted at – at least not without giving it back in equal measure. On this occasion she reined in her instincts and contented herself with giving Muirhead a filthy look before the penny dropped that the two of them were on the same side. She became a little more pliable.

'About eight o'clock onwards.'

'How many people were at the party?'

'About fifteen to twenty. They were all people one had known for...'

'Thank you. Now, was your son at the party. Your son, Charlie, that is?'

'Yes, he was.'

'Did Charlie live in your home at the time?'

'He lived at home with his family, yes.'

'Did he leave the party at any time?'

'Of course not. Why should he want to leave? His family was there and...'

'Thank you. Now do you know when your son went to bed?'

'It was late on. We throw a good party you know. He must have gone to bed about 2.30, perhaps later.'

'Did you see your son the following morning?'

'Of course.'

'Where?'

'At home.'

'Where at home?'

'In his room. In bed. I woke him up.'

'What time would that be?'

'Half past nine – exactly.'

'How do you know?'

'When he had not appeared by nine-thirty, I woke him up.'

'Why nine-thirty?'

'His father had a meeting at ten-thirty and Charlie was going to drive him. He got up, showered, had some coffee and left with his father at quarter past ten.'

'So, between, say, seven and ten, where was Charlie?'

'At home.'

'Sure?'

'What do you mean sure? Why are you asking me...?'

'Mrs Gallagher, your son is on trial for murder. Are you sure?'

'Yes.'

Matthews was quickly on his feet.

'What did your son do for a living?'

'He worked for his father.'

'What manner of business?'

'Buying and selling.'

'Buying and selling what?'

'All sorts of things. Cars, videos, that sort of thing.'

'Stolen things?'

'Certainly not.'

'Certainly not. I see. What about drugs?'

'What about them?'

'Did your husband, does your husband deal in drugs?'

'Absolutely not.'

'Really?'

'Yes, really.'

The pretence at a posh accent was gone. Ma Gallagher was ready for a fight.

'Your husband has a criminal record, I think?'

'Just who is on trial here?'

'Your son – for murder. And you are providing him with an alibi. Does your husband have a criminal record?'

'He was a bit wild, but that was years ago.'

'Has he been in prison?'

'I told you, that was years ago. Many years ago.'

'For violence?'

'No, for robbery.'

'Armed bank robbery?'

'Yes.'

'That's not a crime of violence?'

'No one was hurt.'

'I see. Is your family on friendly terms with the Boyles?'

'We know each other.'

'Answer my question, please. Is your family friendly with the Boyles?'

'No.'

'Why not?'

'I don't know. My husband and Hugh Boyle fell out years ago. I don't know why. It was something to do with the business. I don't think it was that important.'

'Was Kevin Boyle trying to muscle in on your family's business?'

'I have no idea.'

'Your family's drug-dealing business?'

'No. Certainly not.'

'That is why he was killed – isn't it? That's why he was killed by your son?'

'Lies!'

'Lies indeed. Lies told by you in an attempt to cover for him?'

'Utter rubbish!'

'Your son left your home that morning and went to meet Kevin Boyle, his rival in the drug business, in order to shoot him dead and that is precisely what he did'

'He never left the house till he left with his father at ten-fifteen.'

'How do you know?'

'How do I know what?'

'That it was ten-fifteen?'

'I looked at the clock, of course.'

'Why?'

'Why what?'

'Why did you look at the clock? Why was time of such importance?'

'It wasn't. I just looked at the clock. Don't you ever look at a clock?'

'You are here, quite simply, to say whatever you think is necessary to help your son avoid a conviction for murder, a murder he undoubtedly committed'

'That's a lie – and you are the liar. You're a fucking liar. You're just as bad as the other scum in the police. Always trying to cause trouble for us. They've been trying to put Charlie away for years – for nothing. Just because he is his father's son. Now you're trying to do the same. Well it's not going to happen, do you hear me? I will not let you and the rest of these bastards get away with it. Do you hear me? Do you understand me?'

Hilda Gallagher was spitting her words across the Court. All cylinders were now firing.

'Thank you.'

Matthews returned to his seat leaving his victim charged up and ready to take on all-comers. He was quite confident that the jury had the picture. Lord Cowden contented himself by entering a description of the lady's evidence into his notebook in three words, 'A veritable virago.'

Muirhead decided to ask no further questions. It was time to move on to something better – hopefully better. Time for Uncle Eddie.

As Edward Gallagher ambled into Court, Muirhead strove to recall some lines from Gerard Manley Hopkins, Shelley, Keats, W.H. Auden, Siegfried Sassoon, anyone, to encapsulate the cameo in a well-turned phrase. Instead, the strains of the Kinks' song 'Dedicated follower of fashion' rattled around inside his head.

Uncle Eddie was the living embodiment of sartorial ineptitude. The garish check jacket with the eight-inch lapels would have been rejected by most charity shops and even the talking sports jacket himself, Arthur Montford, would not have been seen dead in it. The bright yellow shirt provided an interesting backdrop for the tie – the tie! James Muirhead was a devotee of the adventures of the Starship Enterprise but could not bring himself to believe that a tie depicting photographs of the entire crew, Spock included, was appropriate for a murder trial. Green flared trousers and brown and cream shoes completed the remarkable ensemble.

'It's a bit early for pantomime season. I wonder who his tailor is?', quizzed Anderson.

'Why on earth do you want to know that?'

'I might wander in to his emporium by mistake!'

Lord Cowden rose to his feet to administer the oath, stared incredulously at the vision before him and, sadly, shook his head. Standards! As far as he was concerned the whole world was going to hell in a basket. His golf club now had women members; gentlemen, or rather men, would go out for dinner without wearing a tie; juries actually disbelieved police officers, and now here was a witness, in his court, who looked as if he had taken a detour while en route to a children's fancy dress party. If he had produced a glove-puppet and performed a ventriloquist's act, his Lordship's sang froid would have been ruffled not one whit.

'I swear by Almighty God,' boomed the gravely voice.

Nothing.

Eddie stared resolutely forward. The lights were on but no one was home.

'Repeat after me. I swear by Almighty God.'

Nothing.

'Mr Muirhead, is this witness deaf?'

Muirhead looked at Jack Morton who helpfully shrugged his shoulders.

'Not to my knowledge, my Lord.'

'Does that mean yes or no?'

'I suppose it means, I don't know.'

'I swear by Almighty God.'

Judge and counsel rounded on Eddie.

'Repeat after me. I swear by Almighty God.'

'Perhaps a little slow on the uptake, but undoubtedly not deaf,' offered Muirhead.

A judicial stare was all the thanks he received for this helpful observation.

The rest of the oath was administered, with difficulty and at a funereal pace. His Lordship slumped back in his chair. This had all the makings of a very long day.

Eddie was playing a starring role. He concentrated on every question asked of him, deliberated on the matter and then answered. His use of language was, to say the least, economical. He answered yes or no like a man at judgement day being called upon to justify the most intimate details of his past life. Had his immortal soul been hanging in the balance, Eddie could not have been more cautious. But he was clearly without guile. He was giving the impression that he could not tell a lie if his life depended on it.

'Were you at the party on the night of the 16th?'

'Oh, yes, I was at the party.'

'What was the reason for holding the party?'

'Reason for the party? Oh, yes. It was Frank and Hilda's anniversary.'

'Was Charlie at the party?'

'Charlie? Oh, yes.'

'Did you see him on occasions throughout the evening?'

'I saw him. Oh, yes.'

'Did you see him as the party was going on?'

'Going on. Oh, yes.'

'Do you know if he left the party at any time?'

'Left. Oh, no.'

'Would you have known if he had left the party?'

'Known. Oh, yes.'

'How?'

'How. Oh, yes. He would have said cheerio. Always says cheerio to me.'

'When did you go to bed?'

'Go to bed. Not sure. Small hours.'

'Did you see Charlie when you went to bed?'

'Charlie. Yes. I said night, night. He said night, night, sleep tight, don't let the bedbugs bite. Always does.'

This response baffled Lord Cowden.

'Do not let the what?'

'Let the what?'

'Do not let the...never mind. Carry on.'

His Lordship had been down this road before.

'Carry on.'

'Now, did you see Charlie the following morning?'

'Morning. Oh, yes.'

'Where?'

'Porridge.'

'Porridge?'

'I was eating my porridge when he came in.'

'Came in?'

'Came in to the kitchen. For his breakfast. Hilda was angry. He was not dressed for work and was supposed to be driving his father. Hilda was not pleased. I said nothing. Never do – when Hilda was not pleased.'

'What time was this, when you were having your porridge?'

'Time. Eight o'clock. Always have porridge at eight o'clock.'

'Are you sure about the time? Could it have been later?'

'Later. No, have porridge at eight o'clock.'

This was the one answer Muirhead would not have chosen and he retired to his seat.

Matthews nodded at Uncle Eddie and smiled. He returned the greeting, oblivious to what lay ahead. Matthews commenced

'For how long have you lived with the Gallagher family?'

'How long. A long time.'

'Do you work, Mr Gallagher?'

'Work. I work in the house, keep the cars clean. Frank likes his cars to be clean. I do the garden. I like the garden. Frank says the garden belongs to me.'

'But do you do paid work at all? Do you have a real job?'

'A real job. No. I suppose not.'

'Do the Gallaghers give you money?'

'Money. Yes. If I need it – but I don't need much.'

'The family look after you?'

'Yes.'

'After all, they are your family?'

'My family. Yes. My family.'

'Do you pay rent?'

'Rent. No.'

'Do they buy your clothes?'

'Clothes. When I need them.'

'And provide your meals, like the porridge?'

'Meals. Yes.'

'They seem to be very loyal to you and I dare say you are very loyal to them?'

'Loyal. Yes. Loyalty is important, don't you think?'

'Indeed I do. And no doubt you would not wish to see young Charlie end up in prison?'

'Prison. No. Charlie can't go to prison. Prison is a bad place.'

'You would want to help him if you could?'

'He is my nephew, sort of. Always good to me.'

'I understand. When was the anniversary party organised?'

'I don't understand.'

'When did you first hear there was to be a party?'

'About four o'clock.'

'Yes, yes, but which day?'

'Which day. The day of the party. Hilda told me.'

'So, there was a party to celebrate an anniversary and you were only told about it on the afternoon before it happened?'

'Yes.'

'Was there any food at the party?'

'Food. No.'

'I take it there would be drink?'

'There is always drink in the house. Frank always has drink.'

'So, no food and there is always drink in the house. It wouldn't take much organisation then?'

'I don't understand.'

'It was the kind of party which could be put together at very short notice?'

'I still don't understand.'

'It wasn't a real party at all. It was the Gallaghers summoning people to the house in order to provide an alibi for young Charlie?'

'I don't think so.'

'These people were there to provide an alibi for Charlie while he was involved in the murder of Michael Clark?'

'No, I saw Charlie at the party.'

'Were you constantly by his side?'

'Constantly. No, not constantly.'

'And there would have been ample opportunity for him to leave the party for a time, wouldn't there?'

'I suppose he could have left but I don't think so. Before I came here today, I asked Frank if Charlie had left the party and he told me not to worry that Charlie had been there all the time.'

'I see. He didn't say cheerio to you that night?'

'No. He always says cheerio.'

'Of course, if he had said cheerio, you would have known that he was going out?'

'Yes.'

'So, if he didn't want you to know he was going out, he wouldn't say cheerio, would he?'

'I suppose not. But he didn't go out. Frank said so.'

'Did Frank tell you anything else you should say in court?'

'Anything else. No. Frank told me to tell the truth about Charlie being at the party the whole time and that he was in the house the next morning. Frank knows I can get a bit confused.'

'Indeed. When did you see Charlie the next morning, remind me?'

'Eight o'clock.'

'You are absolutely sure?'

'Yes.'

'When did he leave the house?'

'Left. He would have left about half past eight.'

'Not ten-thirty?'

'Half past ten, no.'

'What was he wearing?'

'Wearing. I think he had his leather jacket on.'

'A black leather bomber jacket?'

'Black leather. Yes.'

'Like the one lying on the table over there?'

'On the table. Yes. Looks like Charlie's.'

'Thank you, Mr Gallagher.'

Muirhead decided against trying to repair the damage. The alibi was leaking like a sieve and any attempt to plug a few holes would look like desperation. He had no intention of appearing to be on the retreat at this late stage of the evidence.

Summoning up all the confidence he could muster and ignoring the Depute's supercilious smirk, he intoned, 'No re-examination, my Lord.'

As Uncle Eddie left the court, he smiled at the dock.

'Did I do all right, Sonny?'

Charlie Gallagher did not respond.

         ●   ●   ●

The afternoon was devoted to the evidence of Paul Tomzack. Forty-two, grey haired, urbane, he held the jury enthralled as he described his dealings with Arnold Warwick.

He had been contacted by Philippe St André who was then serving a sentence of life imprisonment for murder. Tomzack specialised in preparing cases to take before the English Court of Appeal. He regularly received letters from convicted prisoners setting out the most weird and wonderful reasons in support of the allegation that they had been wrongfully convicted. Everything from the judge and prosecutor being masons to claims that the evidence was planted or fabricated by police officers. Some of this could be rejected out of hand. Other complaints had to be taken more seriously. There was something in the letter from St André which made Tomzack think this was one to take seriously – very seriously.

He went to see the man in prison and found himself impressed by the way he recounted the evidence given at his trial by Warwick and his persistent denials that he had ever met Warwick. He had explained all this to his original solicitor and counsel but they had given the impression that they were distinctly underwhelmed by the whole affair. Virtually no attempt had been made to investigate Warwick's past life and only the most formal of challenges had been made to his evidence.

Tomzack had agreed to take the case on and decided to carry out some background research. His firm employed a retired Detective Inspector as an investigator. His inquiries revealed Warwick's past history including previous visits to court as a prosecution witness. It was clear to Tomzack that he had to speak to the man himself.

He had written requesting a meeting and, to his amazement, Warwick agreed. They came face to face in Strangeways prison in Manchester. After explaining the purpose of his visit and outlining the nature of the allegation made by St André, with rising astonishment, he listened while Warwick accepted that his evidence at the trial had been a complete fabrication.

'Did you have to prompt him in any way?'

'Not at all. It was the most extraordinary experience. He seemed quite keen to tell me the whole story. He was more or less boasting about what he had done. What he had achieved – almost.'

'Did he tell you why he had done this?'

'He was quite open about that too. He made up the story and gave evidence in order that he might plead in mitigation in his own case that he had helped the authorities in a major investigation.'

'Did you ask him about the other cases you were aware of?'

'Yes. He was just as open about them. Pure invention on his part. Indeed, he told me there had been other instances when he had given similar statements to the police but had not been called as a witness.'

'What did you make of him?'

'Hard to say. It was the strangest situation I had ever been in. I felt as if I was a part of his fantasy world. If he had told me the time I would have checked my watch and still not been sure.'

'Did you take a statement from him?'

'Not on this occasion. Although he spoke freely, I was afraid that if I took any notes he would clam up. I asked him if I could return later to take a formal statement and he agreed.'

'Did you see him again?'

'One week later.'

'And?'

'Nothing. He sat in the interview room and would not utter a word. He just refused to speak – at all.'

'What did you do then?'

'Well, now I had a real problem. I was in possession of the most crucial information but I could not verify it and it was going to be my word against his. That would not get us through the front door of the Court of Appeal. I was very busy with other cases and it was three to four weeks before I had the chance to visit him again.'

'What happened this time?'

'I had put together an affidavit based on my recollection of our first conversation. However, the meeting started off in the most bizarre fashion. He began to scream and shout that I was threatening him, that I had forced him to make up a story, that his life was in danger. He was ranting so much that a prison officer came into the room. He instantly calmed down. When the officer left, his whole attitude changed.'

'Did anything occur to you?'

'I felt at the time that he was putting on a performance and once he was sure that he had been overheard, he was quite satisfied.'

'What did he say to you?'

'He asked if I had brought a statement for him to sign. When I said that I had, he asked me what he was to get. How much it would be worth. I asked what he meant and he told me he could be in big trouble for retracting his statement, so he wanted big money. He asked for £100,000.'

'What was your response?'

'I told him that this was a ridiculous amount of money and, in any event, I would not pay him for a statement. Not a penny.'

'What was his reaction?'

'He stomped around the room for a time cursing and swearing, mainly about lawyers. He called me a smarmy, smug-faced shitbag. I remember that. I appreciated the alliteration. It didn't take long for the storm to blow over and he changed yet again. He asked for the statement. I handed it to him and he signed it without even reading it. I asked him to read it but he said he was not interested. I decided to read it over to him. Suddenly he grabbed it out of my hand and tore it to bits. He told me I had made it up – that he had never said any such thing.'

'What happened then?'

'The most bizarre event of all. I'm sorry, I keep using the word bizarre, but it is the only way I can describe the whole affair. He asked me for pen and paper and spent the next forty to forty-five minutes, in total silence, writing out the whole story. He handed it to me. Stood up and left.'

'Did he say anything to you at all?'

'Nothing about the statement. He did ask if I would write to the Parole Board and tell them of his co-operation.'

'Did you indicate if you would comply with this request'?

'At first I was non-committal, but he started shouting and bawling that I was trying to set him up, trying to trick him, so to calm him down, I said I would write.'

'Did you ever write the letter?'

'No.'

'Did the matter ever come before the Court of Appeal?'

'No. Philippe St André hanged himself in prison. He left a short note protesting his innocence. He could not cope with the prospect of a life sentence. I still have that man's death on my conscience. I keep thinking I should have proceeded more swiftly.'

'Did you ever threaten Warwick in any way?'

'Certainly not.'

'Or offer him any form of inducement?'

'No.'

'Mr Tomzack, Warwick has described you in this Court as a crook. Any comment you would care to make on that?'

'Yes, but I would offend the members of the jury and no doubt find myself in trouble with his Lordship. Warwick will say anything about anyone. You would have thought by now he might have a conscience but I doubt if he can even spell the word.'

As James Muirhead sat down, all eyes turned to Mike Matthews. When he shrugged his shoulders and blandly uttered the words, 'No questions, my Lord,' it was followed by an audible sigh of disappointment emanating from the jury box. Clearly, one or two had fancied a bit of a battle between Tomzack and the Crown, but it was not to be. Indeed, there was to be no more.

Muirhead closed the defence case, prompting more debate among the jurors.

'We are not to hear from your client, Mr Muirhead?'

'No, my Lord.'

'That is your decision. Very well, ladies and gentlemen of the jury that concludes all the evidence in the case. Apparently we are not to hear from Mr Gallagher. Well, I suppose that is his decision. Or should I say, Mr Muirhead's decision. Tomorrow we will hear speeches from the Crown and the defence and then I will charge you. Please do not begin the process of making up your minds just yet. You will have to give careful consideration to all that is yet to be said to you before you commence your deliberations.'

●　　　●　　　●

McAllister stared at the dashboard clock. 11.10. He had been parked for barely fifteen minutes. It seemed much longer. Time was passing very slowly. The evidence in Gallagher's trial was at an end. Time was running out.

He looked around the largely deserted carpark. There was no pop concert blaring out its so-called music in the Exhibition Centre. Only a dozen cars were parked, scattered around the vast open space. A number were in a line beside one of the centre's buildings. Probably security staff. A few isolated vehicles were dotted around, none of them parked under street lights. These cars tended to arrive, park for fifteen or twenty minutes and then leave. The daughters of darkness were plying their trade. Not one of them was the vehicle he was hoping to see.

One car did attract his attention. It was rocking backwards and forwards on its springs.

'You'll probably catch something, you silly bastard!'

11.15.

Movement across the car park. Two men, young men, furtive, on the alert, looking anxiously about them, heads constantly on the move. They approached a parked car. Conversation between one of them and the driver. A hand placed through the open window. A hand appears from inside.

'Damn!'

McAllister was sitting watching a drugs deal going down and could do nothing about it. If he tried to intervene the buyers would run off and the seller would simply drive away. If he summoned other officers, he would probably scare off his expected visitor, and this was an appointment he had to keep. Nonetheless, it went against the grain to ignore a crime being committed under his very nose. He could not work out the make of the car, never mind the number plate.

The two purchasers hurried away into the darkness with the same degree of agitated alertness they had displayed on arrival.

11.27.

McAllister felt the adrenaline begin to flow. He was taking a risk and he knew it. How often had he told young officers – never go anywhere without back up. Make sure someone knows where you are going. Keep your radio switched on. Do not take chances. If in doubt – walk away. Here he was, breaching each and every one of these rules at one fell swoop. If this was a set up, he was in deep trouble. Mind you, if it went very badly wrong, he would not have to explain his actions to anyone – at least not on this earth.

11.30.

Bang on cue. A car entering the car park. Driving round. Looking. Parking in a distant corner. An N-registered Golf. Time to go.

McAllister walked towards the car. He checked round about but there was no activity to cause alarm. He paused a few yards from the vehicle in order to examine it. There appeared to be no passengers – only the driver. He made for the passenger-door, opened it and got in.

'Good evening, Superintendent. Thank you for coming to see me.'

'It was an invitation I could hardly refuse.'

'Are you alone?'

'Yes. I'm a man of my word.'

'Is anyone listening to us?'

'I'm not sure I understand.'

'I think you do. Are you carrying a microphone or a tape recorder?'

'No. Do you wish to search me?'

'No. I believe you. After all, you are a man of your word.'

'Why do you want to speak to me?'

'Is Charles Gallagher going to be convicted of Kevin's murder?'

'I cannot say.'

'Try, please.'

'The prosecution case is not particularly strong. It has never been very strong. However, there is an eye-witness to the murder who seems quite reliable. He says that Gallagher is the killer. There is other evidence, including an admission to a police officer.'

'So, he should be convicted?'

'It's not as easy as that.'

'I believe that Gallagher's lawyer is very good.'

'He is.'

'How good?'

'Very good. Probably the best.'

The response produced a period of silence as the information was being digested.

'Do you think Gallagher will be convicted? You must have some idea.'

McAllister reflected before he spoke: 'The best people to judge these matters, although it's still to a large extent guesswork, are the officers from the dock escort. Most of them are nearing the end of their police service, which means they have been around for a long time. They have spent hours in court listening to cases. You might say they get a feel for it. I gather that the talk among them is that Gallagher will go down. That's my answer. It's better than a guess – but not much.'

Again there followed a period of silence.

His companion stared ahead, looking through the windscreen as if concentrating on some distant object. McAllister was having great difficulty in maintaining an outward air of calm. He did not wish to reveal his state of agitation but his heart was racing and he desperately wanted to take some deep breaths to enable him to calm down. He could sense that his companion's mind was wrestling with some problem, some dilemma, of profound concern. He was anxious to do nothing to upset the equilibrium of the moment. Something significant was about to happen. He could feel it. He knew it. He would just have to be patient a little longer.

'Do YOU think Gallagher killed Kevin?'

That, he hadn't expected.

'I arrested him.'

A weak response and he knew it.

'If we're going to play games, Mr McAllister, then this whole exercise is a waste of your time – and mine.'

A chance to go on the offensive. He decided to take it.

'Let me remind you, this was your idea. You wanted to see me. You wanted this level of secrecy. I am not in the habit of playing spy games. I am a police officer, not a character out of a John le Carré novel. You wanted to speak to me. If anyone is playing games – it's you. Now, is there something you want to tell me or shall I get out of this car and bring this charade to an end?'

'I am not playing games. I need to know. The reasons are mine and need not concern you. Do you think Mr Gallagher shot Kevin?'

This time the voice was pregnant with sadness. McAllister realised that his offensive had failed. Now the dilemma was his. He would have to answer this question in order to keep the meeting alive. But he had to find the right answer. He feared how his companion might react if he continued to try to be evasive. This was a test to see if he could be trusted.

'When I charged Gallagher, I had no doubt I had the right man. I'm not in the habit of arresting people in the absence of evidence.'

'And now?'

'Now, I'm just not sure. Various things have happened which concern me – have made me wonder. I'm just not at all sure. If I could find something new which convinced me of his guilt, I would not be surprised. If there was something which demonstrated he didn't kill Boyle, that would not surprise me either.'

'If Gallagher was not responsible for Kevin's death, have you any idea who might have been?'

A subtle but important change of language. Much depended on your definition of responsibility. McAllister decided to avoid semantics.

'No. But I would like to speak to Tom McGarry. You knew him, I take it?'

'Of course. You spoke of finding something new, if you could.'

'Ideally.'

Again there was a pause.

'Are you going to find McGarry?'

'I am in possession of some good information. I believe he is still in Glasgow but is likely to try to leave and go, over the water. When he does, we will get him.'

'And then?'

'And then I will interview him?'

'What good do you think that will do ?'

'I won't know till I try.'

'I do not believe that Charlie Gallagher killed Kevin.'

'Why do you say that?'

'What will happen to Gallagher if you discover he did not shoot Kevin?'

'It would depend on how good the evidence was and when I found it. The closing speeches start tomorrow. There may be a verdict on

Monday; Tuesday at the latest. There isn't much time left.'

'What will happen if he is convicted of the murder?'

'This is all a bit hypothetical for me, I'm afraid.'

'Then speculate, Superintendent. Surely as a policeman you know how to do that?'

'He could appeal on the basis of new evidence or perhaps seek a pardon. It would be better if I could do something before the trial is over. But it's getting very late.'

The ensuing pause stretched on interminably. Again McAllister fought to remain calm. Again his companion stared straight ahead – deep in thought. If there were demons battling within, there were no outward manifestations.

'If I give you some information, will you treat it as confidential?'

'If I can.'

'And what does that mean?'

'It means that if you tell me something which discloses you may have committed a crime, I cannot just ignore that.'

'I have done nothing wrong. Certainly nothing illegal. I may speak to you. I will speak to no one else. If you report this conversation to anyone else, I will deny it ever took place and produce a string of witnesses to prove it could never have taken place.'

This statement had a depressingly familiar ring to it.

McAllister had one more gamble to take.

'Obviously, I may have to act upon what you tell me, but the source of the information will remain confidential to me – alone. You have my word on it.'

'Then, Superintendent, perhaps I can help you with your inquiries.'

The next few minutes were to prove among the most extraordinary McAllister had ever known. It was a story he could have dined out on for years. And he had promised to tell no one!

Chapter Twelve

Muirhead prowled around his garden puffing on his pipe and nursing an empty mug. His wife came out of the house and without comment, removed the mug from his hand replacing it with another filled with scalding hot liquid. She received no word of thanks. Muirhead continued with his peregrination.

An observer might have guessed that here was a couple who had had a blazing row resulting in the husband being banished from the house or who had taken himself off into the garden to lick his wounds. The lack of any communication between the two could be taken as confirmation of there being trouble at mill. Wrong.

James Muirhead had been up since 6.30 that morning, composing the speech he would deliver to the jury. It was an exercise which demanded total concentration and which normally caused him to retreat into himself. His wife was well used to the situation.

As the evidence in a trial evolved, Muirhead would note the aspects which were damaging to the Crown or helpful to the defence. These would provide the basis of his jury speech. There was no merit in trying to analyse all the evidence in minute detail. No point in reminding the jury of the material which tended to assist the Crown – unless you had a hell of a good response. Never try to explain away the inexplicable.

He would go over the evidence in his mind, again and again, selecting the parts he proposed to use and framing it for presentation. When he stood up to address a jury, he would have no prepared script. He would not even have the benefit of notes. He would try to talk to the jurors, not at them, in the hope of eliciting some response. As a student of body language he would study his audience as he spoke in an attempt to discover what was going on in their minds. If the response to a particular point seemed positive, he would pursue the matter. If the vibes were bad, he would move on to some other ground which would hopefully prove more fertile.

Fifteen on a jury. It was not his aim to convince them of his client's innocence. He did not require to convince any of them of his client's innocence. If he could create a doubt about his client's guilt in the minds of eight of them, that would be sufficient. That would get the job done. Eight crucial votes.

The speech is the only opportunity counsel has to speak directly to a jury on behalf of his client. There is no telling in advance what the reception may be. Perhaps minds have been made up – one way or the other. It may be that the jurors are confused and require help to unravel the evidential intricacies. It may be that they are genuinely unsure and are open to persuasion.

In a few hours time Muirhead would find out whether his audience was receptive or otherwise. He glanced at his watch. 8.15. Time to go.

•　　　•　　　•

'When you are ready, Advocate Depute.'

'May it please your Lordship.'

Matthews walked to the jury clutching a black leather folder containing his papers. He placed it opened on a shelf in front of the jury box, bowed and began his speech.

'Ladies and gentlemen, it is now for me to address you on behalf of the Crown. In Scotland, persons accused of committing serious crimes are brought before the High Court at the instance of the Lord Advocate. He is in charge of our system of prosecution. He acts in the public interest. Clearly, it is in all our interests that crimes should be investigated, the perpetrators detected, prosecuted and, if appropriate, convicted and sentenced. As one of the Lord Advocate's deputies, it is my responsibility to prosecute this particular case in the public interest. I do not represent the deceased or his family, the police or any particular interest. It is my duty to present all the evidence to you for your consideration and to ask you to return such verdicts as I consider are supported by that evidence.

'It is for you to evaluate the evidence, to decide what to accept and what to reject, and in due course return your verdict. You will be looking for evidence which is both credible and reliable, bearing in mind that people may tell lies or make mistakes.

'There are a number of legal rules which you must follow and although I will mention these in passing, his Lordship will explain them to you in due course.

'Since the Crown have brought Mr Gallagher to court, it is for the Crown to prove guilt. By law, he is presumed to be innocent until proved guilty. That is not to say he is innocent, but he is presumed to be so. His guilt must be established to the standard of beyond reasonable doubt. It is a high standard, but it is not an impossible standard. It does not mean beyond any doubt or to some kind of mathematical certainty. If that was the case, no one would ever be convicted of anything. In the area of human affairs, no one can ever be certain of anything. When you examine the evidence and think about it, if you are satisfied of the guilt of Mr Gallagher, it is, quite simply, your duty to convict. You do not feel sympathy for the victim or hostility towards the man in the dock, however much that may be merited. Duty is above emotion.

'Mr Muirhead, representing Mr Gallagher, is in a different position. He does not have to prove his client's innocence. Indeed, he does not have to prove anything. Basically, his role is destructive rather than constructive. As you have already seen, he will use his considerable skills to harry and pressure the witnesses, to confuse, to muddy the waters, to obscure what in reality is perfectly plain. He does so in a convincing, occasionally dramatic, fashion. All very impressive. It does not make it so.

'When he addresses you, he will impress you with his air of confidence. He will sound very plausible. His presentation has all the art and craft of a great Shakespearean actor. Do not be taken in by it. What you and I are concerned with is substance, not packaging. With evidence. With facts. We are concerned only with the quality of the merchandise, not the glitz of the window dressing. From me, there will be no flowery language, no dramatics, amateur or otherwise, only facts, hard facts to demonstrate that the accused is beyond doubt guilty of the crime of murder.'

Muirhead's eyes bored into his opponent's back. The battle lines had been clearly drawn. Matthews was determined to obtain a conviction and was not about to let anything or anyone stand in his way. His initial onslaught against Muirhead had nothing whatsoever to do with the evidence in the case. It was a blatant attempt to discredit in advance and to portray Muirhead as all wind and no substance. He was trying to tell the jury that he was going to present them with the facts whereas the defence would seek to confuse the issue and bury the facts as far out of sight as possible. In that, he was absolutely right. But it was still unusual for a prosecutor to directly criticise defence counsel in so pointed a fashion. Matthews was out to win.

Muirhead glanced down at a piece of paper which had been passed to him.

'How are the knife wounds in your back?'

He scribbled a reply and returned the note to Donald Anderson.

'He has made the mistake of leaving his knife between my shoulder blades. It will be my pleasure to work it right up his...'.

Anderson smiled.

Muirhead returned his attention to the Advocate Depute.

Matthews had invited the jury to look at their copies of the indictment and was explaining to the jurors the law's requirements for the crime of murder to be established.

'You may think, ladies and gentlemen, that if a man walks up to a motor car and empties a hand gun into his victim's head, this demonstrates a clear, determined, premeditated intention to take life in a cold, callous and brutal fashion. This is as plain a case of murder, indeed, evil murder, as you would ever wish to see.'

Matthews delivered the last sentence, slowly and deliberately, carefully enunciating every single syllable, reserving special emphasis for the word 'murder.'

'It is the Crown's position that Charles Gallagher walked to the BMW, produced a gun and fired it into Kevin Boyle's head, killing him instantly. He was driven to and from the scene by a person whose identity is for the time being unknown. Thereafter, the gun was disposed of and unfortunately has not been recovered.

'Now, you may be wondering what motive Gallagher had for wanting Boyle dead. There is no obligation upon the Crown to establish a motive. Indeed, many killings are quite motiveless. In the present case, I suggest that there was a motive and it was commercial rivalry. The two families, the Gallaghers and the Boyles, have been rivals for many years. They have been at war for years. I do not consider that is too strong a way to put it. Kevin Boyle was perceived to be a threat to the Gallagher activities, probably in relation to drugs and the decision was taken to eliminate him and send a clear warning to the rest of the Boyle clan. Ladies and gentlemen, a clear motive for the commission of the crime of murder.'

It was Anderson who reacted angrily.

'That's totally out of order. Where the fuck does he get the evidence to back up that assertion? You better do something, James. Cowden will let him get away with anything.'

'Take it easy. If I start jumping up and down then the jury may think there is some substance to all of this. We don't want them to put two and two together and come up with the right answer. I'll deal with it – and him.'

Muirhead sat back in his seat, shook his head and donned the mien of a man who could not actually believe what he was hearing. He caught the eye of a juror who nodded imperceptibly as if to say, 'Got the message, son. Got the message.'

The Depute went on to demonstrate from the evidence that this was indeed a case of murder. He lead the jury through the various books of photographs and recalled the scene as it had been discovered by the first officers to arrive. The ballistics experts had described the type of weapon, the number of shots and the range. Professor Walker had dealt with the cause of death and proclaimed the wound non-survivable. None of these matters were in any way contentious but Matthews spared no effort in squeezing every ounce of prejudice out of the horror that had been the murder scene.

'Against the background of this material, ladies and gentlemen, you may have little difficulty in concluding that Kevin Boyle was indeed murdered – by someone. The remaining question is, by whom? Beyond reasonable doubt, the answer to that is the accused, Charles Gallagher.'

There was an explosion in the dock. The background of silence which had enveloped the Depute was shattered. Gallagher shot to his feet and, gripping the dock rail with all his strength, screamed 'NO!' Several jurors jumped and even Matthews was startled. Gallagher had been grabbed by his escort but was making no effort to move. He was pulled back down onto his seat and immediately slumped forward, burying his face in his hands.

'Mr Muirhead, will you instruct your client that if there are any further outbursts I will have him removed from the court. I will not have the Depute being interrupted in the course of his address.'

Muirhead did not move from his chair and made no effort to acknowledge Lord Cowden's instruction and warning. He nodded to his junior who strolled casually to the dock to have a whispered conversation with Gallagher. That the Depute had been interrupted in full flow did not bother him one whit, although he was nonetheless angry at Gallagher. Such outbursts could have an unpredictable impact on a jury.

'He's OK now, James. He thinks our learned brother is a prize James Hunt!'

'At least he's got something right!'

Order having been restored, Matthews returned to his theme.

'Ladies and gentlemen, I turn now to the evidence which, in my submission, demonstrates the guilt of the accused.'

●　　　　　●　　　　　●

Everything was in place. McGarry's flat was completely surrounded. He was going nowhere unless handcuffed to a policeman. One of McAllister's many talents was the ability to plan an operation to the nth degree.

Officers of the Tactical Firearms Unit were stationed on rooftops overlooking the front and back entrances to the close of the tenement which housed McGarry's bolt hole.

Two units of armed officers would simultaneously enter the close from the front and rear. The target flat was on the first floor and, if all went according to plan, the first group would take up position on the stairwell above and below it. The second group would approach the flat and force entry. No warnings would be given. The aim was to catch the occupant completely unaware and deny him access to the weapons he was believed to have in his possession. McAllister had no intention of turning this into Glasgow's version of the OK Corral.

Time to get it done.

McAllister issued the command, 'Go! Go! Go!'

From his vantage point, McAllister could see four officers, wearing police baseball caps and bullet proof vests, hurrying into the building, handguns at the ready. Now he would have to wait.

When the four officers securing the stairwell were in position, the attack team battered the front door from its hinges with a single blow from a sledgehammer and poured into the flat.

In the command car, McAllister waited, and waited.

'What the hell's going on in there?'

'At least there's no shooting, boss.'

McAllister stared at the radio willing it to come to life. Suddenly it responded.

'I think you better get up here, sir.'

McAllister banged his fist on the dashboard in frustration.

'Get going, damn it!'

The car braked hard to stop outside the tenement. McAllister and two other officers hurried up the stairs. At the door of the flat he was waved straight in.

'Nothing, sir. Someone has been here, all right, but they've made a good attempt at clearing up.'

This was not the news McAllister had expected. Hoped for, at least.

'Can you tell if the place was occupied recently?'

'By the feel of it, yes. This is not a flat that has lain empty. Someone has been living here. No doubt about it.'

'Any idea when they left?'

The firearms commander looked around the living room as if soaking in the ambience.

'Harder to answer that specifically. When I came in there was a human smell, sweat, aftershave, stale tobacco and alcohol. You lose that when bodies start moving about the place. But it was there. Some of it still is. You develop a nose for it, so to speak.'

'I do not need a lecture, inspector. I need facts or at least your best opinion.'

'Sorry, sir. Within twenty-four hours, I'd say.'

McAllister turned to one of the officers who had accompanied him into the flat.

'You stay here. I want forensics and finger prints here now. Take the damn place apart if you have to, but I want proof that McGarry has been here. Inspector, you and your men know what to do.'

'Sir!'

McAllister rounded on one of his own men who was leaning casually against a wall.

'Since you seem to have nothing better to do, get on that radio and get Operation Stranraer implemented immediately. Now, let's go.'

❋   ❋   ❋

'The starting point for the Crown is a clear and unequivocal identification of Charles Gallagher as the killer of Kevin Boyle. However much the defence may snipe at him, regardless of the scorn heaped upon his head, no matter how many matters my learned friend would wish to ignore if he could, these facts are there, they are clear, consistent and utterly damning.

'This was no momentary glimpse of a total stranger. No shadowy figure lurking in a darkened background. Barclay Thomson knew Charles Gallagher, knows Gallagher. They were at school together. Thomson watched his former classmate gun down a man in the public street. Initially, it may be that he could not believe the evidence of his own eyes. Is this so surprising? Mercifully, Mafia-style executions are not yet commonplace, even on the streets of Glasgow.

'The defence will no doubt be swift to condemn him for his reluctance to become involved. Again, is this so surprising? He had witnessed a gangland killing in which a man's head had been blown to smithereens. Would any of us, any of you, willingly be a witness against persons capable of such appalling evil? Even when he comes to this court as an honest citizen doing his public duty, he finds himself harangued and pilloried. But he did his duty, ladies and gentlemen. He told you the truth. He told you what he saw and the defence cannot get away from it. Barclay Thomson saw Charlie Gallagher murder Kevin Boyle.

'However, this evidence is not enough by itself. I accept this. I must provide corroboration. A cross-check, just to be sure. Evidence from at least one other source pointing to the accused's guilt. Can I do this? Yes, without doubt.

'I start with the defence case, if I can thus flatter it. Mr Gallagher's position, put simply, is that he was not there. He was at this anniversary party, convened, for some reason, at remarkably short notice.'

'Now who's being fucking sarky,' muttered Anderson, none too sotto voce. This observation attracted a judicial scowl.

'Well, unfortunately, we have heard nothing from Mr Gallagher himself about this, but we did hear from Uncle Eddie. The redoubtable Uncle Eddie! No doubt the memory of his appearance in the witness box will cheer us in the weeks and months which lie ahead... Loyal – yes. Naive – certainly. An alibi witness – no, I don't think so – do you? Uncle Eddie tells us that Gallagher was out of the house at the very time the killing was taking place wearing a leather bomber jacket. Accordingly, he has no alibi. He was out of his house, on the streets and dressed in exactly the same fashion as the killer observed by Barclay Thomson. Coincidence? Mere chance? I don't think so – do you? It is evidence which provides Charles Gallagher with a crucial element in the Crown case against him – opportunity. The opportunity to kill.

'And, subsequently, what is found on a leather bomber jacket owned by the accused? Blood, ladies and gentlemen. Blood! According to the forensic experts there is a very high probability that the blood came from Kevin Boyle.'

'Jesus Christ, this is fucking outrageous!'

This was too much for Lord Cowden.

'A moment, Advocate Depute, I am sorry to interrupt you. Mr Muirhead, kindly direct your junior counsel to be more restrained in his observations. The jury may not be able to hear him, but I certainly can and I for one can do without them.'

Muirhead patted his junior on the arm in a calming gesture.

'Down boy. Don't upset the nasty old judge.'

Like the comment, this rebuke was issued none too sotto voce. His Lordship's fuses were about to blow. Only by a supreme effort of will did he retain his self-control.

'Carry on, Mr Depute.'

Matthews inwardly smiled. So he was getting to Anderson, eh? With a bit of luck he was also beginning to slip under the skin of his learned senior. He would push a little harder.

'Ladies and gentlemen, the defence may enjoy the game but they do not seem to care for losing goals.'

This time it was Anderson's turn to react. He grabbed Muirhead's wrist in order to prevent him leaping out of his seat.

'Easy, Jim, you'll get him.'

This time the words were meant to be heard. Cowden sneered malevolently. Anderson grinned in response. Matthews continued his attack.

'Ladies and gentlemen, even if you had some doubts about the matters I have discussed with you thusfar, there remains the most significant piece of evidence of all. Mr Gallagher has admitted his guilt. He has confessed and, not only that, he has bragged about it.

'Now, I accept that Mr Warwick is a very strange character indeed. A Walter Mitty type of individual, to some extent inhabiting his own private world. There is no doubt, for once, that the defence have many reasonable criticisms they may make of his evidence. Let me speak quite plainly. I have no problem accepting that these criticisms may be made. I have no difficulty in recognising that there is substance to them, or some of them at least. However, the fact remains that Warwick does claim that Mr Gallagher admitted the murder to him while the two of them were in Barlinnie prison.

'If there was no more to it than that, I could see that you might not be overly happy about accepting it. However, there is more to it.

'Mr Warwick did not just tell you about a confession. He gave you details. He knew it was a shooting, in a car. He knew that Mr Boyle had been in a flat occupied by a girl. He used the word "tart." Uncharitable, perhaps, but in the whole circumstances not entirely inaccurate. He knew that the gunman pulled a mask down over his face as he walked towards the car. He knew that neither the car nor the gun could be recovered. Detail, ladies and gentlemen, remarkably accurate detail. Not detail you could invent or guess at. Detail you could only obtain from someone who had been there at the time. He obtained that detail from the man who was there. From the killer. From Charles Gallagher.

'Some half-hearted attempt has been made to suggest that Warwick gleaned all this information from the pages of newspapers. Unfortunately for the defence, it cannot be demonstrated that the witness actually read the relevant newspaper. Yet another attempt at a smokescreen, and that is almost an end of that. Even if some of the detail could be located in press reports, it was detail, all of which was assuredly available to one particular individual. I repeat, the killer, Charles Gallagher. But that is certainly not the end of the evidence.

'It is not just to Warwick that Mr Gallagher chose to unburden his soul. He confessed to a police officer. To Constable Taylor.

' "I gave Boyle what he deserved and neither you nor they wankers will ever prove it. I gave Boyle what he deserved and neither you nor they wankers will ever prove it." A colourful turn of phrase no doubt, but its meaning is abundantly clear is it not? Boasting again, just as he had boasted to Warwick. The words of a braggart. The attitude of a man who is convinced that the law cannot touch him. An arrogant man. But words which disclose a cowardly streak. A man who is prepared to kill a fellow human being in cold blood, but is not himself man enough to face up to the consequences. The kind of man who will shout and scream from the dock but lacks the courage to face his accuser, me, across the court room.

'You heard Constable Taylor being cross-examined. The bullying and hectoring tones. A deliberate attempt to distress the witness by making reference to his father's suicide. Defence counsel have a duty to their clients, of course. But you may wonder whether such tactics as were used against Constable Taylor have any place in our system of justice. Small wonder that the young man was reduced to a state of near collapse.

'No doubt he could have written the remark down in his notebook. But what difference would it have made? How on earth does writing words on a sheet of paper make it more or less likely that the words were said as opposed to being invented?

'No doubt Mr Taylor was over-zealous in his dealings with Mr McPhee. No doubt he is an ambitions young man, but there is nothing at all wrong with that.

'None of this, none of this affects the plain and simple fact that the man sitting in the dock boasted to Constable Taylor that he had killed Kevin Boyle. He did so because he is guilty of the crime of murder.

'Ladies and gentlemen, please consider the evidence. At the end of the day it points all the one way. It has been my duty to present that evidence. It is your duty to return a true verdict according to that evidence. Put aside revulsion, anger, even sympathy for the deceased and his family. The evidence demonstrates beyond reasonable doubt that Charles Gallagher is guilty of the crime of murder. I may ask that you convict him. Justice demands that you do.'

The Advocate Depute bowed to the jury, gathered up his papers and returned to his seat. He made no attempt to avoid eye contact with James Muirhead. The message was crystal clear, even from a toff like Matthews – 'Up yours!'

'After lunch, ladies and gentlemen', from Lord Cowden brought the morning to a close.

●   ●   ●

McAllister checked his watch for the umpteenth time. The convoy of unmarked vehicles was travelling at speed in a south-westerly direction.

'How far from Stranraer?'

'Twenty, twenty-five minutes maximum.'

'Go straight to the port police office.'

'Are you sure he'll turn up?'

'He'll turn up.'

'Maybe we've missed him, boss.'

'No.'

'What makes you so sure?'

'I know.'

'Could be a long wait?'

'Yeah, boss, how long are we going to be here?'

'Until we get him.'

The driver and passenger lapsed into silence. It was clear that McAllister knew something. It was equally clear that he was not sharing.

As his would-be captors were hurrying towards the ferry terminal, McGarry was thinking about his unlawful occasions in Glasgow. He had cleaned his hideaway from top to bottom. His rubbish had been dumped about a mile away. He was confident the place was sanitised.

He had uplifted sizeable amounts of cash from various banks in town. His disguise was in place. No one would recognise him, not even his mother, if he knew who she was. More importantly, the documentation supporting his assumed identity was more than good enough to fool the police in the port unit. He was ready to go. Just one piece of business to attend to.

He parked at the end of a lane which gave him a clear view of three lock-up garages. Too much activity. He would have to wait. He was prepared to take risks but not to be totally stupid. The man was inside. The flashy Mercedes with the personalised number plate. Very understated! He would bide his time. Waiting was not a problem.

Putting his hand inside his jacket, he felt the cold comfort of the handle of the pistol. No need to check that. He knew it was in working order and, more to the point, fully loaded. The safety catch was off, ready for use. And he intended to use it.

Two men left the lock-up, entered a car and drove off. The lane was now quiet. This was as good a time as any. Turning the ignition key forward he checked that the steering lock was disengaged. He had no desire to encounter any delays when he returned to the vehicle.

McGarry left his car and made his way along the lane. He walked neither slowly nor quickly. No need to attract any attention before he had to.

At the first lock-up he paused to listen. Nothing. He passed in front of the open doorway. Two cars, BMWs were in the process of being re-sprayed. What a surprise! No people.

From the next lock-up he could hear voices. Two. Excellent! He recognised both of them. The man he wanted was there. Perfect!

As McGarry turned into the building he pulled the gun from his jacket.

'As they say, ladies, hands up!'

'What the...?'

'It's you...'.

'No sudden movements please. Mistakes cannot be easily rectified.'

McGarry half turned to a quivering mass of jelly wearing overalls.

'You, sit. Sit! Stay there and be deaf, dumb and blind.'

The overalls slumped into a corner.

'Look, McGarry, I'm glad to see you. I've been trying to reach you. You know that, don't you?'

'I told him to sit. I did not tell you to speak. You are not glad to see me, you are shitting yourself. I can smell it.'

'Come on, be reasonable. I've got your money if you just give me time to go and get it.'

'Well now, that's the problem, you see. You've had my money – for too long. I've come to collect, and the time is now.'

'Good. Good. Now we're talking sense. Let's go to the house. I may not have enough cash there, but I can get the rest in a couple of hours max.'

'You misunderstand me, I'm afraid. When I said I had come to collect, I didn't mean to imply I was interested in money.'

'What do you mean?'

'Oh, I think if you try, very hard, you could probably work it out for yourself.'

'You can't. You're fucking mad!'

'Now, that's not clever. You could upset me. Make me angry. Not at all clever. Seriously not clever. Dangerously not clever. If you know what I mean.'

The man in front of him collapsed to his knees and began sobbing into his hands. McGarry looked down at him making no attempt to disguise his contempt.

'Please. Please don't kill me. I'll give you anything you want. Money. You can have more money. All the money you want. I'm sorry if I angered you. I was scared. I thought you had turned on me. For Christ's sake, I'm sorry. Please don't kill me. If you want me to beg – I'm begging.'

'Get up! I'm not going to kill you.'

The sobbing stopped instantly. This piece of play-acting did not endear itself to McGarry.

The man got to his feet and sought to adopt an air of confidence he did not feel.

'I didn't say I was going to kill you, now did I?'

'No. That's right. You didn't say you were going to kill me. I knew we could sort this out like reasonable men. Like businessmen. That's what we are, after all. Businessmen. Now, why don't we go for a drink and talk this over. Yes, that's the idea. We'll go for a drink and talk it over. Reasonably.'

'Stop your raving, for Christ's sake. I just came to give you a message.'

The explosion from the gun and the ensuing screams echoed round the workshop.

Again the man collapsed to the ground. On this occasion he clutched at the remnants of his shattered kneecap.

'Ah good, it works!'

McGarry walked towards the writhing, howling figure.

'Here's the message.'

He calmly fired the gun into the other knee, turned on his heel and made to leave. Before he reached the door he paused.

'Tut, tut! Nearly forgot – again.'

He walked back, picked up the spent cartridge cases, popped them in his pocket and left.

●   ●   ●

'Members of the jury, Charles Gallagher is on trial for the crime of murder, the penalty for which is imprisonment for life. It is these two awful facts which bring you and I face to face this afternoon.'

James Muirhead had opened his address to the jury. He had spent the luncheon adjournment strolling along the walkway by the banks of the Clyde. Not that he cared about fresh air or taking exercise. It was a chance to compose his mind and prepare for the performance which lay ahead. He knew the points he wanted to make. It was time to concentrate on his presentation.

The Crown had set out its stall. The Depute's speech had been impressive. This was a worrying time for the defence. The jury had listened to the parts of the evidence which were most helpful to the prosecution. If they asked for a verdict now, there was a reasonable prospect that they might convict. Muirhead would have to stabilise the situation then go on the attack.

No one knew better than Muirhead that to convince a jury you had to appear and sound as if you believed every word you were saying. You were an actor playing a role. If the critics did not like it they would be swift to let you know. Unfortunately, bad reviews tended to have a drastic effect upon your client.

When he returned to the court building, Muirhead changed into wig and gown, went for the obligatory nervous pee, then headed straight to court. The adrenaline-fed tension was there, but under control. It was a drug which was necessary for the performance. He was ready. There again, he had to be.

'The Advocate Depute has put before you the facts which he claims demonstrates the guilt of the accused. What then is my role? It is not my task to get a guilty man off. As you have been told, rightly, Mr Gallagher is presumed to be innocent and remains so until you and you alone say otherwise. You can only convict a man of a crime, but especially the crime of murder, if guilt has been proved, and proved beyond all reasonable doubt. These are not just words. These concepts are the very foundation of our legal system. Of course they protect Mr Gallagher but they also protect you and every other citizen of this country.

'Proof beyond reasonable doubt is not a matter of ifs, buts and maybes. Before you can convict, there must be no evidence, not a single scrap of evidence, which makes you stop and think, which makes you wonder. If there is – you acquit. I do not tell you this. The law tells you this. The law does not take chances with a man's liberty, for that next to life itself, is the most precious gift we have.

'Every day, you take important decisions in your own life. When you retire, you will take a decision in Mr Gallagher's life. This is the heavy burden the law places upon you. This is why the law demands that you are sure, as sure as you can be, before you bring in a verdict of guilty. It is why you are here. Such decisions are far too important to be left to mere lawyers. They are entrusted to fifteen citizens such as yourself, possessed of experience of the world and using your common sense and sense of fair play and justice.

'It is not for an accused to prove anything. He does not have to prove he was not there. It is not for an accused to give evidence, unless he chooses. Mr Gallagher did not give evidence and you will take nothing from that, despite the Crown's sarcasm. I advise a client and you may think that if he has any sense, he will take that advice. If you want to blame anyone for the non-appearance of Mr Gallagher in the witness box, blame me.

'Let me now deal with the Crown case.

'Mr Gallagher came to this court facing three charges, including two charges of murder. Now he faces but one charge and one charge alone. You may wonder why these other charges were ever brought. They were based on evidence which fell apart before your very eyes. Mr McPhee was bullied into identifying my client by police officers and Mr Taylor in particular on the evidence of Warwick, a deceitful, twisted man who would say and do anything for his own self advancement.

'There was no forensic evidence, no independent evidence, no evidence of any substance linking my client with the death of Mr Clark. These charges should never have been brought. It was no surprise when my learned friend was forced to abandon them. The only surprise is that he did not do so much sooner.'

Payback time for Mr Matthews, and the jury knew it. So did Lord Cowden who was scribbling furiously.

But what of the remaining charge?

'In his speech, the Advocate Depute has poured scorn on the defence and indeed, on me. What a sad situation for a public prosecutor to be in! So much confidence has he in his own case that he is reduced to insults, abuse and attempts at humour which you would have found distasteful. You, ladies and gentlemen, deserve better. You deserve to be treated with respect. You deserve to have the benefit of reasoned argument. That is what you will get from me. The Depute, for whatever reason, has tried to provoke a slanging match. I will not take this bait. I have too much regard for you. You and I will concentrate on the evidence because it is in the evidence that we will see the weakness of the Crown's position.'

'Clever bugger you are, James,' mused Anderson. 'Make Matthews look like a real shit while you're the Mr Nice Guy. I just hope you can keep it going. Appearing to be the good guy is not exactly a role you are familiar with, old chap.'

Matthews sat at the table doing his damnedest not to react to what he was hearing.

'Clever bugger. OK, so you're not going to take the bait. Let's just see what you do with Mr Thomson if you're so fucking smart!'

His Lordship did not have time to be angry at what he was hearing. He was scribbling in his notebook so fast he was in danger of running out of ink.

'Real evidence is something you can pick up and examine for yourselves. When witnesses are relying upon their impression of a situation and their recollection of it, there is always scope for mistake. That is obvious. But fingerprint evidence, scientific evidence, tape-recorded evidence, each have a substantive quality.

'What do the Crown offer? No fingerprints, clearly. No tape-recorded confession, curiously. Forensic evidence, unconvincingly: a spot or two of blood on a jacket belonging to Charles Gallagher. A jacket found weeks after the death of Kevin Boyle. A jacket which could have been cleaned or even destroyed by the man who was so careful that he wore a mask at the time of the shooting and disposed of his gloves, gun and getaway car. This man keeps a leather jacket and does not bother to spend a few pence getting it drycleaned. In addition, you will remember the testimony of Professor Walker, the pathologist, who examined the scene. No evidence whatsoever that any blood sprayed out of the car to contaminate someone nearby.

'But, of course, it goes further. Much further.

'Dr Bruce, the forensic scientist, told you that it was seven hundred times more likely that the blood spots came from Kevin Boyle as opposed to someone else. An impressive statistic – or is it?

'Unfortunately, Dr Bruce could not date the stains. The blood could have landed on the jacket weeks before, or after, the murder. He too examined the scene and could find no traces of blood outside the car, yet three spots are supposed to land on Charlie Gallagher. You know that thousands upon thousands of people in Britain alone have blood which would fit Kevin Boyle's profile. The much vaunted statistics give you not so much as a hint as to how many of these people live in the Glasgow area and at some time over a period of many months have been in contact with Mr Gallagher's jacket. This does not take the Crown to the starting line, never mind into the race.

'What are we to make of Mr Warwick, or Beswick, or whatever name he chooses to use? A liar? A cheat? A man whose ego and arrogance know no bounds? Well, these are the complimentary things one could say about him.

'Arnold Warwick is an odious creature with a track record which demonstrates a catalogue of deception unrivalled in the history of our courts. And yet, and yet, ladies and gentlemen, he was presented to you as just another witness. No attempt was made by the Crown to demonstrate his true character, although the Crown must have known. You are supposed to believe that Charlie Gallagher, in common with many others, found this man so trustworthy, so sympathetic that he chose him as his confidant, his confessor. Never mind a secondhand car, would you buy a second hand for your watch from this individual?

'In common with most con-men, Arnold Warwick is skilled in the art of deception. In Charles Gallagher he saw a chance to do himself a bit of good. You may have little doubt he pieced together his intricate web of lies from pieces of gossip and the pages of the tabloid press. Much as the Crown may try to rubbish this notion, the proof is before your eyes. Give Mr Warwick his due. Treat him with utter contempt.'

Muirhead was now in full flow. He varied the speed and tone of his voice, sometimes raising it to make a point, at others, almost whispering as if sharing a confidence with the jurors. As he was using no notes, he strode up and down before the jury box making regular eye contact with each of its occupants. Whether the audience was on his side or otherwise, it was captive. Muirhead had them where he wanted them.

'Let me remind you of a witness the Advocate Depute, in his wisdom, saw fit not to mention at all.

'Barbara Potter was the girl who was unwittingly used to set up Kevin Boyle. Set up by a man with an Irish accent. Clearly not Charlie Gallagher nor anyone proved to be connected to him. You will remember that she sought to identify Gallagher as being present when she was hired to seduce Kevin Boyle. Damning evidence, if true. In reality, utterly false. She identified Mr Gallagher only because she had been threatened by the man, the man with the Irish accent.

'Time and time again, when you lift the stone you find something nasty lurking beneath.

'And in this case there is surely nothing nastier than the evidence of Acting Detective Constable David Taylor. You will remember him, only too well I suspect. He was the young officer who eventually admitted, was forced to admit, that he leant on Sammy McPhee. This is only one way to describe what he did. It was a blatant attempt to pervert the course of justice – pure and simple. Deliberate and nasty. Mr McPhee may not have a lifestyle which you or I would choose. But who are we to condemn him? What right does anyone have to condemn him or describe him in the pejorative language chosen by Mr Taylor? Who knows what tragedy in his life may have driven him on to the streets? He was entitled to the same respect as any other witness. He was entitled to the same fairness of treatment. He should not have been picked upon and bullied by anyone, let alone a police officer. The conduct of Mr Taylor was as cowardly as it was improper. It was the conduct of a man interested only in self-advancement. A man indifferent to the concepts of propriety, fairness and justice.

'This is the measure of the man the Crown ask you to believe when he claims that Charles Gallagher confessed to him.

'Mr Gallagher was subjected to lengthy interviews, quite rightly, and time and time again he denied any involvement in the murder. All of this was tape-recorded. You are to believe that, during the briefest of interludes when, coincidentally, the recording machine is switched off, Mr Gallagher blurts out his admission. Deliberately. Boastfully.

'Let us assume that he did. This must have been the most momentous event in that young officer's career. Normally in uniform. First experience of CID. He would have bent over backwards to make sure he did everything strictly according to the rules. He would have been desperate to impress by his attention to detail. Wouldn't you? Just so!

'What should he have done, according to well-established procedures? He would have entered this so-called confession into his notebook, there and then, to preserve it for all time coming. What does he do? Nothing. Why? Because he didn't think it was necessary. He didn't think it was necessary to record a confession to murder. Ladies and gentlemen, if you believe that you will believe anything!

'Perhaps he was harshly treated by me in cross-examination. Perhaps it was brutal. But it is a harsh and brutal thing to do to seek to advance your own career by fabricating evidence in such a despicable manner. David Taylor betrayed himself, his father and the police force. You must not allow him to betray justice.

'That only leaves the Crown with the evidence of Barclay Thomson.'

Matthews leaned conspiratorially towards his junior.

'Now it gets tricky for him.'

Her thin smile was not greatly reassuring.

'Ladies and gentlemen, even if you were inclined to accept Mr Thomson's evidence, you could not convict my client. His evidence stands alone and you would have to acquit due to a total lack of corroboration. But even this evidence is fatally flawed.

'Mr Thomson identifies Charlie Gallagher as the killer. He claims that he recognised him. Let us examine the true strength of that proposition.

'If he really saw the shooting, saw a man being injured, his life in danger, he would have telephoned for an ambulance. He did not. He had not seen a stranger he might have been able to identify. He had not seen someone he thought he vaguely recognised. The man with the gun, the killer, was someone he claims he recognised. Someone he knew. Someone he was at school with. And yet, and yet ladies and gentlemen, no name is forthcoming. Why would Barclay Thomson conceal this crucial evidence if, if he had actually recognised the murderer? The answer to this question is, you may think, all too obvious.

'When he found himself talking to the police, he would surely have named the attacker. He did not. He feigns to be a citizen just doing his duty. Yet he would not even give his name and address. He makes telephone calls, anonymously, and only later, much later, does he come forward. Comes forward at a time when he has had every opportunity to be influenced by local rumour. How much better would it have been if his approach had been open and straightforward? Alas, for the Crown, it was not.

'The Advocate Depute, quite rightly, told you the Crown does not require to prove a motive. Equally, the defence does not have to demonstrate why a witness has behaved in a less than honest manner. Ladies and gentlemen, I suggest you would not take any decision in your lives, even a trivial decision in your own lives, based on the evidence of

Barclay Thomson. If that is so, you would surely not use it to convict a man of murder.

'The defence have led evidence to demonstrate that Charlie Gallagher could not have killed Kevin Boyle because he was not there. His mother told you that. Now it would be easy to say that a mother would lie to protect her son and simply dismiss her evidence. Well, the world has become a sad and sorry place if a woman is to be disbelieved just because she is a mother. Yet again the Crown's approach is to pour scorn. You are not allowed to have a party, unless it is planned weeks ahead. Uncle Eddie is portrayed as if he was a simpleton. True, his timing may not coincide with Mrs Gallagher but all that does is to demonstrate that this evidence has not been concocted and can be relied upon.'

'Christ what a bloody whitewash,' muttered Matthews. 'That old fool put his precious nephew out of the house at the time the bloody thing was being committed. Timing not coinciding, my arse.'

'Don't tell me he's getting to you,' volunteered his junior, none too helpfully.

'That will be the day.'

Matthews shot her a filthy look. It did not seem to upset the recipient one whit.

'In this case, much has gone on behind the scenes. You have had only a flavour of it. It is clear that various factions want Charlie Gallagher to be convicted. Their reasons – we know not. Kevin Boyle was a man with many enemies. Someone wanted him dead and was prepared to go to great lengths to secure that aim.

'He was coldly gunned down on the streets of Glasgow. Of course such things are deeply offensive and should not happen. Such an act cries out for justice. Justice, not vengeance.

'The Crown has singularly failed to prove the guilt of the young man in the dock. Moreover it would be a disservice to Kevin Boyle to convict the wrong man of his murder. It would be an injustice to convict Charles Gallagher. Do justice to the living and to the dead. That is all I ask.'

Total silence accompanied James Muirhead as he returned slowly and deliberately to his seat. As he took it, a hundred pairs of lungs exhaled.

'Ladies and gentlemen, on Monday morning I will charge you then you will retire to consider your verdict. Do not begin to make up your minds until you have heard what I have to say. Regard this as a weekend off and come back refreshed. Ten o'clock please.'

As Lord Cowden was leaving the bench Muirhead stared at Donald Anderson who had taken a fit of the giggles.

'What's amusing you? I could do with a laugh.'

'Only an Edinburgh judge could tell a Glasgow jury to come back refreshed!'

Muirhead smiled wryly. Day ten had come to an end.

Chapter Thirteen

The watchers were growing increasingly bored with watching and waiting. They had been in Stranraer since Friday and it was now Sunday. Police officers are accustomed to waiting in the knowledge that it may bear no fruit, but patience was beginning to wear thin. In their various stations, the talk among them was that this operation was a bummer. Only the Boss seemed to believe the target would arrive and he had told no one the basis for this opinion. A diet of lukewarm Coke and plastic hamburgers was making stomachs rumble.

Privately, even McAllister was beginning to have his doubts. Not that he would admit it, let alone show it. The disappearance of the 14.00 hours ferry into the distance had made it difficult for him to continue to exude an air of confidence, especially one he no longer felt. He snatched up the microphone.

'The last boat leaves at 19.35. If you want something to eat, get it now. If you need the lavatory, go to it now. Stay alert. I want everyone on their toes. McGarry will be here shortly. Check the descriptions you have been given and keep your eyes open.'

McAllister would have been more than a little upset if he had heard the soured comments.

'Eat now. Piss now. Keep alert. Britain needs fucking lerts. There's more chance of us getting the fucking knickers off Posh Spice than this git turning up.'

McAllister pondered the situation. If McGarry didn't show, what was to be done? He could not tie up such a large number of officers indefinitely. He was proceeding on the basis of unchecked information and guesswork. He was confident that his target had not left the country. He was a creature of habit and was known to hate flying. The unknown factor in all of this was the end of the trial. Would McGarry want to see its conclusion for himself or would he prefer to be out of reach of the shockwaves? McAllister was banking on the latter.

The officer getting into the back seat beside him brought him out of his reflective state.

'Local CID brought this over. They thought you might be interested.'

McAllister studied the contents of the document which had been handed to him.

'When the hell did this happen?'

'Friday apparently.'

'Why has it taken so long for me to be told? Are they all bloody stupid up there? For Christ's sake does no one ever think?'

'It didn't go to our division. Took time for the connection to be made.'

'Unbelievable! Shot twice. Unknown assailant. No witnesses. Victim cannot identify. That'll be right! He'll identify when I get a hold of him. At least we know what this means.'

'Sorry, Boss, but none of this makes any sense to me. I take it you do understand who's been shot?'

'Of course I do. It makes sense to me. It tells me that the bastard is on his way.'

McGarry was nine miles from Ayr on the A77 and was slowly beginning to calm down, relieved he was leaving Glasgow behind him. He felt no remorse for the damage he had left behind, nor was he concerned at the outcome of any police investigation into it. Even assuming there was one.

Traffic! He hated being stuck in traffic. He had been forced to sit in a queue of vehicles crawling out of the City. Normally he would have carved his way through such an obstruction regardless of the effect upon or the reaction of other drivers. On this occasion he had been a good boy and crawled along with the mugs. No point in attracting the attention of some nosy traffic cop who might delay him even longer. He had built some slack into his timings, so he had gritted his teeth and got on with it, however much it irritated him.

With a virtually clear road ahead, he relaxed and smiled to himself. He would get down to Stranraer and dump this heap of junk in a carpark, paying the appropriate fee so it would not attract attention until he was gone past caring.

He would then have a beer in one of the pubs near the terminal along with dozens of others waiting for the boat. Then he would be off. Simple as that.

The road took him past Kilmarnock and round the outskirts of Ayr and on down the coast. Only one small problem remained. Beyond Turnberry he came to the town of Girvan. He turned off the main road and parked. Leaving the car, he strolled along the harbour wall. His hand was in his jacket pocket gripping the handle of his pistol. He paused, looked around him and, when satisfied he could not be observed, pulled out the gun.

'Time for you and I to part company, my old friend.'

He stroked the handle and almost caressed the cold metal. Its feel was very familiar, almost comforting. McGarry was not a man given to sentimentality but he was almost saddened by the prospect of parting with the gun. It had served him well over many years. It had faithfully carried out his wishes and, more to the point, had never let him down. It had saved his life on more than one occasion.

He looked at the gun, the water, then back to the gun.

'No. You deserve better. Anyway, I might just need you. However, you I don't need.'

He threw two spent cartridge cases into the water.

He returned to the car. In the side-door pocket was a duster. He wrapped the gun in the cloth and placed it in his suit carry.

'Right. Stranraer and home.'

❊   ❊   ❊

McAllister leaned forward to pick up the mike but was beaten to the punch when the radio crackled into life.

'Target has just entered the terminal. Target has just entered the terminal. Wearing dark calf-length raincoat – belted at waist. No hat. Brown leather suit carry.'

'Keep him under observation. When he goes to get on the boat, take him down. No unnecessary risks – but take him down.'

McGarry had checked the approach to the terminal and was now taking in all the surrounding details. Senses on full alert. Nothing unusual. Nothing to make him feel uncomfortable. He had timed it to perfection, as ever. The boarding of the boat was underway. He would join the rest of the foot passengers, nice and calm, get through control, and off we go. Two middle-aged ladies were making their way forward. Perfect. McGarry tagged along just behind them. Everything was going according to plan. It always did. As he walked casually along, he thought with satisfaction of the man he had taken care of. It would be some time before he could walk, anywhere.

A combination of over-confidence and sentimentality were about to prove his downfall – that, allied to the lack of eyes in the back of his head.

A piercing scream coincided with the ground rushing up to meet him. He fought to move his arms but they were being twisted behind his back. He hit the ground with a thump and a heavy weight landed on his back knocking the breath from him. The rough surface tore at the right side of his face. He could see nothing other than pairs of feet shuffling around in front of his eyes. Before his mind could analyse what had just happened, the cold metal against his temple answered any questions he might have had.

'Armed police officers. Lie still and you will come to no harm. I will show you my warrant card.'

McGarry had no need to read the plastic card which was dangled in front of him.

'We are going to place handcuffs on you and then carry out a body search. If you lie still, you will come to no harm. Do you understand?'

'Just get me off the ground before you tear my fucking face off.'

The handcuffs were applied and McGarry could feel hands rubbing across his back and down his legs. When he was turned over the process was repeated on his chest. Looking up, he could see faces, none of which he recognised. Faces, strange faces, and the barrel of a gun which was still being pointed at his head.

'He's clean.'

He had no difficulty in realising that he had been stupid, but more to the point, careless. Very bloody careless. Well, they could do what they liked. They had nothing on him and they would get nothing out of him.

Two men hauled McGarry to his feet and he found himself face to face with a suit.

'Now you, I do know!'

'Thomas McGarry, my name is Detective Superintendent McAllister. I am detaining you on suspicion of a crime punishable by imprisonment, namely assault. Other than supplying me with your name and address, you are not obliged to say anything but anything you do say will be noted and given in evidence. You will be taken to Glasgow where your further rights will be explained to you. You will then be interviewed under tape-recorded conditions. Do you understand?'

McGarry had nothing more he wished to say at this particular point in time. He was paying little or no attention to McAllister but was preoccupied with the man standing just behind him holding his brown leather suit carry. A chill crept over him as he realised the enormity of the situation.

The bag!

While McGarry was being placed in the back of a police van, McAllister returned to his own car to make contact with Stewart Street Police Office. He intended to treat his prisoner as a maximum security risk and Stewart Street had all the necessary facilities. While he thought it was highly unlikely that anyone would seek to mount a rescue bid, this man had taken some catching and he was taking no chances.

By detaining him, he could only hold McGarry for six hours before he would have to charge him with something or release him. However, he had already made up his mind that he was not interviewing this man in a local police station.

As he reached his vehicle, two officers came rushing up to him. One was sporting a bullet-proof vest and a baseball cap bearing the logo POLICE. The other, one of his own sergeants, was carrying a leather suit carry.

'Problem?'

'Not exactly, Boss.'

'What, then?'

'I thought you might find this interesting. This bag was dropped by McGarry when he was snatched. We were searching it, and we found this.'

He opened up one of the side pockets. McAllister could see an object with a distinctive shape, wrapped in some kind of material.

'You're thinking the same as me, Boss. He couldn't be so stupid.'

'Or so arrogant. Get one of the boys over here with his camera. I want this examined now and the procedure photographed, every step of the way.'

'Do you want to go to the office?'

'No. We do it here, right now.'

Within two minutes, the photographer had arrived and indicated that he was ready.

The bag was re-opened, the package removed and slowly and carefully unwrapped. The repeated exploding of the flash gun confirmed that every detail was being recorded.

'It's a nine millimetre self-loading pistol. Browning. Do you wish me to check to see if it is loaded?'

McAllister shook his head at the stupidity of the question from a man authorised to carry a gun.

'Get on with it.'

Rubber-gloved hands picked up the weapon which was handled with a degree of respect amounting almost to reverence.

'Safety catch is on.'

A click was instantly followed by an ammunition clip springing out of the base of the pistol grip. The officer pulled back the slide and looked into the weapon.

'Nothing in the gun, sir. It's empty. However, there is at least one cartridge in the clip.'

He gently placed the gun down on the material which was spread on the bonnet of McAllister's car. He then proceeded to extract six cartridges from their holder.

'All apparently live, sir.'

'Right. You two get that lot to Glasgow, now. I want ballistics tests. If there were bullets found at the scene of Friday's shooting, carry out a comparison. If none were found, take the bloody place apart until you get them. I also want a comparison with the bullets from the Boyle murder.'

The two officers glanced at each other incredulously.

'Just do it! I don't give a damn if you and ballistics are up all night. I want a report on my desk first thing in the morning.'

'Boss, the Boyle bullets are productions in court. We can't get them till tomorrow morning at the very earliest. Even then, surely we'll need to get permission from someone? We may not be able to get our hands on them till the trial is over.'

McAllister reflected for a moment.

'Leave that to me. Get on with what we do have. I'm going to have a few words with our Mr McGarry. I still want a report first thing tomorrow morning.'

McAllister strode to the police van which was being guarded by two uniformed officers. Perhaps he was getting somewhere – at long last. At least he was in a position to make the man think. A man who thinks is a man who worries. A man who is worried is a man who might just be inclined to talk.

'He inside?'

'Sir. Handcuffed to two cops as per your orders.'

'They are not cops. They, like you, are police officers. Now, get your notebooks out, come with me and write down everything you hear – and you better hear everything.'

With that, he climbed into the back of the vehicle and sat down opposite the dejected figure. McGarry stared at the floor.

'Thomas McGarry, I am releasing you from detention...'

The eyes came up, slowly. The look, a bizarre mixture of suspicion, controlled elation and pure hatred. Even McAllister had never experienced anything quite like it. He had confronted people who had carried out the most horrific acts. Deeds involving the kind of violence which would shock even devotees of the sickest of video nasties. Some could be described as mad. Some were quite simply bad. Some demonstrated not so much as a vestige of remorse as if what they had done was all in a day's work. Never before had he felt himself to be in the presence of genuine evil. The eyes burned into him as if seeking to inflict harm. He shivered involuntarily.

'...you are now under arrest.'

Suspicion and elation disappeared leaving only the hatred.

McAllister kept his face impassive and his voice flat.

'I am now going to prefer a charge against you.'

He intoned the words of the caution: 'The charge is that you did, on this day, in Stranraer, have in your possession a firearm and ammunition without being in possession of a firearms certificate contrary to the Firearms Act of 1968. Do you understand the charge?'

McGarry's eyes spoke volumes but his lips did not move.

'Do you have any reply to the charge?'

Only the eyes spoke.

'Very well, you will now be taken to Glasgow.'

McAllister climbed out of the back of the van, then turned back.

'You will speak to me – soon.'

McGarry raised his hands and formed his fingers into the shape of a gun. He spat on the floor.

'Get him to Stewart Street!'

As he walked away, McAllister smiled.

'So I've rattled your cage. And with a bit of luck, I've only just started.'

It was six o'clock in the morning. McAllister could contain himself no longer. He had arrived in Glasgow shortly after midnight and confirmed that McGarry was securely locked up. He had permitted himself a glance at the man in his cell. McGarry had had his clothes taken from him and was clad in a white paper overall. He was lying facing the wall. He could detect not even the slightest movement. However, McAllister had no doubt that the man's senses were functioning on full alert. McGarry was aware someone was there and knew exactly who it was.

He stared again at the police file on his desk. He now knew all that the records could tell him about Thomas Joseph Aloysius McGarry, but there were too many unanswered questions. Far too many!

Still nothing from ballistics. He glared at the phone. He needed a favour, and how! Even at six o'clock in the morning. Especially at six in the morning.

A sleepy, 'Hello', answered his call.

'Bill, I'm sorry to trouble you, it's Grant McAllister.'

'Grant…what time…for God's sake it's six o'clock in the morning…it's the middle of the night. I take it this is not a social call?'

As he spoke, his voice was becoming more alert. Bill Scott was the second most senior official in the Procurator Fiscal's Department in Glasgow. The two men had known each other for many years, indeed since their careers began. Bill Scott was as straight as they came.

'Bill, I need a favour…a big favour.'

'You're not in trouble, are you, Grant?'

'No, not at all. This is business, not personal.'

'I'm awake now. Go on.'

'You may want to get yourself a cup of coffee. This is going to take some time.'

'Business first. Then coffee.'

McAllister set out the detailed background while the fiscal listened in silence.

'That's some story, Grant, but you don't seem to have too much evidence to back it up. There's an awful lot of theory.'

'That's why I need a favour. I want to examine the bullets from the Boyle murder but at this stage I want to keep it private. It's the charge today so I don't imagine anyone will be referring to them. I need you to authorise their transfer into my custody. If the result is negative, no one need ever know. There will be nothing to know.'

'And if the result is positive, which is fairly unlikely?'

'You will get all the information. It's not for me to decide what to do with it.'

'What do you really think?'

'I just don't know. That's why I want to do the tests.'

'To say the least of it, this is pretty irregular.'

'I appreciate that. I'm not doing anything illegal or underhand. I'm trying to do my job.'

'Should we try to halt the trial or at least delay it?'

'As you said, there is no evidence. I can only speculate till I have some facts.'

There was a pause while Scott mulled over all that he had heard.

'OK, Grant. Obviously I trust you. When we both end up in the shit you won't try to run away?'

'No chance.'

'Meet me at the High Court building at half-past eight. I'll make the necessary arrangements.'

'Thanks. I owe you one.'

'Almost certainly.'

* * *

Yet again the public gallery was packed. The level of commotion indicated that the watchers anticipated they were about to witness something momentous – eventually. When the defence arrived to take its place at the table, the Crown team was already seated. It had an additional member. A new face. As Gallagher was brought into the dock, Anderson leant over to Muirhead.

'What's Bill Scott doing here?'

'I was just wondering that. I didn't know he had any interest in this case – till now.'

The entire company was brought to its feet by a cry of 'Court' which greeted Lord Cowden's entry onto the bench. His Lordship settled into his chair, turned to face the jury, waited for silence, then the gravelly voice began.

'Ladies and gentlemen of the jury, you have now heard all the evidence and the speeches on behalf of the Crown and the defence. Shortly you will retire to consider your verdict. Yours, not mine.

'You and I have separate functions. I will tell you the rules of law which you must apply and you will take these from me without question. The evidence, on the other hand, is a matter for you and you alone. You must decide which witnesses to accept and which to reject. You may accept a witness in whole, in part or not at all. Before you accept the evidence of a witness you must find him or her credible and reliable. Even a truthful witness may make a genuine mistake. If you reject a piece of testimony for any reason, just put it out of your mind.

'It is your assessment of the evidence which counts, not mine and certainly not counsel's. You have heard their addresses and the exchanges contained therein. If their submissions assist you, good and well. However, you should concentrate on facts, not rhetoric, clarity rather than hyperbole, common sense rather than flights of fancy.

'There are certain fundamental rules which apply to this as to every other case. Let me deal with these now.

'It is for the Crown to prove its case. The burden of proof is shouldered by the Crown throughout the trial and it is for the defence to prove nothing. The accused pleads alibi. He says he was elsewhere. He does not require to prove this.

'The standard of proof is beyond reasonable doubt. This does not mean mathematical certainty. When you have considered the evidence, and thought about it carefully, if there is some matter of substance which makes you doubt the guilt of the accused, then the Crown has failed to discharge the burden of proof and you will acquit. If you have no such doubt, it is your duty to convict. Use your common sense. You will not be swayed by sentiment, revulsion or the prospect of punishment so improperly referred to by Mr Muirhead in his address. You must and will act as judges, judges of the facts.

'You must find corroboration, evidence from two separate sources pointing to the guilt of the accused. There need not be two eye-witnesses. Murderers do not normally seek an audience. If you find two pieces of evidence which point to the guilt of the accused, beyond reasonable doubt, it is your duty to convict.

'This does not apply to the accused. He need prove nothing and, of course, does require corroboration. If, in the whole body of evidence led by the Crown or the defence, there is material which causes you to have a reasonable doubt, you are entitled to acquit.

'Now, the accused did not give evidence. There is no legal obligation upon him to enter the witness box. The law decrees he is entitled to remain silent and his silence does not amount to guilt. You may have wished to hear from him and hear what he had to say. You may wonder what, if anything, he had to hide. Put such thoughts out of your mind. The accused has offered the defence of alibi and some evidence has been led in an attempt to support this. An accused does not require to prove he was elsewhere. However, if you believe this evidence, you acquit. If it merely raises a reasonable doubt in your minds, again you acquit. However, in the absence of evidence from the accused himself, you may find it easier to accept the Crown submission that the alibi evidence should be rejected. It is a matter entirely for you. But let me stress this. Even if you reject the alibi defence, that does not of itself mean that the Crown case is proved.

'Ladies and gentlemen, will you now look at your copies of the indictment. The charge remaining before you is a charge of murder, the most serious charge in our law.

'Murder in our law is constituted by any wilful act causing the destruction of life, whether intended to kill, or displaying such wicked recklessness as to imply a disposition depraved enough to be regardless of consequences. The language may seem archaic but it has stood the test of time. However, to put the matter quite simply, if a man discharges a firearm into the head of his victim, you may have no difficulty in concluding that he intended to kill his victim. Consequently, such a deed would undoubtedly amount to the crime of murder.

'Now, when the trial commenced, there were two other charges on the indictment. The Crown have withdrawn these as the Advocate was perfectly entitled to do. Why he did this is his affair. No doubt there was some very good reason why they were initially before you. He does not have to justify his actions and this has no bearing on the one charge which remains.'

As his Lordship's address was proceeding, Grant McAllister was pacing his office. Agitation had been replaced by impatience and excitement.

He was in possession of the first ballistics report. The knee-capping bullets had been recovered from the knees of their victim and were fired by the gun found in McGarry's suit carry. He had him by the balls but was not ready to squeeze – just yet. No need to rush. McGarry was not going anywhere for a very long time.

Footsteps approached his office and he turned to see Joe Johnstone striding towards him carrying a file. Johnstone was head of the firearms section. A former army weapons instructor, he had spent his life studying guns and the science of ballistics. What he didn't know about the subject could be inscribed on the head of a pin. Given any encouragement, he would talk guns till the cows came home. He had the habit of using ten words when one would have sufficed. Joe Johnstone was a man who could bore for his country.

'Well, Joe?'

'I thought I'd bring this over personally. Too important to entrust to one of the underlings. I knew you would be anxious for the results and I didn't want to keep you waiting. Time can be of the essence in these cases. You'll want to catch the bird before he flies the nest, I dare say. I thought you'd prefer to see the results rather than just a telephone call. No room for misunderstanding when you see it in print. Sometimes, down the phone, people can get the wrong end of the stick. Too desperate to hear what they want to hear, that sort of thing. I take it this is fairly important?'

'Joe – what is the bloody result?'

'Here. Read it for yourself.'

McAllister took the report and began to study it with the utmost care.

The first three pages described the comparison test which had been carried out involving the bullets and cartridge cases from the Boyle killing and test firings from the weapon recovered at Stranraer. The barrel of a gun imparts distinctive marks to a bullet as it passes down its length. Each barrel is unique. When cartridges are ejected from a self-loading pistol the metal of the gun will leave equally distinctive striation marks on the metal of the case. These are as unique as fingerprints and enable experts to establish if a particular bullet or cartridge was fired by or ejected from a particular weapon. He turned the page and studied the conclusion.

'The bullet fragment recovered from the head of the deceased was nine millimetre and of typical fired appearance. It had been significantly damaged by contact with a hard surface and was unsuitable for comparison purposes.'

'Damn!'

'Read the first paragraph, eh? Don't worry, it gets better.'

'The cartridge cases from the test firings of the Browning pistol were compared with the cartridge cases found at the Boyle locus. The striation marks on the cases caused by ejection from the weapon were examined under a comparison microscope. In our opinion they were identical and we have no doubt that the cartridge cases found at the Boyle locus were fired from the Browning pistol found at Stranraer.'

'Got him!'

'I told you it got better. I always believe in saving the best for the last. Keeps people interested. Builds up the tension.'

'Thank you, Joe. Is there any doubt?'

'Relax. None at all. The gun you found at Stranraer killed Kevin Boyle. You lucky bugger.'

'Yes. Maybe so. But now my problems really start.'

McAllister picked up the telephone.

'David, you and Tom go and collect our Mr McGarry and take him to an interview room. Tell him nothing. I'll be there momentarily.'

Joe Johnstone was leaving the office.

'Joe, thanks. I appreciate it.'

He received a wave of acknowledgement.

'Now to work!'

⚫   ⚫   ⚫

'Ladies and gentlemen, as I indicated, the evidence in the case is for you and not for me. I intend to say nothing about it. You have heard the arguments, the pros and cons rehearsed in the speeches of counsel. These are serious matters and they merit serious consideration.

'The Crown must prove, beyond reasonable doubt, that the accused is guilty of murder before you can convict. Mere suspicion will not do.

'The Crown rely heavily on the evidence of the witness Barclay Thomson. He positively, you may think very positively, identified the accused as the killer. Was he in any way shaken in cross-examination? Are the criticisms of him justified? Does he really have a reason to lie, to fabricate his evidence? If he is lying, he is a wicked, wicked man indeed. It is a matter entirely for you to resolve. If you accept his evidence, there is ample material to provide you with the necessary corroboration.

'There was bad blood between the families and perhaps a motive based on commercial rivalry, if I may thus generously put it. You have the bloodstains on the jacket, a jacket owned by the accused and similar to that worn by the assailant. You have the admission to the witness Warwick – a colourful character indeed. Particularly, you have the confession to the young police officer, Mr Taylor. You will remember he, tragically, lost his father. You will also recall, I have no doubt, the ferocious attack mounted against him and decide whether you thought that was justified or possessed of any merit.

'No doubt Mr Muirhead conceived this to be his duty in terms of his instructions. And, no doubt Mr Taylor made mistakes. Surely we all make mistakes. The enthusiasm of youth is especially prone to error. But did he really lie, would he really lie about such a vital matter? You may think that this would be a very difficult prospect to contemplate. If you accept his evidence, then clearly that would take the Crown a very long way towards proving its case. A very long way indeed.

'You must, of course, remember everything Mr Muirhead said to you in his powerful address and give it such weight as you consider appropriate. The special defence of alibi is supported, albeit to a limited extent. However, I think it right to say that Mr Muirhead placed more reliance upon his attack on the Crown case than he did on the alibi. I leave all these matters with you.

'Ladies and gentlemen, there are three verdicts open to you, guilty, not guilty and not proven. Not guilty and not proven are acquittal verdicts and have the same effect. The accused walks free and cannot again be tried for this crime. I can take your verdict from you at any time. You should not rush to judgement, but there is no minimum period you should devote to your deliberations. I can accept a verdict which is unanimous or by a majority. However, if your verdict is by a majority, then at least eight of you must be in favour of guilty before you may bring in such a verdict. Please elect one of your number to chair your deliberations, if you have not already done so. Your spokesman or spokeswoman should be ready to announce your decision when you return to court with your verdict. Will you now please retire and consider your verdict on the charge of murder which remains against the accused, Charles Gallagher.'

The macer approached the jury and, having advise them to take their notes and copies of the photographs with them, ushered them through the door and into the jury room. When the last juror filed past him he closed the door and locked it, before hurrying onto the bench to lead his lordship back to his chambers. It was five past eleven. The trial of Her Majesty's Advocate against Charles Gallagher was over. All that remained was the verdict.

●　　　●　　　●

Early afternoon and a phone call had advised McAllister that the jury was still deliberating. It was time to turn the screw.

McAllister sat down at the table opposite the sullen figure of Tom McGarry who displayed no reaction to his arrival.

'Is the machine ready to go?'

'Yes, sir.'

'Switch it on, please. This is interview room two at Stewart Street Police Office. The time is now 2.25. My name is Superintendent Grant McAllister. I will ask the two other officers present to identify themselves.'

'Detective Inspector David Craig, Strathclyde Police.'

'Detective Sergeant Tom McSherry, also Strathclyde Police.'

'Mr McGarry, will you state your full name please...no response. I confirm that Mr McGarry is present. Inspector Craig.'

'Yes, he is here and has declined to give his name.'

'Sergeant McSherry.'

'Mr McGarry is present and has declined to speak.'

'Mr McGarry, you have already been charged with a contravention of the Firearms Act of 1968. I am now going to ask you questions about a shooting which took place in Brown Street in Glasgow last Friday. You are not obliged to answer these questions but if you do, your answers will be tape-recorded and may be given in evidence in any subsequent proceedings. Do you understand? Again, no response. Very well.

'Mr McGarry, were you in Brown Street last Friday when a man was shot twice?

'Do you accept that a Browning self-loading pistol was found in your bag when you were detained at Stranraer?

'Mr McGarry, bullets were recovered from the scene of the shooting in Brown Street. These have been compared with the Browning found in your possession. Do you understand me?'

McAllister stared intently across the table. You're struggling, you bastard. You're beginning to panic. You are trying not to show it but your eyes tell me otherwise. I've got you and I know it. More to the point, you know it.

'Mr McGarry, this is a serious matter. You do not have to answer my questions, as I have advised you. That is your legal right. However, it may be in your interests to do so. Ballistics experts have examined the Browning and the bullets from the shooting. They match. They match exactly. The bullets were fired by your gun. Now, do you have any comment to make, Mr McGarry?

'Then I will ask you about another matter. You still do not have to answer but if you do your answers will be tape-recorded and may be given in evidence.

'Ballistics experts have also carried out tests to compare the Browning found in your possession with cartridge cases found at the shooting of Kevin Boyle. Will you confirm that you knew Kevin Boyle? You were employed by him at the time of his death? You were his bodyguard, his minder? Why were you not with him when he was murdered, as one might have expected?

'Mr McGarry, the bullets which killed Kevin Boyle were fired from the Browning, from your gun. Now, do you have anything to say?'

The two men stared at each other in silence. McAllister had decided he had said enough. It was time to wait – for as long as was necessary. He held McGarry's stare.

Come on you bastard.

Come on!

Come on!

'Switch the machine off.'

'I can't do that.'

'Then take me back to my cell and you get fuck all. Now switch the machine off.'

Chapter Fourteen

Bill Scott sat forward at his desk listening intently to every word; occasionally shaking his head in disbelief he felt no need to interrupt.

'That's quite a story, Grant.'

'Certainly, I thought I had seen and heard most things, but nothing to match this.'

'Did you have any idea that he was the one intimidating Muirhead?'

'I wondered, but only because of the Irish accent and because he had disappeared so soon after Boyle's death. It seems the man tried to get the job done on the cheap and when that failed, he sent for McGarry. He was desperate for Gallagher to be convicted. Oddly enough, if he had just left things alone, there's a fair chance that would have happened.'

'And Clark?'

'That was purely personal. The Mad Dog had been as good as dead for a long time. Apparently he had been sent to work over a young pusher who owed money to the Gallaghers. Got a bit carried away and killed the poor bastard. We'll find him in a missing person's file somewhere; I have no doubt. Just another junkie who disappeared. Unfortunately, he was McGarry's nephew. Having dealt with Kevin Boyle, McGarry decided to tidy up a loose end – simple as that.'

'Who else was involved?'

'That, I suspect, we will never know. McGarry has only told us what he wants us to know because it suits him. He is no grass.'

'What you haven't explained is why he turned on Kevin?'

'Easy. The oldest reason of them all. Money. What's the situation at the trial?'

'Jury is still out. That's over four hours. Why did McGarry talk?'

'Hard to say. For long enough he wouldn't say a word. As I told you, he would only speak off-tape. Then he gave me the whole story, or what he claims is the whole story.'

'Do you think he would repeat it on tape or make a formal statement?'

'No way. No point in asking him.'

'You took notes?'

'Yes. We've got a fairly detailed record. He didn't object to that for some reason.'

'Why did he tell you?'

'Again, hard to say. I think the answer is revenge. He was paid for killing Kevin. Fine. But then he was hired to lean on Muirhead. The man tried to renege on the deal. McGarry took this as a personal slight. Hence the shooting.'

'A personal slight! I'd hate to see him taking offence.'

'He realised we had him for possession of the gun and the garage shooting. Then, when the bullets matched the Boyle killing, he knew he was finished. I am convinced he decided that, if he was going down, he wasn't going down alone. All done for revenge – pure and simple.'

'How sure are you about all of this?'

'I am as certain as I can be. Charlie Gallagher is a nasty little shit. He should have been locked up for half of the things he's been in to. But he didn't kill Boyle. I have no doubt about that. However, he'll be back, no doubt.'

'What do you want to do?'

'I need warrants.'

'I'll arrange that for you. What about your Mr Warwick?'

'Leave him for the time being. He's going nowhere, after all. Maybe we should actually let him spend some time in Gallagher's company.'

'When all this comes out, he's going to find prison detrimental to his health, anyway.'

'Someone else's problem.'

'Quite. And Thomson?'

'I think I may have a word with him. His name meant nothing to McGarry. It could be he simply made a genuine mistake. Could be he's a publicity seeker. Maybe he was harbouring some old grievance. Who knows?'

'What do we do about the trial?'

'I don't see what we can do at the moment. If he's acquitted, we have a problem. If he's convicted, then we have a major problem. Either way, we can't solve it just now. I have to deal with the other matters first.'

'You'll have your warrants within the hour. Best of luck!'

Just as McAllister was leaving the fiscal's office, Bill Scott answered the telephone.

'Thank you. I'll let him know.'

He replaced the receiver.

'Message for you – from the court.'

●   ●   ●

The three lawyers walked along the corridor towards the front door.

'What do you reckon, James?'

'God knows. By the look of them, it's been fairly lively in that jury room. They're arguing about something but whether it is a verdict or just a piece of evidence, who can tell? Christ, they could still be arguing about who's going to be the foreman!'

The court had re-convened at 4.45.

His Lordship was growling at the jury: 'Ladies and gentlemen, there is no pressure of time being placed upon you. You will be given as long as is necessary to enable you to reach your verdict. However, it is nearly five o'clock and I have no doubt that your deliberations will be tiring. I do not wish to know what stage you have reached, but if you feel there is no prospect of being able to return a verdict within, say, an hour, then I shall direct you to stop for the day and arrangements will be made to provide you with overnight accommodation in an hotel. Can you indicate if you expect to be able to return your verdict within a reasonable time this evening?'

The collective shaking of heads conveyed the answer – in the clearest possible terms.

'Very well, ladies and gentlemen. In a moment or two the court will adjourn. When you return to your room, please do not discuss the matter further. The Clerk of Court will come to you and explain what is to happen. Please let me stress that when you are in your hotel you must not talk about the case with anyone, and you should not permit anyone to talk about it with you. At ten o'clock tomorrow you may continue with your task. Tomorrow morning, please.'

His Lordship left the bench. Day eleven had come to an end.

James Muirhead looked across the table. Mike Matthews raised his eyebrows. Muirhead shrugged a 'who knows' gesture and led the defence team out of the court room.

'Stupid question I know, but what do you reckon, Jim?'

'Yeah, it's a stupid question.'

The response was made kindly and without a hint of irritation. Muirhead smiled wryly.

'All we know is that they are split. By the look of them they've had a fair argument going. But at least some of them must be on our side. Who can tell what is impressing the convictors – Thomson, Taylor, the blood? Anybody's guess. It depends on how many sheep are in the middle and which side has the better powers of persuasion and the greater stamina.'

'It's a lottery, isn't it?'

'Sure is. That's why we try to stack the odds in our favour.'

'Still a bloody gamble!'

'Are we going for a beer?' chipped in Anderson.

'Now that is a stupid question!'

The three men laughed, wearily.

* * *

'Davie, the DI wants to see you, pronto. Maybe he wants to welcome you back, personally like!'

David Taylor ought to have detected the thinly-veiled warning. Unfortunately, since his mauling in the witness box, he had been off work and had only returned to duty that morning. He had been unsure what to expect but had been pleasantly surprised, and relieved, that no one had made any comment on the near disaster which had befallen him. Police officers are not noted for their sensitivity or for respecting the sensitivities of others. What could they do anyway? He hadn't admitted doing anything that was illegal, really. So, he had noised up a witness. So what? It happened all the time. Witnesses regularly needed a gentle reminder of what was required of them.

At worst, he could face a disciplinary charge. What with being his father's son, the suicide and all that, they weren't going to do much to him. A slap on the wrist. Be a bit more careful in future, that sort of thing. Hardly a problem. Certainly nothing to worry about. Might have to do some more time in uniform. Pain in the arse. He was too good to hang around with the plods. The CID would want him back. After all, they liked guys who knew what was what, knew how the game worked, knew the score.

By the time he got to the Detective Inspector's room, he had a spring in his step. His over-confidence had prevented him giving any real thought to the reason for the summons. Had he been less cocky, he might have been better prepared. He might even have taken a moment to wonder why the DI was seated behind his desk flanked by two officers who were plainly not of junior rank.

'Morning, or is it afternoon, sir, you wanted to see me?'

Confident.

'Yes, Taylor, would you care to sit down?'

'No, thank you sir, I'm just going out on a job.'

'Very well. I take it you know who I am?'

'Of course, sir. I also know you were a pal of my dad. He often mentioned your name.'

Taylor thought he would throw in a bit of grovelling for good measure.

'These officers are Detective Chief Inspector Ward and Detective

Inspector Thomson of the Disciplinary Branch.'

Here we go, thought Taylor. The slap on the wrist. Better show a bit of humility and contrition.

'Good afternoon, sirs.'

Suitably formal.

'They have something to say to you. Before they do, as a senior officer as well as your father's friend, I want to advise you that you are entitled to speak with the Police Federation Representative. It might be in your interests to take this advice. What these officers have to say to you is a serious matter – serious for you.'

Sadly, Taylor failed to take the hint, so generously offered. He did not even notice the hostile body language of the two strangers.

'No, thank you, sir, I am quite happy to deal with this. I have nothing to hide.'

The Detective Inspector shook his head, in resignation. The two strangers looked more relaxed.

'As you please. Mr Ward.'

'Constable Taylor, I am Detective Chief Inspector Ward and this is my colleague Detective Inspector Thomson. We are officers of the Disciplinary Branch. I am about to prefer a charge against you but before I do so, I must advise you that you are not obliged to say anything but anything you do say will be noted and may be given in evidence. Do you understand the caution I have just administered?'

'A charge! What charge? No, I don't understand.'

'I will put the charge to you in a moment. Do you understand the words of the caution?'

'Yes. Yes, of course.'

'David Taylor, the charge against you is that you did on 16th July 1997 in the High Court of Justiciary while giving evidence on oath in the case of Her Majesty's Advocate against Charles Gallagher, falsely state that said Charles Gallagher had admitted to you that he had killed the late Kevin Boyle, the truth being, as you well know, that he made no such statement, and thus you did commit perjury. Do you understand the charge? Do you understand the charge?'

Taylor understood only too well. He could not comprehend the scale of his predicament, but he understood the nature of it.

'Yes.'

'Do you have anything to say in answer to the charge?'

'I think I had better see the Federation rep and a lawyer.'

'Anything else?'

'No. I have nothing to say to you.'

'Very well. Mr Taylor, you are now under arrest. You will be taken to the uniform bar where your rights will be explained to you. For the moment, I think you had better sit down.'

The short brutal procedure was at an end.

Automatically Taylor did as he was bid. He looked in turn at each of the men opposite. If he hoped for a hint of understanding, sympathy or compassion, he was hoping in vain. The Disciplinary Branch officers showed no sign of any emotion. Detective Inspector David Craig shook his head and looked away. Taylor realised he was alone. Completely alone.

●   ●   ●

As David Taylor's little world was collapsing about him, Grant McAllister and Tom McSherry were heading to Miller Hill, a private hospital on the outskirts of Glasgow. Before leaving his office, McAllister had made a phone call – largely a one-sided conversation for most of its short duration.

'That's all I can tell you, I'm afraid.'

'I understand. You are sure – this time?'

'Yes. I'm sorry.'

'I believe you are. When are you going to see him?'

'Within the hour.'

'May I be present?'

'If you really wish.'

'I do.'

'Then certainly.'

'And the other matter?'

'No verdict.'

'I don't envy you.'

'I believe you don't.'

On arrival, they made their way to room B12 where they had arranged to meet with the physician who was in charge of the subject of their visit. The doctor was chatting to a uniformed officer who was stationed outside the door of the private room.

McAllister took the doctor aside and explained what he intended to do.

'Any problem with that?'

'Medically, none at all. He is fit enough. I suppose you will want to take him into custody?'

'As soon as possible.'

'It will be some time till he is fit enough to be moved to...?'

'Barlinnie.'

'Barlinnie. Does it have a hospital unit?'

'It does. It's not as comfortable as this place, but it is adequate.'

'Even at that, I would not wish him to be moved for a week yet, perhaps ten days. His leg injuries are very serious. He must be kept immobilised in order to give them the best chance to heal.'

'I have no problem with that. I may have to increase the level of police presence.'

'Superintendent, he's not exactly going to run away.'

'I appreciate that, but I am about to charge him with a serious offence. I have a duty to make sure that he is held in secure conditions and indeed I must have regard to his own safety. That is the responsibility of the police, not the hospital.'

'Yes, I see that. Very well. I will insure that everyone here co-operates with your men if they respect the fact that he is my patient and is still entitled to our best medical care.'

'I would not have it otherwise.'

'Right, Superintendent, I'll leave you to get on with your work. I take it you do not need me to be present?'

'Thank you, no. That will not be necessary.'

McAllister and McSherry entered the room to find a man lying in bed with his legs in plaster. A woman was sitting by the bedside. The patient turned to look towards him with an expression which was less than welcoming.

'It's manners to knock before coming in. This is a private room in a private hospital.'

'We are police officers.'

'I would never have guessed. No one else wears such cheap suits and shows a total lack of manners. Save your breath before you start. I've already told your lot, I'm not saying anything, and I'm not answering any questions.'

'I'm not here to ask you questions. My name is Detective Superintendent Grant McAllister and this is...'

'I don't care who you are, I'm not talking to you.'

'...this is Detective Sergeant Tom McSherry. Are you Paul Boyle?'

'Read the name on the door, if you can.'

'Mr Boyle, I have a warrant for your arrest.'

'Very good. And what am I supposed to have done? Parked my car illegally? A smash and grab raid perhaps? Gun running? My legs are smashed to fuck and you come here because of some poxy warrant for some shite or other, just because my name is Boyle. Well, take your warrant, shove it up your arse and get to fuck out of here.'

'Mr Boyle, I have no intention of going anywhere until I have completed what I have come to do. I am about to prefer a charge against you. You are not obliged....'

Paul Boyle affected an air of casual indifference while he was cautioned. He looked round his room in a bored fashion.

'Do you understand the caution?'

'Fuck off. Fuck right off.'

The woman at the bedside had remained silent. Now she spoke. Gently but very firmly.

'Paul, please do not swear like that, at least not in front of me. I think you should listen to what these men have to say. You're not a child any more. Now, please try to behave politely and like an adult.' The voice trembled only slightly.

'You should be supporting me, damn it. Why are you taking their side?'

'I'm not taking sides and I think I have supported you long enough.'

As Paul looked at his mother he could see tears welling in her eyes. Somehow she seemed to know what was about to happen. A knot tightened in the pit of his stomach.

'The first charge is that you did between 16th March 1997 and 18th July 1997 in Glasgow and elsewhere conspire with Thomas McGarry to intimidate James Muirhead one of Her Majesty's Counsel in Scotland, threaten him and members of his close family with violence and attempt to induce him to act contrary to his professional duties to his client in the case of Her Majesty's Advocate against Charles Gallagher and you did attempt to pervert the course of justice. Do you understand the charge?'

Paul wanted to say something, anything, smart, witty, appropriate, but the fight was slowly draining out of him to be replaced by a rising tide of alarm.

'It's nonsense.' Weak.

'Very well.' Contemptuously dismissive.

'The second charge against you is that between 1st January 1997 and 16th March 1997 in Glasgow and elsewhere, you did conspire with Thomas McGarry to murder your brother Kevin Boyle. Do you understand the charge?'

Nothing.

There was nothing to say and nowhere to go. He looked towards his mother but Annie Boyle was staring at her hands which were demurely folded in her lap. If she had words of comfort for her son, she kept them to herself.

'Do you understand...?'

'I'm not stupid.' Limp.

'Do you have anything to say in answer to the charge?'

'No.' Defeated.

'Very well, Mr Boyle, you are now under arrest. When your medical condition improves you will be removed to Barlinnie prison. In the meantime you will be permitted to remain here. You are now in police custody and officers will be stationed outside your door. You will be allowed access to members of your immediate family but only under supervision. Other visits will be entirely at the discretion of the police. Do you understand all that I have just said to you?'

'What do you care?' Petty.

'I will take that as a yes. You are entitled to have a solicitor notified of your arrest. Do you wish me to notify a solicitor?'

'You'll never prove it. Any of it.' Defeated.

'I'll take that as a no, and we shall see, Mr Boyle. We shall see.'

McAllister turned to leave the room. As he reached the door he was halted in his tracks by an unexpected question.

'Where's McGarry?'

McAllister looked towards the bed and half-heartedly forced himself to stifle a sneer.

'Don't worry, Mr Boyle. He'll be waiting for you – in Barlinnie.'

McAllister left the room without waiting for a reaction. He had savoured the moment long enough.

In fact, nothing was directed towards him. As the door closed, Paul Boyle turned towards his mother and silently mouthed a single word.

'Why?'

Annie Boyle rounded on her son with a ferocity which was as unexpected as it was unfamiliar.

'Why? Why? You dare to ask me why? You tell me. Tell me where I went wrong. Tell me how to get rid of the pain. Tell me why you destroyed your father. Tell me how I am to cope with what is going to happen. Tell me how to get your brother back. Tell me why you killed Kevin.'

'I didn't kill...'

Annie began to slap her son about the shoulders, her screams and tears fusing into one.

'He did it to me! When we were young he kept doing it and no one stopped him.'

Annie froze.

'Night after night. He made me do it. I felt so dirty but he wouldn't listen. He wouldn't stop. I prayed that you or dad would find him, make him stop, but you never came. You were never there, when I needed you most. I still wake up expecting him into come in to my bed. I hated him, mum, I hated him!'

Annie Boyle's demeanour suddenly changed and she placed her hands on her son. 'There, there, my wee man. I'm here now.'

* * *

The two officers were in the hospital car park before either spoke.

'Why did he have his brother killed? If you want to tell me.'

'No point in keeping it a big secret. Kevin had been moving into the drug scene. Old man Boyle never touched the stuff. He knew the dangers involved. Paul was trying to get the family into more legitimate ventures, or at least semi-legitimate. Drugs did not feature in his financial plan. Plus, Kevin was becoming dangerous. He was snorting the stuff as well as selling it. He and his mouth were out of control. He kept bragging that he was about to take over the whole Glasgow drug scene and would be worth millions. He became a business liability, pure and simple. The killing was no more than an act of rationalisation, to adopt the jargon.'

'Christ, that makes it sound almost respectable.'

'It was anything but!'

'I know. Cold-hearted bastard to have his brother slaughtered for the sake of business, if that's all it was.'

'I'm not totally convinced either. McGarry sensed there was some other problem between the two. Didn't know what and nothing was ever said to him. He claims that Paul hated Kevin and this drug business was an excuse rather than a reason. We'll look into it, but...'

'So how come we did Gallagher?'

'That will take a bit more explaining. In fairness, the Gallaghers were obvious suspects. When we received the tip-off from the mysterious witness...'

'Thomson?'

'...Thomson, the whole investigation went charging up what turned out to be the wrong track. Warwick and that idiot Taylor derailed it completely. Made it look as if we had a reasonably strong case.'

'And Clark's murder?'

'That was an internal matter. Act of revenge by McGarry for something Clark did in the past. He didn't just kill him. He butchered him. Almost certainly enjoyed the experience.'

'Evil bastard!'

'Precisely that. The Clark case was always weak against Gallagher. I was not convinced that we should have gone ahead with it. Crown counsel's instructions. There was only the partial identification and the general circumstantial evidence. I just wasn't convinced. Then young Mr Taylor got himself involved, this time with McPhee.'

'He's in deep trouble.'

'Taylor! I intend to make it my business to create a new category of trouble for that idiot. Not just for what he was up to, but for what I suspect he did to Bob. By the time I am finished with him...'

'Three lives lost!'

'And one nearly fucked up by us. Get on the radio and find out if there is any news from the High Court.'

'One thing intrigues me . How did you get wind of all this?'

The look indicated there would be no answer.

'OK. One thing really does intrigue me. Boyle's mother. She sat calmly throughout the whole thing. You would have expected her to go crazy when you effectively charged one son with the murder of his brother during the trial of the killer. Pretty fucking crazy situation. It would be some shock for anyone. But there was no shouting and bawling. No reaction at all. Strange as it seems, it was almost as if she was expecting it.'

The look told him all he needed to know.

●   ●   ●

James Muirhead walked calmly along the corridor towards counsel's robing room. He ignored the clamour going on round about him as the press fought with each other to grab interviews with the Procurator Fiscal, the police, Jack Morton, the rival families, the court cat and anyone who was prepared to provide them with a one-liner on the verdict.

Outside, the members of the waiting crowd were becoming animated as the news spread. Their number was being swollen as the public gallery decanted into the street. A heavy police presence was there to keep the rival factions apart. Some of the press were already mingling with the spectators hoping to pick up a choice piece of reaction. Across the road, at the edge of Glasgow Green, television cameramen were awaiting their reporters. There was time to make the six o'clock news. Time – but only just. Photographers crowded round every door. There was one picture every one of them wanted. Failure would not be readily explained to their editors.

The macer was packing away the productions, mystified as to why one seemed to have gone missing. The jurors were attending to a most important task – collecting their expenses.

Lord Cowden had been whisked away in his official car, his expression betraying his view of the matter. Mike Matthews was walking to the train having made a phone call. He would go home later – a deal later.

For the last time in the case, James Muirhead sat in the same carver at the same round table in counsel's retiring room. He was alone, and very much alone with his thoughts. Jack Morton and Donald Anderson had gone to see Charlie Gallagher in order to deal with the formalities consequent upon a verdict.

Muirhead reflected on the events of the past few weeks. He had defended many clients charged with murder. Some had been convicted when he felt they should have been acquitted. Some were acquitted when the evidence suggested that such an eventuality could only exist in the realms of fantasy. You just could not tell what a jury would do, what would influence them, lead them to be for you or against you.

For over twenty years this had been his life. He thought he had seen it all. But there had been nothing to match this one.

Witnesses being nobbled, a super grass, perjury by a police officer, all against the background of the long-standing rivalry between Glasgow's leading criminal families.

Kevin Boyle dead. 'Mad Dog' Clark dead. A senior police officer committing suicide. Hugh Boyle reduced to some kind of gibbering wreck. And shadows. Everywhere you looked, shadows. Moving. Manipulating. Shadows you could see but never get close to.

The man with the Irish accent, and the gun. The bloody gun! This mysterious stranger who had threatened him and his family, who had tried so hard to force him to betray everything he believed in – fairness, impartiality, justice. Muirhead shivered involuntarily. For the first time he wondered.

Just how close had this man come to getting to him, influencing him, controlling him? He could never betray a client, no matter what the risk, no matter what the danger. But he had been afraid and fear can make a man do strange things. Could fear have influenced his decisions without him realising? And if it did, what effect may that have had on the man who sat behind him in the dock? The man had placed his trust in him, although he would never have admitted this. Trust, the one thing you could never betray.

Enough of this thinking. It was bad for you. He had a phone call to make.

'Superintendent McAllister.'

'As you might say, I take it you recognise my voice?'

'Indeed. Well?'

'Not proven, by a majority.'

'Close.'

'Close enough.'

'Congratulations.'

'That's a strange thing for you to say. As my former client might say,

I just fucked up your case.'

'Quite the reverse.'

'I don't understand.'

'No, there's a lot you don't understand. Can we meet for a drink later? There are some things I think you should know.'

'Is my family still in any danger?'

'No.'

Muirhead was weary and really wanted to go home, to his family, to a bath and a decent bottle of claret. To normality. That would have to wait. He had a feeling he wanted to hear what McAllister had to say to him.

'I deserve a drink now that this is all over. Bar of the Moat House, eight o'clock?'

'Bit upmarket for a policeman's salary.'

'Charge it to expenses.'

'I'll be there.'

McAllister replaced the receiver.

'So you think it's all over? Well, Mr James Muirhead QC, for some of us it's only just beginning. Some of us have to prepare for a murder trial.'